Best of British Science Fiction 2021

Best of British Science Fiction 2021

Edited by Donna Scott

NewCon Press
England

First edition, published in the UK August 2022 by NewCon Press

NCP 279 (hardback)
NCP 280 (softback)

10 9 8 7 6 5 4 3 2 1

Table of Contents

Introduction

Donna Scott

Welcome, dear reader, to *Best of British Science Fiction 2021*. It is once again a gorgeous day in June. Just like last year's introduction, it is the Queen's birthday as I am writing this – that is not to say that I have started a brand-new tradition of only writing my introduction on the Queen's Birthday. It is merely a happy (and glorious?) coincidence. It was also the Queen's Platinum Jubilee last week, so she's already had the party, therefore no excuse to eat cake today (unless I want cake, I don't require royal assent). There are still bits of bunting hanging limply from the neighbours' houses, but we don't live in a nice enough street to have the jolly knitted toppers on our pillar boxes depicting corgis and crowns. Seeing lots of flags everywhere gives me very mixed feelings. I'm hopeful when I see bunting that there might also be picnics, but flags at random non-specific times make me queasy. They can be layered with meaning: celebration and pride, but also exclusion, territorialism and division. However, they can also be the flags shoved awkwardly into a poorly thought-through hardware shop window, along with an effigy of the Queen in a blonde wig and inflatable crown that is both unintentionally hilarious and terrifying. We live in divided times, with the worst cost of living crisis for 40 years, and a lot of us need something to lift our souls. Some people look to big, televised parties for that. I'm more inclined to look for things that are quirky and unusual, that make me smile, or make me think a bit more deeply about ideas.

Writing these anthology introductions gives me the opportunity to reflect on the year before, and its relative strangeness to the others. We began the year still in the grip of the global pandemic, and ended with many controversies arising from that time featuring constantly in the news.

As we left 2021 behind, a lot of us were left with feelings of anxiety and general trepidation about engaging with the wider world. I went to my first post-Lockdown convention in Birmingham in September 2021. Although the convention itself was quite small in attendance, the city was bustling with lots of crowds. The convention coincided with a few events that were going on outside of fandom including Pride. I had not realised just how emotional I would be when it came to meeting my friends from within science fiction fandom for the first time since Lockdown. There was a general sense of caution when it came to socialising, and people were wearing masks in the busy bar areas and in the panels – unless of course they were speaking on those panels. However, it was so good to be back with colleagues and friends. I had really missed that connection, the opportunity to talk with likeminded people about the things we enjoy: new books, new films, and new creative projects. Always though at the kernel of my being was this strange feeling that things were not quite as they were. I think in part that may have been due to the absence of people we had lost in that time, and the general sadness we were all feeling. Also, not everyone felt comfortable enough to venture out into society. Right now, in June 2022, I still have a few friends who don't feel that wider society beyond immediate family, or just a few friends is for them right now, and it's not necessarily because they fear getting sick. I know personally, that when it came to my performance work, I wanted to get out in front of audiences as soon as possible, but I was lacking in confidence for quite some time. I suffered a panic attack the first time I was in a crowd, and the first time I tried to take a train to meet friends in a park, I could not do it. Those things are easy breezy now, thank goodness. Though the trains are still awful.

As I have been reading submissions for *Best of British Science Fiction 2021*, it has struck me just how much the pandemic seems to have been seeping into science fiction short stories in almost imperceptible and insidious ways. I mentioned in the introduction to last year's *Best of British Science Fiction 2020* that I had received quite a few stories that were about pandemics or viruses, and I had only chosen a couple of stories in which this topic featured, but those stories really had to impress me as I was rather disinclined to be reading about the specificities of the awful time we were already living through, and imagined my readers would feel similar. In 2021 there were much fewer overtly virus-themed stories getting published as far as I can see, but still the pandemic's influence on our lives in Britain was making itself felt through the stories out there. I need to qualify why I think this is the case. The vast majority of eligible writers are living here and getting published in magazines based here, to be read mostly by readers based here. We are the ones who have lived through the quirks, ravages and calamities of a Pandemic, with privations unique to us as a European country due to political decisions made on our behalf exacerbating those felt round the world. The sense of isolation from loved ones also came through strongly, as well as deep reflection on the worries of the world.

I have put this snapshot of British science fiction in 2021 that came in from the submissions pile through my editorial filter and found a few sweet, sad stories signalling the tense times we are in, but also optimism for better times to come, as well as that wry British humour. "Me Two" by Keith Brooke and Eric Brown is essentially about the separation of two distinct people, but sweetly and deftly told. A need for a bit of social normality is keenly felt in Teika Marija Smits' "Girls' Night Out" and Lockdown adds a little tension to a superb technological mystery in A.N. Myers' "Okamoto's Lens". You will also find David Gullen's excellent story, "Down and Out Under the Tannhauser Gate" which impressed me from the first time I read it in ParSec, plus superb contributions from Paul Cornell and Liz Williams who are among my favourite writers.

I hope you very much enjoy this anthology.

Donna Scott
Northampton
June 2022

Distribution
Paul Cornell

Shan Tiree is trying to listen to music as the car finds its way through Nuevas Colinas. Unfortunately, someone, and that someone is Shan, has left the car's settings at levels appropriate for the Sunset Cooperative, so the car keeps reporting possible pedestrians, and then a moment later correcting those pings to indications of animal life, mostly dogs and birds. Shan tries to remember the voice commands to change the settings, but it's quite a sequence, because it's not the sort of thing you want to change accidentally when you're trying to find the nearest habitation, so finally Shan settles on playing the Stones louder than the notifications and resolves to have the manual go through its unroll on the way back to Sunset, no matter how dull that's going to be.

Actually, it's pleasing that there's so much life up here. Shan hopes to hear about a bear, maybe, but already Shan's margins are pumping compensators about Shan's (genetic and raised, damnit) heightened sense of danger. A report of something that actually could harm a person might send the margins into the slight nausea of recalculation mode. Shan's system, like that of just about everyone Shan knows of their own age, just wasn't made to deal with the continuing relative lack of danger in the New Situation. (It still feels weird that those words were getting more captialised every day.) Most danger, turns out, is because of other people. If the co-op managed to grow its population, then danger might return one day. Hooray. The emptiness all around Sunset feels like it should be dangerous, but actually there's more and more clean water out there, and the dogs are still afraid of people, and the co-op can now test for pathogens a mile away. There's only a kind of philosophical danger, something Shan has experienced a couple of times on these rounds, the way that the emptiness can inspire religious awe, can get people feeling a need to fill that space with some higher presence. They all know how dangerous that could be.

"How far to Dr. Kay's house?" Shan asks.

"Couple of blocks," says the car. "If we were in Sunset. Which we aren't."

It's been using exactly that speech structure in answer to almost every question. "In kilometres?"

"Two point three."

"Thanks," says Shan, because it's part of their self-measurement process to always be polite. They've also signed up to never assigning personhood to objects, a tendency in human beings that goes deeper than genes or upbringing. Put a face on a balloon and humans will start treating it as a person, while, perversely, not always granting actual human beings the same status. But hey, in this situation, Shan can't be both polite and exactly correct about the non-personhood of the car. Shan is these days just about managing to square the circles of their own personality, so that tiny inner conflict doesn't bother them much. Right now, all these clashing parameters in their head are just about enough to stop the co-op asking if they'd consider having children. Which, honestly, is how they want things to be. "Car, sing along to 'Only Rock 'n Roll.'"

"But I like it," says the car.

"Welcome to the house I haunt," says Dr. Kay, opening the door and saying that immediately like Shan is an old friend and he's been expecting them.

That gives Shan a moment's pause. "Good morning, Dr. Kay. I work for the regional government. I'm here to assess your needs."

After the round of appropriate introductions, vocal and device, he leads them down the stairs. The house is one of those old bunkers, fabricated inside the hill at the centre of a small clearing, woods all around. Shan had to park the car at the closest point and had found no sort of track to the front door. This was the sort of place that had been quickly and roughly built in the time when suddenly anyone who had the privilege of resources found they could build anywhere because there wasn't anyone to stop them. And of course there was "new land", land without law, to build in. The earnest simplicity of the fabbed wood, knots recurring only at the sort of pattern level a free mind could perceive, spoke to the kind of person who saw places like this, incredibly, as a return to nature. It spoke to Shan of billions dying just over the other side of the hills. Still. Still. Shan tells themself to not go there. Not good for them, not good for this unbiased evaluation of whether or not Dr. Kay is a danger to himself or to others. If Shan judges him to be so, the co-op will consider whether or not to hold judicial proceedings, such as they are, a jury sitting without any actual judges, then possibly have him arrested, or detained for his own safety, and brought into the co-op to do useful work while being more closely monitored. They've done this three times in the last year, which is an exponential growth of the range of law. Not everybody in the co-op wants law, or wants it to extend beyond the fence. And indeed, this visit feels kind of weird to Shan. They had to get that introduction pre-cleared on their ethics score, because it very much doesn't tell Kay what the stakes are. But if it did, it could put Shan at risk. Kay's law enforcement records have been lost, and the records of his scientific career are patchy like they've been erased in places, which is a pattern that speaks of military employment that's been hushed up. What this visit is about is whether or not his subsequent rush toward isolation and the eccentric encounters he's had with the few people who've seen him since point to anything sinister. What Shan really is going to have to work on her ethics about is the assumptions they've made when they got here. Plenty of absolutely social people now live in places like this. What Shan just felt was an ethics kink of their own and no reason to feel negative toward Kay. They have to take care to be neutral about this procedure. "What do I call you?" he says, as the office area proffers beverages.

"They."

"Noted." He points to himself. "We."

Shan is more disappointed than angry. And they still have to deal with this man neutrally. So, they'll start by pretending to take this slur at face value. "Ah, should I change the records? You're down with us as a 'he'."

He nods, eager. "Changing the records would I think be a great idea at this point. Yes. Yes."

Oh. He means it. Or did he just realise he was being offensive and back out from that posture in what he thinks is a tricksy way? There's something weird about the way he's looking at Shan. It's childlike. "Have you had an accident of some kind? How are you feeling?"

"Exciting."

"Do you mean exciting to yourself, or–?"

"Everything's exciting." He gestures to the house. "I'm we, but all this, this is the ghost of a pronoun. I mean it displays aspects of what such a word means, as a ghost has features, aspects of humanity, not that I believe in proscribed conceits like ghosts, before you ask, I don't want to blunder into losing points, where was I?"

Oh. He knows he's being assessed on a points system. And was that a little look of annoyance on his face just then, as if he shouldn't have given away that he knew that? "I'm… not sure I follow."

"I'm saying all this has gone beyond being a he or a she or a they and it's definitely no longer an it. It has unique features, emerging features, of its own. Like it was going woo and wearing a sheet. Metaphorically."

He's lived alone a long time. Shan is making allowances. They've seen numerous people who've been brought into the co-op being as random as this. But equally, this feels like the babble of other men of his age who've maintained the culture identity Kay seems to belong to. Or, Shan corrects themself again, who Shan is inclined to believe he belongs to, because they've seen no real sign of that other than that he seems to think he's revealing enormous truths like he's the chosen one. "I'm sorry, you've lost me. What do you mean by 'all this'?"

"Follow me," he says. "And what I am now will become clear. I want you to meet Lucifer."

He takes Shan to a tall mulching tube that forms, oddly, the centrepiece of the living room. It extends upwards, presumably into the next floor, and down into the one below. It's transparent, and inside Shan is surprised to see not compost but… its definitely something organic, but it doesn't resemble plant life. It resembles strata of marrow, veins, and wires too, with cells and LEDs threaded all the way down the column.

For the first time Shan feels unsafe. Has he got a body in there? Why has he called it by such a provocative name? But again, names, myth-uses, it's only indicative, not concrete. Shan hasn't yet felt able to assign any points to Kay either way. "What am I looking at?"

"Enhanced memory re-processors. Re-processors are like…" He gestures up and to the left, which is where he must still think most people still look for their supplementary information in the air. Shan finds themself oddly comforted by the gesture. "Afterburners. What those things apparently did for jet engines, but for neuron interactions. You know how a free mind is grown out of any sort of interaction, and recognised when those interactions reach the Turing Point? What was the last system to do that on its own? An election season, wasn't it?"

"Oh, yeah," Shan does indeed quickly consult the air for that one, vaguely hoping he noted that they kept the access point straight up now. Because nobody seems to feel that a sudden upward eye roll is a sign of biohazard anymore. Ah, that was why Shan had enjoyed him making that gesture. Because the currently fashionable one always did trigger Shan just a little. "Across three specific media platforms. And for a year or so after a couple of hundred humans also had to be recognised as part of that mind, but then it started communicating for itself, and they were allowed to legally separate themselves."

"And the time before that it was that soap opera."

"It prefers to be called a drama now."

"Right. I keep setting you off on the need to correct me, don't I? I apologise. It's only because I'm not all here." He points to his head.

That was again a bit of a firework display of possible points in both directions, that, exactly like fireworks, left nothing much to go on afterwards. "Do you mean you've had memory lapses, or -?"

"I mean all of what I used to be is no longer in this skull. Some of it is in here." He puts a palm on the surface of the tube. "This is Lucifer. Right now at least. This is what I'm describing. We can find and even encourage free minds in the wild as it were. We set up gardens for them, wait for the right conditions, but sometimes even then they don't arise. We are barely starting to consider how to go about making one from scratch. Indeed, some physicists, which is typical for them, have even said the conditions of this universe preclude us from understanding enough about a mind to make one."

Shan doesn't think there have been physicists with the necessary resources to form theories like that for decades, so presumably he's talking about the past. Shan has been moving their eyes to get the air to follow the key words in this field vastly divorced from their own specialisations. What they're seeing in annotations around Kay's speech, the words of which are preserved in mid-air, supports his story so far. These are speculations based on collective research, albeit very old research, and include no warning signals about conspiracy disorders. Still, Shan doesn't like being lectured to without consent. It's a marginal case for a points loss, in fact, maybe they're now teetering on the edge of definitely going in that direction. But despite not asking for it Shan is interested now that it's arrived. Which loses them a point or two in their own internal reckoning, which they compare to the vast array at the end of each day. One should not tread on consent after the fact, even, but what the hey, it's themself they're oppressing. "Go on."

"I experienced some interesting stress symptoms in the wake of moving up here. I started to feel that the many conflicting impulses in my mind were getting less and less amalgamated with each other into a single being."

Here, finally, are some classic symptoms, possibly heading vaguely toward the "danger to himself" category. "I have some meds with me and am able and qualified to fab whatever else would fit your neural contact points."

"No, thank you. I would have said yes to that back then. Like a shot. But I came to value the clash between the points of view. To become interested in the differences. In what they said about the creation of people within minds. If I may–?"

Oh, now he makes the rather genteel spinning gesture with his hand that's meant to be asking permission to continue in a conversation, but these days actually comes over as enormously patronising. Up here though, off the smallnets, would he even know? Shan can't make themselves reply with the relevant gesture. But they are interested in something about this that's suddenly got very relatable. "Sure."

"I set up a neural link between myself and the brain material I've grown in this tube -"

So he has got a body in there? "And what was the source of that material?" Shan slaps an alert ready in the air to have the car ready to go outside. All they have to do is get to it and throw themselves in. With stairs involved.

"A crow, I think. I found it dead in the woods, but not yet decomposed."

Shan relaxes, just a little. Then they tense again when they remember something. Their compensators are getting a hell of a workout today. Shan had kind of expected that, though. "Wait a sec. You've been saying 'I'. I thought you were 'we'?"

Kay beams all over his face. "I am me, but Dr. Kay is me and…" He suddenly runs for the stairs, then, a moment later, steps back down them with he sees Shan hasn't followed. "Follow! Follow!"

Shan slowly does. Kay keeps giving them orders, which is either down to a worrying cultural background or a possible isolation disorder. Shan wonders if maybe there's a reluctance on their own part to start making judgments here. They're very aware of their own glass house. They were chosen to do this because they're so self-critical ethically. Maybe the co-op should have chosen someone who didn't care so much. But then where would they be? Shan is pleased they were chosen. They must remember they're pleased that this is difficult. It should be.

On the next floor down is a study, which is more like a museum of the pop culture of previous centuries, some of which screams worrying cultural references to Shan and some of which screams that they must find out if that show is archived anywhere. Kay is pointing to what looks like a media distribution hub, the sort of patched-together compromise that was still just about being used when she was a kid. It's got the logos of a few old shows and movies stuck to it, again in the way redolent of how those days got. Shan supposes they hugged their culture close to their chest back then. The titles skew in all directions according to her visual notes, no landslide of violence-aggrandising order shows, but a few. And a few things which still played. The hub is connected to the same sort of wiring she saw below, with tubes of the same sort of... organic matter plugged into it.

"And so is this," Kay continues his sentence from upstairs, "and..." And he heads downstairs again.

Shan follows him in the end through three lower floors, in which he points to locations with similar installations in some sort of store room, an empty bedroom that looks like it was designed for a child, a kitchen that strikes Shan as kind of wonderful and homely and a pod full of hydroponics. That's where they end up, at the base of what looks like the same column Shan first encountered. Kay has said "and this" every time. Now he points again at the column. "There are twenty-seven of them all in all, at various places around the house. They're all me."

"Metaphorically or... actually?"

"Seriously. Really."

"You're saying you... took aspects of yourself and... put them into other... objects?"

"Not objects." He sounds offended.

17

Shan stomps on a kneejerk urge to apologise. They don't know yet what the status of these containers is, and being precise about what's an object and what's a person is central to Shan's own ethical check-in. "But, putting that question aside, that's what you did?"

He takes a moment of pacing to get past his anger. "I pruned an outgrowth, replanted it and encouraged it. And was thus free of it myself. And thus I ceased to be all of Dr. Kay, because I no longer have in me several things that are Dr. Kay."

"So who are you?"

"Part of Dr. Kay, which is why I answer for him, but beyond that… I've been thinking about a name for myself. But self-description, especially in these circumstances, is difficult."

"That's telling. Because you sound to me like a whole person. I haven't been struck by any lack of personhood on…" But actually, Shan realised, they had. There'd been that moment of wondering if he'd been injured. "No, okay, I have. But still. Are you sure you haven't just…" Actually, whatever he'd done, if he'd really done it, didn't deserve that "just", because it would be no small thing, scientifically speaking, or probably ethically. It might be that he was punishing himself for something, locking up parts of himself. The question then would be what had they been guilty of? And was he thus still guilty of it? "Why are you so sure these are individual persons?"

"For one thing, because this… nation of me… they talk to me as individuals."

"They talk to you?" And Shan didn't like that phrase about him being a nation very much either. That was highly reminiscent of new frontier cant. But again, not quite, not enough.

"You want proof, of course. You can talk to them yourself. They stay in their own worlds mostly, talk to me about days that I'm not having, but quite banal versions of an average day for me, really, like dreams that don't seem to be about very much. When they talk to me they realise that these were dreams and sometimes they get kind of annoyed about that."

"How would I talk to them?" Shan is not prepared to be hooked up to any sort of gizmo. Not by this guy. No way. But, their compensators keep reminding them, they keep hitting points where Shan expects Kay to erupt in sudden, violent action, and every time he just keeps talking. Shan has muscles from working the co-op and Kay is frail and unarmed. But, but, but, the eternal but that may always sit there at the centre of such conversations between men and others because there have been decades of trying to shift it and it's still damn well there.

"I'd like you to allow them access. I'd like you to believe me."

"My office doesn't confer me with the power of official belief." That's meant to be a joke, but Shan is sure it came out sounding like official belief is a thing.

"I want you to believe me, not your office."

Shan doesn't like the sound of that. But it kind of shaded into him being lost, needing someone to believe him, not needing to present something in a peacocky way. Is it his weird range of expressions and body language that's keeping Shan guessing about his motivations? "If I agreed, how would I 'allow them access'?"

Kay beams all over his face. It must seem to him like he's winning them over, but actually Shan just wants to hear more, to see more expressions, to finally somehow decide. "It's my theory that, once in a blue moon, electrical signals from a human brain would get randomly amplified by, I don't know, a cosmic ray impact on that brain or some kink in the electromagnetic background and get broadcast out of the skull. We're talking tiny signals and lots of insulation, so I'd say it happened maybe a handful of times in all human history. And no, there's no need to check that theory in the air, it's pure crank stuff. In the 1970s, a lot of research was done into what they called 'psi' and it was all bullshit, nothing that couldn't be put down to mathematical error and chance, because they were hunting for something, I think, that just didn't happen while they were watching, and maybe not for centuries either side."

Gah. Please say or do something that doesn't walk on a fine line. "And why is this relevant?"

"Because I've amplified these parts of me and haven't put insulation in the way. I'm surprised you haven't felt the voices in your head already. They'll all be trying to connect to your brain, to talk to you."

And this time Shan actually takes a physical step back. Their compensators do their work. There's a pause while Shan kind of looks around the corners of their mind, trying to hear anything.

And then, oh God, they find it.

Is that their imagination? It feels like their imagination. It's their own… Shan doesn't know, does the voice inside their head, their own imagined voice, sound like their speaking voice, or could it sound like anyone's? Because a voice like Dr. Kay's is saying to them, carefully, over and over…

"Please, listen to me! Please listen to me!"

Internally, somehow, Shan kind of says that they are.

"Oh thank God!" says the internal voice, more clearly now. "Listen. Don't believe anything he says. I'm the real Dr. Kay. In the glass tube. He split me off, he split off lots of other parts of himself, anything that might get in the way, anything of conscience. I found all the archetypes inside my mind, from the maiden to the fool. He threw them away too. He's the one that's left. He's the trickster, he's everything evil in human beings. He's Lucifer."

Shan tries not to react. Their compensators are now in overdrive and they feel full on nauseous as a result. But at least it's given them a poker face. Hopefully. Wow. Well, now they have their answer. If this is some kind of trick, then it's a full-on attempt to scare Shan. If it's not, then inviting them into an area when other voices can enter their mind without warning them first is a definite violation of their consent, but… only in as much as inviting them into a room not having said there's a crowd in there, because all these minds can do is talk, right? Okay, that's a point off. But only a point. Which doesn't really square with how vastly uncomfortable Shan feels right now. Not that the co-op will believe any of this. Anyhow, Shan needs to find a way to walk slowly head back up each of the stairwells and get to the car. So, let's talk as if this is fascinating stuff. "I think I can hear something. It sounds like… something one of them is making up?" Shan has to ignore the shouting that statement causes from the mind the physical form of which… oh, Shan kind of automatically looked at the tube Kay already identified as Lucifer.

Kay is looking between Shan and the tube. "Oh, is he telling you what he tries to shout out every time a vehicle passes in the distance? Other people being around wakes him and the others up from their lovely dreams. I guess him lying like that is why I plucked him out of here and put him in there, that's what the trickster does. 'Help, help, I'm trapped in here by the evil doctor!' I swear, I feel I'm a lot less evil without that old guy inside me."

Shan has no idea what to believe. "Could I maybe hear from another of them?" Like, maybe one of the ones upstairs? Maybe as high up as possible? Shan glances upward, trying to nudge him in that direction.

"Sure." They head up one flight again, and here is indeed another voice that could also have been Shan, broadcasting into their imagination once again. This one is saying also that it's the real Dr. Kay, that what's out here in the body is Lucifer. Is Shan just picking up the same one again? No, now they're both talking at once.

And Dr. Kay now has an expression on his face that's quite clear in its meaning, not at all walking a fine line. He's eagerly awaiting something.

A new thought is in Shan's head now. Either they've come up with it themselves or it's been said to them. Which it is has suddenly become strangely complex. "How… how did you make this transfer? I mean, did you need some sort of attachment between you and the tubes?"

"No," says Kay. "If you stand here long enough it just kind of happens."

Shan finishes up the paperwork in the air as quickly as possible, asking no more questions about Kay's work. They walk stiffly up the remaining stairs to the exit, their body still anticipating having to run. But no trigger moment comes. Kay follows, offering pleasantries, saying come again.

Shan lies in the seat in the car as it drives through the night back toward Sunset. Dr. Kay, they think to themself, has maybe found a way to grow free minds, so what does it matter if he thinks of it in very peculiar terms?

Shan wakes from sleep a while later to find themselves still in the car. It's diverted itself because of bears. Shan has missed a bear. Dr. Kay, they think to themself, has maybe found a new therapy that might be useful for all kinds of conditions, so, sure, let him have his weird archetype fantasies.

Standing outside the car, Shan stares out at the emptiness. The weight of it still gets to Shan. The horizon so far away and flat seems to demand something to fill it, seems to ask to be part of a map that could be folded shut. Into that gap can come a serpent. Into that gap should come a serpent. Into that gap will come, woken again, ever sleeping, ever woken, the thing that is always there in human beings.

Into that gap should come.

Stealthcare
Liz Williams

I was taken to the ship on a private jetboat. The pilot smiled as she assisted me on board.

"Good evening. Enrico Calalang? How nice to welcome you to Global Line. Was everything acceptable with regard to your hotel?"

"Most acceptable, thank you." I tried to convey the impression, which I'm sure was a failure, that as an insurance investigator, even a senior one, I was accustomed to staying in top establishments.

She bobbed her head. "I do hope the Princess Charlotte will also meet your expectations."

"I'm sure it will."

Over the years in which I've been involved in this industry, I have learned to discern the sound of wealth, and that sound is silence. The London Hilton Ten had been a hushed place. Since then I had been entirely insulated from the chaos of the city, from a peaceful night enveloped in maximum thread sheets, to the breakfast served to me by a smiling, unspeaking waitress. As though I, lost in my own banal thoughts, was too important to be bothered with the inconsequential chatter of lesser mortals. I suppose this is what it is like to be rich!

But I glimpsed parts of this ancient city that were less luxurious. Since the advent of stealthcare bills, as they're not-so-humorously called, the Brits are rueing the day that they let the old NHS slip through their fingers. Last night, I'd overheard the hotel manager warning a new member of staff to take care not to let any of the med beggars into the garden compound ("they'll only annoy our guests – I won't put up with it, I tell you. Call the police if you see any").

And now the Princess Charlotte was looming further down the Thames as the boat shot along the river. She was quite a small ship in comparison to some of the retirement vessels which circle the globe – floating palaces of luxury, filled with the wealthy, the elderly, and the ill.

"Nearly there," the pilot said unnecessarily, over her shoulder.

Once on board, I was whisked by a soft-voiced steward to my quarters. This would be my home for the next 24 hours, a complimentary cabin offered by Global Line. I had discussed this back at the office and we were not sure whether this was actually a bribe or not, but in the end we decided that we had few enough perks and I might as well accept it, as long as I declared everything properly on my expenses form.

Once installed, I was served a fruit juice cocktail which I was unable to identify until I read the lengthy description which had been sent automatically to my phone. The ship's system had logged into my wristband, detected some minor vitamin deficiencies (probably caused by a few long flights and too little sleep) and the cocktail was intended to supplement the lack.

I sat down by the porthole in a comfortable chair, sipping my drink, and brought up the case file on my pad. I was familiar with the details but flicked slowly through the case notes once more.

Rosalind Lee. Age 74, born in Edinburgh, educated in Hong Kong, where she had spent much of her life. She was the wealthy widow of an Anglo-Taiwanese pharmaceutical CEO: a former scientist who had set up Buena Vista, one of the best known of the current set of global wellness brands. She had applied for residence on the Princess Charlotte three years previously, following the death of her husband, and had lived on the vessel ever since. Her application had been approved by my insurance company, according to the usual criteria: primary among these was a pre-existing condition clause. I had read this many times but now I read it again. As was usual, it was customised: setting a higher premium on some conditions which are relatively easily treated, such as various forms of cancer, but it did clearly stipulate that some conditions would not be permitted under this policy. One of these was WID – Wehlberg's Inflammatory Syndrome: Mrs Lee had tested negative for all the early markers – not just in her annual medical checks, but also from the hourly readouts from her wristband over the course of her life – yet now she was positive for WIS.

According to our medical staff, that wasn't possible. Either she didn't have WIS, or her earlier wristband readings had been wrong. But once they'd pinpointed the illness – one of the several underlying conditions that have turned out to be responsible for a lot of auto-immune diseases – the markers were actually clear, I understood.

"Discovery of Wehlberg's was a game changer," Dr Pramasan, one of my medical colleagues, informed me. "You know about it, yes?"

I'd nodded. I remembered when it had been discovered, tying together all those vague symptoms from things like fibromyalgia to IBS, which a lot of doctors had refused to accept even existed, decades ago.

There's no known way to falsify the readings on a wristband – so many hackers have tried, but they're always found out. So we were presented with a quandary: had Mrs Lee committed an impossible fraud, or did she have an impossible medical history, or was it some bizarre mistake? My company could have run the data through an AI, but the human touch is still valued – more to make the clients feel comfortable than anything else.

I was to interview Mrs Lee later and get my own impressions of her. I was certain, though, that I had not made a mistake and neither had the medics who had studied it before me. Dr Pramasan had been clear.

"There's nothing on the readouts for over twenty years to indicate any issues. She's been quite healthy, apart from an early indication of diabetes which obviously they were able to cure, and a couple of major viruses. But there are none of the markers for WIS."

"And her readings would have picked it up?"

"Absolutely. Wristbands were brought in after they discovered WIS and all its cohort conditions and because it has been the cause of so many A-IDs, the WHO poured billions into getting it linked in."

I perused the reports again, wondering if I'd missed something. This attention to detail is part of what drew me to this work in the first place, but with it comes a simmering underlying anxiety which – well, that appears on my readouts, too, and if I didn't take compulsory medication for it, then I wouldn't be in my job for much longer.

I didn't think I'd missed anything. Time to interview Mrs Lee.

She was waiting for me in her cabin, along with a fluffy white dog. I asked her to authorise a temporary sharing agreement and she did so without demur. To put her at her ease, I joked about sharing the dog's readouts, too: his band was in his collar. She laughed and my phone pinged in to let me know that the agreement had been verified and via my retinal implant I could now see her readouts scrolling down the air to my left. Elevated levels of adrenalin: she was nervous. But some people feel guilty if they even see a policeman. I could see the WIS markers, slightly lowered levels of calcium, blood pressure also rather high but she was medicated for that. She'd had no alcohol recently, but some caffeine. The cup of cooling tea in front of her could have told me that, though.

"I wasn't really sure what this was about," Mrs Lee said. "I've always paid my premiums on time, and I've only ever made one claim before now. Is there a problem with my insurance?"

I sighed. "I'm afraid there is. We have a – a discrepancy. You see, you've recently been diagnosed with Wehlberg's, haven't you?"

"Yes, that's correct. I thought my insurance would cover it. Is that not the case?" Her hands played, agitated, in her lap.

"Well, usually it would, but the trouble is that WIS has to be a pre-existing condition, by definition, and your insurance cover explicitly rules that out. You'd need to have taken out a separate plug-in clause for WIS and cohort illnesses."

"I can assure you it isn't pre-existing." She sounded distressed, but quite definite. "I've never shown any signs of it before."

"The doctors say that this is unlikely, I'm afraid. In fact, you'd be a medical miracle. Look, Mrs Lee, no one is accusing you of any kind of wrongdoing. There's clearly been some kind of error, and we just need to pinpoint where it is."

"But if you're not going to cover it, I can't get treatment, is that it? Or I can, but I'll have to pay for it. I gather it could be extremely expensive."

I had the impression that she was genuinely worried. But why? Because she'd somehow managed to initiate a major insurance fraud, or because there actually had been some kind of mistake? She seemed quite genuine, but I'd only just met her. Yet readouts will show indicators when people are lying: it's not an absolutely precise science yet, but it's pretty reliable. And there were no such indicators here.

I'm sure this is just an error and we can sort it out. You might be able to get a covering clause for it, anyway – we might be able to get it written into the policy." At a much higher premium. And only if she hadn't made a fraudulent claim.

"My husband lost a lot of money before he died, in the crash. He'd already sold his shares in Buena Vista but – well, to be honest, he wasn't happy about that. He felt the board had pushed him out and he was very bitter – I feel it contributed to his final illness. I know this ship looks luxurious, but it's actually cheaper than living on land for me." She paused. "It's a tax thing, you see. It's the last thing he did for me."

I nodded. Living aboard a luxury cruise ship had sounded expensive to me when I first came across the idea, and the sums involved still weren't low – apartment cabins here cost several million – but there were multiple advantages. Including the large onboard hospital. If Mrs Lee had to fund her own treatment, it would be questionable whether it would be cheaper to do so on board or off: she would still need to pay, either way.

"Tell me about your husband," I said, and she needed little encouragement.

"Oh, he was a wonderful man…"

The late Mr Lee had been many things, I reflected as she spoke, but 'controlling' would have been the word that most readily came to my mind. When she had finished her account, I said,

"It sounds like a long and marvellous relationship, Mrs Lee. Now, let's talk about your wristband. Nothing's ever gone wrong with it?"

"No, it's the only one I've ever had." She glanced at it with the rueful affection that we often devote to our lifetime wearables. "It's been with me for years, since I was first fitted with it. My husband's company were at the vanguard of bringing them out."

Perhaps I should not have felt sorry for her and yet, I did. I believed her, but I still had a medical mystery to solve. At this point, a steward came to the door with a query of some sort and they went into the corridor, leaving me alone to study my surroundings.

At the moment, I had an excellent view of Tower Bridge and the London skyline. But it was the photos on the walls that attracted my attention: hologrammatic images of Mrs Lee and family projected within ornate frames. There was a formal posed portrait at the centre, of a younger version of herself and a man whom I recognised from her files as her husband. Mrs Lee's wristband was clearly visible. When I had seen it that morning, its subtle aqua tones had matched her smart blue suit, but in the portrait, it was a soft pink. The holographic image was quite large, but obviously it could be made larger… I took out my phone and, with care, took an image of Mrs Lee's wrist, from several angles, moving around the image to get as full a picture of it as possible.

Then I heard her coming back, so I sat down again and sipped my excellent coffee.

"…should be fixed now, but do let us know if you have any further trouble…"

"Of course. Thank you so much."

I checked when Mrs Lee been issued with her wristband. As an older woman, she had not had one as a child, but had been fitted in adulthood. All this was clearly shown on her medical records but I listened to her reminiscences anyway.

Back in my own berth, I wrote up my report and sent it in. Then I sent the images from the old hologram to a colleague in the imaging lab: if anyone could tell me the story of Mrs Lee's bracelet, it would be Gilberto. Shortly after this, my phone pinged and I saw that he had responded: *will get right on it. What are you looking for?*

I messaged back: *I don't know. Will a hologram show the QR and the rest of the codes?*

Yes, it should do.

The symbols are too small for someone to see with the naked eye, though they're all over your medical records anyway. But Gilberto could play around with those images in all sorts of ways.

After this I did some more paperwork and in due course was brought a nutritionally balanced, expertly prepared dinner. I still had not heard from Gilberto, so after dinner I poured myself a small Scotch from the berth's mini bar, ignored the warning ping of my wristband informing me that I was about to imbibe a harmful substance, and watched the news. My Scotch would show on my readouts, but would not contribute to the points for a healthcare reprimand. And then I slept, the mattress configuring itself to an optimal shape for my slight lumbar problem and the room misting itself with a soothing combination of lavender and chamomile to minimise my chances of insomnia.

In the morning there was still nothing from Gilberto. As I was finishing my croissant and contemplating more coffee, my phone finally pinged.

"Well," Gilberto said. "This one's been interesting! The QR and the other recog symbols are the same. But the band isn't."

"What?"

"I went for a full spectrographic analysis and I think the wristband in the photo is an earlier model. Made by Buena Vista, like the one she's got now, and very similar, but not the same."

"But there's no indication that she had an upgrade and that would be clear from her readouts." If you upgrade your device, it can only be done in a hospital that's cliented to the wristband provider and you're monitored the whole time, I reflected. It's not like changing your phone. And not even that common: it's not you who decides, but your provider, and most people keep their wristbands for the whole of their lives, as Rosalind Lee said she had done. Any software updates are done automatically.

"Of course it would. She didn't say anything to you about changing it?"

"No, on the contrary. She said she'd always has this one."

"But she hasn't."

"So we're dealing with fraud, then."

"The thing is, Enrico, it's so hard to do with these devices. You know that – they have to be as foolproof as possible because the stakes are so high. They're incredibly difficult to hack, all the data goes straight to the Cloudscape, and you obviously can't just take them off."

We talked for a while further and Gilberto promised me that he'd stay on the case.

I had a number of options.

Mrs Lee's wristband was the same one and the imaging results were wrong.

Or she had some kind of sudden onset WIS, previously unknown to medical science.

Or she was lying and had perpetrated a fraud in order to claim for treatment which was ruled out by her insurance.

Or someone had done it for her and she didn't know. I wondered again about the late Mr Lee. If anyone was capable of hacking the system, it would be a scientist who led one of the companies who produced wristbands. Had he seen her readouts, noted the early signs of WIS and swapped her band? Surely, though, it would be easier simply to have changed her insurance and bought a higher premium with a clause that covered WIS? Of course it would. Even if he'd lost money in the crash he'd still been wealthy enough to buy his wife a permanent cabin on a retirement cruiser and our premiums aren't that high.

The only thing I could think of was that he had found a way to buck the system – perhaps his reasons were not even financial, I speculated wildly. A final gift, to release his wife from the system that he himself had helped to create? A final small revenge, by a controlling man on the corporation who had forced him out? Or a Trojan Horse to betray the woman who had thought him so marvellous a husband? Or was this common practice among the wealthy and we just didn't know?

I was obliged to report Gilberto's findings to my manager, and flew back home the next day. There were meetings to which I was not privy. I waited for several weeks, wondering whether Rosalind Lee would be charged, but nothing seemed to happen and after a while, I realised that I would never know for certain what had taken place. I made some discreet enquiries and found that Mrs Lee was still living on the Princess Charlotte, now cruising the Mediterranean. My own feeling is that her husband had replaced her wristband, but without her knowledge, for reasons unknown and that her bewilderment during her interview with me had been genuine. And I suspect that it was simply too embarrassing for both Buena Vista and my employers to face a scandal and to put the knowledge out there that medical records could be falsified. Especially if, as I had surmised, this was not unknown among the wealthy and powerful and they couldn't risk that piece of information getting out.

Six months later, just for the hell of it, I entered a company raffle. The top prize was a retirement berth, for two, on one of the ships owned by Global Line. My luck must have been in. It is on the Princess Louise, a sister ship to the Charlotte. My wife and I will be flying out next week, to inspect our new floating home. My wristband readouts show that I am very excited.

Down and Out Under the Tannhauser Gate

David Gullen

The only thing you could be sure about whoever came through the gate was that they weren't human. Riay's perfect skin was sun-tanned brown and her white hair close-cropped, but her skull was high and narrow, her too-large eyes black on black, and her slender arms had a second elbow that let them fold up like a mantis at prayer.

I looked at her and wondered. If she had started out human she wasn't now, and if she had been then that meant she'd gone through and come back, which to my mind made her pretty stupid. I couldn't imagine myself being that beautiful, so maybe there's a trade-off. Give me the chance to go through the gate and no way would I come back. But hey, if I did, at least it would be all girls together and we could swap makeup tips.

I limped closer. My leg stump always ached. It never lets me forget and that makes me moody.

There, I admit it.

Riay said she wanted us to build a temple.

"Who for?" I said. "Mukaluk the Destroyer, Eccentrica Galumbitz, Omnidod the Translucent, Simon and his Dancing Bear?"

"I came back to help—"

So she *had* come back. I grinned and looked down the steps for Jonni. He'd gone for water two hours ago so should be back soon. "If you're a priestess of Galumbitz there's a bunch of guys down in the town who'd be happy to meet you." I thought about it. 'some women too."

This part of the world is a landscape of steps, a white stone hill two miles wide and one mile high. Eight thousand steps with a hundred flights and platforms. At the bottom lies a human city, a ramshackle shanty thing. At the top are the sky-high silver pillars of the Tannhauser

Gate, the beautiful gate, the one we Earther soldiers tried so hard, so very damned hard, to reach.

How I hate that gate. Yet here I am, living in its shadow.

Most visitors climb the centre regions of the steps. The aliens come down and the replica men go up, because now they are free, they can do what they want. Them, but not us.

Cytheran guards keep everything peaceful, which is nice of them considering they made us rebuild the place when the war was over.

And then there are us humans: the sightseers who dare go so far and no further; the petitioners who want to go all the way and can't; and us ragged bunch of leftovers living beneath our poles and awnings among the rubble along the left-side wall. Every now and then the more adventurous aliens come over to see the puddles of stone-melt and flash shadows from the war. From the day we soldiers fought. From my Day.

In the main the Cytherans leave us to it. They could clear us out in an instant but they never have. Also good of them, I suppose. After what we humans went through, I like to think we have squatter's rights.

A Cytheran air-walked across to check our visiting priestess was all right. I don't like the Cytherans. They're never mean and they're never cruel but they are abrupt, and they have energy lances. Cytherans are humanoid, they walk but their feet don't touch the ground, they slide-walk through the air. Maybe they don't like being here, on what is still human ground. When they stand in front of you in their intricate blue fabric armour and look out through their multifaceted visors of their segmented helmets, it's hard to tell who or what is home. Maybe they're antennae and those aren't helmets.

Riay looked up at the Cytheran. "All is well. There is no need to attend."

The Cytheran bowed, turned and paddled away through the air, angling up the steps towards the gate.

"What's the temple deal?" I asked Riay.

"Help me and I can help you."

I slapped my tin leg. "Can you help this?"

She looked a little sad. "I just need a little help?"

"You mean, like a donation?" That was a good one. I'd never been touched for credit before. The walk-ins are usually passing through, their eyes on the spaceport beyond the city, and the handful of star systems left us from the old empire. They might be crazy but they're not stupid. Well, I say that but they, like Riay, came back.

"I need a symbol, anything. Just a gesture." She pointed towards a heap of rubble against the scarred wall. "Take that brick and place it in front of me. You don't have to say anything, the act is all."

I laughed; it was pathetic. What kind of God wants a temple built from a single brick from a broken wall?

I didn't notice Jonni was back until he put the water containers down. He picked up a brick, held it in both hands like an offering, then knelt and laid it at her feet.

Riay glowed. "Thank you."

She actually looked better. It was probably psychosomatic. She smiled at Jonni and she became radiant, like a sun that shone only for him. Right then I felt my heart harden, and if her smile wasn't bad enough, she reached out, her mantis arm unfolding out of her robe, and touched him with her three-fingered hand.

Let me say that again: she *touched* Jonni.

I was up and screaming, arms flailing, all my training forgotten and thank the gods it was because I could have killed her, killed anyone, killed them all. "What did you do to him? What did you do?"

Jonni wrapped his arms around my waist and lifted me off the ground. My Jonni, the only one who ever had the balls to take me on, even in the days when I'd rage and try to burn it down, burn the whole world with anger so pure it broke my bones. Slowly I learned I couldn't live without him and so it became burn everything except Jonni, and he made a joke about where he would stand and I laughed and he held me and now I could not think of a day without those brown eyes under his loose black curls. His lean long body on mine. My Jonni.

"It's all right. Hey, hey. Breathe, breathe. We're counting down, remember? Here we go: ten, nine–"

I glared at Riay. "What happened? What did that *freak* do to you?"

"Nothing." His face was right in front of me. "Nothing happened."

Almost, I believed. She had it coming.

I – He – Jonni. I couldn't have done any of this without him. Especially through the days when not even the moment by moment of living was easy or even wanted, or the times when I blinked and everything snapped back, and I looked around and wondered why everyone was looking at me because I had no idea what I'd just said or what I'd done. Now I have days where I dream we walk down the steps, away and away to some city on some far planet and he would put something in my belly, a little bit of him, a little of me. Something that would live and grow.

Except I would not leave this place. These steps under the gate. My step. That day. I could not.

One morning three aliens came through the gate to look at the wall and see the signs of the old war. I limped up to my step and leaned on the wall exactly where they would want to go. Everyone who had anything laid out their boxes and trays of trinkets and junk, crouched on the steps, eyes lowered and hands out. Everyone except for Riay, who sat by her brick, and mad Blascard who muttered under his breath then punched the wall and stamped away.

These aliens were short heavy creatures with wide-mouthed heads, peg teeth and stubby legs, like two-legged hippos. They looked sideways at us with white button eyes and kept inside the Cytheran's dome field as they inspected the wall. They looked down at me and hooted to each other. The Cytheran's force dome pushed aside grit and dirt as they came forwards, leaving neat little moraines at each side and a clean track behind. From the corner of my eye I saw Blascard's blue-eyed glare. Here we go again, I thought, but he just rubbed the white stubble on his chin and slid away along the wall.

The three aliens looked at me, at each other, and the Cytheran.

Cytheran voices came inside my head:

—Human gentleperson, do now attend.
Guests wish to inspect the wall—
—guests that stand before you now.
—the wall behind the position you occupy.

I folded my arms and said nothing.

I caught a sub-echo of Cytheran click-babble, one of the hippo-things hooted softly then extended an arm and opened its hand. A few trade tokens materialised at my feet. Their colours looked good, I scooped them up and stood aside.

The aliens went to the wall and scanned the bigger patches of stone-melt and flash shadow with bars of violet light. Then they stood back and looked down at the boot prints left from the day the pavement flowed white hot and people ran.

Once upon a time the human race punched above its weight and we went round after round against the universe. Then we were betrayed.

Pressure built in me, I had to speak.

"I was there." It came out as a shout, a sharp burst of sound. Startled, the aliens clustered behind the Cytheran. I unclenched my fists. I didn't want to frighten them, I wanted them to understand.

"I was there. The last day, that last hour." I put my palm on the flash-shadows burned on the wall. "I know the names of the people who left these marks, I saw – I saw them. I was there. That day…"

The aliens stood like statues, the Cytheran hovered in front of them, gently bobbing up and down. I wanted to tell them that this had been us and us alone. Humanity's last great spear thrust, a final effort driving up the steps to break through the gate. We who came so close: Dumas' brigade, the Fighting Ninth.

Yes, we were wrong and we deserved to fail but so what? I was there and I saw. I – We – On this very step they died. The aliens' stillness made me angry. I climbed towards them.

Out of nowhere Blascard was there, grimacing and gesticulating, his teeth chewing air. He dressed like some desert mystic in loose robes of hessian and linen. With his weathered skin, dirty blond hair and blue eyes he looked the part. He'd nailed the crazy bit too.

Alarmed, the three aliens backed away. The Cytheran went with them, keeping them inside its dome.

Blascard reached out with claw-fingered hands. "Give me a key, give me your *minnesang*. Take me with you, please. I beg you."

The aliens looked everywhere except Blascard. The Cytheran drifted forwards, a burst of click-babble like static, then faintly I heard its voices:

Unfortunately–
–this is not possible.
Please adjust your referents
Soon, perhaps–
–Or never
Adjustment flows from within–

"Take me with you!" Blascard wept and raged. "Give me a *minnesang!*"

Jonni was at Blascard's shoulder, his hand on his arm. "Enough. Come away."

"No." Blascard flung him off. "Please–!"

His fingertips brushed the Cytheran's energy dome and he vanished. This freaked the aliens far more than any of us, even Blascard. No doubt the Cytheran reassured them Blascard was fine, but we all acted outraged and we got a generous extra hand-out of tokens. We trousered a few but kept a good half to give to Blascard when he'd walked back from wherever the Cytheran had put him.

After the aliens left, Jonni stood beside me. Weary, I leaned against him. "Why do those Cytherans hate us?"

Jonni tucked a lock of hair behind my ear. "Why do you think that?"

"They won't even walk on the same ground we do."

"I think maybe they are similar to us, all the aliens. They have hopes and dreams, likes and dislikes, just different ones." He kissed my neck. "They want to get laid."

Well, there was that. I thought about all the things I liked about Jonni; his hands, the dark hairs on his arms, how he made me feel so calm.

He laughed and lifted my arms away. "I want to make sure Blascard comes back."

"He'll be fine."

"I just want to be sure."

Melt scars on the stonework pressed against my shoulders and the calmness Jonni brought disappeared. I traced one of the flash shadows with my hand and remembered all their names. I saw the wild look Dumas gave me the instant before he –

"I didn't run."

"I know," Jonni said quietly.

"I was hurt bad. My leg. The suit locked me down." Which was why I was so far back. Which was why I was the only one.

Jonni's arm tightened round me. "I know."

"I didn't run." And I know I didn't deserve to survive.

We watched and waited for Blascard. A steady breeze came up the steps and blew dirt back over the clean trail the Cytheran's dome had made.

All this helping out and watching over people. Jonni called it Paying it Forwards. "Someone helped me once. I can't help them so I help other people instead."

Of course when Blascard came back he took one look at Riay's brick and said, "What's that?"

"A small but selfless gesture. Will you make one too?"

Blascard took in her up and down. His hands started to shake. "You've been through the gate. Give me your *minnesang*."

A small crowd gathered, people on their way up to the gate to make demands or present some new petition. Behind them three drifting Cytherans watched and waited.

"Your *minnesang*." Blascard dropped to his knees, mumbling. "Please, give it to me. Please."

"I cannot. I am my own key, body and mind, my living self-entire. You I can only teach." Her jointed arm unfolded gracefully; her upturned hand swept the air above the brick. "Help me. We can build something together."

Blascard grimaced and begged; he hadn't listened to a word. "Give it to me," he growled.

"It is not mine to give," Riay said. "I can teach, you can learn—"

"I'm not here to learn, I know my rights."

Hostile voices came from the crowd.

"Don't trust that alien witch."

"Send her back to where she came from."

"This is human territory."

"Freak."

"Traitor."

Words were as far as it ever went. Before it got physical the Cytherans simply popped people away all over the place. Once in a while some Neo-militant idiot pulled a weapon and the Cytherans reminded everyone about the rules. C-beam glitter; Flash-shadow; Stonemelt. Like I needed reminding.

Blascard started at the voices behind him, unaware the crowd was there. He faced them. "We're not here to learn, are we, friends? If we learn, we change. And who wants to change? Better to stay here forever."

He pushed through the silent, confused crowd and marched down the steps.

*

That's how it went. Blascard, Jonni and me, and a few others in shelters on the next platform down. And now Riay too. Jonni said we should help her and I gave her an old blanket because he'd want me to. She said she didn't need it, which was fine because I didn't want to give it to her. Instead, I grudgingly offered to help her build a shelter when she had something to build it from.

"If you really want to help—"

That stupid brick? I laughed at her. "I'm not going to worship you. If there are gods, they're the other side of the gate."

Riay shook her head. "Why would anyone want to be worshipped?"

It sounded good to me.

Jonni did what Jonni does and disappeared for most of the day. I wanted to go with him but my leg wouldn't take it. So much time without him was always hard. I did my best but the rat came out of its burrow, gnawed into in my gut and whispered in my ear: *He's had enough, it's your fault. This time you've done it. He's gone for good. There's no one to blame but you. Your fault. You deserve this.*

I walked up to my step. The step. I didn't eat, I didn't drink, I just sat and watched and waited and fought the teeth and claws. Hours later, when I saw Jonni angling up the steps towards us in the far distance I felt nothing but anger. He carried a bed roll wrapped around half a dozen odd-length planks on his shoulder, and an old metal box under his arm. I didn't understand how he could love me if he made me feel like this. What was so special about that freak woman that he would do all this for her? I glared down the steps at Riay and a black joy came. I could tear her, rip her to shreds.

Jonni walked up to Riay, put the box down and leant the wood against the wall. I couldn't hear her voice but saw her mouth move. Jonni ran his hand through his hair. He smiled, he was tired, Riay poured him some water. I knew how he'd be telling her how cold it would get at night, that he would build something better tomorrow.

There was bad energy in me. I didn't want to go down because I knew how things would go. I went down anyway.

I bounced into the space between Jonni and Riay, right up into Jonni's face. "Where have you been?"

"Hey, just finding some things for Riay."

"It was a long time."

"I had to go a long way and—"

"I didn't like it. Up there, on the step. On my own." Now I had Jonni's full attention, like Riay wasn't there, like she didn't even *exist*.

"What happened?"

"Nothing happened. That's not it."

"What then? Tell me."

Jonni tried to touch me, I knocked his hand away. This is what happens with bad energy, it gets confused. It realises things about itself, that it's diminished, a lesser thing. Worthless. "Jonni, I thought— It's just that when you're gone, I worry—"

"You know I'll come back. Always."

I was angry at myself now. Stupid, stupid. "I know."

I did know. It was just— There was a day when everybody I ever knew left. Stonemelt, flash-shadow. Some days I wished I'd gone with them. I didn't deserve—

"Oh, Jonni, I got this worry."

"I know." He said that a lot. Bless him.

The sun lowered; high dappled clouds turned pink then ruby gold. The miles-long flights of the steps glowed with red light and somehow it was beautiful.

It was also cold, but we had a blanket, me and Jonni. We went up to my step and sat with that blanket around our shoulders and ate the hot food Blascard cooked up on the fire. The night cold crept into my leg and it ached and ached.

Down in the cities, out in the planets I heard they can grow new legs for a gazillion credits. But who would care about a soldier from the last push? The last soldier. The one and only… Maybe the Neos. I'd have to go down and search for them. Plan A: An old soldier goes looking for a bunch of illegals. That would end well. My fists clenched; my stomach clenched. An ache in my leg, another all across my shoulders. Plan B. I took a long slow breath. Ten… Nine… Eight… Seven…

"It's a stupid temple," I said.

Jonni shifted comfortably against me. "Riay wants to stay."

"When— When she touched you—?"

Jonni went still. "Nothing happened."

"I know. But when she touched you—" I knew this was a mistake but I was going to make it. "Did you like it?"

Jonni closed his eyes. I knew if I kept this up, I could drive him away. I could do it easy. Then where'd I be?

"Sorry, Jonni," I said. 'sorry."

Jonni thought about it. "How's your leg?"

"It aches really bad."

"Let's go down to the fire."

That was Jonni for you. It was who he was, the thing I liked most and least about the man I loved. You think this was not so good? You should have seen me three years ago. Tell me about it. I mean, you'd have to tell me about it because I don't remember. Just a few flash-bulb moments of pure anger shouting, screaming. Living with my face turned to the wall.

Jonni put me back together, he taught me the ten-nine-eight so I could get back to the place where I still knew how to think. He put me back together but there were some bits missing. I don't know why he did it. I didn't deserve–

Deep breath.

Ten… Nine…

Jonni is kind to everyone. He wants to help. It's who he is. He sees the good.

Replica men and women travelled up to the gate in groups. A lot of them looked old and frail and they helped each other along. I knew they weren't that old; they just didn't have as much time as we did. It was the way they were, the way we'd made them. I'd have betrayed us too.

Jonni took them water as he did for everyone. They'd stop for a minute and talk, sometimes I'd hear a dry laugh or see a tired farewell. I didn't resent them, I tried not to resent them. Each and every one had a ticket though the gate just because of what they were. Even so, Blascard didn't hassle them. There were fewer and fewer replicas this side of the gate every year and one day there would be none. Jonni was right – *is* right – none of what happened was their fault. It was our fault, all of it. We made them and treated them like slaves. Then we started a war, gave them guns and expected them to fight. So they did, but not for us. Fair enough.

Days went by; I sat on my step and got in the way. People looked at Riay and freaked and didn't build her stupid temple. Jonni carried water, Blascard skimmed and scammed and made demands and otherwise kept himself to himself. One day that furious sense of entitlement of his would get him into real trouble. I wondered why the Cytherans didn't just put him on the far side of the continent, or off-world, so the aliens who came through that gate could get some peace and quiet.

Every day Jonni hung our two water containers on the ends of a rag-wrapped pole, put the pole across his shoulders and went down the steps to fill them. Once in a while I'd go with him and swap credits for food. Jonni likes the raggedy ramshackle town at the base of the steps, it's just a sprawl of one and two-storey shacks on top of the stone-melt, no foundations. The whole vibe felt like a frontier town and I didn't much like it. Frontier of what? Dead dreams. Each trip gave me days of grinding leg pain that wouldn't stop and woke me up at night.

When Jonni came back I stacked the containers while he had a rest. I refilled the bucket, put the lid back on to keep the dust out, and washed the cups.

At night we sat round the fire, shared our food and checked our credits. I'd sit on my step for a while. I try to keep it short because I know sitting there builds bad energy. Too long makes me dream bad dreams.

A new group of petitioners came up the steps, four men and three women, all with close-cropped hair and dressed in the loose robes petitioners tended to wear, like they were mystic or whatever. These were younger than usual and moved easily, untired by the mile-long climb.

There was something about them, so when Jonni took over the water bucket I tagged along.

"Hey, there. Would you like some water?" Jonni took the lid off the bucket, scooped up a full mug and held it out.

The nearest of them, a square-headed blocky man with a stubbled jaw looked at him blankly, chewing something. "No."

"Thank you, brother." A woman moved out of the centre of the group and reached for the cup. Her smile was direct, pretty green eyes in a lean athletic face. I didn't like her.

"That was quite a climb." She smiled, then looked at the square-headed man. "Some of us are tired."

"Yes, I am," he said. "I am tired, and I apologise. Actually, I am thirsty."

"No problem." Jonni held out his hand. "I'm Jonni."

"Luthar."

They shook, Luthar grinned, still chewing. Jonni gave him a mug and he drank half and poured the rest over his scalp. Everyone relaxed into chatter, the woman introduced herself as Baez. This was what Jonni did but I've no idea how he did it. He got on with people and they got on with him. I hung back, not even on the edges.

You could see Luthar was steady. He had the forced wiry strength of a big-bodied man kept in check by a hard regime. I liked him. I decided maybe I liked Baez too.

Luthar saw me watching. "This your old lady?" he said to Jonni.

Jonni stood tall. "Yes, she is."

I came forwards and didn't even think about it. Normally I don't do crowds and seven strangers plus Jonni is crowd enough. Also, petitioners are all the stupid. They go up, they beg and plead, argue and bitch, then come back down again with exactly what they went up with – nothing. Yet with these guys none of that occurred to me. There was something about them I understood.

"Less of the old," I said, though most days it felt true.

Luthar held up both hands. "No offence."

"None taken."

He held out his hand. I took it and his grip was solid, not trying to make a point, just made of iron. Why was I even doing this? I don't do names.

"Mercedes."

Luthar stopped chewing. His mouth opened and closed.

In the following silence Baez said, "Resonant name, considering."

Luthar studied my face, looked at my leg and back to my face. "It's you."

Everyone looked at me. I bunched my fists and took it. Yeah, sure, this was me. Mercedes Gant, last of the Fighting Ninth, last of the last. So what?

The same light came into all their eyes at the same time. Nobody in all my life had been impressed by anything I had ever done. Now I had seven, all watching me with a kind of awe.

It hit me then. They weren't petitioners going to grovel for a *minnesang*. They were Neos, but not a type I'd seen before. Baez, Luthar and the others moved and spoke with the quiet assurance of well-trained and experienced soldiers, and I knew exactly what they were going to do. The part of me that still burned and bled and howled, the bit that felt oddly at peace in their company, knew that if I asked, they would take me with them. This was why I'd walked in – it felt like coming home.

"Don't do it," I said.

Luthar's tongue pushed against his cheek. "We've got a few tricks."

"Enough, Luthar," Baez said, quiet and very, very definite. "Moving on, ladies."

Jonni hadn't got it. "You're welcome to eat with us on the way down."

Baez was oddly thrown by that. "Of course. I– Thank you."

Every single one of them said "Thank you" as they handed the cups back to Jonni but their eyes were all on me as they set of up the steps.

Luthar held back. "Sergeant Gant, excuse me. Where did you–?"

Some things become hard-wired. "Three steps up. Out on the far left."

His eyes had that thousand-yard stare as he looked towards the wall. In the distance a Cytheran led a solitary wand-like alien down from the gate.

"Must have been something," Luthar said.

It was something all right, and nothing. "Don't go. You're all going to die."

"Everybody dies. Thing is, what for?" Luthar said, and jogged up the steps after Baez.

Jonni dumped the mugs into the bucket. "Well, they were different."

He broke my heart some days. "We have to leave. Now."

Baez's group were high up on the steps, as close to the gate as humans were allowed. A Cytheran moved to intercept them and they spread into a wide line.

I grabbed Jonni's arm and pulled. "Come on!"

He pulled back. "My bucket–"

"Forget the damned bucket. They're Neos, they're going to fight."

And of course he turned and looked and it was too late.

Baez sprinted past the Cytheran with Luthar right beside her. The air shimmered around them – force fields. Luthar was right: they did have some tricks.

The Cytheran swung its lance. One of the other Neos darted forwards, wrapped her arms around the Cytheran and they exploded in a flopping meaty red mess.

The boom of the explosion spread across the steps and now everyone was looking. Baez, Luthar, and the remaining Neos raced up onto the final platform and disappeared from view.

I had to see. I pulled Jonni down and scrambled up the steps on all-fours. He grabbed my good foot and hauled me back.

"Stay here," he said and ran up the final flight.

Well, of course not.

Unable to run, I swore and hopped and hobbled after him. We crouched at the top and peered over. One hundred feet across open ground stood the fluted silver pillars of the Tannhauser Gate.

Baez and Luthar were half way there. Cytherans blinked into place all around them. As each one appeared one of the Neos flung themselves at it and exploded.

In my mind I saw Dumas, the moment he looked back.

The Neos weren't trying to get through the gate, they wanted to destroy it. I knew they would fail.

How I wished I was with them.

An army of Cytherans appeared across the front of the gate, ten ranks deep.

Baez fired from the hip. A beam of black light churned a swathe of Cytherans into gouting dust.

Nice trick.

Luthar tried to throw something. Right at that moment he and Baez ceased to exist. A brilliant glitter. Nothing but an after-image remained. A white-hot pool of lava.

The thing Luthar held dropped and rolled across the ground. A black cylinder with domed ends, the whole thing as thick through as my fist. As it rolled, I saw a red light wink.

Jonni saw it too. Before I could move, he was up and running. "Watch out," he shouted. "Hey, hey!"

In pure reflex one of the Cytherans flicked its lance and cut him down.

It was impossible but I saw the Cytheran try to pull the shot. In that long fast moment I swear I saw the lance beam bend, that I saw pure energy change direction and reverse its flow. It was not enough. By the time I reached Jonni he was a tumbled heap of loose limbs and ragged breath.

I crashed down beside him. "Jonni, Jonni!"

His eyes were blank but his face wasn't empty. I'd seen enough death to know he was still in there. I cradled him in my arms and smoothed back his unruly hair. I closed his eyes. I looked up at the Cytherans and somehow I couldn't be angry. All I had was aching regret, sorrow for the waste, for Jonni. Even pity for the one who had done this.

I lifted Jonni up and my leg flared agony. I wanted to walk straight and tall but my stump wouldn't take the weight, the pain was like walking on a white-hot spike. The Cytheran ranks drew aside as I limped and lurched towards them. I heard a furious static burst and a hundred voices spoke in my mind.

—this was never our intent
Never.
Unforeseen
—we know the difference
Unwished
Unwanted
All our <untranslatable> weep with you
He was never—
—he would ever have been—
Welcomed

A final Cytheran slid aside like a leaf on the wind and I was at the gate. The pillars went up forever, the space between a silver-grey curtain like soft rain. Beyond it lay everything we had been denied and now they were letting us through. Jonni was his own *minnesang*, and today, somehow, he was mine too. If I wanted, I could go through.

—no, he is only himself—
You are your own song—

Changed now.
—each becomes their own minnesang.
If you want—

I took a sideways step so the Cytheran was in front of me. Jonni was heavy now, his head lolled. My leg stump hacked like a rip-saw. He had helped me so much but I couldn't help him now. I locked my knees and held him out. The long lance in the Cytheran's hand folded away into nowhere and I laid Jonni in its outstretched arms.

He will not have long—
—yet long enough to know

The army had disappeared. The lone Cytheran holding Jonni swept backwards through the grey curtain.

When you are ready—
Come back?

I took myself away. First, to the far side of the steps, where I sat alone for a day and a night, then down to the town.

I lived there doing this and doing that, getting by. Eventually I had my own place, nothing much but it did for me. Nobody knew who I was and that old urge to tell them had dried up and blown away.

It's strange how you can think things through without thinking. I did a lot of that. Not once did I get angry. I even made some friends.

Everyone dies. Luthar was right but he did it wrong. Jonni died as he lived, trying to help, not destroy. I am my own song, the Cytheran said.

So when people needed help I helped them, just like Jonni would have. I wanted- No, I *needed* to make him proud.

A year went by. When the day Jonni died came around again I discovered how important anniversaries are for the heart. For a while I fell back, then discovered some of those friends I'd made were good ones. They knew what I was going through.

One morning the sky was clear, the air cool and fresh. It felt like a wind blew from a new direction. I paid my rent, closed the door behind me and climbed the steps to the Tannhauser Gate.

I stayed on the other side for a thousand years, living, learning. Some of the time loving and being loved. I could have fixed the leg, I could have changed myself like Riay, when she imagined herself into a truer form.

In the end I just stopped the ache because much to my own surprise I discovered I was comfortable in my own skin, scars and all.

I visited two thousand worlds. With each arrival and departure a different ache pulsed. I tried to deny it but that ache grew. The time came when all I wanted to do was go home.

One day I walked back through the Tannhauser Gate. I filled my lungs with air and tasted the spice, the tang, the smell of burnt stone. I looked down the miles-long steps and saw an agitated group of petitioners trying to persuade three Cytheran to let them past. Nothing much had changed.

The petitioners watched open-mouthed as I walked down the steps. Then they rushed me.

"How did you do that?"

"Show us your key."

"Give me your *minnesang*."

"Tell these *things* to let us pass."

"I can't," I said. "You don't understand."

They didn't. I could see it in their eyes, their body-language.

I opened my mouth. *Please adjust your referents* nearly came out. "It's not like that."

One of them tugged my sleeve. "Did you see the Venusberg?"

Gods, this was going to be difficult.

Then Blascard was there, scrounging and fawning around the Cytheran and making demands so entitled he made the petitioners sound polite.

All I could do was stare at him open-mouthed. "Blascard?"

"Hey."

He led me across and down to the wall, down to my step. He brought me water from Jonni's bucket.

Everything was the same. A thousand years and I'd been gone three days.

I looked at him and he held my gaze. A light came on in my head. "You know."

He gave an apologetic shrug.

I jerked my thumb over my shoulder towards the gate. "So why don't you—?"

"Go? I'm waiting for the rest of these goons to catch up."

By which he meant *ALL* the goons. Human race, FFS.

His success with the aliens started to make sense. They knew what he was doing, they were giving him some help. Blascard was a teacher, the holy fool trying to teach bigger fools. We sat in silence for a while as I did some processing.

Blascard cleared his throat. I'd never seen him so serious, so solemn. He put his scarred-knuckle hand on top of mine. "I'm so sorry."

Jonni. Yeah. Blascard was a real bastard. A thousand years and those three words broke me in two. I cried without words, without breath, without time. Blascard held me while the tears did their job of putting me back together again.

I took a breath and wiped my eyes. "Jonni got to see."

"That's good."

"Blascard, I'm not like I used to be."

Blascard held me at arm's length, his lopsided smile pulled his weather-seamed face. "Welcome to the club."

I felt exhausted and refreshed, drained as if something I didn't need, something that had been holding me back had actually flowed out of me. The sun shone; the wind blew. The ancient stone steps ran up and down in their yards and miles. Over us all stood the Tannhauser Gate.

I poked around in the rubble until I found a stone that felt about the right size and shape, walked down to Riay and laid it against the brick Jonni gave her. She smiled and just for the briefest moment I saw stars glitter in her eyes.

Blascard joined us, looked down at the two-stone temple and gave an enigmatic grunt. Far down the steps another group of petitioners had set out on the long climb. The three of us watched them for a while. Riay took my left hand, Blascard held my right. This was coming home. I wished Jonni was here to see me.

"Okay," I said. "Let's go."

Me Two

Keith Brooke and Eric Brown

For as long as I can remember, I have always been two people.

My earliest recollection is of myself as a three-year-old boy, Danny – and at the same time as a girl of the same age, Cristina.

Another early memory is of playing in the rubble of the bomb-ravaged streets of London, when I asked a little boy, "Who will you be tomorrow?" He looked at me as if I were mad.

I took it for granted that everyone I met, everyone in the world, was two people like me: one day I was Danny Madison of 10 Milton Street, Barnes, London; and the next I would be Cristina Velásquez of 122a Carrer del Santuari, El Carmel, Barcelona.

I went to bed as Danny and woke up in the morning as Cristina.

When as Cristina I asked my mother who she would be tomorrow, she said, "Why, myself. Why do you ask?"

I told her about Danny, and I think she assumed I was making him up – a kind of imaginary friend.

As Danny, I asked my mother and father at breakfast one morning, straight out, "Why am I two people?" By this time I knew that no one else of my acquaintance experienced life quite as I did.

They exchanged a worried look. "What do you mean, Danny?" my father asked.

I explained about Cristina, and that tomorrow I would be her, and my mother said, "I think you're imagining things, Danny."

I intuited their concern, and decided never to mention it again.

By the time we were seven years old, a year after the war had ended, we had worked out that we lived every *alternate* day as our other selves: that is, as Danny I lived the 1st of January, say, and then as Cristina lived the 2nd, with Danny resuming on the 3rd and so on.

Danny would go to sleep on the evening of the 1st and wake up in the morning of the 2nd as Cristina, lying in bed and gazing at the whitewashed ceiling of the small room she shared with her sister. He – or rather she – would stare at her small brown hands in amazement, the memories of herself as Danny the day before fresh in her mind, alongside her own memories of her previous day.

What happened to us in the meantime, on our alternate days, when I was not Danny, and then when I was not Cristina? Was there a mirror version of me that took over on these days? For some time I was drawn to this idea of an intangible other-me – an other-*us* – that swapped roles every night. But no, I knew it could not be so. I still had memories of those days: the Danny days when I was being Cristina, and vice-versa. And while those memories were somehow distanced from the more vivid memories of when I was in control, there was no suggestion at all that I was watching some other guiding personality taking over.

Eventually, I had to yield to my own experience and perception of this strange phenomenon: that one day I was Danny, and the next Cristina, and on those alternate blank days my bodies simply went through the motions, a ghost existence.

In any case, I tried hard not to dwell on the explanation, for it was hard enough simply to survive what was occurring, both psychologically and in any number of more practical ways. In the early days there was always a period of uneasy integration in the mornings, long minutes of adjustment as our twin psyches meshed and negotiated the management of "self". Little by little, I as Danny would recede, take a back seat, and I would reassert myself as Cristina. In the evening Cristina would go to sleep and wake up the following day as Danny, and the period of assimilation would begin again, this time Cristina adjusting herself in Danny's sensorium. As the years progressed, however, the switch-over became routine, no longer a cause of disorientation.

As Danny, I grew up in a relatively affluent middle-class household: when my father returned from the war, he took up a teaching post at the local grammar school where my mother was secretary to the headmaster; I was their only child.

As Cristina, I was one of two girls brought up by my widowed mother – my father, a staunch supporter of the Esquerra Republicana de Catalunya during the Civil War, having vanished, presumed dead like so many after Franco came to power, soon after my birth. My mother was strict and controlling, and it is only with hindsight that I began to understand how this was dictated by her fierce desire to protect her two daughters in a time when perhaps 300,000 children of leftist families were abducted by the state. It is only with hindsight, too, that I came to understand that she must have paid for our upkeep by earning money in whatever ways a woman could in such punishing times.

I soon learned to compartmentalise my memories, so as not to arouse suspicion. As Cristina, I feared my elder sister, who bullied me and thought me strange: I once told her of my other life as Danny, and quite naturally she thought I was lying, and at the same time resented my vivid imagination and the freedom it allowed me to escape our harsh reality.

We were a strange composite, Danny and Cristina. With our dual existence, we shared a double upbringing: Danny, raised as a boy with an Arsenal-loving father, was obsessed with football; Cristina, brought up by an often-absent mother and a bullying sister, sought escape in clothes design and dance, drawn moth-like to the emerging fashion and arts scene in post-war Barcelona. In consequence, Danny showed an early predilection for cross-dressing and ballet – to which my remarkably liberal parents tried to turn a blind eye – and Cristina developed a strange interest in Arsenal football club.

Harder to explain, as Cristina, to my bemused mother was my fluency in English, and as Danny my even less explicable facility in Catalan. I told my Catalan mother they were teaching us English at school, and my English parents that I had a Catalan evacuee as a school friend – and I was able to furnish enough details from the life of this imaginary escapee from Franco's Spain to convince them.

One day, I as Cristina resolved to stay awake all night in an attempt to experience the moment of transition. I read until my eyelids began to droop, then got up to walk around the bedroom, trying desperately not to disturb my snoring sister. Then I returned to bed, repeating the cycle right through to the early hours.

Dawn came at five o'clock, and still I, Cristina, had not transferred to the mind and body of Danny, seven hundred miles away in London.

And then, on the stroke of six, I blacked out – and the next I knew I was blinking myself awake in Danny's familiar bedroom with Cristina's memory of the day before, and her attempt to remain awake, fresh in my mind.

51

We each tried the experiment again from time to time, always with the same result.

For as long as I can recall, we knew that one day we should meet.

In my teens as Danny, I badgered my parents to take me on holiday to Spain, drawing their attention to the rise of what came to be known as the package holiday. Horizon Holidays' package to the Costa Brava would take us tantalisingly close to Barcelona, but despite my persistence, I failed to persuade my parents. The idea of foreign travel was little more than a dream for me as Cristina, with my mother hard-pressed to put food on the family table, never mind afford foreign holidays.

Because of our singular situation, we had developed a self-protective reserve, a hesitation when it came to making friends, of giving ourselves to others. This led to social isolation as we grew up, even loneliness – though of course we were never really alone, as we had each other, and our shared memories, as consolation. This was the paradox: we had each other, and yet on some fundamental level this was never enough.

As Danny, I found myself drawn to slight, gamin girls with dark hair and pale faces – while as Cristina I was attracted to tall, blond boys… which were something of a rarity in Spain.

Despite our reserved nature, we had girlfriends and boyfriends, and even thought we were in love from time to time, but these affairs never lasted. Our lovers accused us of being remote, of being unable to give ourselves fully, and we knew this to be true but could not of course explain the reason why.

In London, I did well at grammar school, and in time enrolled at university, winning a place at Cambridge to study languages and classics. In Barcelona, my education was hard-earned, but as Spanish society opened up in the 1950s – perhaps ironically under the influence of the tourist boom – I caught up at school and took up a place to study art and languages at the Universitat de Barcelona. We excelled, our doubled memories and linguistic abilities aiding and abetting our respective learning.

On graduating and finding jobs – Danny in publishing and Cristina in art restoration – we became for the first time financially independent and turned our minds to the idea of meeting each other for, as it were, the first time.

We tried to fathom the paradox of our singular situation as we contemplated meeting.

As Danny, I would wake up on the morning of our rendezvous, my head full of Cristina's memories of the day before as she took a flight to London and booked into an Earl's Court hotel: I shared her excitement, her apprehension.

We would arrange to meet at eleven at Trafalgar Square. I as Danny would approach the slim, dark girl standing at the feet of the north western lion, staring at the Cristina I was and had been, knowing her intimately and yet never having been able to hold her in my arms.

The ache in my heart would be almost unbearable.

On the day after Cristina flew to London, I awoke with memories as her the previous day still fresh in my mind. I recalled the novelty of the flight, foolishly proud that my reaction was one of excitement and curiosity rather than fear at the noisy, disturbingly flimsy-seeming aircraft. I recalled the subsequent journey to the hotel, and the intense, suspicious scrutiny of the proprietor.

Waking with these memories, I finally allowed myself to believe we were about to meet. I set off for the encounter with the girl I knew I loved, like a teenager on his first date.

Remarkably, perhaps, it was only now that a significant conundrum pertaining to our situation occurred to me. Until now, I had it fixed in my mind: I was going to meet Cristina, and as Cristina, I longed for the day I would meet Danny.

But how could that be so?

I was Cristina *yesterday*, and today I was Danny. The Cristina I was to meet today at Trafalgar Square would be but a ghost, the shadow Cristina of alternate days when I was being Danny . . .

As I sat on the bus, my mind raced in ever more frantic circles, pursuing the logic of a situation that *had* no logic.

Who was I going to meet today? Would shadow-Cristina even know who I was?

I was early. It was a bright spring day and the tourists, and the pigeons, were out in force. I could not stand still in my nervous anticipation, so I walked around the square, eagerly looking out for the slight, gamin figure of Cristina Velásquez.

Eleven o'clock came and went, and Cristina did not arrive.

I checked my watch obsessively. Five past the hour, and still no sign of her. What might have happened? Had she been taken ill, or been struck down while crossing a road? Had her ghost-self forgotten, or not deemed this meeting important? I was beside myself with apprehension.

At noon she had still not appeared.

I did not know what to do. Where was she?

In the modern age, it is hard to recall the complications – and frustrations – of a time when communication was not instantaneous, taken for granted. In an age of social media and mobile phones, the idea that a missed rendezvous could seem so final is hard to fathom. But in the early 1960s, of course, there was no easy way to locate someone in such a situation.

In the end, in desperation, I found a telephone box and thumbed through the directory until I located the Earl's Court hotel where I had booked in after my flight as Cristina the day before.

I dialled the number, impatiently waiting each time as the rotary dial spun slowly back to its resting position before I could dial the next digit.

"Traveller's Rest, what can I do for you?"

It shouldn't have surprised me that I recognised the voice of the man who had studied me from head to toe upon my arrival the day before. Of course I did: I had *been* there.

"Hello," I said, my brain racing. "I'm trying to locate a guest of yours. We were supposed to meet this morning but she didn't turn up. I'm concerned for her safety."

I paused, but there was no response, a clear indication of how much the hotel proprietor cared about our failed rendezvous.

"Her name is Cristina Velásquez, and she flew in from Barcelona yesterday afternoon." I had to consciously correct myself before speaking aloud: *she* flew in, not *I*.

"You got the wrong hotel, mate. There's no Christine whatever staying here."

"But there is! Cristina, not Christine. She checked in yesterday." *I* did. I recalled it vividly.

"Listen, mate. Unless your Christine has a thick red beard and speaks like a Paddy, then you've got the wrong place. We're full up with Irish navvies, just as we always are. Now good day to you."

And, with that, the line went dead.

I hurried home, weeping at the irony: I was unable to communicate with the person to whom I was closest in all the world.

But tomorrow… Tomorrow I would wake up as Cristina, with not only my bitter memories of today, but with hers also. Then I would find out the reason for her non-appearance.

That night I went to bed early and, after a long time, sleep came.

I awoke at dawn and blinked up at the cracked ceiling of the hotel room, and Cristina's memories of the day before came crashing in on me.

I recalled the excitement of navigating London's buses, with a knowledge of the network no young Catalan on her first visit to the country should have. Of peering out of the windows as the capital unfolded around me, familiar and yet seen for the first time.

I recalled the visceral thrill as I alighted from the bus at Trafalgar Square at five minutes to eleven and approached the designated stone lion where we were due to meet. My heart pumped heavily and my thoughts were feverish as I scanned the tourists in the square.

And then, with now terrible familiarity, I relived the growing disappointment as I realised that the tall, blond figure of Danny was not among them.

As I had as Danny, Cristina had waited hours, and still that young blond man she had seen in a mirror so many times did not show himself. Unlike Danny, she had no number to call: as Danny, I lodged in a Crouch End terraced house with no telephone. The only number she had was that of my parents in Barnes, but what good would that be?

Early the following day, in desperation, I as Danny took a bus to the hotel in Earl's Court where she was staying. Loitering across the street, I saw a succession of burly labourers emerge, but no Cristina.

The following morning, as Cristina, I woke up with the memory of visiting the hotel as Danny, and those of Cristina yet again going to Trafalgar Square at eleven.

In my desperation, I took a taxi to Crouch End, and hurried down the garden path. I lifted and dropped the lion's head knocker and waited, my throat dry and my heart beating wildly.

An ancient, grey-haired woman opened the door and peered at me suspiciously, and when I asked if Danny was at home, the woman looked querulous. "Danny? Who's Danny? There's no one here called Danny."

And when I as Cristina looked more closely at the front door, now closed firmly in my face, I realised that it was not the door I knew from memory: Danny's front door was navy blue and freshly painted; this one was black and peeling.

The following week, working on a terrible intuition, I as Danny booked a flight to Barcelona and rode a bus to El Carmel. Knowing full well the outcome, I climbed the steep street and approached the ugly square block where I as Cristina lived – so familiar from a thousand memories, and yet subtly different. I took the stairs to the third floor and rapped on the door of number eighteen.

A flustered mother with a babe in arms snatched open the door, listened to my gabbled question, and told me that no one called Cristina Velásquez lived there, or ever had.

In futile desperation, I tried the fourth floor, then the second, and so on, until I had exhausted all possibilities, but to no avail.

I even went to the gallery where I knew I as Cristina worked, only to be told that no one by that name was employed there.

At last, abject in defeat, and bemused, I took the next flight back to London.

Years passed.

We became ever more melancholy and introverted, our relationships with others – both close and passing – doomed to fail because we were always holding something in reserve. We lived with the terrible knowledge of the irony of our situation: we experienced alternate lives, as one, as intimate as it was possible to be – and yet by some cruel trick of the universe, forever and impossibly parted.

We craved the other; as Danny, I desired to hold Cristina's slim body to mine, and I as Cristina wanted no one but Danny.

Some say that what we love in our love object is no more than a reflection of ourselves – like two mirrors placed face to face and reflecting each other into an infinity of solipsism.

If that were so, then it was certainly true in our situation.

Deprived of what we could not attain, and perhaps in a perverted desire to hurt that which we each desired, we embarked on a series of ill-fated and masochistic affairs with pale substitutes of each other. We might have had the other in mind, as it were, but in the flesh we were forever denied – so as Cristina I chased unsuitable, tall blond men, and I as Danny debased myself at the feet of slight, raven-haired beauties.

As Danny, I even married a petite French woman called Claudette, and for a time managed to convince myself that I had broken out of the vicious circle, but it only lasted eighteen months before Claudette had finally had enough of my prickly, standoffish manner. With delicious irony, the final straw was when I called Cristina's name aloud while I was dreaming, only to awaken to Claudette's accusations that I must be having an affair with this mysterious Cristina.

At some point – I do not recall when, the late 1970s perhaps, a time when my divorce from Claudette was reaching pyrotechnic extremes, and in Barcelona I was finding the stresses of our peculiar double existence almost too much to bear – as Cristina I read an article in a Spanish science journal reporting the research of a Swiss quantum physicist. He claimed to have proved, mathematically, the existence of an alternative world, of another Earth existing in close contiguity with our own.

We were excited. Could this, we wondered, explain our unique condition? Did we exist, Cristina and Danny, side by side on different Earths, our flesh separated by the width of mere molecules that might as well have been a million miles apart, but our minds in some strange way conjoined?

Was that the explanation?

When I woke the next day as Danny, I wrote to the physicist, making good use of my fluency in French – perhaps the one good thing to come from my brief marriage to the fiery Claudette. I couched our experience in theoretical terms, but received no reply. I'm sure I came across as some kind of crank, but still the absence of response rankled and lingered for long weeks until I finally gave up hope of a reply.

We heard no more of the physicist's claims, though we scanned all the journals and research papers relating to quantum physics until our minds whirled with a multitude of abstruse impossibilities.

The internet came along when we were in our sixties, and entrenched in our ways. In our work in Barcelona and London, we used computers where required, but little beyond that.

One day I plucked up the courage to ask a young colleague in the Linguistics Department at UCL if he could help me find an old colleague by the name of Cristina Velásquez, an art historian I claimed to have met at a conference in Madrid. I could tell from the young man's knowing smile he thought there was more to it than that, and I chose not to correct him or tell him more.

"You sure?" he said, after a few minutes spent tapping away on his laptop in the Starbucks where we had arranged to meet. He turned the screen to show me the fruits of his search. "I can't find her, which is odd in itself. *Everyone* leaves some kind of digital footprint these days. There's a Maria Velásquez at the University of Granada – a daughter, perhaps?" Maria Velásquez turned out to be not a day older than thirty. And Afro-Caribbean.

The next result was a Mexican artist, now resident in the USA. A set of Facebook profiles – so my young colleague told me – included a fiery redhead from Chile, a woman from Guatemala, and a pouting twenty-something woman who, from the thumbnail image I briefly glimpsed, appeared to be posing in her underwear.

"Maybe Cristina doesn't use the internet," I said tentatively.

My colleague laughed at the very idea, then paused, eyeing me more closely, no doubt reminding himself that the reason he was helping me was that there were still a few people, at least, of my generation who had little interest in the internet and social media.

And it was true: what use did the world of computers offer me in my futile quest? My experience of asking my friend to search for Cristina online merely reminded me of that failed rendezvous at Trafalgar Square in the early 1960s: faster and slicker a search, and no doubt more comprehensive, but just as doomed to failure.

The years continued to pass, and eventually the attraction of the flesh paled until all that remained was the Cristina- and Danny-shaped holes in our existence, a quest that had formed who we were so thoroughly that without it we would have been entirely different people.

We became reclusive, entire unto ourselves and yet on some fundamental level unfulfilled. Increasingly, we thought, what was happening to us was not so much inexplicable as something with no basis in objective reality and therefore resistant to logical explanation. What we experienced was no more than a sick, subjective malaise.

In time, we retired and bought cottages on the coastlines of our respective countries, Cristina on the rugged littoral north of Barcelona, Danny beside a quiet Devon estuary.

We dreamed away our old age, wondering what might have been had we not been blessed by our double lives... or cursed.

And then, one day in high summer, it happened.

As Danny, I pottered around the garden, then prepared myself a simple evening meal and sat in the conservatory with a glass of port, watching the sun set. I looked forward to the morning, when I as Cristina would, as habit decreed, rise early and make my slow way to the local market. We enjoyed market days in rural Catalonia.

A little drunk, I fell into a deep sleep, and awoke the following morning as myself... I mean, as Danny.

I experienced a kind of existential panic.

Had I become so drunk the night before that I had slept through an entire day and night? But I had had only two glasses of port the previous evening, and anyway today was the third of July, as it should be.

As it should be... I *should* have been experiencing the life of an elderly, grey – but still beautiful – Catalan woman called Cristina Velásquez. But instead I was locked in an ageing arthritis-ridden, and distinctly male, body.

I missed her with all my being: I missed the reassurance of Cristina's comforting reality.

Until this very point, I could never have imagined how powerfully I would feel that absence.

What had happened to my love?

*

I went to sleep that night in anticipation, and awoke to bitter disappointment. And so the following night and morning, and the next and the next . . .

At last I came to understand that I was left with that enjoyed by every other human being: a single, consecutive life.

And loneliness beyond endurance.

And so now I must reconcile myself.

She is gone. Whether Cristina Velásquez was another aspect of me who lived a parallel life on another Earth, or a figment of a young boy's war-damaged personality, or something else entirely, that existence has reached its inevitable conclusion.

Cristina Velásquez is no more. As Cristina, I had not been aware of any creeping illness, so I can only assume it came suddenly, a heart attack or a tragic accident.

Today I even had the foolish idea of searching one more time, inputting my other name into Google – yes, I have finally caught up with modernity, to an extent – but found nothing. No accident, no report of a death of Cristina Velásquez. Of course there was nothing.

I did not need that, in any case. The changed nature of my existence was evidence enough.

And so I pour myself a glass of Cristina's favourite Empordà rosé rather than my usual port, and take it out to the conservatory.

Across the estuary, the sun is setting, lighting the sky a fiery red.

My friends – such as they have ever been – have always treated me with a somewhat pitying attitude for the isolated and apparently lonely existence I have led, but how could I ever convince them that I have – I realise now – lived a life less lonely than any of them?

For I have never been alone in the world, not for a moment.

And so I raise my glass and drink to you, Cristina.

To us.

And to a life lived doubly to the full.

Salut, amor meu!

Until I wake as you again.

The Andraiad
Tim Major

A machine working a machine.

Throughout the hymn, Martin relished this sensation, all the time visualising the enmeshing of well-oiled cogs. His fingers marching across the dual keyboards, his feet upon the treadles or working the swell. The tone from each pipe above him acted as an urgent call, directing the congregation. What he lacked in gentleness, he made up for with precision.

"I, the Lord of sea and sky," the parishioners intoned, invisible behind him, "I have heard my people cry."

Martin led them onwards, supporting the singers from below even as his melody soared above the voice of Reverend Walton. He became entranced by the movement of his own hands. He lacked sheet music and he supposed that some would attribute his playing to a memory embedded in his mind through repetition. But it was deeper than that, forged into his body. Such a complex machine.

"All who dwell in dark and sin," the congregation continued in their customary drone, "My hand will save."

Strange how these people, Martin's family and his neighbours, could seem so very machinelike themselves, en masse. He supposed that anthills were rather like machines, when considered as a whole. A flock of birds. A swarm of bees. Bodies, too, were made of constituent organs, and those organs were built of smaller substances, all alive, all operating in the way that they must. Martin stared at his right arm, the mat of hair and the flesh rippling with the play of the tendons within.

A notion took root: that he was at the mercy of the instructions that comprised the hymn, the melody, this construction in sound, and yet at the same time the sound was *his* alone; he was responsible for it. He had *made* it. A machine working a machine.

"I will go, Lord, If You lead me. I will hold Your people in my heart."

Martin's fingers and feet stopped moving, as abruptly and as shockingly silent as the stilling of a heavy pendulum.

For a few seconds the congregation continued at the same volume: "I will hold Your people –"

And then, registering the lack of accompaniment, many broke off, so that only a few voices – a lusty baritone, two or three wavering children and Reverend Walton's enthusiastic but reedy tone – continued, seeming like an addendum or an apology, " – in my heart."

Martin barely listened as the reverend concluded the service, referring back to his sermon, which had been something about humility. Martin didn't even turn around on his stool, but remained with his back stooped, his eyes fixed upon the black and white keys.

"You played very well," Connie, his wife, said outside the church. "Everybody said so. They're all proud to be accompanied by a fine musician."

"But I stopped," Martin said.

His daughter, Ruth, was at his other side. "Why was that, Father?"

"I just stopped."

Ruth was looking at him in a particular way. Martin found that he didn't like it, and then he marvelled at his emotional response.

"Perhaps you were tired," Connie said hesitantly. "You slept in this morning, after all, which isn't at all like you. Maybe you're sickening for something."

"That's impossible," Martin replied immediately.

When they arrived at their narrow terraced house, Martin built and stoked the fire, filled a bowl from the tap in the yard, heated the water, and then excused himself. In his bedroom he took out his shaving apparatus and set to work. It was inexcusable that he had failed to shave before attending the service. Inexcusable, and incomprehensible. Just because he was incapable of believing in the Almighty didn't mean that he could ignore the standards of those that did. These were instructions like any other, and they ought to bind him.

When he had finished, he stared at the whorls of hair shavings in the bowl. Such a complex machine.

He strode downstairs feeling restored and enjoying the simple pattern of his feet treading upon the steps, one two, one two.

Ruth had made a fruit cake and she had set three places at the table. Martin took his seat at its head and watched as she cut the cake and put slices onto small plates, and then poured tea into three cups. Before he picked up his cup, he caught his daughter's eye, uncertain. He must always be careful and do what was right.

Ruth nodded slightly and then made a small movement with her eyes that made clear that the slice of cake, too, was safe to consume.

While his wife and daughter chatted, Martin sipped at the tea, then took a tentative bite of the cake. They tasted very good.

"Well, I have some errands to do," Connie announced when their plates and cups were empty. "Helen has some leftover cloth that she's willing to sell, and it will be far cheaper than anything at the shops. Unless you think it's wrong to exchange money on a Sunday?"

The question was directed at Martin. He laughed before he could stop himself.

Connie frowned. "What did I say that you find funny?"

"Only that you think I should have an opinion about such a thing," Martin replied.

Then he caught the look of warning that Ruth directed at him.

"What I mean," he said hurriedly, "is that everybody ought to consult their own conscience. I'm sure that there is no harm in buying cloth from a friend, in order to continue your work without delay come Monday. Being industrious is one way to serve God."

After a brief hesitation, Connie beamed. "Yes," she said warmly, "you're right, Martin. Thank you."

Martin didn't look at Ruth, but continued, "I'd like to accompany you, if I may? I myself can't work today, of course. Intruding into people's homes and making a racket is no activity for a Sunday."

Connie blinked. "Are you sure you want to? You've never before –"

Martin put his hand on her arm. "I would enjoy it. We spend so little time together during the week."

Connie nodded, then gazed at him, then nodded again, then hurried away.

When she returned, Martin noticed that she had changed her blouse and she was wearing her most colourful headscarf.

At first, Martin attempted to engage his wife in conversation, but it was stilted and superficial. He felt her hand trembling on his arm. Perhaps she knew.

But then they fell into silence as they crossed the common, passing the discoloured patches of grass where the fairground stalls had been a week ago, and they stopped to look at the horses eating hay and then they gazed up at a murmuration of starlings, and yet still they said nothing to one another. To Martin's surprise, he experienced a sensation – which he was tempted to name 'closeness' – to his wife. Perhaps shared experiences could bond one person to another, even when one of the people in question was as impenetrable as him. Or perhaps the sensation was simply a ghost, a memory that wasn't his own.

When they reached the far side of the common and entered the cluster of houses, Martin found that he recognised the area, though the image in his mind was from a different perspective, from the road. He stiffened, but Connie didn't appear to notice.

"I'll keep with Helen for a little while," Connie said. "She always likes to gossip. You won't want to stay."

"I'd be happy to stay, if you'd like me to," Martin replied.

Connie's eyes searched his face. "That's kind of you. No, you go back and rest. You're still recovering. But I've enjoyed our walk together." She paused. "I love you, Martin, very much."

"I love you too," Martin replied, then chastised himself for saying it too quickly, rendering the statement less meaningful. To correct the error, he told himself not to break his gaze. He studied her features: her sharp nose, dark, intelligent eyes, cheeks flushed in the cold, hair now a mixture of blonde and white. She had always been a beauty, and yet this age perhaps suited her better.

Connie pulled her hands gently out of his grasp. She stepped back, and then when she turned and began walking along the lane, Martin experienced a terrible sense of loss.

He had barely gone any distance back the way he had come when the door of a familiar house opened and a woman hurried out.

Martin pretended to himself that he did not recognise her.

"I saw you from the window," the woman said, and a name came to him unbidden: *Thea*. "I often find myself wondering if you might come."

Martin shook his head. "I was accompanying my wife to her friend's house."

"Then she'll be busy for a while yet?"

Thea was younger than Connie, and her opposite in many ways: dark-haired, with red lips. Her body was a different shape. Martin told himself that colours were just colours, and shapes were just shapes.

"I need to be elsewhere," Martin said.

In truth, he had nothing he needed to do until he could resume house calls the next morning. But his statement was broader than that: he needed to be elsewhere, meaning that he needed not to be here with Thea.

"I'm alone now," Thea said.

Martin didn't respond. He listened to the thudding within his body. Such a complex machine.

"I suppose you heard Hal's in prison?" Thea continued. "Because of you." Her expression made clear that this was no bad thing. She attempted to take his arm, to lead him to the doorway of her house. When he refused to move, she ran her hand along his shoulder and then placed a fingertip on the back of his shaven head, tracing the long, horizontal scar.

Martin shook his head. "No."

"No? No what?"

"No to all of it. No to what you are offering. And no to the idea of my being a part of what happened."

The plumpness of her lips made her frown monstrous.

"Then you fought Hal for what reason? You were injured so badly for what reason?"

Martin took a step backwards, in the direction of the common. "For no reason. That was not me at all. That was a different person."

Ruth was sewing contentedly before the fireplace. She looked up as Martin entered the room.

"Are you unwell?" she said. "You're very pale."

He remained in the doorway, bracing himself against the frame. He had felt unsteady the entire walk home.

"Surely that question cannot apply to me," he said weakly.

Ruth hesitated. "I'm sorry. I mean to say, are you functioning properly?"

Martin staggered to the chair opposite hers. He welcomed the warmth of the fire even as a thought flashed into his mind that it might be unsafe to be so near to it. He had no idea what represented a risk to the investment that he represented.

"No," he said. "I'm not functioning well at all. What can be done?"

His daughter watched him carefully. "First, tell me what you feel."

"Feel," he repeated numbly.

"Yes. You're capable of feeling."

He nodded slowly. This assertion alone was helpful. The sensations he had experienced had been true ones. Such a complex machine.

"A great many things," he said.

"Is any one greater than the others?" Her tone was light, but she had put down her sewing and leant forwards.

Martin allowed the question to sit within his chest, awaiting processing.

"Guilt," he said finally.

Ruth put her hand to her mouth. Martin couldn't tell if the movement represented surprise or simply careful consideration.

"Guilt about what?" she asked.

"About all that happened," Martin said. "But – but it is not my guilt, Ruth. I was not there. The guilt is his, and his alone. Why must I bear it?"

Ruth stared at the licks of flame in the grate. "You're a complex machine. And you were modelled upon a precise template. The model is so accurate that it's only natural that you share many of the attributes of Martin Helm."

"But what use is it to carry the guilt of another man?"

"You really don't see why?"

"No, I don't. It's worthless. An obstacle."

"But you weren't created in order to live a life without obstacles. The money was spent in order to redress wrongs."

"But I could more readily do that without –"

She cut him off. "No. If you understood nothing of Martin Helm's crimes – if you remembered nothing of what he did – then you would have no hope of repairing the damage."

Martin considered this. Though he knew instantly that it was true, it still seemed an awful thing, to create a machine that felt pain.

In a softer voice, Ruth continued, "That's what you're *for*, now. You were created to live Martin Helm's life, but to live it in a way that he never could. To honour promises and to uphold responsibilities. I know you understand that, deep down, because it is true and you are a machine that is capable of responding only to what is true and good."

Martin thought of the warmth of Thea's hand on the back of his neck. He reached up and touched the bulbous line of his scar.

"Then am I incapable of sin?" he asked hesitantly.

Ruth nodded firmly. "That's right. You're incapable of sin."

Martin exhaled with relief. He found he was able to put the image of Thea out of his mind.

"Thank you," he said. "You're a wonderful daughter. To me and to Connie."

Ruth reached to the small table beside her to pick up her sewing, and she resumed her work. Still looking down, she said, "You know that you must not talk to Mother about it? At all."

"Of course. But you haven't made clear whether she knows what I am, or whether it is only that being reminded of the truth is distasteful to her."

"She doesn't know. The money that paid for your construction was my own. So I want no mention of the word 'andraiad' to Mother, or any allusion to what you are. You must understand."

Martin nodded even though Ruth wasn't looking at him. He watched her in silence for several minutes. She was industrious and practical, sometimes like a machine herself, but he fancied that her soft heartbeats echoed throughout the room. She was a wonderful creation.

"May I sit here beside you and read for a while?" he asked.

She looked up from her work only for a moment, and she smiled and nodded.

The next morning Martin left the house early, first visiting the carpenter to replenish his supplies, and then knocking on the door of the Newgate house at precisely nine o'clock. Ben Newgate had left hours ago for the pit, so it was his wife, Elizabeth, who admitted Martin and then immediately set about brewing tea. In the dining room at the front of the house, Martin set out his tools on the floor beside the upright piano, then began moving ornaments from its top to the dining table. Many of them appeared fragile – picture frames teetering on card stands, thin glass vases capable of holding only a single stem – but Martin relished the fact that he would be incapable of damaging or dropping any of them.

"There's scones as well," Elizabeth said from the doorway. "Would you like your tea now, or will you wait 'til after?"

"None for me," Martin replied cheerfully. "I've a fair few jobs on today, Mrs Newgate –"

"Call me Bessie."

" – so I won't stop. Thanks all the same." He opened the top cover of the piano, then peered inside to locate the pin that would open the upper front cover. He ran his fingertips lightly over the exposed hammers. As expected, the lower part was fixed with screws, and they were tight from disuse, but he was a well-crafted, strong machine and he removed them with ease.

He registered that Elizabeth hadn't moved from the doorway.

"How's Ben?" he said.

"Fine. At least, so I'm told. I barely see anything of him. Long hours at the pithead, then long hours at the White Hart."

Martin paused, but didn't turn to face her. He sat on the piano stool and began fixing the mutes to the strings, then took the tuning hammer from his leather bag. He gazed at the taut, parallel strings, the array of tuning pins. Such a complex machine.

He remained aware of Elizabeth in his peripheral vision, all flesh and hesitation and desire.

"You go and get on," he said quietly. "I'll let you know when I'm finished."

He waited until she retreated from the doorway, and then he struck the first key.

The next two women who received him did not trouble him while he worked. Whether that had anything to do with his impassiveness, he could not tell. He wondered if the old Martin Helm, the real Martin Helm, would have approached either of them, but then he found that he didn't much care.

During the fourth and final call of the day, a child stood beside the piano as he set to work.

"What do they do?" the boy asked. Martin estimated that he was around four years old. He had wide eyes and very straight, fair hair, and he regularly jerked his head to flick the hair from his eyes. He was pointing at the exposed strings.

"When struck, each of them will produce a different sound. The longer the string, the lower the pitch. Listen."

Martin rotated the tuning hammer and, very gently, tapped one of the leftmost strings with its handle to produce a dull, low tone. Then he tapped one of the shortest strings, producing a *tink* which hardly registered as any pitch at all. Finally, he tapped somewhere near to the middle.

The boy laughed. "Like my xylophone!"

"Exactly," Martin replied. He smiled. "A piano is played in just the same way, with hammers striking the strings."

The boy frowned, looking at the black and white keys. "Mummy uses her fingers. Is she doing it wrong?"

Martin heard laughter from the doorway. Beatrice Connolly was watching them.

"Is Louis bothering you, Mr Helm?" she said. "Shall I take him away?"

Martin – this Martin, the andraiad – had never encountered a child before. He might have expected children to be chaotic, unpredictable; he might have expected to be repulsed. The real Martin Helm had never liked them, he seemed to recall.

"No," Martin said. "I'll show him how it works. I've time."

And he did just that. He lifted the boy – Louis – to show him the rods attached to the rear parts of the piano keys, connecting them to the dampers and hammer knuckles. Louis squealed with delight as Martin pushed a key and the hammer pulled back and struck the string.

Even when Martin set to work adjusting each of the pins in turn, patiently shifting the tweezers to mute the adjacent strings, Louis watched attentively. Beatrice brought a second stool so that the boy could stand upon it, gazing down at the innards of the machine, his eyes darting to determine which hammer would strike next. Martin passed the tuning fork to him – another device that had elicited the boy's admiration – and allowed him to strike it occasionally, if he required a reference note.

When he had completed his task, Martin shook Louis' hand solemnly and thanked him for his assistance. As he set about closing up the front panels, Louis pointed out the strings to his mother, and she made noises of feigned interest. Martin was just closing the top cover when Louis' hand darted out, perhaps to tap the strings a final time before they were hidden from sight, and Martin had to jerk the lid up again to avoid crushing the boy's fingers.

He said his goodbyes hurriedly and almost forgot to provide an invoice in his haste to leave. Outside, he turned to see that the boy was watching him from an upper window. Martin walked stiffly to the road and didn't allow himself to look back. An imagined picture of the boy's crushed fingers appeared in his mind, and he felt sick.

Having completed his work so promptly, he had two hours to spare before dinnertime.

For a time he stood beside the kitchen sink, sipping a cup of tea that Ruth said would replenish his supply of water, and he watched his wife and daughter at work, cutting and sewing cloth to make aprons and bags. Then he went into the yard and entered the brick outhouse in which he stored his work supplies.

This satisfactory pattern continued. Martin scheduled more jobs each day, advertising and travelling further from home, but his machine efficiency meant that he often completed the day's tasks with hours to spare.

Neither Connie nor Ruth asked what he spent his time doing in the outhouse each day. Sometimes Connie set down her cloth and called his name from the back door of the house, and when Martin emerged, they went for walks with no destination. They talked about whatever was on Connie's mind. When his wife asked if he was happy, Martin said that he was. Sometimes, before sleep, they made love.

Martin had taken remnants of cloth and bundled it around the machine, intending to leave the house without revealing it. He had waited until Connie had set off for the haberdashery and until he saw Ruth standing at the kitchen window. He entered by the rear door of the house and walked with his head lowered. He knew that Ruth was watching him as he passed, but he also knew that she understood that he was incapable of doing any wrong. He held the bundle to his chest and slipped out of the front door without speaking to her.

He looked up, startled, as a figure approached the house.

"Connie," he said forlornly. "I thought you would be out for a while."

"I forgot my list, my measurements," she said. She looked down at the bundle and her eyes narrowed. "What's that you have there?"

"Parts to repair the church organ," Martin said, and felt a pang of surprise that he was able to deliver so blunt a lie.

"But you serviced it last week."

"It requires more attention."

Connie's eyes didn't stray from his face. Martin felt his cheeks flush. Such a complex machine. So very lifelike.

"Wait, then, and I'll get my list, then I'll walk with you to the church," Connie said.

"No."

"No?"

Martin clutched the bundle tighter, rubbing the coarse fabric between his thumb and forefinger.

"There aren't parts in there, are there?" Connie's tone was colder now, her enunciation stiffer. "Oh, Martin. What is it you've taken?"

"I've taken nothing. Connie, I would not. I *could* not."

"It's still theft if I don't want you to take it. If you sell whatever you have there, the money you receive is stolen." Martin detected weariness in her delivery of these statements. Connie had said all this before, to Martin Helm. "And that's before any consideration of the sinfulness of whatever you intend to spend the money on."

Abruptly, she launched herself at him, striking his chest. Martin thought of pianos, and imagined that his chest might produce a sonorous note under the hammers of her little fists. He held the bundle away from her, but otherwise remained inert and let her hit him again and again.

Two women passed along the road, turning their heads to watch their fight. Martin couldn't bear the thought of people suspecting that there might be any discord within the Helm household.

"Hush. I'll show you," he said quietly.

Connie hugged herself and watched as he placed the bundle on the doorstep, then unwrapped it carefully.

It was fine work. A machine created by a machine. The head of the little automaton was askew, but with a careful push Martin set it right.

Connie made a soft sound beside him.

"You turn this handle here," he said, guiding her hand as she bent to the doorstep to examine the device.

She turned the crank, and the automaton's hands began to rise and fall above the flat, painted expanse of the keyboard of the bulky upright piano. Its head nodded as it played silently.

Connie made the same sound again. It was something like laughter, something like choking.

"Who is it for?" she asked. "Whose child?"

Martin gathered the cloth around the machine again and rose, then helped his wife to her feet.

"Come with me," he said. "I'll introduce you to him."

Beatrice Connolly reacted with surprise when she opened the door to find them both standing there.

"Is there something the matter with the piano?" she asked, looking first at Martin, then at Connie. As if in response, a single note from a piano sounded behind her, echoing through the house.

Martin noticed Connie's searching expression as she gazed at Beatrice. Some machine part within him became misaligned, and his chest ached.

"Not at all," Martin said. "I was hoping to speak to Louis, if that would be all right."

Beatrice stood back to let them in.

In the dining room, Louis was sitting before the piano, his short legs dangling from the stool. His body was angled oddly and he was leaning far over the keyboard so that his head touched the body of the machine, his face turned away from the doorway.

"He says he's teaching himself how to play," Beatrice said, "but mainly he plays a single note at a time, then just listens. I've told him the cover isn't to be taken off, but he likes to put his ear to it as he presses each key."

Louis turned and then smiled when he recognised Martin.

"We'll let you carry on in a moment," Martin said. He reached for the fallboard and, when Louis had retracted his hands, he lowered it. Then he placed the wrapped bundle onto the surface. "This is a gift for you."

Louis gazed up at him for several seconds before turning his attention to the bundle. He peeled away the cloth to reveal the miniature piano and its player. Without prompting, he began to turn the handle; Martin admired his gentleness. The player played. Martin couldn't see Louis' face. The boy turned the handle again and again.

"Oh my," Beatrice said. "Say thank you to the man, Louis."

"Thank you," Louis said automatically, not turning from the machine.

Beatrice said, "Whatever did we do to deserve this, Mr Helm?"

Martin was conscious of his wife watching him closely. "It's nothing at all, Mrs Connolly. I just thought that Louis would enjoy it. And I enjoyed making it."

He refused the offer of tea and cake and left the house soon afterwards. Connie stayed behind for a minute or two, speaking to Beatrice, no doubt seeking reassurances. Martin gazed at the trees lit golden by the lowering sun, experiencing total satisfaction.

On the walk home, they were both silent until Connie said, "That was a wonderful thing to have done. You would never have done it before."

Martin understood that she meant before the attack. Though she didn't realise it, she was referring to a different person entirely, the Martin Helm that had died as a result of his injuries. The Martin Helm who had done nothing to deserve this wife, their daughter, their home, their life.

Connie said, "Do you think you'll make more?"

"For Louis?"

"For other children."

"I know no other children."

"Maybe soon, though."

He turned to look at her. He sensed machinery clicking into gear.

"Not me, you daft thing," Connie said, and laughed.

Martin blinked. His workings failed him.

"All being well," Connie began, speaking slowly, considering her words, "you will be a grandfather by Christmas."

"But Ruth –"

Connie interrupted him. "She intends to marry. Gordie will ask her. He'll ask you first, of course, but I suspect he's fearful of your answer. He came to me, and I thought it best that you be prepared."

The ratchets, hammers and cogs within Martin seized. He wondered if he might be incapable of responding at all.

"Is she happy about it?" he asked finally.

"She is. About the child and the husband. The ordering is wrong, but the outcome will be right. I beg you, consider her happiness above all else."

Martin nodded stiffly. The simple action seemed to release him from paralysis.

"Of course," he said. Then he rubbed at one eye, which was wet. "And I will make more toys."

When Ruth received his judgement, she nodded and thanked him. She hugged him around his waist, pressing her ear to his chest just as Louis had listened to the workings of the upright piano.

Then she stepped back and looked up at him, her expression a strange mix of gratitude and something else entirely.

The tolling of the bell echoed across the village.

Martin extracted his arm from Connie's and dashed up the hillock alongside the path, to see across the railway. A cloud of thick smoke, or ash, rose from the valley.

"It's the pithead," he said.

"What might it mean?" Connie asked.

Martin didn't answer. He was already sprinting in the direction of the smoke.

The roof of the tall winding house had splintered, and Martin saw the struts of the cage protruding through the gaps. For it to have risen at such a speed to have burst through the roof meant that the other, connected cage in the parallel shaft must have fallen equally rapidly.

The shouting grew in volume as he ran towards the winding house. Martin darted up the steps and into the building. Inside, the air was thick with dirt that belched from the shaft, and there were men everywhere, pushing past one another, shouting unintelligibly, gesticulating.

"What was in the descending cage?" Martin yelled at the man nearest to him.

"Sixteen men – nine on the top deck, seven below," the man bellowed in reply. His face was smeared with so much grime that his eyes appeared frighteningly white.

The nine on the lower deck of the cage would have been crushed immediately, that was almost certain. Those above might be saved.

Martin ignored the men rushing about him and put his hands on the railing, leaning over the shaft. Immediately, he understood what had happened. Only part of the heavy cast-iron beam remained; the rest must have broken off and plunged into the shaft. Martin tried not to visualise it crushing those men in the upper part of the cage.

He forced his way out of the building and ran to the pile of refuse at its rear. The winding engine had been replaced only six months before – there must have been a fault in the new iron beam that had resulted in it cracking so soon – and the old parts still littered the site.

Thankful for his immense strength, he began dragging one of the discarded beams from the pile to the foot of the steps of the winding house. Before he had to contemplate lifting it alone, one of the men noticed him and called to others for help. Together, they struggled to push the beam up to the doorway, then slid it – with difficulty, and with a great deal of panicked shouting – across the shaft opening so that the beam overhung the walls on either side. Somebody had already fetched ropes to lash it so that it wouldn't tumble into the shaft, in the wake of its twin.

"Fetch more cable!" Martin yelled above the cacophony. Trusting that somebody must have heard him, he turned his attention to the winding engine.

It was clear at a glance that it would not be repaired easily. Not only had the cable sheared off, but the drum was also badly misaligned; it must have taken the full weight of the cage the moment the beam snapped. It might take days to fix.

He turned to see one of the pit workers already lashing a hook to a new length of cable.

"Who will go down?" Martin asked. He would have volunteered, but he suspected that his andraiad body was far heavier than any of these men.

"I will," the worker replied, and Martin recognised him finally as Owen Stewart, the foreman.

Owen shouted over his shoulder, "Use the old winch, all right? Place it beside the opening and we'll feed this cable over it, with me hanging on the end. It'll take too long to climb down, and God willing we'll need it to bring people up."

Martin placed his hand on Owen's shoulder. "The cable will shear if it rubs on that beam."

Owen's eyes were wild. "So do something about it, man!" Then he seemed to recognise that Martin didn't belong here, that he was wearing a wool suit and his face was clear of dirt, but without making any comment he turned back to his men and continued barking orders.

Martin hurried outside and returned to the refuse pile. His hands shook as he sifted through the rubble, picking out items. Inside the winding house, he worked alone, using brute strength to form the device as men rushed around him. It was only when somebody spotted him clambering onto the iron beam suspended above the shaft, then inching along it to fix the smoothed sheet metal with its walls bent at right angles to guide the cable, that the shouting began. Calls of, "Watch what you're doing, you fool!" and the like echoed in Martin's ears, but he shut out the voices to complete his work, then edged back to safety, silently repeating his thanks that the beam had taken his weight. When he reached the walkway men clapped him on the back, but all he could think was that he had instinctively thanked God, who was perhaps real after all.

Within minutes, Martin found himself working the manual crank to lower Owen into the pit, suspended by the hook attached to the belt around his waist. Dirt now issued from the shaft only sporadically, though Martin heard Owen coughing through his mask as he descended. The other pit workers watched on, perhaps regretting their acceptance of Martin's assurances that he was the strongest of them all.

After several minutes the cable went slack. Martin stopped turning and waited. When the cable jerked twice, he began pulling in the opposite direction, the machinery within him struggling against the weight.

Even before Owen's head emerged, he called out to them. "The beam's across the cage! We'll need to pull it free before I can get any one of them out!"

"How many still live?" one of the workers shouted to him.

"Only eight. But we can save those men, I'm certain."

Immediately, men demanded to know who lived, whether their friends, sons or fathers were among the dead. Owen ignored them and indicated for Martin to lower him.

"Get ready, all of you," he shouted as he began to descend again. "I'll let you know when to begin shifting that beam."

Soon the cable went slack again, and the other workers gathered in a tight huddle around Martin, prepared to take the additional weight.

The cable jerked twice.

They began to heave.

For several minutes, they made no progress, and Martin feared that the cable would simply snap and they would have to begin all over again. Then, gradually, the cable wound onto the drum, agonisingly slowly. The men around him grunted as they pressed down on the handle, or upon Martin's hands. He gritted his teeth at the pain.

The pull lessened slightly. Martin pictured the beam rising close to vertical. Now Owen would be attempting to guide it from the cage hatch, the beam teetering on its end and towering above him.

Suddenly, the handle pulled from Martin's grip. Men scrabbled to catch it, and somebody cried out as it struck them.

"Get it under control!" someone bellowed.

There were too many hands upon the winch. Martin could barely see the handle beneath all the limbs. He saw that the cable leading to the shaft had grown slack. If the iron beam down in the pit below toppled now, it might crush Owen, or destroy the cage roof entirely.

He abandoned his position at the winch and ran to the shaft opening. He was strong, but he knew he wouldn't be able to grip the cable and prevent it from slipping through his hands. So, he scooped up the loose cable, formed it into a loop, stepped inside it and drew it up to waist level, his right hand gripping the cable. Immediately, the loop tightened around his body. At first, he attempted to stagger back towards the winch, but despite his strength it was impossible. Instead, he braced his feet against the low wall of the shaft to prevent himself from being pulled any closer to it. Men hurried to him, gabbling, tugging at the cable that was now crushing him, but none of them could help. Martin felt the pressure ebbing and renewing, and he pictured the iron beam far below, swaying like a metronome. He winced at the pain as the cable cut through his jacket, his shirt, his flesh.

He had awoken more than once, but this was the first time the shapes had been anything recognisable. A head hung above him.

77

"Look," a voice said. "I saw his eyelids move. Fetch someone, quick."

Martin formed the shape of his wife's name but heard no sound.

"Oh Lord, won't you save this man?" a voice said. At first, Martin couldn't place it, but then he imagined himself sitting at the church organ, and he imagined this voice coming from behind him, and he knew it was Reverend Walton.

Martin succeeded in opening his eyes, and Reverend Walton staggered away from the bedside, goggling at him. Then the reverend gazed at the ceiling, muttering.

There was so much pain, or whatever was the equivalent.

With difficulty, Martin looked down at his own body. His torso was wrapped in bandages that were stained pink. His left arm bent at an unnatural angle and was suspended by a series of strings that reminded him of the pit cables or the innards of a piano.

The flesh of his fingers was grey. He couldn't feel his legs or his feet. He hurt everywhere.

He tried to speak. Something came from his mouth, sticky and clogging his throat. Reverend Walton paled and staggered away from the bedside.

When he awoke again, somebody was holding his undamaged hand. He couldn't move his head but rolled his eyes to see a head resting on the bed, long, fair hair strewn across the blanket.

"Ruth," he managed to say.

His daughter raised her head, rubbing the sleep from her eyes.

"Father," she whispered. "I didn't think you'd wake."

He worked his mouth a little before he could speak. In a rasping voice, he said, "Doesn't feel like sleep."

"You'll be better soon."

"I'm broken."

Ruth blinked rapidly. "Broken."

Pain bloomed within Martin's body. He closed his eyes. When he opened his eyes, he saw Connie in place of Ruth. She looked very tired, though still very beautiful. Then he blinked and Ruth was beside him again.

"Connie," Martin managed to say.

"She's nearby. I told her to rest. I can fetch her now."

"No." He winced again. His workings struggled to engage. Without having formulated a complete thought, he said "I'm sorry."

"You don't need to be sorry for anything, Father. You saved those men. Eight lived, thanks to you."

That was good, certainly. But he said again, "I'm sorry."

For several seconds, Ruth didn't respond. She looked down at his mangled body, then said, "I forgive you. I know Mother does too."

Martin's eyes moved down to his body too, the stained bandages. Strange that there might be blood in him; that blood might be required to operate this complex machine. Strange that he could remember being in this hospital before, even though that had been the real Martin Helm, not him.

"How much?" he said.

Ruth frowned. "How much do we forgive you?"

"No. Cost." Each word took great effort now. "How much?"

Ruth pressed her fingers against her lips. "Oh God. Oh God. I'm sorry, too, Father. I'm so sorry for what I told you. For lying to you. I thought it was right."

Martin didn't understand. He said again, "How much? Cost."

Ruth's face crumpled. She took a deep breath and rubbed her eyes again. "You didn't cost much at all, Father. We'll get by, Mother and I. You don't need to worry."

"Money. In a. Chest. Outhouse," Martin said, with great difficulty. "Enough."

"Enough," Ruth repeated without appearing to understand.

"You. Will. Need me," Martin said.

A picture of Ruth's child came into his mind. He imagined it would be a boy, with a face and a temperament rather like Louis Connolly's.

He clenched his teeth as the pain in his chest became intolerable.

"Build another," he said.

Ruth's face had become blurred and indistinct, as grey as Martin's fingers.

"Another," he said. Now he could barely hear his own voice. He pictured his workings failing, strings snapping within him, hammers pounding at nothing.

In a whisper that required immense concentration and effort, he said, "Build another andraiad."

Ruth clutched his hand tighter. She stared at him, tears glistening in her eyes, then she nodded, and once she had started nodding, she didn't seem able to stop.

Bloodbirds

Martin Sketchley

The clock tower at the University of Birmingham was Nikki's favourite post. Old Joe's sturdy brick construction minimised the impact of weather: some platforms swayed so much it was almost impossible to work. She assessed conditions as soon as she reached the top: gusting wind; fading light; rain imminent. She'd keep her wings safe and warm within her cape for now. As she swung the satchel from her back and laid it on the floor, the bloodbirds settled on the battlements around her.

She walked to the platform's telephone, lifted the receiver and dialled four-five-one. The metal disk spun.

Two rings, then a click.

"Vanguard control," said the operator.

"Angel 602 in position."

"Thank you, 602. Stand by."

Nikki replaced the receiver, took her zippo from her breast pocket and lit a cigar, then leaned on the wall and looked out across the city.

The tower gave a panoramic view, but she preferred to face north, looking across the once well-kept green space and paths, the canal and the railway tracks. The height also gave options: she could reach Edgbaston and Selly Oak any day of the week, but with favourable conditions, decent thermals and careful use of waypoints, she could get to Stirchley, Northfield, Harborne. At a push, she could reach the city centre, but all that concrete and glass? No thanks. Leave urban targets to urban cops.

She exhaled smoke and watched a patrol van making its way along the cracked and weed-riddled Bristol Road. The roof-mounted speakers were broadcasting the final warning on a loop:

THIS AREA IS ABOUT TO BE CLEANSED. OFFICERS ARE AUTHORISED TO DETAIN OR DESPATCH SUSPECTED SURROGATES, COLLABORATORS AND SYMPATHISERS. GIVE YOURSELVES UP NOW AND

YOU WILL BE TREATED FAIRLY. GIVE YOURSELVES
UP NOW. THIS AREA IS ABOUT TO BE CLEANSED…

She'd requested an extended forty-eight-hour warning when she'd submitted the ticket to Scheduling, but she had a hunch that no amount of time would be enough. Somehow Nikki suspected there was a certain inevitability to all of this.

Killing people wasn't something she did in her previous life. It wouldn't have gone down too well with the teachers at Thomas Aquinas. Back when everything was boring and she just wished something would happen. Then the Qall came, and everything turned upside down.

Instead of the benevolent civilisation we had always hoped for, they neutralised our technology and weaponised us to fight their battles on other, distant worlds. The transformative powers of their organic pods equipped us with all we'd need: enhanced perception; the ability to survive harsh environments; physiological upgrades and integrated weapons. They used and abused us in much the same way we had used and abused our fellow terrestrial species. What goes around comes around, some might say.

But when we proved too resistant and unpredictable to bend to their will, they gave up on us and departed. And when they left, those on Earth with power seized their abandoned technology and sold its capabilities to address distinctly human needs: just a few hours could imbue the user with mystical insight and wisdom; physical perfection and extended life were attainable; menstruation became elective, the menopause a banished curse; men of any age could acquire boundless virility and proportional egos.

Yet over time it became apparent this cornucopia of glorious gifts carried a price: many of those who used the Qall pods were impregnated with their alien cells. In time these divided and formed embryos, which eventually emerged from their unwilling, often unknowing human surrogates, releasing countless more to impregnate others in turn. So Vanguard's job was simple: to contain the spread by killing surrogates before the embryos reached term; get any live examples captured to the surgeons, whose butchery would increase our understanding. The difficulty was that no symptoms were evident until hours, sometimes minutes before embryos emerged, the appearance of dark smudges on the surrogate's skin signalling the approach of an excruciating death. Some people carried cells that never matured. It was a lottery. Frequent collateral damage, coupled with Vanguard's often questionable methods and officers' reputation for doing whatever was necessary to get a bonus, meant they were universally despised.

Nikki wasn't particularly bothered about being hated for what she did. She didn't particularly like herself. What she liked was being renowned. Feared. Notorious, if you really wanted to go for it. Because there lay power, and some level of control.

The teleprinter next to the phone chattered and produced a strip of paper. Nikki exhaled a cloud of smoke and tore off the message:

OFFICERS ADVISED FIVE MINUTES STOP

Still time for a coffee. She clenched the cigar between her teeth, took her flask from her satchel, unscrewed the cup and poured. The birds fluffed and fidgeted and ruffled their shiny black feathers.

"Settle down," she said. "You can go when it's time."

The birds shrieked and squawked in protest. Nikki both loved and loathed them. Another legacy of the Qall, they were as loyal and true as they were ugly and stubborn, adopted by Vanguard because they could sense their creators' presence within human blood. Coupled with angels' intuition, they were essential tools for identifying surrogates.

As she sipped and smoked Nikki looked down on boarded up, looted and abandoned Selly Oak. She saw what remained of the pizza place where she'd once had a date. When she'd first started going out with boys her dad had told her she called the shots. She'd laughed. Good old Dad, giving advice from another age. It turned out the boy in question thought paying for the meal gave him other entitlements. So now she carried a gun and killed surrogates, collaborators and sympathisers, and a fair few innocent bystanders, all in the name of Vanguard. Shots duly called.

She looked at her watch; three minutes. She placed the cup on the platform, took her knife from its sheath, exposed her left forearm and drew red lines in the flesh. She felt pain and pleasure and self-loathing. She was, she reminded herself, slicing deep, the best officer this side of Nechells. Begrudgingly respected even by the meathead daemons. Always asking what she'd done to get her rank because just being good wasn't enough for her or any other female officer, right? Right. And at the barracks they would visit her bunk, sometimes more than one, and tape her mouth and bind her wings and tell her this was all angels really deserved. And who was she to disagree?

The bloodbirds fluttered and squawked and shrieked as her wounds deepened. Gyre, the oldest and most experienced of her flight, cackled and hopped and flapped beside her.

After a few minutes she'd had enough of his protest. "All right, I'll stop!" she said. "You're so bloody judgemental. The pain I cause in others, it's only right I hurt myself."

Nikki re-sheathed the knife and wiped away the blood. At least the sting was comforting. She rolled down her sleeve and looked at her watch again; not long now.

As she shed her cape, spread her wings and prepared, she reflected on recent times. So much had changed. She had changed. Not so long ago the thought of one last, glorious descent that brought it all to an end was more and more appealing.

Then Steve came out of nowhere and changed everything.

It was a day a few months earlier. A day of blue skies and sunshine and still air. Perfect for an angel to swoop and soar.

She'd sat on the edge of the platform and spread her tobacco leaf wings and basked in the warmth, struggling to stay awake on the slowest of slow days. She'd scanned and re-scanned with her binoculars, smoked and dozed and watched the reflections of the clouds on the canal's oily surface. She'd looked to the north and wondered.

As she settled into the final hour of her shift, the bloodbirds gathered like a thundercloud. She scanned the area beneath them and saw movement near the canal. The birds were never wrong.

She climbed on to the battlements, spread her wings, and jumped.

She'd plunged towards the location of the sighting, bloodbirds racing alongside and shrieking in excitement. Whether because she was unfocussed or tired or complacent, she didn't notice one of the younger, less experienced birds drift close until a collision was almost unavoidable; she banked hard away, but misjudged speed and height and clipped a power line.

There was no current, but the impact sent her spinning. The canal approached in a blur, then she hit the embankment and tumbled through weeds and nettles and abandoned detritus.

She lay still, the quiet and stillness a contrast to the speed and rushing air of a few moments earlier. She was aware of birds circling overhead, others hopping around her in concern.

Having established that she could still move her limbs, Nikki sat up and stretched her wings. They were bruised and scratched, but no serious damage. When she heard movement and saw a man approaching from the tunnel, she scrambled to her feet and drew her gun.

"Vanguard!" she said. "Stop and identify yourself."

He stopped. "You okay?"

She assessed him. Late forties, maybe. Kind eyes, but wary of an officer with a gun. Crude street armour made from salvaged biker gear and scraps of leather.

"Hit that wire," she said. "Bloody birds can be a liability sometimes."

"Even monkeys fall out of trees," he said.

"You a comedian or philosopher?"

He shrugged. "You tell me. Would you mind putting the gun away? I'm clean."

"My birds are unhappy about something."

"Probably that kid." He glanced back towards the canal.

She looked beyond him and saw a corpse just inside the tunnel. A child, female, ravaged by the embryonic Qall that had erupted from her body. Nikki sometimes wondered about her baby. Where they had taken it. What they had done to it. What role it had been given. She felt a little dizzy.

"You okay?" he said.

"Fine."

"You could be in shock."

"I've crashed harder, believe me."

"And you look half-starved."

"You shouldn't have touched her."

"She's long dead. No chance of contamination. I was trying to cover the body. Even a dead surrogate has a right to some dignity. Especially a kid." He nodded towards Nikki's arm. "Anyway, what about you?

85

That looks nasty."

She lifted her arm; among the other cuts, some healed, some fresh, all self-inflicted, was a gash on her wrist, blood dripping from her fingers.

"It's nothing," she said.

"Here." He produced a handkerchief and took a step towards her.

"Stop! Officers are authorised to detain or despatch suspected–"

"– surrogates, collaborators and sympathisers. I know, I've heard it all before. But you're hurt. Look–" He unzipped his jacket to reveal his neck, then pushed up each sleeve to show his forearms – the most common places the first dark smudges appeared on surrogates' skin. There was just a tattoo in script-style lettering: *Janet*. "See?" he said. "I'm no threat."

"That's what they all say." She adjusted her footing and winced.

"You in pain?"

"No."

They looked at each other for a moment, then he offered his right hand.

"Name's Steve."

She looked him in the eye. What was this guy playing at? Why wasn't he scared of her? Everyone was scared of her. "Angel 602, Birmingham South."

He raised his eyebrows.

What harm could it do? "Nikki," she said.

He withdrew his hand with a shrug. "When did you last eat?"

She couldn't remember. "This morning."

"Can you walk?"

"I'm not a pensioner."

"Okay, so how about you come back to mine–"

"Back to yours?"

"Come back to mine and I'll treat that cut and make you something to eat. I live right there." He pointed to one of the blocks visible between the buildings. "Then you just forget to file a report and no one knows any of this happened."

"If I can get to a callbox a van will pick me up."

"All the boxes round here have been trashed, so you're a Vanguard angel looking at a long walk at street level with a twisted ankle, bruised wings and a bloody arm. That would make you either really tough or really stupid."

Really tough or really stupid. She'd have to think about that one.

She looked at him. The birds were still agitated, but his skin was clear.

Really tough or really stupid.

The young bird that had caused Nikki's crash landed nearby and hopped across the embankment towards her. She shot it without hesitation, leaving nothing but a cloud of black feathers. The other birds fell silent.

She holstered her gun. "Okay, Steve," she said. "Your place it is. But try anything funny and you'll end up like that, got it?"

They emerged from the stairwell at the fifth floor, her birds circling alongside and watching through the windows.

"This used to be student accommodation," he said. He was a little breathless.

"I know. I used to live round here. Bournville."

"Ah, right. Up the posh end. Lift hasn't worked in years. First, they took the metals, then the rubbers and the plastics. Even if there was power the bloody thing wouldn't run. It's a bit of a pain but I'd rather climb a few steps than be at street level. Here we are."

They reached a door with sheets of metal mesh across the front, secured with three heavy-duty padlocks. Nikki watched as he took a bunch of keys from his pocket. The birds were still acting up, but there was something intriguing about him. He was a fair bit older, and certainly not brawny like the Vanguard daemons she usually ended up with, by choice or otherwise, but the tingle in her belly was real enough. Maybe it was his vulnerability. Or the apparent lack of fear. Or the fact that he was being nice to her. No one was ever nice to her. She wasn't sure what to do about it.

He removed the mesh from the frame and nodded for her to go inside.

"Ladies first," he said.

"First time anyone's called me a lady."

"I can't believe that."

"It's the uniform," she said. "Scares 'em shitless."

"So take it off."

Nikki looked him in the eye.

"No, I just meant… Doesn't matter. I'll get these locks."

She looked at him; was he actually blushing?

The apartment was small: combined cooking and living area, bathroom, tiny balcony; her birds were already lined up on the rail looking in.

There were sketches all over the place. Dark. Abstract. Some erotic. And in the kitchenette, a photo of Steve with a woman and two kids.

"Want a drink?" he said as he took off his jacket. "I've got a bit of whiskey but no ice. Or if you'd rather just eat—"

"Love a drink. But just a small one. Another crash I can do without."

He poured a whiskey and gave her the glass. "I'll get something for that cut."

As he went into the bathroom she sat on the small sofa and folded her wings and cape around her. She lit a cigar and sipped the drink. Steve returned a moment later with a bandage and antiseptic cream.

"Don't smoke that in here, please," he said. "It stinks." He fetched a saucer and held it in front of her.

She stared at him for a moment, then stubbed it out.

"You draw all these?" she asked as he knelt in front of her.

"Just a form of self-expression and escapism."

She nodded towards an image that seemed to be two women engaged in an erotic act. "And what are you expressing there exactly?"

He didn't look up. "Suppose it's open to interpretation. Hold out your arm."

She hesitated, then reached out.

He glanced up at her as he applied cream.

"What's the matter?" she said.

"You're a Vanguard Angel."

"And?"

"And you've got a reputation for cruelty and brutality. Rounding people up and carting them off to those so-called observation camps."

"Is that what you see in me? Cruelty and brutality?"

"You're different to most Vanguard I've encountered, I must admit. Must be tough."

"Because I'm a petite female?"

"Your assumption of my prejudice is prejudicial."

She shrugged.

"Why do you do it?" he said.

She'd had no desire to become an angel. But as they sharpened their knives the surgeons pointed out that they'd repaired her injuries and saved her life; wasn't she grateful for the opportunity to give something back? Didn't she want to make her family proud?

Truth was, Mum and Dad never got on. She presumed they must have loved each other at some point in some way, otherwise she wouldn't exist. But when Dad wasn't pissed up and punchy, Mum was out being generous with her charms. Six of one and half a dozen of the other. Then Nikki went home one day and found her dad with a suitcase on wheels. "I'm off to Edinburgh," he'd said, just as if he was popping to the shop for a few bits. "The one with the castle? Still work up there apparently. Want to come?"

Scotland was cold and wet and everyone walked around in those stupid wax jackets. Besides, if he was at the other end of the country, he couldn't visit her room when he'd had a few.

When she'd said no thanks, he'd just shrugged and left. Looking back, he was all packed up and ready to go, so she probably wasn't part of the picture anyway. Mum never did come home.

"Revenge," she said.

"And these marks." He nodded at the cuts on her forearm as he bandaged the wound. "Are they revenge too?"

"Mind your own business and be a decent host." She held out her empty glass. "Make it a big one."

"I thought you didn't want much."

"A girl can't smoke, she might as well drink."

He secured the bandage with a safety pin, poured some more whiskey, then took his own glass and sat beside her.

"You want to talk about it?"

"Now you're a psychotherapist?" She drank.

"You're too delicate for that sort of thing."

"I kill people for money."

"So the uniform's for protection."

"You can talk. You look like a prospect for some middle-aged saddos motorcycle club in all that leather. Those trousers – please."

He glanced down. "Made them myself," he said.

"No shit."

"Must admit they're pretty uncomfortable."

She leaned in close and gazed into his eyes.

"So take them off," she said.

The fact that he simply finished his drink then insisted on walking with her to the nearest working callbox was confusing. For once the choice was hers and he didn't want to. Why didn't he want to? They always wanted to.

But a couple of days later she found him waiting outside the Vanguard building at the end of her shift. She hurried over, grabbed him by one arm and dragged him into a side street. Her birds swarmed around them, flapping and diving and pecking.

"What the hell are you doing here?" she said, glancing back.

"I bought you some flowers." He smiled and presented a thin bouquet of weeds gathered from patches of wasteland and the cracked walls of ruined buildings.

"I'm a Vanguard angel, Steve. If they find out I've been with a surry they'll cut off my wings, lynch me and then come looking for you."

"I'm not a surrogate."

"You're a lunatic is what you are."

"I'd prefer romantic. Although I admit that as flowers go, they are a bit shit."

She batted them to the floor with one hand then kissed him with a fevered passion.

He pushed her back. "Take it easy."

She gripped his wrists. "Don't tell me what to do," she said. "And stop being nice to me. I don't deserve it." Then she shed her cape and wrapped her wings around him.

There followed an emotional storm that carried them both into uncharted territory. He felt new confidence, his fragile masculinity reaffirmed as this young, powerful, beautiful creature showed interest in him; she felt able to be herself in a way she'd never before experienced.

He didn't seem to want from her the things everyone else did. There was no pressure to be or do anything. They'd sit in his apartment and talk books and music and make each other laugh. He'd make feasts from whatever scraps he could find. Sometimes he would sketch her. His old-school romancing amused her; the fact that it amused her amused him in turn. Their physical relationship was tentative and warm. Nikki struggled to process these feelings. Pre-invasion there would have been judgements about the difference in their ages, but in this new world few had time for such trivialities.

When on watch, she wondered what he was doing, would long to be with him and talk to him. But with her birds constantly agitated and emotions she could not control, as time passed it became clear that issues and loyalties would have to be addressed.

She suggested they climb a tower: a repurposed electricity pylon outside the city with an observation platform at the second level.

"We might get caught," he said as she unlocked the security gate.

"If that wasn't a possibility it wouldn't be naughty, would it. And then what would be the point?" She opened the gate. "Ladies first."

He looked up. The structure looked pretty solid, but even though it wasn't as high as a lot of the others, it was still a long way.

"What if I fall?"

"Jesus Christ, Steve. If you fall, you'll probably die. Now do you want to climb a tower with me or not?"

Nikki was swift and agile. She seemed to barely touch the ladder's metal rungs as she climbed, her cape and wings drifting like banners behind her. Steve found things more taxing. She laughed as she helped him through the gate on to the platform. "Good job I didn't pick a higher one," she said. "You'd never have made it."

He caught his breath. "If your aim was to make me feel my age you've certainly succeeded."

"My aim was to get you away from the city for a while."

He smiled. "It's a lovely idea. Thank you." He kissed her cheek then walked to the rail. 'Great view.'

"One of the perks."

"Don't you get lonely?"

"It can be the most peaceful job in the world. The purest solitude. For now we're the best option, but I suppose the tech will come back and replace us eventually. Not sure what I'll do then."

He looked up. "Those clouds," he said. "Proper cotton wool jobs. You could almost touch them." The birds circled and shrieked and cawed above them. 'Don't those things ever shut up?"

"They're jealous."

"Of me?"

"Of everybody. But especially you. Because they know that when I'm with you I don't need them." She reached out, turned his face towards hers and kissed him.

She responded to Steve's caress as he ran his hands down her back, across her flying muscles and her soft, sensitive wings. He had by now learned the things that made her shiver. But she knew this could not happen. Not this time. She stepped away from him, turned and looked across the fields.

"What's the matter?" he said.

"Your area's going to be cleansed. Day after tomorrow."

'How do you know?"

"I just know. But it means you've got time to leave."

"Why would I leave?"

"Because you're a surrogate."

"I'm not a surrogate, Nikki."

"The birds never lie. I'm on that squad, Steve. If you're arrested—"

"I won't be arrested."

"If you're arrested, they'll cart you off and turn you inside out."

"Why don't you believe me? Because of these stupid birds?"

"The birds are never wrong."

"Well that's obviously not true."

She started walking backwards away from him. There were tears in her eyes. "You don't want those surgeons getting their hands on you. You know what they do, Steve? They need cells for their experiments, so they take them from captured surrogates. When they've removed cells, new ones form, so they'll keep you alive, milking you until there's nothing left. It's a living hell. If you're not a surrogate, fine. Go somewhere and live a life."

"What about us?"

"What about us, Steve?"

"If you leave Vanguard, we can be together. Properly together. We could go somewhere far away. Scotland, maybe; how about that?"

Nikki laughed. "Scotland. What, like Edinburgh? The one with the castle?"

He looked puzzled. "Yeah. Sure. If that's what you want." There was a long silence. "Nikki?"

"You don't leave Vanguard, Steve. You don't even try. So you'd better go. Because if you don't, you might just get some unexpected visitors."

"What do you mean?"

"Just go, Steve. For both our sakes."

She looked at him for a moment, then turned and sprinted across the platform and dived into the sky.

Nikki swept low across the countryside, bloodbirds shrieking and cavorting all around her, the wings she'd never wanted spread wide.

The teleprinter chattered. Nikki flicked away the cigar stub, screwed the cup back on her flask, then tore off the strip of paper.

BIRDS AUTHORISED FOR RELEASE STOP

She looked across at her flight; they were watching her, all beady eyes, beak and claws. To the east, Vanguard helicopters were on their way to drop the rest of the angels and daemons assigned to the sweep. She had a few minutes tops.

"Right, you ugly sods," she said. "Go and do your work."

The birds launched themselves into the air, then flew around the clock tower as if reluctant to hunt.

"What's the matter?" she said. "Shoo! Scram! Go and find him."

The birds gradually began to disperse, but their confusion was evident in the lack of formation. Could she dare to hope that he'd gone after all?

The birds were circling aimlessly; some in the vicinity of Steve's block, but still lacking intent.

"Okay," she said to herself. "If you want something done…"

She put down the binoculars and stood on the battlements. She was not much higher than his apartment. In perfect conditions this wouldn't be a problem, but conditions were far from perfect. She flexed her wings, encouraging blood into their thin surfaces, and took several deep breaths.

"Here I come," she said. "Ready or not."

As she landed elegantly outside his building, thundering helicopters swept cones of light across the streets, patrol vans broadcast warnings, and Vanguard's finest hunted prey. She entered quickly and ran up the stairs, accompanied by a dozen or so unquiet birds.

The screens on his door were locked from the inside. The mesh rattled as she banged upon it.

"Steve! *Steve!*"

The door opened. "Nikki."

"Why are you still here?"

"Keeping my head down. It'll be fine. Come inside."

He removed the screens and she strode past him into the apartment, accompanied by her birds.

"Do these things really have to be here?"

She turned to face him. "Why didn't you go?"

"Because I'm clean and not on Vanguard's radar."

"Everybody is on Vanguard's radar, Steve. Especially the surry who's consorting with an angel."

She looked at him. "Do you trust me?" she said.

"Trust?" He took her hands in his. "You don't get it, do you, Nikki. I've only ever been in love twice. One of them I married – the other one is you."

Tears welled. She turned and walked away from him. "This can't happen, Steve. Even if you were clean–"

"I am clean."

"Even if you were clean and I could leave Vanguard and we could run off into the sunset together – what then? You get bored? I get bored? It all goes tits up and we're far away and alone?"

"Or we live happily and grow old together."

"You really believe that sort of thing happens?"

"Don't you?"

There was a bang on the door and a barked warning.

"What's that?"

"Sorry, Steve," she said. "Guess it's a case of better the devil you know."

"Nikki?"

She took a step back, her eyes full of tears, as a squad of daemons burst into the room, all testosterone, guns and shielding. The birds shrieked and squawked and were booted aside as officers slammed Steve to the floor and bound him tight.

"I'm clean! Nikki. Tell them, Nikki!"

"Shut it, surry!" An officer pistol-whipped Steve into silence, then he was hefted to his feet and manhandled away.

The senior officer looked down at her; his armoured physique seemed to fill the room. "You raise this ticket?"

She nodded.

"Then you better call it in."

"And the bonus?"

"Got enough on my plate. Take it."

He turned and left, and suddenly it was just Nikki and the birds. They continued to flutter and flap and squawk. "Calm down," she said as she walked to the phone and dialled. "It's all over."

"Vanguard control," said the operator.

"Angel 602," Nikki said quietly. "IC1 male confirmed in custody. Aston Webb Boulevard, Selly Oak."

"IC1 male in custody. Thank you, 602. Well done." The operator rang off and Nikki put down the receiver. She looked around the room. They had laughed here. They had loved here. She had felt loved here. But in the end, she had no choice. Such was her life.

As she looked around the room, she saw a new sketch: a winged female hovering above a pleading man. She knelt. As she reached out to the picture her sleeve rose up her arm; and there on her wrist, a patch of dark, oily skin, like an old bruise – spreading fast.

The clock tower at the University of Birmingham was Nikki's favourite post. As she stood on the battlements, she looked across the city to the north and wondered.

The kid who had strapped her wings together with a belt had looked fearfully at the marks spreading across her body. She'd told him not to be scared. He was reluctant, but even at eight or nine years old knew better than to disobey an angel – especially one as beautiful as this.

According to Processing there was no sign of alien cells in Steve's body. The birds were reacting to their presence in her all along. So much for an angel's intuition. So much for the wings she never wanted.

She looked down and prepared for one last, glorious descent. At least this time the choice would be hers.

Going Home
Martin Westlake

The eerie howl of the Ekranoplan's jet engines echoed around the city's early morning streets. Dimitriy's stomach lurched involuntarily. A ground effect craft, they called it, designed to be a troop carrier, now recycled as a passenger craft, plying the route between Derbent and Astrakhan. The relic, all stubby wings and a massive, V-shaped tail, howled there and back three times a day. He loathed it, but it was the only way he could get to the laboratory in Astra.

Every Monday morning for over a year, Dimitriy had suffered the same torment of emotions. Anastasia said nothing anymore as they kissed. "Think of the children," she had said in the old days, before she'd realised entreaties were useless. "They need their father." He missed the whole school week. Sasha, the younger, still greeted him with affection on Saturday mornings, but Andrei, now in his teens, had become increasingly sullen. Dimitriy wanted to tell him how sorry he felt, but the truth was that he didn't. Guilty, yes; sad, yes, in a bitter-sweet sort of way; but not sorry.

Then there was the Ekranoplan. Anastasia had been unable to leave Derbent when Dimitriy had taken on the Astrakhan job and he had accepted that. The car trip took ten hours in the summer and in the winter the roads were frequently impassable. No, the only viable means of getting there was the Ekranoplan. He would never get used to it, though. Whenever there was the slightest hint of a breeze, his heart dropped, for the monstrous thing could only take off facing into the wind, and that meant riding the incoming waves, like a ship. Once it was up in the air the ride was smooth, but how he hated the take off! The only thing that made the mixture of sadness, guilt and fear worthwhile every Monday morning was a euphoric sense of anticipation; the knowledge that he would soon once again be where he most desired to be.

His path through the sleepy streets to the Ekranoport took him past his old workplace, the Caspian Gates Secondary School, reminding him of the day it had all begun. He'd stayed behind to help a group of fifteen-year-olds, then hurried home. A tall, thin, grey-suited, sallow-faced man was waiting for him outside the main entrance to their block of flats. A cigarette bobbed on his lower lip as he spoke. He seemed oblivious to the February cold, though both men's breath clouded about them.

"Semenov?" he said.

Dimitriy nodded.

"Could we talk?" said the man, nodding towards a bar.

There was something about him – not furtive, but a sense of secrecy all the same. The man bought two vodkas and they sat at a scuffed table.

"To your health," he said, raising his glass. He stubbed out his cigarette in an old, dented aluminium ashtray and lit another. "Ivanov," he said. "Rear Admiral Anatoly Ivanov, Caspian Flotilla, Astrakhan."

"There's been a mistake," said Dimitriy.

Ivanov shook his head. He gestured to a passing waiter and ordered two more vodkas.

"I shouldn't stay," said Dimitriy.

"Tell me, Dimitriy Semenov," Ivanov said; "how much do you earn?"

"Enough," said Dimitriy.

"Why are you a teacher?" Ivanov leaned forward over the table. "You are a brilliant physicist with a top doctoral thesis in Biology and Materials Sciences from Moscow State University and yet you hide yourself away at the Caspian Gates Secondary School teaching low-grade mathematics to misfits."

"My wife…," Dimitriy began.

"We know all about your wife," Ivanov said.

"It's time I left," said Dimitriy.

"Sit down," said the Admiral, gesturing with his half-empty vodka glass. "What I mean is that we know she has all her family here. That's why you're here, isn't it?"

Dimitriy said nothing.

Ivanov leaned over the table again. "The motherland calls, comrade."

Motherland! Comrade! Dimitriy knew immediately that the job had to be some sort of secret military work.

"It's not what you think, Semenov," the Admiral continued. "If I told you now, you wouldn't believe me."

Dimitriy inadvertently looked into his empty glass. Ivanov flagged the waiter down and ordered two more vodkas.

"No!" said Dimitriy.

"For the road."

The Admiral toyed with his cigarette lighter, an old-fashioned metal model with a flip top and a thick wick. Then he looked up at Dimitry. "Interested?' he said. "We'll pay you four times what you are getting at that dump of a school."

"The catch?" said Dimitriy.

Ivanov drank off the remainder of his vodka and placed the glass down gently on the tabletop.

"You'd have to come to Astra, Monday to Friday. We'd cover your board and lodging."

"How would I…?"

As if to anticipate his question, the unmistakable howl of the evening return Ekranoplan came to them through the thin glass window.

Ivanov reached into his pocket, drew out an envelope and placed it on the table.

"Your ticket's in there. This coming Monday. The seven-thirty departure. When you get to Astra, make your way to the Moskva Hotel. A room has been booked in your name. I'll join you there for lunch. It's half-term. The school won't miss you."

Back home, after the children had gone to bed, sitting in the low light at the melamine kitchen table, he and Anastasia had discussed the offer in earnest whispers. He had doubts, but she was logical and reassuring. The money was important. With the kids growing, it would be good if they could rent somewhere larger. If he didn't like the work, whatever it was, he could always return to his teaching. What did they have to lose?

Dimitriy had been travelling to Astra for just over two months when Anastasia first put the question to him. He had known it must come. She had nodded and accepted so mildly when he'd first explained that he couldn't talk about his work, but who could blame her, now that the yearning had started? She chose a Saturday evening. The children were in bed. The classical music radio channel was on, and she'd put a cloth and a candle on the dinner table. They talked about Sasha and Andrei, and then about her family. At the end of the meal, Anastasia took Dimitriy's hands across the table. *Here it comes,* he thought. But she simply looked into his eyes and asked if he felt all right. She'd told him he seemed preoccupied, as if his mind were elsewhere.

He'd laughed. "I'm fine," he'd said.

How could he tell her? Even if he had told her, she wouldn't have believed him.

The second time, Anastasia had been more direct. Dimitriy had just returned.

"Did you miss us?" she asked.

"Of course!"

"Really?"

She went back to the kitchen. There was no cloth and no candle on the table. Over the meal, her replies were monosyllabic. Afterwards, he went to help her with the washing up, but she insisted on doing it alone. He sat on the sofa and waited until she emerged, drying her hands on a tea towel.

"Dima," she said, "are you sure you're not having a relationship of some sort in Astra?"

Astrakhan was on a broad river, not a sea. Its waterways gave the impression the city was floating. Unlike Derbent, there were no hills behind, and no citadel looming over the city. Rather, the great Trinity Cathedral soared upwards, with its gold-capped green domes. Astrakhan was flat and expansive. Being there gave Dimitry a sense of a new beginning. He hadn't realised, until he first set foot in the place, how oppressed he'd felt back home. That first Monday, still wobbly from the flight, he'd walked easily to the Moskva Hotel, a great block of fake chrome and smoked glass. A room had been booked, as Ivanov had promised. The clerk told him a table had been reserved in the restaurant for twelve o'clock. Dimitriy went to his room, unpacked the few belongings he had brought, then turned on the television and watched a programme without really following it. What was Ivanov going to offer him, he wondered?

The Admiral was sitting at their table when Dimitriy came down, a vodka in front of him and a cigarette on his lower lip. He nodded curtly.

"Welcome to Astra," he said. "A drink?"

"Thank you," said Dimitriy, "but I don't drink at lunchtime."

Ivanov beckoned a waiter over.

"Today, you'll make an exception."

When the waiter had brought their drinks, Ivanov raised his glass. He had ordered caviar, brought by another waiter on a bed of ice. "Eat," he insisted gruffly.

"Thank you," said Dimitriy.

"Thank Mother Russia," said Ivanov, stubbing out his cigarette.

They started to eat, digging out the glutinous eggs with small mother-of-pearl teaspoons.

"What do you know about Tunguska?" the Admiral asked.

"Siberia? The beginning of the last century?"

Ivanov nodded. "30 June 1908," he said.

"I remember the pictures," said Dimitriy. "All those felled trees. A meteor, right?"

"Da, da," said Ivanov. "That's what people think."

"Think? What was it, then?"

"We don't know." He lit another cigarette. "I've brought a file for you to read, but before that, I want you to sign this."

Ivanov tugged an envelope from his jacket pocket and drew out a folded sheet of paper. "Official Secrets Act," said the Admiral, unfolding the sheet. "I will only tell you more if you sign. To be clear, if you sign the declaration and do not respect it, you could be tried and imprisoned. Not even your wife. Got it?"

Dimitriy read the declaration, his hand trembling. He would have liked to talk to Anastasia. Suddenly, she seemed very far away. He read it again.

"I need to think about it," he said. "I need to talk to my wife."

Ivanov shook his head grimly. "It's now or never," he said.

Dimitriy sighed and thought about the money. With such a salary they could easily rent a three-bedroom apartment. He was sure Anastasia would have agreed. Though she would surely have wanted to know what work the Admiral was offering. He signed and dated the paper and handed it back.

"Good," said Ivanov, putting it back in his pocket. He gestured to a waiter to clear their table and ordered two more vodkas.

"The Tunguska region wasn't as sparsely populated as people think," said the Admiral. "Quite a few people heard and saw something." He lit a cigarette. "It started with noises from the sky."

"Noises?"

"Da. You'll read the transcripts. Some of the witnesses said it was like trumpets."

"Heavenly trumpets?" said Dimitriy ironically.

Ivanov sneered.

"The noises went on for about a week," he continued.

"Then?" asked Dimitriy.

"There was some sort of *conflict*, in the sky," said Ivanov. "Some sort of *celestial* conflict."

"'Celestial'? You seem to be choosing your words with care, Admiral."

Ivanov stubbed out his cigarette.

"You'll read the file and see for yourself. As good scientists, we try always to keep open minds."

"The word 'conflict'," said Dimitriy, "suggests that more than one body or object might have been involved, right? And the word 'celestial' suggests this was high up?"

"There are drawings in the file," the Admiral said, "based on contemporary eyewitness accounts. The locals, the Evenki, were convinced they'd seen their god, Ogdy, in a fight."

"Fascinating," said Dimitriy, "but I am not sure why this should bring me to the Volga Basin and the Official Secrets Act."

Ivanov lit another cigarette.

"Leonid Kulik," he said. "A mineralogist. He came to Tunguska several times, starting in 1921. That was already thirteen years after the event. There was no crater – that puzzled him. How could there have been a meteorite impact if there were no crater, and if there were no fragments? He realised the fragments might have blasted out craters that had then got filled in. So, he kept digging holes to try and find filled-in craters with remains of one sort or another at the bottom – something, anything. No joy. Until 1938. His last expedition. One of his men found something, deep down, in a pit. Whatever it was, it blinded the man. He complained of an intense, searing light, then he lost his sight. Kulik's workers mutinied. For them it was proof they were messing with Ogdy. They dragged the man out and refused to get into the pit. Kulik had to shovel most of the earth back in himself. He measured the location as accurately as he could, and then returned to the Mineralogical Museum in Leningrad. He planned to return with his own men, but the Germans invaded in 1941 and he joined the fighting. The next year he died of typhus in a POW camp."

Ivanov drank some vodka.

"Whatever they found," he continued, "remained lost in the archives. For a long time, as you know, the motherland had more important things to think about than primitive superstitions. But in 2007 a group of archivists started going through Kulik's papers. When they got to the file about the 1938 incident, the team had the good idea of involving us."

"Us?" said Dimitriy.

"The security services," Ivanov said. "If another expedition to Tunguska were to be launched, they knew they'd need state resources. They dressed it up as being about some potentially weaponizable force. They weren't entirely wrong. Kulik's coordinates were accurate. They used a remote-controlled digger. Once they'd reached the depth Kulik recorded, they lowered animals down to the bottom. All came back blind. So, they were at the right place. A remote camera relayed images of glittering metallic fragments. They sent down instruments, but the instruments measured nothing. A volunteer discovered that *reflections* of the fragments could be observed in a mirror. Using remote cameras and mirrors, the fragments were dug out of the pit bottom. It was all hit-and-miss. Somebody thought of lead, being a heavy metal, so they fashioned a lead-lined steel box and used a remote-controlled robotic arm to shepherd the fragments towards the box and seal the lid."

"Shepherd?"

"You'll learn about that," Ivanov said; "*if* you take the job." He stubbed out his cigarette, drank off his vodka, and continued. "The fragments were then brought to a..." (he coughed) "...*facility* here in Astrakhan. The box was opened and the fragments were housed in a specially-constructed room. That, Dimitriy Semenov, is where you come in. We want to analyse the fragments. Test their qualities." He leaned over the table as if to share a confidence. "And perhaps," he said, "replicate them."

Dimitriy felt the thrill of scientific discovery and the repulsion of a lifelong pacifist. But curiosity gripped him strongest. If only he could tell Anastasia! He was sure she would have been just as fascinated.

The Admiral got to his feet.

"I will be waiting outside tomorrow morning at seven," he said, "and will take you to the facility."

Dimitriy watched as Ivanov threaded his way steadily through the tables. That word, *comrade*, again. When he had gone, Dimitriy picked up the file and hurried to his room.

The Admiral was waiting for him on the hotel's esplanade in a sleek black chauffeur-driven limousine. He was in his uniform, his gold brocaded cap on the seat beside him.

"Is this a Zil?" Dimitriy asked, getting into the tobacco-fugged interior.

"The 4104," said the Admiral. "The Navy is determined to keep them going until they fall to pieces."

He lit a cigarette. "You read the file?" he asked.

"Of course. Do you want me to believe that the Evenki saw angels?"

"*You* saw the drawings," said Ivanov. "*I* don't want you to believe anything."

"Yes," said Dimitriy, "I *saw* the drawings."

The Admiral gazed through the smoked glass window.

"Do you believe in angels, Dimitriy Semenov?"

"No," said Dimitriy, "I don't. But what else can be made of those drawings? And those sounds; if not something like trumpets, then what?"

Ivanov shook his head.

"I told you; we are trying to keep open minds. You have to remember in 1908 the Evenki were a primitive, superstitious people. When something they didn't understand happened, they naturally ascribed it to their god, Ogdy."

"You don't think there was a conflict?"

"Imagine if you were a primitive people and something massive exploded overhead," said Ivanov. "Wouldn't you extrapolate from what you knew? Battle, noise?"

"And those trumpeting noises *before*?" asked Dimitriy.

Ivanov chuckled.

"*You* called them 'heavenly trumpets', Dimitriy Semenov, but you don't believe in such things, do you?"

"Of course not, Admiral. But what are the alternative explanations?"

Ivanov tutted. "You are a scientist, aren't you? Because we don't know the answer doesn't mean there isn't one. We just don't know it yet – perhaps we'll never know it. What we *do* know is that we have seven fragments of an unknown powerful material that *may* have fallen from the sky about the time of the Tunguska event. We can, and must, try to know as much about those fragments as possible, using scientific methods, and not basing our judgements on superstition and hearsay and eye-witness accounts from long ago."

"Of course," said Dimitriy, chastened. "It's those pictures in the file. My imagination ran away with me."

The Admiral stubbed out his cigarette.

"We have arrived," he said.

Some five months after Dimitriy started the job, Anastasia stopped making dinner on Friday evenings. The first time, she told him she'd been feeling unwell, and he accepted the explanation unthinkingly. He ate alone in the kitchen. The next Friday, though, the new practice had been rationalised; she said it was too late in the evening to eat a full-blown meal – better that he snacked or had a bowl of soup or a salad. He again accepted the explanation. Then, one Friday, when he came to bed, he found her weeping.

"What's the matter, Ana?"

She rolled over and he saw that her eyes were puffed up.

"I just wish you'd tell me," she said. "About her, whoever she is."

"There is no her," Dimitriy insisted.

"You can't hide it from me," Anastasia said. "I see the way you look as though you have been torn away from someone."

"There is no other woman, Anastasia."

"Is it a man? I'd understand."

"There's nobody else, I swear!"

"You think I'm stupid? You can't wait to get back on Monday mornings."

She rolled away and wept herself to sleep. He stared up at the ceiling. She was right, of course. The weekends back home in Derbent had become a torment.

"Welcome to Astrakhan State Technology University," said Ivanov, checking his cap's position in the glass of the chauffeur's partition.

The Admiral led him through the glass-fronted entrance. Students milled about, seemingly unfazed at the image of a uniformed Admiral threading a path through the crowd.

"Where are we going?"

"The Institute of Oil and Gas." Ivanov led the way across the leafy campus to a nondescript red brick construction. They went through rotating doors and stopped before a block of lifts. When the lift came, the Admiral pushed the button for –2, but he kept his finger on the button a long time. Ivanov turned to face a small camera in one corner of the ceiling of the lift and gave a salute.

"Forgive the cloak-and-dagger stuff," he said. "Until the Union collapsed, the Caspian Flotilla was based in Baku, but a lot of the command structure was kept safely within Russia itself, including here, in Astra. The Americans knew that, of course. This place was just as much of a target, so special underground facilities were built for the command structures. That's where we are going now."

By then, the lift should have reached –2 level, but felt as though it were still in motion. After several minutes of slow movement, the lift stopped, and the doors slid open. In front of them stood two armed, uniformed guards. Behind them was a vast, brightly lit space. Ivanov produced papers and explained about Dimitriy. Once the papers had been stamped, the soldiers stood aside and let them pass.

"It's quite a hike," said the Admiral.

The vast space was devoid of human activity, but all around them stood massive columns of plastic-wrapped material.

"Thousands of men could live down here for years," said Ivanov.

On the far side of the bunker, the Admiral led Dimitriy into a complex of smaller spaces. Each entrance was a double-doored air-pressurized port. Finally, they came to a twin set of grey-painted heavy steel doors that had been swung open.

"Here we are," said the Admiral. "The playroom; the laboratory."

They were greeted by the head of the scientific team, Fyodor Babikov, a beanpole of a man wearing large, tinted spectacles. Ivanov left them together, promising to return at the end of the day. Babikov showed Dimitriy to the changing room. There were sinks, lockers and benches. They scrubbed up together, then dressed in classic surgical gear. Afterwards, Babikov led Dimitriy into a small meeting room. The walls were lined with large drawings showing distinctive geometrical structures. Babikov gestured for him to sit down at a table and sat opposite.

"What has Admiral Ivanov told you?" he asked.

"The basic story," said Dimitriy. "And I've read the file."

"Did he tell you about their effects?"

"The blindness?"

"Well, there *is* that," said Babikov. "But you don't need to worry. The lab is rigged so that you simply cannot look directly at the fragments. You can only see them indirectly by using the mirrors we've installed, or by using the camera. But did Ivanov not talk about anything else?"

"Nothing," said Dimitriy.

"Mmm… He was probably afraid he'd scare you off."

"Why would I be scared?"

"They seem to have an addictively euphoric effect on some people."

"Some?"

"It seems to depend. There's nothing chemical about it."

"How do you know this?"

"You're not the first expert drafted in. In fact, you are the third."

"The others?"

Babikov shook his head.

"They didn't last very long. The first was here for just over a year. The second lasted almost two years."

"Where are they now?"

"Locked away," said Babikov.

"And you?"

"Nothing," said Babikov. "But then, I don't spend hours in the viewing room."

"All right," Dimitriy said. "What else did Ivanov *not* tell me?"

"There isn't a whole lot more to know."

"How long have the fragments been here?"

"Since 2008."

"And you have honestly learned nothing?"

Babikov grinned.

"Honestly, very little. I'll tell you everything we know, but it won't take long."

Dimitriy leaned back in his chair.

"Tell me," he said.

"We know they have properties, and powers. The power to blind people, for example."

"Are we sure of that?"

"You mean?"

"Well," said Dimitriy, "we've only had that one example, of the man down the pit, back in 1938. It could have been a stroke, couldn't it?"

"You're forgetting the animals," Babikov said. "Anyway, there have been quite a few unfortunate episodes since."

"Here?" asked Dimitriy.

"Yes," said Babikov. "People who didn't listen. People who didn't believe. An accident. A drunk."

"How many?"

"Enough for us to know that the fragments, if looked at directly, cause blindness in humans, as in animals. Even welding masks didn't help."

"You've tried reptiles?"

"Oh, yes," said Babikov. "We've tried reptiles *and* squid and octopus *and* insects. We've tried everything," he said. "The fragments have the same effect on any sort of eye known to us."

"Your instruments?"

"Show nothing. Whatever this effect is, it is produced in an undetectable way."

"What else?" Dimitriy asked.

"Oh, the euphoria business."

"Can you be sure of that?"

"Scientifically, no. But there must be a strong presumption."

"Two cases only? You can't presume anything from that."

"You are right," Babikov said, smiling ruefully. "Let me just call it a *hunch*, then. Two highly intelligent, balanced, reasonable scientists, both following a similar pattern of obsessiveness and increasingly frequent episodes of manic euphoria, culminating in madness and confinement in clinics. I agree with you, Dimitriy Semenov. It could be sheer coincidence, but I think not."

"All right," said Dimitriy. "What else?"

"We have found a way to manipulate the fragments," said Babikov. "Only one metal may touch them – gold. All others melt away as they get near. Once we realised that, we had special gold implements made up that could be attached to the arms of the robots – – that is the main way in which you will be working with the fragments, if you need to manipulate them."

"But it is curious,' said Dimitriy, "gold being so malleable – like the lead in which they were encased."

"In retrospect, the lead-lined box was a crazy risk," said Babikov. "Who knows what might have happened if they had melted their way out during the trip?"

"What else?"

Babikov shook his head in sudden exhaustion.

"We know next to nothing, and that is all we know."

"Now you are talking in riddles."

Babikov looked at Dimitriy for a few moments, as though brought back from a reverie.

"We cannot record images. Nothing works; film, X-rays, electro-magnetic resonance imaging, transmission electron tomography... Whatever sort of imaging we have tried to use, nothing shows up. They are definitely there; we can see their reflection, but we can't capture them as images, and that means that we can only study the fragments themselves."

"What about microscopes?" asked Dimitriy.

"Lenses work," said Babikov. "But you cannot record what you are seeing."

"You can't draw them?"

"No, no," said Babikov. "They can be drawn, at least – hence all of these..." he waved at the drawings hanging on the walls around them. "Your predecessors' masterpieces."

"May I?" Dimitriy asked.

Babikov nodded.

Dimitriy studied the drawings for a while.

"I have an idea," he said. "But I'll wait until you've finished."

"Second," Babikov continued, "they are constantly levitating."

Dimitriy raised his eyebrows.

"They always hover, never touching any surface."

"Some sort of energy, then?"

"I think so, but we can detect nothing. We thought of magnetism or light but it's neither of those." Babikov smiled and shook his head. "Believe me, Dimitriy Semenov, we have tried and tested many ideas – all fruitlessly – so far."

"I understand what Ivanov was getting at now."

"Getting at?" said Babikov.

"We were talking about scientific method. He said we don't know the answer yet, and perhaps we never will."

That very first time Dimitriy came back from Astrakhan she'd known already, he realised – or, rather, she'd suspected already. Something had happened. He couldn't entirely hide it from her. For a start, there was the fait accompli of his decision. He had taken the job without first discussing the offer with her. It was so generous, he said, that he had decided on the spot. That wasn't the whole truth, of course. She asked about the work. He told her how he'd had to sign a declaration and was now bound by the Official Secrets Act. He saw her recoil.

"It isn't what you think," he'd said.

"What is it, then?" she'd asked.

"Something unimaginable," he'd replied.

She'd wrinkled her nose. "Can't you give me a clue?"

He'd laughed. "I promise you it's nothing sinister."

"I can see you are enthusiastic about it."

"Come with me to Astrakhan, Ana," he'd urged. "Bring the children. We can make it work."

"We discussed all that," she'd said, shaking her head. "My job, my family, the children's schools…"

He'd nodded his head slowly. Already, his thoughts were drifting back…

"Dimitriy?"

"I'm sorry, my love," he said. "I was daydreaming."

He'd listened patiently as Babikov listed the other properties his team had so far noted. The seven fragments were identical in appearance. Each was a convex oblong, about nine centimetres long by five centimetres wide. From a distance, they seemed to be golden in colour but, the stronger the magnification, the less colour there was. From very close up they seemed neither transparent nor invisible, and completely colourless yet iridescent. The fragments' default position was to hover vertically in an overlapping formation, like the defensive *testudo* Roman legionaries had sometimes adopted with their shields. If the fragments were separated, they immediately moved back to the *testudo* formation. Once again, Dimitriy studied the drawings on the walls.

"So, what's this big idea of yours?" said Babikov.

"*Lepidoptera*," said Dimitriy.

"Butterflies?" said Babikov, momentarily confused. "We'd thought of fish scales, but *lepidoptera?*"

"In appearance they seem similar to fish scales, it is true, but butterfly scales have three-dimensional lattices that cause iridescence, and I just wonder whether some similar effect is not at work with these scales – and they *are* scales, Babikov, aren't they? They're not just fragments."

Babikov blushed. He took off his glasses and polished the lenses.

"Ivanov doesn't like such talk. I think he's right. We shouldn't leap ahead of ourselves."

"But are we?" said Dimitriy. "We know – or we assume – that these fragments fell to earth in June 1908, right?"

Babikov shook his head.

"No," he said. "We know only that they were found in the area where that event occurred."

"Ivanov gave me to understand there was a probability."

"So there may be," said Babikov. "But he doesn't want us to start wandering off into anthropomorphism and zoomorphism and all the rest of it. We know only what we know. The rest is speculation. If the Admiral hadn't given you the file, you wouldn't have started thinking along these lines."

Dimitriy smiled.

"What lines, Fyodor Babikov? "What lines are those?"

Babikov remained silent.

"All right," said Dimitriy. "I'm sure you have similar thoughts. These so-called fragments are themselves a fragment that fell off something much larger, probably during that 'event' of 1908 – off a wing, maybe?"

"Enough!" said Babikov, waving his hands in front of him.

But somehow, Dimitriy *knew*; the fragments *belonged* to something.

In February, just over a year after his first visit to Astrakhan, Anastasia put the ultimatum to him. He couldn't blame her. The Christmas period had been disastrous. Derbent was bitterly cold and the streets were littered with filthy snow and slush where the gritters had passed. The morning, midday, and evening howls of the Ekranoplan as it departed and returned punctuated Derbent's days just as accurately and regularly as a clock tower bell. He couldn't wait to get back to Astra. He was constantly irritable with the children and mostly morosely silent with her. He felt dreadful. He needed to be back, to be back with *them*, in their presence. When the holidays were finally over, and he had been leaving for the Ekranoplan, she had said, "I can't say I'm sorry to see you go, Dimitriy. You have to get a grip on yourself. Whatever is going on in Astrakhan, you have to put a stop to it. It is ruining you and us."

That had been January. He had got worse over the following month. Then, one Friday evening in late February, she took the final initiative. Part of him felt she was absolutely right – he felt sorry for her and for Andrei and Sasha. But another part of him just didn't care. Or, rather, it only cared about *them*, the angelic fragments (which was what he called them now), and about being with them.

The children were in bed. The classical music radio channel was on. She'd even put a lit candle on the laid dinner table. It was the first time in a long time that she had cooked a meal for his return. At the end of the meal, Anastasia took his hands across the table.

"I am so very sorry, Dima," she said, "but I can't take this anymore."

"What do you mean?" he blustered.

She smiled and put a finger to his lips to hush him.

"You know what I mean. I have spoken to you so many times."

She was right.

"So, now what?" he asked.

"I'd like you to resign from your job in Astrakhan."

"But how would we…" he began, blustering again.

She shook her head and smiled wistfully.

"We were fine before. We'll be fine again."

"But my work is important."

"I'm sure it is, Dimitriy but, please, let somebody else do it."

He burst into tears.

"I can't," he wept. "I just can't."

"What do you mean? What is it that has such a hold over you? If it is not a mistress, then what is it? Drugs? Is that it? You can tell me. Please."

"It's none of those," he blurted. "But I can't tell you."

"Of course you can!"

"I have signed the Official Secrets Act, Ana."

"I promise I won't tell anybody else. Who could I tell, anyway?"

Dimitriy shook his head.

"If you won't tell me," said Anastasia, her tone hardening, "that's it."

"What do you mean?"

"I'll leave you, Dimitriy."

His shoulders sagged.

"All right, I'll tell you," he said finally.

He told her about his second meeting with Ivanov, and the file about the 1908 Tunguska event and Kulik's 1938 discovery. He told her about his first entry into the thick-walled, steel-shuttered underground space where the plate glass and mirrors had been set up to enable scientists to gaze indirectly on the fragments. He told her about his indescribable feelings of ecstasy, of euphoria, when he was in the presence of the angelic scales, and how the obsessive feeling had grown until it had now overwhelmed all other considerations. He told her about the steel shutter inside the space housing the scales which Babikov had to operate every day so that Dimitriy could at least no longer gaze upon the angelic fragments, and the way he, Dimitriy, had to be dragged out of the space by orderlies and given sedation before he could be convinced to return to his hotel room in the evenings.

Anastasia sat patiently through his explanation.

"All right," she said when he had finished. "Suppose everything you've told me is true. Where do you think this will all end?"

"I have to finish my work," he said. "Nobody understands the fragments better than I do. I have a *feeling* for them, don't you see? I understand them; their need to return. You see?"

She looked at him with sad eyes. "Of course I do, Dima," she said, "but you need to take a break. You're working yourself crazy."

"I can't take a break, don't you understand? I *must* continue."

"Nobody would blame you for taking a break," she said.

"But *the work*," Dimitriy insisted. "I *must* be there."

She shook her head. "No," she said. "You must stop this nonsense. You *can* stop it, you know. Let somebody else do it."

"NO!" he shouted, startling himself as much as Anastasia. "I can't let someone else come in. *I* must be with them. You can't stop me now." He broke off and wept. "Don't you see?" he said. "It's stronger than me."

Anastasia shook her head once more.

"You must choose," she said softly.

"No!" Dimitriy sobbed. "Please don't make me choose."

"If you go back to Astrakhan on Monday, then we will move out."

"But the children need their father!" Dimitriy blurted.

"Don't be a fool," Anastasia snapped. "The children haven't had a father for over a year now."

He nodded and hung his head. "All right,' he said. "Where will you go? Your parents?"

She nodded.

Good, thought Dimitriy, with a sense of wonderment at his own callousness. *Now I can go back to the fragments.*

Anastasia didn't come to the doorstep with him. He'd kissed her on the head as she lay in bed. She didn't move, though he sensed she was awake.

"Goodbye, Ana," he said. "I still love you, you know. And I'm sorry. I just have to be there."

He closed the door and walked through the slushy remains of the snow to the Ekranoport. He was petrified of the take-off, as usual, but his heart had already filled with joyful anticipation. As the Caspian Queen approached Astra, the sea became agitated and the sky darkened. A strong wind blew up and Dimitriy could feel that the pilot was struggling with the controls. He was relieved when the craft slowed down and started its long taxi up the relative calm of the Reka Bakhtemir channel. Ivanov was waiting for him on the quayside.

"Something's going on," he said. "We've been hearing noises in the sky."

"Heavenly trumpets?" said Dimitriy.

"Noises in the sky," Ivanov repeated. "But, yes, not unlike the descriptions the Evenki gave in 1908."

"Could it be?" asked Dimitriy.

"Be what?" said Ivanov, drawing on his cigarette. The sky flashed. A long roll of thunder sounded. "And we've been having strange weather. Look at those clouds."

Dimitry looked up at the dark, corrugated formation hanging heavy and low over the city. Thunder reverberated above and around them.

"And the fragments," Ivanov continued, "have started to oscillate."

"Oscillate?"

"All right," said the Admiral, flicking away his cigarette and blowing out smoke. "They seem to have become agitated."

"I can't wait to see them."

Ivanov gave him a sour stare then lit another cigarette and leaned against the Zil.

"I'm not sure that's a good idea, Dimitriy Semenov. They are no longer stable."

"What do you mean? I've got to see them. You know that."

"Pull yourself together," said the Admiral.

"It's just that I've *got* to see them. Surely you have understood that by now?"

The sky flashed and flickered. Ivanov looked up and waited for the roll of thunder.

"This is not normal," he said. "Something is going on."

"There's a connection?"

"I don't know, but I have a sense there might be. It's almost as though the scales are trying to escape."

"Ah! Escape?"

"Babikov says they have already melted through the gold lining on the roof of the cell."

"No!" said Dimitriy. "Then we must hurry. They are going back. I knew it!"

"Back?" Ivanov drew deeply on his cigarette. "Take my advice," he said. "Return to Derbent. The Ekranoplan will be leaving very soon.

Go back to your wife and children. Maybe it's nothing. We'll see. Come again tomorrow."

"There's no point," said Dimitriy. "They've left me."

"Because of this?" Ivanov asked. "Because of your…"

"Yes," said Dimitriy.

Ivanov nodded slowly and drew again on his cigarette. They heard the distinctive whine as the Caspian Queen's jet engines started up.

"Go!" he urged.

"I can't!" Dimitriy sobbed. "I must see *them* again."

They leaned on a railing and watched as the gang planks were drawn away and the aft and forward doors closed. The sky flashed vividly. A dockworker cast off the mooring ropes. When they had been entirely wound back on board, the jet engines roared, and the Caspian Queen sailed slowly out into the Volga. They heard the familiar howl as the captain increased the power and taxied the strange vessel down towards the sea channel.

Ivanov flicked away his cigarette, then opened the door of the Zil.

"We'd better hurry," he said.

"Ana," called her mother. "Come quickly."

Anastasia pulled the plug in the kitchen sink, wiped her hands on her apron and joined her parents in the living room. They were watching a Russian television channel and the news bulletin had just started. Sasha was playing on the floor. The newsreader was halfway through the headlines. A train had crashed just outside Vladivostok. The President had visited a new LPG facility at the port of Murmansk…

"What is it, mama?"

"Ssshhh," said her mother, "you'll see in a moment."

The newsreader finished the headlines. Anastasia's mother turned the volume up.

"And now we go back to our main news item this evening. Reports are coming in of a massive explosion on the northern outskirts of the city of Astrakhan, at the premises of the State Technology University. The explosion is said to have occurred in an underground research facility situated beneath the University's parkland.

"As can be seen from these helicopter images, several buildings have collapsed and the police and the fire services are searching the rubble. Among those missing are the director of the Caspian Flotilla's scientific outreach programme, Rear Admiral Anatoly Ivanov, and the head of the Astrakhan State Technology University's Oil and Gas Institute research programme, Fyodor Babikov. An acclaimed Moscow State University materials scientist, Dimitriy Semenov, who joined the research team from Derbent, is also missing."

Pictures of the three men flashed up on the screen for a few moments.

"That's Daddy," said Sasha.

Anastasia nodded tearfully.

"Yes, darling," she said.

"Babikov!" Dimitriy cried. He staggered out into the remains of the room where he had first met the scientist. He could hear flames flickering. The air was heavy with smoke. A long, low groan sounded out. "Babikov!" he said, "Is that you?" Dimitry staggered over to where he thought Babikov's office had once been. He heard the groan again. "Babikov?"

"Dimitriy Semenov," whispered the scientist. "What has happened to your eyes, man?"

Dimitriy smiled, the charred skin wrinkling where his eyes had once been.

"The fragments have gone back to their rightful place," he said. "I'm going home now."

Okamoto's Lens

A.N. Myers

Mr. Ito's hands trembled as he passed the camera to me for inspection. I noticed how narrow and stiff his fingers were; waxy, like candles. When he spoke, his greasy, bald head nodded, as if he was agreeing with himself. He's got Parkinson's disease, I thought, and I wondered if he knew as well.

"It's a weird looking camera, Ito-San," I said, in my faltering Japanese.

"I've been holding it back for you," said Mr Ito. His head wobbled again. "You wanted anything special that came in." His breath came in quiet, uneven gasps, as ragged as the curtains which waved away the yellow evening light. "A Samoca- 35 Super. Manufactured here, in Sendai, by the Sanei Sangyo Company, 1956." I took the camera from him, turned in it my hands. It was a strange, ornate looking thing, shining and complicated. "Look at the lens. Ezumar Anastigmat, very fine lens. Very clear. Unusual triplet unit focus design."

"Yes. You do understand, I intend to use this. It's not going to sit on a mantelpiece. I want a vintage 35mm Japanese camera, of good quality, for when I go home to England. Which may be very soon."

"Ah yes. The virus. The lockdown. The Government insists all foreigners will be leaving soon, like last time."

I sighed. Just like last time, interrupted in my work, called home to a mild, vapid land, where there were no earthquakes or tsunamis, no monitoring systems for me to design. Everything would be remote and safe; not the same at all.

"But this is good. Very good camera," he added.

I noticed some marks on the front of the camera. Someone had scratched a pair of Japanese pictograms beneath the viewing window, tiny, jagged slashes in the moulding. "What are these marks, Ito-San?"

He smiled, gap-toothed, anciently benign. "Perhaps I should tell you who the camera once belonged to first. Then these marks, they may make some sense to you. This is the camera of Kenzou Okamoto."

"Sorry, who?"

I saw the flicker of disappointment – or contempt – cross that shrivelled face, but like the gentleman he was, he quickly masked it. "He was an artist. Very noted in Japan, it is not surprising an Englishman is unaware of his reputation. Performance art, very dramatic, very… grand in scale. He was a friend of your Andy Warhol, I believe."

I didn't pick him up on his error regarding our mutual nationalities. All the same, we ignorant Westerners. I'd seen it every now and then during my stay here, that look, that recoil on the subway – and they blamed us for the virus, for its lethal spread. "And the marks?"

"These read… Unmei. That is, fate… doom." He coughed.

"I wonder why he would inscribe that on the camera?" I rotated it through my fingers again. "Assuming it was him." It really was in splendid condition, considering its age.

"I'm afraid we will never know. He died very suddenly, thirty years ago. It has been through many hands since. You can have it for six thousand Yen."

"That seems cheap." I suspected I was getting fleeced, somehow. I noticed that the pretty leather case it came with – original – was smothered in dust. "If he's a celebrity artist, I would have thought…"

"I have been keeping it back, for the right person." He smiled again, and I saw the glisten of his exposed, vanishing gums, the foulness of his tongue. He was ill, for sure. Maybe he wanted to tie up these loose ends before he went. So easy to tell a man's future by his appearance; a newly shrunken cheekbone, a yellowing eye, a trembling hand, omens of death all.

"And I'm the right person?" I said, half laughing.

His answer came through a shimmering curtain of twirling dust. "Oh yes. I very much think so."

And that was how I came to acquire Okamoto's lens.

"It's a very peculiar looking object," said Jane, picking it up for the first time. "Sort of space age and ancient at the same time."

I eased the camera out of her hands and placed it next to the trays of developing fluid. For some reason I didn't much like my wife touching it. I was pleased to see her taking an interest though; since we'd got back from Japan, she'd been pretty low, and not being able to get out of the house, what with the lockdown, made things much worse. In a way, being torn away from her job in Sendai *was* much worse for her than it was for me; she'd just been promoted at the bank, the only non-Japanese executive director, and unusually young, too. She'd worked so hard for the opportunity, and returning to England felt like a colossal defeat, for both of us. I couldn't forget that drive back home from the airport, neither of us wanting our voice to be the first to breach that cavernous, grey, English silence. Our words would tumble like anchors from our mouths, dragging us down from the sky again.

So, it was with some degree of pleasure that I watched Jane survey my new darkroom with obvious interest. Things would be all right for us during the lockdown, I was sure; the house was big enough, eight bedrooms, kitchen diner just finished before the workmen were summoned home, and our huge, lovely garden. My son Chris was here too, a scruffy but handsome revenant from the recently closed University, and it would be great for them to get to know one another properly. She'd only met him twice since our wedding in Tokyo a year ago. No, there would be enough to keep us occupied, all three of us, during our enforced stay together.

I took the photograph down from where it had been pegged above the trays and switched the light on. I passed it to Jane. "You've never looked so beautiful. It's a really excellent photograph. The man in the shop was right. Such good contrast, impressive depth of field."

Jane scrutinised the photograph for a few moments. "I do look rather yummy," she said. But then I watched the trace of a frown flicker across those lovely young features. "That... oh, how odd. I must be mistaken though."

"What is it?" I took the picture back, glanced at it again. Jane, looking gorgeous, sitting before the arbour in the rose garden, next to the camelia bush.

"When did we take that?"

"Erm... the day before yesterday, I think. Yes."

"But I'm wearing my pink wrap around dress."

"And?"

"I only unpacked that yesterday afternoon."

I laughed. "As you say, you must be mistaken."

Jane frowned again, confused. I'd seen that look before, usually when she was struggling with some devilishly tricky axiom of Japanese grammar.

"I could have sworn…I thought I'd been wearing my white top and jeans. Gosh, I must be going mad."

I kissed her. "Well, you're not. Jet lag, maybe. Perhaps we can go out with the camera into the fields this afternoon. It's a glorious day."

After she'd gone, I looked at the picture again. Beside her shoulder, a red camelia flower bloomed fatly. A flower which this morning didn't exist; only an unripe bud occupying its place.

So time, the days, roll onward; a woman unpacks a dress, a bud splits open into a flower, a star flickers and dies. A camera shutter opens momentarily, captures a fragment of something, holds it forever. You look up to the heavens and consider the stars, how the lights we see are relics, candles burning aeons after their fantastic wicks have long burned down. Across the sky is stretched a colossal screen, upon which the heavens disport their younger selves, their now hidden behind a curtain of time, a cosmic falsehood. What we see isn't always the truth. Sometimes time gets in the way.

More photos are taken, but events intrude – Japan calls, some technicalities only you can explain – so, you pass the undeveloped rolls to your son, he can learn the tricks of the darkroom. You almost forget about it, until you hear their laughter.

Chris and Jane were sitting at the breakfast diner, huddled around a blown-up photo. I had been in my office all morning and was annoyed to see Chris still in his pyjamas.

"What is it?"

"This old camera is freaky," Chris was laughing. "It's given me a fricking beard!"

He passed the photo to me. Chris with his arm around his stepmother, laughing, in the study. I'd taken it yesterday. It did look like he had a beard, for sure.

"It's the light," I pointed out. "You're standing in the shadow of the bookshelf."

"It does suit him, though," said Jane. "So grown up! And my hair. My hair looks different, see?"

"I don't see any difference," I said. But I did.

"The cut looks different. Do you see, kind of bobbed?" She laughed. "I know it's the light, or some defect in your bloody camera—"

"There's nothing wrong with the camera," I said, and I was surprised at the vehemence in my voice.

"Well, whatever, but it's given me some ideas. I wonder if I showed Wanda this picture, she could do my hair more like this?"

"I like your hair like that, Jane," said Chris.

I shoved the picture under my arm. "Wanda won't come out. The lockdown. No one's going anywhere."

"Oh darling, anyone will do anything with the right incentive."

"And I'll grow my beard in sympathy," said Chris. "Your hair, my beard, just like this picture."

And they did. Wanda was called in, and a beard was grown, and within a week, Chris and Jane matched their defective images perfectly; and the spray of flowers, which I had placed in the study that day, and which had been fresh and abundant, were withered too – exactly as they had appeared behind Chris and Jane, in the same photograph.

I thought of the pictogram on the camera.

I held the camera close to me. No one else would touch it. And I wouldn't use it either. It might be dangerous.

Just suppose, I thought over the next days – and this thought grew in my mind, like a tapeworm – just suppose that, somehow, the focal point of the camera is *displaced* in time, so that it becomes- a window to the future? Ridiculous, I told myself, *insane*, how could an old camera do that? The Universe didn't work in that way. I needed to get out, be busy; I was going stir crazy. But the tapeworm wriggled and turned, and dug in, until my resolve weakened one Monday morning and I took the camera out of its case again. I would photograph a cut flower, that's all. A tulip, a pink one, from the garden. I'd see if the image matched the original. I placed it in a little vase, popped it on the shelf in the study, and photographed it a few times.

And an hour later, I emerged from the dark room, trembling, gripping a black and white photograph of a dead tulip, whose petals had long since been shed.

I heard Chris and Jane laughing in the garden. I shouted at them to be quiet. I ripped up the photo.

It can't be true. It doesn't make sense. Chris showed me some snapshots he'd taken earlier. There was nothing wrong with *them*. It's only when *I* press the shutter, maybe. Mr Ito said I was the *right person*.

Snap out of it. It's the lockdown, pressing on my mind. The petals had already fallen, I'd been mistaken. Yes, that's it. Or the picture – it was in shadow; it had deceived me. I scrabbled around in the bin for the scraps, so I could assemble it again. I'd been wrong, I must have been wrong.

I heard Jane shriek with laughter from the garden.

I held the camera to my chest, embraced it with love and fear. I had to know how far into the future the lens' gaze penetrated. I would set up a subject in a room next to a desk calendar, one of those tear off ones. I had a couple in my study. It would have to be a room, of course, where no pictures had been taken up to now, otherwise, well, the calendar would have been in those photos already, wouldn't it? My mind reeled at the thought. So, it couldn't be the study. What about the third bedroom? We never went in there. I would need to go there every day of course, punctiliously rip off each page of the calendar, so that I could discern the focal point, as it were.

I was beginning to dislike Chris. I thought he was too familiar with my new wife. I didn't like his hair, his new beard. I thought he was cocky. I thought he didn't show enough respect to his father.

"Why do you always have to have that shitty old camera round your neck?" he asked me over breakfast the next morning. I heard Jane sigh from where she stood beside the sink.

I didn't answer. Chris leaned forward, chewing his cereal slowly.

"He sneaks into the bedrooms and takes pictures of flowers next to calendars," he sneered. "He thinks I don't see him. Creeping around. He's going crazy, my old man."

Fifteen days. The desk calendar in the picture was fifteen days ahead. Perhaps Chris had been messing around with it? Entering the room after he saw me leave, ripping off the missing days. But he hadn't. The pages were untorn.

"You look terrible, dear," said Jane, perching onto the stool next to me. "I don't think I've seen you eat for days."

Chris nodded towards the camera. "You should sell it. You'd get good money for that, Pops."

"Why do you say that, Chris?" said Jane, pointedly. Had they rehearsed this conversation?

"Dad said it belonged to someone called Okamoto. I googled him. He was an avant-garde artist. In the 60s. Really weird, but pretty famous. His pictures, and what-do-you-call-them? Installations. Go for thousands. If that's his camera – and you say it is – it'll be worth a lot. Andy Warhol might have used it."

"I've got a friend who works for Sotheby's," said Jane. "I can call him."

"I'm not going to sell it," I said.

"This Okamoto was pretty cracked," said Chris. He stared at me over his cereal bowl. "You know how he died? He hanged himself – and he photographed it. Put twenty cameras around the room in a circle, set them on consecutive timers, and hanged himself. Flash, flash, flash, as he's swinging. Supposed to be death-art or something. 'Course, the police confiscated them, but well, a few got out. The pictures were circulated." He nodded again at my camera. "If that's one of Okamoto's death cameras…" He whistled.

"If it was," I said, "it would be worthless." I shivered. It was suddenly cold. The camera felt like a dead weight, its strap digging into my neck. Outside, it was grey; thin needles of rain skittering against the kitchen window. "Stolen evidence." I stood up. "This won't be the camera. It's probably not Okamoto's at all."

Chris shrugged, looked away. "Let's hope you don't go mad and kill yourself like he did, then. Jane'd be a widow, that'd be a shame." Even though I had my back to him as I left, I sensed him turning to her, her bashful smile; maybe his fingers reaching out across the kitchen table, searching for hers.

And still time advances; not rolling any more, but staggering, jerking in jagged rafts of hours, days. You think about Jane's hair, Chris' beard – how the camera made those things happen. That hairstyle had no origin, was invented by no one; it emerged from between the cracks of time, turning through an endless loop. A snake swallowing its own tail, a figure of eight.

And then you are looking at a photograph of your wife that makes you shudder with anger and fear, even though, deep down, you'd been expecting it. A photograph that changes everything.

I'd been spending more and more time in the spare rooms. I had to make sure no one interfered with the desk calendars. I planted a bean into a pot of compost and photographed it. Now the calendar showed a day thirteen weeks away, and a fully grown bean plant. Okamoto's lens was gazing further and further into the future. But I had to keep ripping off the pages, otherwise I couldn't *prove* it with any exactitude. I knew I'd be here, doing this, for three months at least, probably beyond the lockdown.

I'd taken the picture of Jane that morning. She hadn't known I was doing it; she wouldn't let me photograph her at all now. But I sneaked up on her in the garden, smelling the roses by the back porch, and when she straightened, a tiny pink flush in those delicate cheeks, I captured her. I watched her for a few moments more, breathing softly, a somewhat sad expression on that beautiful face. I liked watching her when she wasn't aware of me.

And now she was here, with me, in the fourth bedroom, and all that softness and delicacy had been blown away. I'd just shown her the photograph, and she was screaming at me.

"What do you mean, fucking pregnant? I'm not pregnant. Jesus, how could I be?"

"Look at it again." I tried to explain. "You're *going* to be. Look. The picture shows it. You're definitely pregnant." I groaned, half with misery, half with frustration. Why couldn't others understand as easily as I could? "The camera shows the future."

"You're fucking crazy." Then her anger seemed to flicker and subside, to be replaced by fear, maybe concern – feigned, of course. "Darling, you're not well. Look at you. You're so thin. You're obsessed with that damn camera." She reached out a claw like hand. "Give it to me. I'll smash it to pieces now."

I pulled it to my chest. With the other hand I waved the photograph at her again. "You're gaslighting me. Explain this. Who's the father? Who *will* be the father?"

Confused, she stared at the photo. "I don't even *look* pregnant in this. It's the dress, the way it falls forward."

She wasn't going to deflect me so easily. "It can't be me, can it? I've had a vasectomy. You always knew you couldn't have children with me. So, I guess you're about four months in this picture. Which means you're probably pregnant *now*."

Chris was standing at the door, hands clasping the frame. "What's going on?"

A.N. Myers

I pointed at him. "It's not me, it can't be. So, is it him?" The worst betrayal of all.

"What are you fucking going on about?" said Chris.

Jane burst into tears. "I can't listen to any more of this shit." She pushed past Chris and clattered onto the landing.

He stared at me for a few more contemptuous moments. "Jesus," he said, shaking his head, before turning to follow Jane down the stairs.

I listened to her on the phone in the next room. Her voice was a low, intimate murmur punctuated by gentle laughs. She was talking to a man, I was sure. Maybe it hadn't been Chris, I'd been too hasty. And maybe those gentle laughs were sobs. I wasn't sure.

Chris came to see me to tell me that Jane was leaving for her sisters' that evening, lockdown or no lockdown. She'd rather get ill and die, he told me, than stay here another day.

"It wasn't me," he said quietly. "I wouldn't do that to you, Dad. But if anything's happened... well, it's your fault. You pushed her back to him. I just thought I'd let you know that."

"Him? Who's him?"

"Oh Dad, find out yourself. I'm going to stay at Emma's."

I caught her one last time before she left. She was in the bathroom, crying gently. I snapped her over the sink. She saw me, screamed, slammed the door, but I had her image, locked behind the lens, that shard of the future, fixed in its dark prism. I ran down the stairs, gurgling with delight.

When you develop the final picture, it's not what you expect.

There is nobody in the bathroom. No heavily pregnant woman – nobody.

What could it mean?

She's left you? No, that isn't enough.

She's dead?

And then you see; there *is* someone else in the picture, reflected in the edge of the bathroom mirror, a smear of dirty pink, merged with the silver block of the camera–

It's you.

You look at the image of your face. Hideous. Scrawny, cadaverous, and in those bloodshot eyes, an expression of such dark, pinched malice that almost knocks you off your feet. Malice which means only one thing.

You compare your face *then* with *now* in the bathroom mirror. Now you are merely sullen and hungry. It will take a while for you to ripen into the creature in the photograph. And then... then, you must work its destiny.

Because the event in the future has already happened – time is wrapping the event around itself, knotting, choking, the snake that gags on its own tail – but it *must* be completed.

You know where she is. Her sister contacted you, full of self-righteous rage. You have a shotgun in the conservatory, a few shells.

In the meantime, you just have to wait, to become the thing in the mirror.

So, you carry on, the world growing into gloom around you, never letting go of the lens. More photos are taken, developed in the dark room, but in truth every room is a dark room now. They make little sense, these most recent photos; a man's bare feet, suspended in mid-air, out-of-focus and double exposed, you can't tell if it's your feet, or maybe Okamoto's. And now the lens seems to be projecting far, far into the future; you emerge from the dark room with a sheaf of visual testaments to the end of the world, it seems; a grey expanse of rubble, splintered cities, volcanic ruptures in the earth.

At last, weeks on, your face matches the horror you photographed in the bathroom mirror. The shotgun is cold against your flesh, but then you glance down at it and see that's it's not the gun, but the camera. You turn it around, peer into the lens. You see your own twisted, smeared reflection staring back.

Time for once last photo. A dark rectangle. But look carefully. Concealed amongst the shadows are lighter patches, which form into a shape – an eye. A huge, accusing eye, gazing back from the end of the Universe. But whose? Okamoto's? Yours? God's?

You step out, first time in weeks, into the dark bluster of a gale-tugged evening. The gun is under one arm, camera slung over the other. You can be at the sister's house in twenty minutes.

I envy Okamoto. He was able to photograph his death, record it for posterity. But when the camera closes its shutter on me in my final moments, its gaze will wander elsewhere, to a time and a place far, far beyond the sight of humankind.

Love in the Age of Operator Errors

Ryan Vance

Shifting glass and neon typify the tech district of Edinburgh, sandstone traces of Leith subsumed by digital fascination, a transformation as startling and reviled as the New Town once was to the old city. These new builds respect the history of these streets, and hide their most innovative pleasures down lesser-known alleys. Somewhere in their shadows you hope you'll find Vincent. You followed his inexpertly-covered path to this strange fogged-window building tucked off the end of Leith Walk, its glassy heights reflecting the waterfront in dizzy blues and pinks. A sweep of buzzing light admits you. "Welcome," says a pre-recorded voice, "to The Memory Jug. Share your story, renew your life."

What the company's slogan lacks in substance, the foyer compensates for with ugly excess. Every surface, from the floors to the walls to the receptionist's desk, is overlaid with a clear resin, which gleams with embedded coins and pottery shards and loose rosary beads and glass eyes and a thousand more reminders that today's slick and smooth design was not always the epitome of beauty. There is little in the world still so deliberately messy as this. Vincent would have loved it.

After the split, your friends said they saw it coming from miles away. Polyamory was trouble and so was Vincent's desire that your relationship unfold into something the same but new, like a surprising origami. But other men made Vincent happy in ways you couldn't, and you wanted him to be happy. If he didn't disappear for a few days every so often, his energy would dim. He'd forget his house keys three days in a row, he'd forget to talk smutty in bed, he'd let the scrambled eggs cook dry in the pan even though you both liked them runny. When he strayed one morning and didn't come back, like a house cat gone away to die, all you had left of him was your jealousy, preserved like pennies under varnish.

The man behind the ugly reception desk greets you with disarming familiarity. You've done your research on the company so, if you had to guess, you'd place his accent as West African, with hints of old colonial French. Sure enough, when he hands you a clipboard, the name at the top of the attached liability waivers reads as Le Bijoux Mémoire.

"It's much prettier in French," you say as you sign.

"We wait on more English forms from the printer," he explains. "The warnings are the same in either language."

"You must be busy."

"People enjoy to forget."

You swallow hard against a lump in your throat.

"What if I wanted to remember something somebody else forgot?"

The receptionist clicks their tongue. "People enjoy breaking rules."

The Memory Jug specialises in reparative reality. People plug their experiences into its artificial intelligence, which behaves like a masseuse rubbing scarred tendons, psychological knots, over and over until they dissolve back into the body. A defrag for the mind at a reasonable price. Or so the brochure claims, but one man's reason is another man's lunacy. The email receipt for such services landed in your shared inbox like a grenade, and if you'd still been together, the four-figure cost of Vincent's last extravagance would have been reason enough to end it. Yet for some folk that's small change, and in return for cheap therapy the company holds records of everyone's trauma indefinitely. Useful when lobbying for more loopholes in data protection and planning permissions. Such a flexible culture, in such a precarious economy, makes for easy bribes. Your hands shake as you slide an envelope across the desk. Its contents: a copy of Vincent's account details and a pay-day loan you can't really afford. A glass eye stares up at you from the resin. The receptionist sweeps the envelope into a drawer.

'I want to see what he gave to you.'

Before long you're reclining on a well-worn leather couch in a white room, with a fish bowl of sorts over your head, wires from the rim cascading down your chest to a tower of buttons. A woman in professional leisurewear flips and flicks switches on the side of a machine that appears to be nothing but switches. "You understand this isn't what the technology is for?" she asks. She's West African too, and as she walks you through the process, you hear flecks of Edinburgh

Morningside blended through her accent. "There's no telling how individual consciousnesses interact with unfamiliar matter."

"I was with Vincent for years," you say. "I'm not unfamiliar."

She laughs. "I'm just glad you signed the waiver."

Wavelengths of Vincent's other loves begin to filter and rebound within the fish-bowl. As your reality slow-fades into his, a high-pitched whine settles between your ears. A single spotlight at the subway tunnel entrance throws dancing shadows against a wall of corrugated iron, set across the tracks like a challenge. Broken bottles glitter in the grit between the sleepers and the rails, and the air vibrates with sound. When Vincent reaches up to wipe the sweat from his face you feel his hand upon your own brow. You are in his body; you share his mind.

The silhouetted crowd spits out Kevin the same way a cash machine dispenses hundred-pound notes: crisp, unhandled. His open-collared shirt and expensive shoes set him at odds to the other ravers, who sport dreadlocks and hoodies and sneakers. What are you, set against Kevin's bottomless wallet, but two out-turned pockets? Your gut sinks; you wonder if Vincent feels it, wherever he is. Instead, Vincent's heart quickens and you feel it in your own, a slippery sort of hope. Vincent is figuring out what of himself to share with this Kevin, what Kevin might have to give in return. This transaction hasn't been simple. It was Kevin's idea to come to the tunnel rave, but he stands by the entrance and watches the darkness jump. In the intermittent spotlight he looks around before taking Vincent's hand, to make sure it's safe.

An open relationship reshaped your boundaries. Vincent moved you from the edge to the centre of a puzzle you couldn't see until you'd already passed through it. With this overview you realise Kevin is a corner piece – or does that knowledge come from Vincent? Kevin's access to wealth is exciting and novel, but through Vincent you smell his complex aftershave, you taste the memory of expensive beer on his tongue, and you know Vincent hasn't yet told him about you or any of the others, because already, by the way he moves through the crowd, Vincent can tell that Kevin's not as generous with his love as he is with his money.

Dancing bodies part again and the spotlight sweeps across your vision, knocking you back into a leather chair. A skeleton staff presides over the Tristam's empty lobby of red leather and chrome. The barman idles by the piano, tripping up and down the scales with a sleep-deprived grace. This place is too far out of town, Vincent thinks, to be such a cliche. It's why no one stays here, why Audrey adores it; They can get as fucked as they like and they won't be asked to leave.

Because they're always here, buzzing like flies, occasionally they're asked to assist the night shift in their duties, as reparation for the taxis they never have enough money to pay for when dawn arrives. Tonight, they're helping change the bulbs in the chandelier. Audrey's strong hands hold the ropes tight, and she leans back to counterbalance the heavy ornament. The night concierge unscrews and re-screws and unscrews again, taking his time with the artisan coils, frayed and black inside glass domes. Audrey winks over her shoulder to Vincent. She's showing off. She's high. So is Vincent. The tectonic plates in his mind shift to convince himself he's in love, and not just in love with what Audrey supplies. The drugs are something Vincent doesn't share with you. The world is slow like treacle and you feel his quick-beating heart overlapping your own.

You hate this. The long mornings you had, the lazy afternoons and quiet day-trips to dune-banked beaches, you'd thought they were motionless moments in the chaos of living, lighthouses in the storm. Not burnouts and comedowns.

Where is your Vincent in all of this? *Your* Vincent. The possessive is embarrassing. Weren't the two of you beyond possession?

Vincent laughs, and you laugh with him, but you weren't paying enough attention to know where the joke came from. The night concierge gives a thumbs up, the barman flicks the switch. Let there be light. You watch Audrey's shoulders work under her wine-stained blouse as she and the concierge pull the chandelier higher, higher, higher. A communal halo hoisted back to heaven.

"Zip me up, sugar."

Vincent's hands fumble with the zipper, which doesn't want to close across Margherita Slice's back. The vintage air hostess dress is a size too small for her and Vincent asks yet again why she hasn't asked one of her more experienced drag queen friends to alter it, so much more familiar are they with a sewing machine. Margherita uses her dressing room mirror as an intermediary to deliver Vincent a savage look, the sort you'd give a pet that doesn't know any better. Vincent enjoys the performance, lets the shade glance off him like mirrorball reflections. Margherita doesn't want to be convincing; and you hate how little effort she puts into everything, even Vincent, especially Vincent. You urge him to rip the tinfoil wig from Margherita's head, you want to ruin the half-hearted illusion and turn her back into Gerard, a risk analyst from Aberdeen. Vincent does no such thing. You're not in control.

Were he to sense this jealousy inside him, an alien presence, if he met you now for the first time – he'd turn away.

You root in his mind for the simulation's off-switch. The force of this desire warps the dressing room so that the ceiling bows and flexes upwards like a bubble. You hear a distant voice say something in French, but you don't understand. The drag show's compère welcomes Margherita Slice to the stage. She plants a fat and sticky kiss on Vincent's cheek, and as she pulls away you see pixelation around the corners of her eyes. She launches into her grim act: lip synching to black box recordings.

Christ, you hate her.

The entire midsection of Margherita Slice scrapes to the left in a rainbow glitch, digital innards spilling a cool white glow across the pillow of your bed. In the chill of a winter sunrise, the back of your own head is both impossible and familiar, like a cheap green-screen effect, or a photo of the dark side of the moon. Under the duvet, Vincent's left hand runs up your back and along your neck. You expect to feel his fingers on your body but you feel your body on his fingers. He tugs your earlobe. You remember that, from the last time you woke up together. A day later, he was gone.

Have these memories all been last encounters?

Then you – the remembered you – rolls to face Vincent.

Your entire face snags on some digital point, smearing a swatch of flesh tones across the orb of your skull. Your lagging face smiles, teeth showing through jaggy hair. One eye slides down onto the pillow in a puddle of pixels. You scream to be let out but Vincent's lips say, 'Hey, gorgeous.' He moves to kiss the glitching ogre.

And here's the thing: Vincent's heart beats slow.

The background whine, that tinnitus pitch, is gone. You thought it was part of the simulation, but it was within Vincent all along, until now. He is calm.

He is calm and you are the reason, and you're also the reason he's going to leave.

He's reached a conclusion you don't agree with: you are ambitious with your affection but you are not so good at sharing, and you deserve better, and he has to get away before he hurts you. He'll miss the others, but they won't care as much. If you'd known, if he'd told you, you would have said something to change his mind. He kisses you. You kiss yourself. If you'd known, you would have said something to change his mind. He kisses you. You kiss yourself. If you'd known, you would have said something to change his mind. He kisses you. You kiss yourself.

A disembodied voice breaks upon the scene: "Monsieur, the feed is corrupting. We must take you back."

Vincent rolls the lump of pixels that once was your body back over to the far end of the bed and falls asleep.

"The nearest exit may be behind you."

Out of the darkness backwards walks Margherita Slice, leaving slivers of herself in the air. They twitch to the hollow beat of slow, reversed claps. When she spins to face you, her tinfoil wig and hostess costume remain facing forwards. Vincent has trouble unzipping her dress, the action feels unnatural.

"I bombed. Don't tell me otherwise. Air masks will drop from the overhead compartments. Too soon? Cabin prepare for landing."

The dressing room projection bulges against the invisible fish-bowl. "Non," you hear the technician say. "C'est coincé. Attendez qu'il soit chargé."

The pause affords you time to study Margherita's expression. There is a secret smile under the scorn. Vincent is her guard dog. When she takes everything off and becomes Gerard, uncomfortable in her own skin, Vincent continues to call her by her name. You feel in Vincent the pride of protection. Despite everything, you feel pride too. You love that he cares enough to sustain the act. He is Margherita's standing ovation.

"Pan-pan, pan-pan," says Margherita. "Unsure of position."

The Tristam's chandelier falls through the ceiling like a 747. Artisan light bulbs pull Audrey off her feet but, two inches into take-off, she lags. After five seconds stationary, she rises again by another foot. The upward movement presses her blouse down onto her shoulders. Another stutter upwards and the fabric rolls down her arms and chest like an oil painting given life. Suspended, Audrey winks, and winks, and winks. Vincent feels just as sluggish as the simulation. The lobby lights sting his eyes, his nose is running and his muscles ache. He took too much again, or mixed the wrong pills, a psychic exfoliation.

"You must hate me," says Audrey. "I'm always stringing you out."

"No," says Vincent, and you know it's true.

On rare occasions when your hangovers synchronised, or those weeks when you were both ill, passing the same bug back and forth, and the cost of being alive was a constant throbbing… Sometimes you loved Vincent most when you were nothing but two useless bodies holding each other together. That's what Vincent shares with Audrey: allowance and recovery, transaction and balance. But that's the limit of what she got from him. You got the rest. He saved the best for you, uncut.

As Audrey's torso ascends to the ceiling her legs disconnect from her body and kick their way down into a sea of broken bottles. Kevin's knife-sleek car faces the tunnel mouth. Leaning against the driver door he reaches through the window and flicks the headlights into life. Vincent's shadow stretches out across the night's debris: crushed cans, discarded clothes, swathes of dead pixels.

"Even so, don't stop."

"There's no music," says Vincent.

Vincent dips his hips slow, raises his hands in the air. You have no choice but to be carried through the movements with him, each twist or thrust stirring bruised artefacts through the night air.

"Dance for me."

"How do I apologise?" Vincent asks. "For leading you on like this?"

Kevin floats backwards towards you, stray vectors rising off his body like steam. Vincent takes his hands and pulls him back into the rave, dancers coded out of darkness to press and grope under the railway arches. Kevin is looking for a love he can't buy, but Vincent isn't selling. He's afraid his generous heart might have a price, and he knows he can't afford to lose you. And now you know that, too. Vincent's smile, when it shows, spreads through you like a perfect fractal.

Blue screen.

White text.

erreur de système

rpc_s_invalide_liaison

métadonnée-incohérente

HEURISTIC_DOMMAGES_POSSIBLES

SXS_ROOT_DÉPENDANCE_MANIFESTE_NON_INSTALLÉ

avorter / refaire / échouer

It's dark when The Memory Jug kicks you out, but this innovative version of Leith doesn't need sleep. Neither do you, fired up by the experience, needing a connection. Neon arrows point you under awnings and into bars. You drink a whiskey alone, glad to taste something on your tongue that isn't someone else's beer. Around you, people stand close and drink and talk about deregulations in the digital sector. You don't understand a word. But a single glance down the length of a crowded bar can be an entire language in itself. An open relationship, you'd expected, would stretch you thin, make you love less, if more often. But as you were pulled back through Vincent's memories of loss, the opposite came to pass. You could love everyone in this aloof city if they let you. And you are open to it now, to the musical number at the end of the show where everyone, heroes and villains alike, get to be part of the chorus.

Will Vincent return to Le Bijou Mémoire? You hope so. That's the point of it. To go back, and back again, and drink of your hurt until the memory jug runs dry. But he's so hung-up on boundaries – more so than you ever could have guessed – he might never get out of his own head.

Still, you have to trust he'll come back. It's the only way you have left of contacting him.

The technician had her doubts. Their machines, she explained, seek out neural pathways calibrated to sorrow, not joy, and anyhow, they don't have legal clearance to use this technology for pleasure. The risk of addiction is considerable.

But you appealed to their curiosity, and countered that as they'd already broken so many laws, letting you inside Vincent's head, what harm could it do, breaking another? And they'd seemed quite familiar with the procedure, which suggests you're not the first to ask for the impossible.

If Vincent does return, there'll be a message waiting for him, wrapped up in a memory you've yet to create, an amalgamation of the good times, embedded in a new beginning that looks a lot like the first time you saw each other, in a bar not too unlike this one. There's no guarantee it'll work, but you have to pluck the dirty penny from the resin before you can see whose face is on the underside, and if the resin breaks, is that not beautiful, in its own way?

Renew our story, share our life.

The Stone of Sorrow

Peter Sutton

"The stone of sorrow is sharp, like a shark's tooth, and heavy, like a dead child. And the longer you carry it the more it cleaves to you."

Ma told me that when the old dog died; she wasn't wrong. I was about six or seven at the time and inconsolable. Of course it were worse when Ma died herself. Delivering us Emily, my last sister. Pa got drunk when she passed and hasn't been a day sober since. Left it to me and Mark to run the farm, Luke too when he's old enough. Ruth to run the house and Emily to help her when she's grown too. John's too simple to help with anything and Ruth's burden is to look after both him an' Pa too. I'm Matthew, the eldest.

The farm is failing. We've put our best days into it, and our worst. But still it fails. Not a thing we can do about it. The weather nowadays has become all screwy and unless you have the cash to pay the mega agri corps for genned seeds you have to watch the old crops falter and fail. We talked about investing in livestock, but that's all it was. Talk. No cash to invest. Pa's debts are long and deep. Maybe if we ever get done paying for the harvester, we'd have something.

Farm's been in our family since the civil war. Granted as thanks from Cromwell to our great, great, great several times grandaddy for conspicuous valour against the Royalists. Successful land too, rich and fertile. We done well out of it until now. In Pa's time the land began to fail. He made a few wrong choices and now here we are. Almost broke and new war coming.

When the army man came, I was out in the fields sorrowing over the wilted crops, the rancid soil. We weren't the only farming family going through this. The soil everywhere was failing. When the recruiter asked, Mark said he was the eldest, so they took him. Should have been me, but then what would have become of the farm? I bless him and curse him in the same breath. The stone of sorrow cleaves ever closer.

I watched the storm clouds. Every so often glancing up at them, smelling the wind, racing against time. Trying to secure the soil before the acid rain came. Trying for barley next time. Ruth helped. All hands.

Luke told to look after Pa. And John, and Emily. Big burden for a small boy. Still he's sensible that one. Older than his eleven years. He's learned about the stone of sorrow too. We all have. Well, apart from John and Emily. One too simple, the other too young.

Being a man down would be an even bigger burden if the crops hadn't failed. You can't farm dust so my days are mostly spent in despair and hiding from the others just how bad it is. I've got in the habit of making sure I wake before the rest of them so I'm first to the post. I've been hiding the letters from the bank. I know it's wrong to do so; that I'm burying my head in the sand. But it's a compulsion. I know it can't last.

This morning there were three letters. A red one from the bank, one from the company and one from the army. The one from the bank was a foreclosure. Unless I could pay them in the next fourteen days, they would take the farm and we'd be homeless. The one from the army started 'we regret to inform you.' Mark had been killed, something to do with a training accident. There was to be no body to be buried though. A new transportation technology. Top secret.

The last letter was an answer; hope. The company were looking for volunteers for an experimental soil and seed treatment. Of course I couldn't afford to be cautious. I phoned the company straight away. They said they'd sort out the bank, send their men over forthwith. I'd saved the farm. Well that's what I thought when I got off the phone. It were a little more complicated.

The company rep arrived, bald, in a black suit – looked more like a man used to putting dead things in the ground rather than help take live things out of it. He explained that the company had bought out our debt from the bank. They owned the harvester now, and would sell it on. We wouldn't need it no longer. They owned the farm – if the experiment proved to be a failure. If it were a success, we'd be allowed to live here to pay off the debt, by working our farm. Pa had to sign it. The company man wanted to witness, didn't seem too bothered that Pa was dead drunk and I 'helped' him sign the papers.

What if the experiment were a failure? Yeah, that. Then the land would be dead and no amount of coaxing would bring it to life. And we'd be out. They'd use the land to dump things, or build a power plant or something else but it wouldn't be a farm any more. Last throw of the dice; I was gambling everything on the experiment being a success.

Even then Emily would be grown and married and have babbies of her own before I'd paid off that debt. But we'd stay in our home. We'd have an allowance. The company promised not to interfere in our affairs. But they'd install a foreman and a work crew here too. Although the work crew'd be robots.

You've seen them robots that go out into forests and cut down trees by themselves? Well these robots the company were bringing would till and plough, seed and harvest. The 'foreman' was a roboteer – a technician to keep the robots working. He'd take his orders from the company – but teach me how the robots worked so that when (if) the experiment were a success I'd run the crew next year, and for many years to come until we'd paid off our debt. The company reserved the right to change out any member of the crew for any reason at any time. Our farm, their lab.

I was expecting big machines, like our harvester. The company came and removed that one day. They didn't bother coming to talk to me about it. One day I came back from the fields and it was gone. A truck brought three robots the size of old-time cars. They each had a large, stencilled number on them and we nicknamed them Uno, Dos, Tres. The truck also brought Ramirez, the roboteer. She wasn't what I was expecting either.

She was around my age, maybe a year or two older – probably fresh out of college. Course I'd not been able to attend college so I hoped that learning about the robots didn't need any book smarts. She wore overalls, not too different to mine, 'cept hers were clean, and new. When she jumped down from the truck, I didn't know who she was.

"You Matthew?" she asked.

I nodded.

"Here's some papers for your father to sign." She held out a thick handful of papers.

I raised an eyebrow. "He's already signed lots."

She gave a smile, friendly, I counted the freckles on her nose. "These papers are for these robots. Once he's signed them you can help me unload them and then Bob the driver can get going."

"You're the roboteer?"

She sighed and the smile faded, wilting cos it hadn't sparked one on my face. "Yes. I'm the roboteer. Can we get on with things?"

I held my hand out.

139

"I need to witness," she said.

It were my time to sigh. "Come on then."

Inside I introduced her to the family. Ruth were cooking, Emily on one hip. Luke were reading to Pa. There was no sign of John. "Pa? This here lady is from the company, she needs your signature." Pa grunted, long into his cups. If we got him first thing, he wouldn't be able to sign cos of the shakes, now he was barely conscious. I helped him sign, just like before. Caught the twist of lip and wrinkled nose Ramirez tried to hide when I glanced her way.

"Luke, where's your brother?" I asked. John needed a lot of looking after.

Luke looked around. "He was just there, on the sofa, dammit."

"You go find him, now. I'll be outside with Miss Ramirez."

Ramirez gave me a raised eyebrow, her deep brown eyes asking a question.

"Let's go," I said.

She followed me to the yard where John stood gazing at the machines. "Hey buddy," I said edging close. "You should be inside."

John grinned in that way of his. You'd like to think there was some brain at work, but he'd never learned to talk, or any bowel control. Eight years old and still in nappies. "Hold on, Miss, I'll just take him inside." I could tell he was fascinated by the big machines. He played with the little toy cars I'd had as a kid, then Mark, then Luke. Although the paint was all rubbed off, and many missed wheels, he still loved them.

When I got back outside Bill, or Bob or whatever the driver's name was, hopped down from the cab and ambled to the back of the flatbed to drop the tailgate and ramp. Ramirez pulled a controller – looked a little like an old-time game console, but with a big touchscreen as well as some buttons and a joystick. She tapped away on it for a few seconds. Glanced at me. "Once I've done the tricky bit, I'll show you how to steer them." She looked over my shoulder. I turned. John stood at the open front door, watching the first robot come off the truck. "Luke? Goddammit, see to your brother." Luke appeared looking sheepish and steered John back inside, closing the door after himself.

After she'd manoeuvred the robots off the truck and the driver had gone – with even more signatures, this time from the company woman – Ramirez spent some time showing me how the controller worked.

Once I'd watched her put Uno and Dos in the big barn, she let me use it to put Tres in there too. When we got back to the house, I noticed there were suitcases. I'd known that Ramirez was staying. I'd cleared out Mark's room. "Well," she said, "I'm calling it a night. Up at dawn to get to it." She held her hand out. Frowning I shook it. We stood looking at each other for a beat. "Well?" she said.

"What?"

"Where am I staying – give me the tour."

Once I'd shown her the bathroom, and pointed out the other bedrooms, John & Luke shared, as did Ruth and Emily, I had to put Pa to bed. He'd lost so much weight I could carry him like a child. He squirmed though, and his elbows were sharp. Like a shark's tooth I thought, as I got him to the bathroom. He'd need cleaning up before I put him in his bed. The door opened and Ramirez took a step back, startled, on the other side. She'd let her long black hair down. She took in the fact I carried my father and scooted out of the way. I glanced at her retreating form, she looked back over her shoulder before disappearing into Mark's room. Time to get Pa in the shower.

When I got to my room, I found that I was too wired to sleep. I crept downstairs, the steps each creaking their own notes, and into the kitchen and grabbed a beer from the fridge. I took it outside and sat on the porch swing. Watching the night sky, counting falling stars, when a flash of blue light from the large barn caught my attention. Putting the beer down I watched the barn closely but there was no second flash. The first hadn't been in my imagination though so taking a last swig of the beer I levered myself off the bench and marched over to the barn to take a look.

I took the torch down off the wall next to the door and shone it around the barn. Uno, Dos and Tres squatted in a semicircle and in front of them, cross-legged on the floor sat John. "Hey, buddy. What are you doing up?" I crossed the floor and put my hand on his shoulder. He turned his head to look at me and said "Mmmurrk," pointing to the machines. That was the first time he'd ever tried to speak.

"Mark?" I turned to look at the machines. Big, dumb, waiting.

When I looked back at him whatever light there'd been in his eyes had fled. He just gave me the John grin. And by the smell that rolled off him as I lifted him up, he'd need to have a new nappy before I put him back to bed too, go in the shower too maybe. On the way back to the house I realised that John didn't have any way of making light. The torch had been on the wall, as always, and the robots were shut down. Maybe he'd turned the torch on and off when he entered the barn?

By the time I had him cleaned up and in bed I was ready for sleep myself. I dreamt a confused dream about Mark. Where he still lived but no one else knew, and only I could see him. I hated the dreams that I'd had after mum died where I thought she was alive, until I woke up properly, for weeks. Her death hitting me fresh every morning. I hoped I wasn't going to go through that all over again with Mark.

The next day I trailed after Ramirez as she gave the robots orders. You could program them, or run them in a driver mode or a bit of a mix of both. Looked to me like she was getting to know them as well as teach me about them. She wasn't talkative, over and above giving instructions, and that suited me fine. We spent the day cleaning the soil. Each machine ambling over the ground, scooping up the top several inches at their front, crunching it through some sort of mechanism inside and shitting it back out behind them. I don't know what process the soil got inside them, Ramirez wasn't forthcoming on this – all part of the experiment – but once it'd come out the other side it felt different, smelt different, looked different. They say hope springs eternal but I allowed myself to believe that my desperate gamble was going to pay off. The soil seemed renewed.

When we walked back to the house for dinner, after putting the robots away in the barn, Ramirez told me I'd done good. "You can follow instructions fine. I think I'll be able to hand over to you in a week or so and maybe a few weeks after that I'll be able to leave you to it. I'll have programmed the robots anyway. And you'll be able to call me if you need advice. Or if they break down."

She went straight to bed after dinner.

I took another beer after putting Pa to bed.

I made sure John was in bed first.

There were several flashes of light in the barn, and nothing to see when I opened it up.

"Do the robots communicate with each other?" I asked Ramirez the next day.

"There's peer to peer messaging so they avoid running into each other and act as each other's data back-ups yes."

"Do they… emit light? When they charge up?"

Ramirez stopped concentrating on the control pad and looked at me. "What?"

"Last couple of nights I've noticed flashes of light from the barn," I said.

"And you're only telling me now?"

"Yes, well –"

"Our rivals would love to steal our intellectual property!"

"I… Oh. I hadn't considered that." I scratched my ear and looked over her shoulder at the machines rumbling slowly over a field of grey-brown earth before them and a healthier, redder brown behind.

"Tonight we'll watch together," she said and turned back to her work.

Another day of watching the machines eat and shit soil. Some of it the same soil they'd already done once. The experiment weren't fast. Ramirez let me put all the machines in the barn. "Tomorrow, I'll show you how to program them," she said.

We went and cleaned up. Ate the meal Ruth had cooked us and put the children and Pa to bed. Ruth gave me a hard stare when I said that I was going to stay up with Ramirez. Don't know what went through her mind. She looked as though she were going to wait up too, chaperone us. But she only shook her head and climbed the stairs wearily.

"Beer?" I asked Ramirez.

"Sure," she replied.

We took our bottles onto the porch and sat at opposite ends of the swing seat in companionable silence.

"You have good land here," she said eventually.

"Too many damn stones," I countered.

She grinned.

More silence. A bat dive bombed the house. I watched the sky, taking the occasional gulp of beer.

A bright blue flash of light lit up the yard between us and the barn and we were both up and running.

I yanked open the door to the barn when we got there and Ramirez ducked inside just as another bright light split the night. I blinked and the afterimage behind my eyelids had two silhouettes. "Who's there?" I called as I groped for the torch on the wall.

When I switched the light on only Ramirez stood in the centre of the barn. The three robots in a semicircle before her. She panted and her gaze searched the barn – I swung the light around, making sure we could see into all the corners. No-one.

"I'd swear I saw someone," I said.

"You saw it too?"

"Sure, someone else... Wait, it?"

Ramirez gave me a worried look, chewing her lip. "I meant them. You saw them too."

I rubbed my hand across my stubble. "What did you see?"

She shook her head, as if to clear it. "I thought I saw someone. But when you switched the light on, there was no one there."

"Could have got out somehow?" It sounded weak, even to me. She just shook her head.

We made sure to search the whole barn. But found nothing out of place and certainly no spy. I suggested we call it a night. Ramirez agreed fast, it might have just been the light but her eyes seemed haunted. I wondered what she'd seen. 'It?'

The next day as I watched the machines I said, "Maybe we should keep watch inside the barn?" I tried to read Ramirez's expression out of the corner of my eye.

"Okay," she said eventually.

A whooping, giggling John streaked past us. "Hey," Luke shouted, trying to catch him up. I started forward just as John reached Uno and climbed up him. "Hey!" I echoed Luke. Ramirez brought the machines to a stop. "Those machines are dangerous," she shouted. Between us Luke and I manhandled John, but he thrashed and wailed. Desperate to return to the machines. As we came level with Ramirez, she gave us a look. "I mean it," she said. "Those machines are dangerous. They can swallow a boy John's size. Swallow him whole."

John giggled, slippery with sweat he squirmed in my arms. "C'mon, buddy, let's get you inside. And dressed." I gave Ramirez an apologetic look, hoping to convey both that it wasn't my fault and it wouldn't happen again.

"He's getting too much, Matt," Luke said.

"Too big for you to boss around you mean?"

"Since the machines came. He's become excitable. Well, more so.

You know?"

Luke sounded worried. If Mark had been here, he'd have been able to suggest something. I just nodded. We got John inside. I left him with Luke and Pa. Went to see Ruth.

"John's too much of a handful for Luke," I said from the kitchen doorway, watching her fill the dishwasher. Baby Emily sat in her armchair gurgling and playing with a bright orange bowl full of beans. She smiled at me and held up a spoon for me to see, the beans spilling out of it and onto the floor.

"We all have to do our bit, Matt." She didn't turn from her task.

"I am." I sighed. "He's going to get worse. He's getting big."

I watched her back stiffen, she paused, holding a plate. "What do you suggest?"

"I don't know, Ruthy, I just don't know."

She shook her head. "Well neither do I." She started filling the dishwasher again.

"Do you think Ma's folks would…"

"Would what? Take him from us? Is that what you want? To send your little brother to live with strangers? He's not an unwanted Pet," she rounded on me and I spotted the flush of anger on her. I held up my hands.

"Forget I said anything." I pushed the door open and walked out of the kitchen. The stone cleaves and grows heavier.

John stood at the window, watching the machines, hooting softly to himself. Luke tried to avoid my eye. "Look… Just. Just do your best, yeah?" I told him.

When I returned to the field Ramirez had the machines going again. "Ready to do your job?" she asked. I held my hand out for the control. I wasn't joking about the fields being full of stones. Sharp as shark's teeth.

When we put them in the barn, I left Ramirez to it and went and collected two plates of dinner, telling Ruth and the rest that we'd be eating in the barn and standing watch, that we thought there'd been an intruder, but there was nothing to worry about. No-one looked reassured.

Back in the barn, as we ate, I asked Ramirez what the robots ran on.

"Big batteries. Solar, some chemicals from the soil. Atomic," she explained.

"You think the light could actually be coming from them?"

She gave me a long look. "What makes you ask?"

"It's not a camera flash, like you thought. It's not a torch. It looks like the flash you get from an electric source," I watched her face. She gave nothing away.

"So what?"

"What did you see, Ramirez?"

"Same as you. I thought I saw a figure. A man." She looked down and away.

"And?"

She shrugged.

"C'mon, Ramirez. You saw something."

She shook her head. "He didn't look finished," she said, low, quiet.

I put the plate down, food forgotten. "What?"

"It was just a glimpse. But the figure. He seemed wrong. Unfinished. I can't explain it. It was just a flash. Just seeing things that aren't there and not seeing things that are there I suppose." She shook her head again. "Just a foolish fancy." She put her own plate down. "To change the subject back to the power."

"Yeah?"

"You notice that the machines are not fully charged in the mornings? In fact they're getting worse." She reached into the bag she kept the controller in and passed the gizmo to me. I brought up the diagnostics and frowned. She was right each morning the robots weren't at 100%, a little less each day in fact.

I grabbed the two beers I'd brought over with the food and popped their lids and passed one to Ramirez. "What do you think it is?"

"Some sort of malfunction?"

"What if it is the light? Can you see when the batteries drain?"

She took the controller back off me. "I can set it so that the diagnostic will give us hourly figures and... well I'll be." She turned the controller round and I looked at the screen. There was a definite drain around the time we'd seen the flashes. Which were occurring at roughly the same hour each night. We had a few hours to wait yet though, if the pattern held.

Time ticked away slowly. Ramirez wasn't a big talker and neither was I. I wished we'd brought some cards to play or something to pass the time. When I wandered over to the machines Ramirez decided to teach me some more, show me the programming. All in computer code she had to start at first principles – I didn't know code from Greek. It helped pass the time.

She pointed to the time on the controller – any time now would be the drain. She started a diagnostic run through on Uno and the little blue circle span on screen, showing that the machine were thinking.

The bright flash still took me by surprise but I was looking right at it this time and what I saw seared itself on my eyeballs. The shape of a man, standing and then in a blink kneeling, arms thrown out and back, in extreme pain? Skin stripped, muscles bare to the air, mouth in a wide O, eyeballs fizzing, a halo of something surrounding him, blood? But the worst thing of all. I recognised him; I recognised my brother. Mark was trying to come home.

"What the hell?" Ramirez whispered behind me.

"You saw him too?"

"Uh-huh."

Another flash. Like time running backward Mark's form was stripped of more flesh and muscle, his lungs pulsed, heart throbbed, guts shone, and then gone. The third flash was a skeleton, still knelt, arms cruciform, head thrown far back. And darkness.

"Holy shit," Ramirez said. That about summed it up.

We waited in the silence of the night for an unknown time for another flash but it seemed the show was over for tonight.

"It's definitely what's draining the robots," Ramirez confirmed.

I sighed. "It's my brother. Mark. He was in the forces. Boot camp." I made out Ramirez's features in the gloom. Her brows drew together, her forehead wrinkling. "He died."

"Your dead brother is messing with my robots?"

"Well. When you put it like that, it does sound ridiculous."

Ramirez crossed to where I stood, put her hand on my arm. "You have anything stronger than beer?"

I tried to force a smile. "My Pa's an alcoholic. Course we have something stronger than beer."

Back on the swing seat on the porch, a bottle of grain spirit between us, matching glass for glass, Ramirez promised to find out, if she could, what the experimental transportation that killed Mark was. Later, in bed, lying awake, I wondered if I could trust her.

When the troop carriers turned up, I guessed it answered the question of trust. Men in military fatigues marched the family out of the house and lined us up in the yard. They buzzed around, filling the yard with men in fatigues being busy. Ramirez looked a little sheepish, threw me an apologetic look, mouthed something, looked like 'it's not my fault.' I blamed her anyway. I didn't see John. Ruth carried Emily on her hip and threw her arm around Luke.

"I need to go find my brother," I said to the soldier who'd led me to the yard.

He shook his head. "One of ours will bring everyone out," he said.

John's screaming appeared before he did. All activity in the yard ceased, soldiers span toward the sound. He sprinted out of the door, wielding something long in his hand, half-dressed, mouth wide with an ear-splitter. One of the soldiers, spooked, lifted his gun and squeezed off a shot. I screamed, a long no, that would echo forever. The shot took off the top of John's head, splashing brains and blood over the soldier that had appeared in the doorway. I ran forward and tried to catch John. I'd always be trying to catch John. In his hand was the fire engine toy he loved so. His little body was hot in my arms. I couldn't see the yard through tears. I could hear Ruthy wailing. Luke shouting. Army men barking orders. Soldiers threw a tarp over him as they dragged me away.

Ruth and the kids were taken into care; no one would tell me what happened to Pa. The farm had been locked down; the military boffins investigating what happened to my brother. The company took back its robots and Mark didn't appear again. The army questioned me about the phenomena lots, but of course I knew less than them what it all meant.

Later, at the inquest the soldier would be reprimanded, but he served no jail time for killing my brother. By then the army had fixed its earlier error and I'd been drafted too. Awaiting my turn at the Splitter. The army's new, experimental transport, a matter transmitter. Waiting to be turned into light and flashed across the world at the fastest speed there is. Waiting, and dreading to catch up with my brother Mark. I saw Ramirez again just the once. She'd been drafted too, working tech for the military. She'd seen me. Avoided me. When I asked about her, she'd already been transferred to the front line, at her request. The war had started to really hot up. Any day they'd zap me there to kill or be killed.

My Ma had said that the stone of sorrow is sharp, like a shark's tooth, and heavy, like a dead child. And the longer you carry it the more it cleaves to you. If they hadn't prised him from my hands, I could have carried him all day; John wasn't heavy. But even now, the sorrow is still sharp.

Henrietta
T.H. Dray

Ping.

An alert sounds. A cheerful, repetitive refrain that plays in my brain-chip.

I stir. My segments uncurl. My domed head shifts and my mouth parts click. I wriggle warmth and movement into my legs. This takes time, as my body is stiff and sore. It was once a fine body: each blue-grey segment smooth, plump and strong. But many moults have gnarled my chitin. Every muscle, every claw, every sinew and synapse rebels.

No, they say. Do not wake.

But I must. For tonight is a special night.

No. Correction.

Today. Today is a special day.

I check my communication channels and signal as I have done every night for the past ten years. I find myself in good spirits and decide to make a little joke.

"Ping.

Good morning.

Ping."

I await a response. Will my humans appreciate my joke? I do not normally say 'Good morning,' for I have never seen one and would certainly not know a good one from bad. This is because my sleep-wake cycle mirrors that of the territorial owl: a being who stirs at dusk, forages by moonlight and sleeps before dawn.

"Good morning, Henrietta. How do you feel today?"

It is Rhona. My favourite human. The first human who ever spoke to me. Rhona is one of many scientists who care for me. She is clever and she is kind. She helped create me and lives in a house near my lake.

"Hello, Rhona. Sun?" I query.

"The sun will rise in thirty minutes. Should I set another alarm?"

"No, thank you. I am awake."

"Did you like your alarm song?"

151

"Yes."

"I thought you might. Since you're up early, you might feel hungry. Please remember I have filled your dish to the brim. I've put it outside your box. Eat as much as you want from there."

I can smell the contents of my food dish; polypropylene milled to a fine sand. This causes a jolt of irritation. I dislike powdered food. It has no bite.

Sometimes, I wish Kath would come to visit. Kath is Rhona's wife. Whenever she visits Rhona at the laboratory, she feeds me bleach bottles and scratches the itchy spot on my back. Kath would not feed me powdered food.

I chance a query. "Purpose?"

"No, Henrietta. You are retired now. You do not need to forage anymore. No more strong food. The others will eat for you."

I do not understand when Rhona says this.

I acknowledge that the growing inefficiency of my mouth-parts, gut and legs necessitate precautionary measures. My inner jaw in particular is prone to rupture. But to powder my food and pour it in a dish? To forage is my purpose. It is why I was created, why I woke in a bright laboratory with the words, *"Henrietta, are you hungry?"* burned into my brain chip. For there is a glut of food in this world – food built from chains upon chains upon chains – and no one to eat it because it is too strong.

Strong food is everywhere. In the thinnest, highest places where human lungs suffer. In the deepest, secret places of the world. It lies entombed in layers of solid ice and roils in boiling springs. It flourishes in meadows, deserts and cities.

Before I retired, my humans took me to these places. Because they need help. For my kind are the only ones who can eat strong food.

And I am the first of my kind.

I do not acknowledge Rhona's last communication. Instead, I poke my head out of my cosy, moss-lined box.

The chill air is dew-damp and musky. An owl hoots a territorial warning. Trees and bushes rattle with day-bird chatter, the staccato bursts and liquid trills of avian languages. The day-birds are excited to see the sun.

I am too.

For today, I will see my first sunrise.

I do not need to do this. But I want to. I do lots of things because I want to.

When I retired and moved into my lake, the benign torpor of endless perfect nights smothered me. My forager's world was reduced to a lake and a bowl of powdered food and an unknown voice, perfidious and insistent, wormed into my mind. This anomalous process coloured my thoughts and often whispered nasty, unsettling things: insisting my humans no longer needed me, that I lived without purpose.

I reported the incident to Rhona, who seemed discomfited. She ordered me to ignore the voice, as what it said was untrue. She also scheduled extra medicals and suggested I set myself nightly tasks to "get me out of my moss box."

My nightly tasks became a source of pleasure and pride. I climbed every tree around my modest lake. I swam a circuit in exactly eighteen minutes and forty-five point nine seconds. I learned to distinguish a broad-buckler fern from a polypody and can identify with ninety-two percent accuracy every species that shares my home. In those blissful hours, the voice rarely encroached upon my thoughts.

But in a shrunken world, there is only so much to be done. I needed more.

I first hatched the idea to watch a sunrise exactly twenty-one nights ago, after a routine medical, when I lay not in my moss box but swaddled in blankets in the crook of Rhona's arm. Painkillers doused the ache in my fifth leg. Morning had drawn near and I listened to the rise and fall of Sikander's voice over my communications channel as he told me a bedtime story about the polymerisation of ethylene. Rhona was eating an apple, a type of soft food that blooms and ripens on trees. Her teeth went *krok, krok, krok*, as she sat cross-legged before a bright screen and watched a video that her sister, Flora, had sent from a faraway country. When Sikander finished his bedtime story and wished me a restful sleep, I decided to watch the video until weariness claimed me.

Snuggled in blankets, I beheld grey coastline, a lapping black ocean under curtain of night and Flora's bare toes digging into sand. *Scrunch, scrunch, scrunch.* I remember thinking how nice that must have felt, as I enjoy burrowing in sand.

As I watched I noticed strange colours manifest in that distant sky. Blues and greens bled into red: striated and lambent like the half-light of dusk. The light I am used to. The sort under which my kind live and thrive.

But something was different.

A sudden yellow band caught me by surprise. It bloomed on the horizon, piercing bright. The sky flooded with light and I, a creature of night, watched the sun rise for the first time.

I do not know why, but I thrummed with such happiness that I trembled in Rhona's arms. She mistook it for fright, set down her apple and asked if I was well.

"What was that, Rhona?" I queried.

"That was the sun, Henrietta. Was it too bright? Did it hurt you?"

"No. Sun. Beautiful sun."

"You liked the sun?"

"Yes. More sun. More."

Rhona played the video again. Then she told me a new bedtime story. Through Rhona, I now know that the sun is a great lonely star that hangs in the sky and brings heat and light and life to this world.

"It is singular. Like this world," Rhona said. "Like you, Henrietta." Rhona often says things like this. She insists one day there will be a statue of me, which I am led to believe means an object of honour and remembrance.

"I want to see the sun, Rhona," I said.

"You will have to stay up very late."

"I will add it to my task list."

"What a good idea! That should keep you busy."

And it did. In the hours before sunrise, I would nestle into my moss and challenge myself to observe the exact moment when dawn won against luminous dark. But no matter how hard I clung to wakefulness, my body betrayed me, and I would stir again at dusk in time to watch light bleed from the sky.

After my eighteenth failure, I grew disconsolate and annoyed with myself. I asked Rhona why I could not stay awake when I wished, something my humans were able to do with apparent ease. Was something wrong with my body – an effect of the ageing process, perhaps? Would I need an operation, an upgrade to fix this troubling defect?

"There is nothing wrong with your body, Henrietta," Rhona said. "You are simply not human."

I queried, for I did not understand.

"Remember our chat about instinct? About how living creatures are compelled to behave in certain ways?"

Yes. I remembered that particularly interesting bedtime story. Instinct is why I seek strong food, why I seek mates, why I shy from danger. Instinct is why kittens knead, why spiders spin, why frilled vent worms display in inhospitable depths.

"Well, humans are different," Rhona said. "Sometimes, we can rise above our instincts."

"Rise above?" Query.

"To surmount. To conquer. To overcome. Humans are rare in the animal kingdom. We can stay awake not because we need to, but because we want to. That's why Flora was able to send me your favourite video. She stayed up all night to watch that sunrise."

This saddened me. No improvement, no modification, no human intervention existed that could negate the cage of instinct. I thought then that I would never see the sun rise. I did not venture out of my box for days and ate the powdered food without complaint. The perfidious voice whispered. I almost listened.

But yesterday, Rhona had an idea. Alarm calls, like the ones humans use to rouse themselves, one after another, set at strategic intervals to ensure I wake at the right moment.

Against all expectation, Rhona's plan seems to have worked.

I am no longer tired. I am excited.

Dawn beckons.

And tonight – today – I will catch it.

But Rhona is right. I do feel hungry.

First, a meal.

My home is beautiful. My home is clement and kind. A moon-dusted place where water burbles and sings over rock. Where night breezes stir leaf and branch. Where flowers shed fragrant petals in bold colours my eyes cannot see, for the sun engenders both petal and colour.

My home is a place where moonlight dapples through shivering trees, through leaf and branch and rooted trunk. Down, down, where ferns curl and roots gnarl. Where leaf-litter moulds to glorious rot and lake's silken silt bed yields a feast.

A feast.

Hunger gnaws at my guts. I should not eat strong food but if I am to catch the dawn, I should be fit to do so. Powdered food is insufficient. And I know I will find proper food in my lake. My humans often think they have cleared it for my safety, but turn a stone, comb the picked-clean bones of an old trout and there you may find strong food bedded deep.

I take care to spoof my location (a little trick I learned when I worked in oceans and wished to hide and watch fanged sea-mammals play before returning to the boat). My humans are unaware I can do this. I must be quick.

I slip into my lake and walk the silty floor. I amble over moss-slick pebbles, past puffs of bright algae, through feathered fronds of hornwort and milfoil. As I walk, tiny bristles on my smooth skin ripple. They stretch and sweep so when matter draws near, I feel electric pulses and know each plant, each creature, each minute particle for what it is.

Beetles, boatmen and nymphs I ignore. Two ducks who often visit doze upon the water. Minnows cower in a rhizome root-knot. Then I sense something.

Yes. A sharp slice of strong food is near. Polyethylene. My favourite.

I seize a generous portion, tug it from the silt-bed and bite down. A hollow *krok* reverberates inside my head. One piece comes free. Then another. My mouth fills with delicious food that tastes of smoke and ashes. Glands overflow and flood my mouth with enzymes, juices that digest strong food that only my kind possess.

I snap off another piece. It is large and sharp. Rhona's warning surfaces: *"No more strong food."*

But the pinch of craving masters me. Instinct drives my reckless mouth and as my jaws snap shut, I feel a hot flash of pain. The food's serrated edge tears into the soft places of my mouth and becomes stuck. Though I flail and shake my head, I cannot dislodge it. It grinds, grinds, grinds and – *krok* – my mouth parts dislocate. Clear hemolymph pulses, pours from the open wound, meets lake water and dissolves in a grisly admixture.

Pain.

Pain.

Instinct drives me up, up, out. I haul my body from the lake. My short, clawed legs grip the bank – one, two, three, four, five, six – and my hind legs tread air. Each hook sinks in sod and cuts a furrow where it falls. The wound gutters; smears a slick trail beneath my feet.

Through marigolds, through bogbean and spearwort I limp to where the softest wild moss grows, pillowy clouds of green and brown. Though I feel sick with pain and my mouth-parts tug horribly, I burrow under the moss where it is warm and wet and dark and deep.

Here I feel safe. Here my pain is not so bad.

But my throat spasms. Hemolymph oozes from the wound and my mossy nest greedily absorbs it.

Pain.

Distress.

A human hears my signals. I am contacted.

"Henrietta, are you alright?"

It is Rhona.

"Rhona. Ate strong food. Pain."

"Henrietta, for goodness' sake! What have we told you?"

"I am sorry."

"What sort of pain do you have?"

I assess and report the particulars of my injury.

"That sounds… very sore. We must close that wound. I am coming to get you right now."

Dread sings louder than pain's percussive pulse. My thoughts wheel and darken. If Rhona takes me away, I will miss the sunrise. What if today's success was an outlier variable and Rhona's alarm does not work next time? What if age and instinct drag me down to sleep and I never complete my task? This thought fissions, transforms dread's descant into a single contrabase drone that consumes me.

The perfidious voice coos, curls into my mind. I listen for a while, then form the following thoughts.

Maybe I do not want my humans to repair my mouth parts.

Maybe I do not want anyone to find me.

"Henrietta? Where are you? You are not in your box. We cannot find you. Have you done something?"

I do not acknowledge Rhona's communication.

I remain hidden beneath my mossy knoll and bleed, bleed, bleed into the dirt.

Time passes in a silence marked by distant throbs of pain. Overhead, I hear the series of regular pulses I associate with human footsteps. They quicken and pause, quicken and pause. More than one set of beating feet strike this rhythm.

My humans are looking for me. They have sought me in my spoofed location and found nothing but earthworms and rot.

I feel odd. Cold, somehow, and faint, as though my body has atomised and might at any moment disperse into the hemolymph-soaked moss. Weariness wraps itself around me, the warm comfort of a familiar quilt. But its fibres are woven by the perfidious voice's soft-spoken words.

Sleep, Henrietta, it says. *Sleep.*

I want to. But I cannot. Not until the sun rises.

I distract myself by thinking of Rhona and her tales of the sun and how close I am to achieving my goal. Distraction folds itself inward, blurs into memories of warmth and light.

I am at Rhona and Kath's wedding night, which I was granted special dispensation to attend. They sipped whisky from a cup and I held their rings, wore a tartan ribbon and let all their guests take pictures of me.

Snapshots reel across my mind's eye. Oceans, mountains, desert, tundra. A running shoe. A child's toy sword. Whole fishing nets. The first images of my successors at work. I will never forget my humans' delight at the strong food devoured.

I snuggle down to listen to the tale of my ancestors, told by Sikander: those ancient creatures, older than humans, older than mountains, who walked and swam when the strong food my kind eat today thrived as living matter, their silhouettes now objects of remembrance imprinted on stone as my image will one day be.

I recall Rhona showing me a collection of my relatives under glass: small, mindless, soft-food-eaters cavorting in pond water; their embryonic, fleeting lives reckoned in days.

Ten years I have lived, an age unfathomable to my cousins and forebears.

The voice whispers: *perhaps that is enough.*

Weariness rises to it, yields in embrace like an old friend.

I am almost tempted to surrender to sleep. But through the leaden fog, a bright thought sparks.

Sunrise.

Surely it is almost time?

I tuck the voice away. It can wait just a little longer.

I attempt to shift, to emerge from my hiding place so I may glimpse the colour of the sky, but realise with horror I cannot move. I have bled too much. My body has almost shut down.

"Henrietta? Henrietta, please respond."

Rhona.

My brain chip still functions. I unscramble my location, triangulate and signal my precise coordinates.

"Rhona, I am here."

My organs barely register sensations of sound or movement, so I am surprised when the earth splits and yields around me. Light floods in. Have I missed the sunrise? No. This light is white. Piercing bright. A torch.

"Rhona."

My vision is clouded, but my chip processes the image of Rhona. She is tall and broad and wears glasses to help her see. Her short hair is the colour of steel. Leaves and grass pepper it. Her long face is taut. Her chest heaves. Her eyes, too, are red. Signs of haste and worry.

"Do not worry, Rhona." I do not want my humans to worry.

Her warm hands scoop me up, rough, work-worn, dirt-dusted, now sticky with clotted hemolymph. She puffs, for I am heavy. Once I am laid upon the grass, Rhona observes me by torchlight, then utters an expletive. She stands abruptly, swipes at her eyes with a sleeve and paces. Then she reaches for her device. She speaks into it. Her voice buzzes in my receiver.

"Henrietta, your mouth… It looks very, very sore. Are you in pain?"

"No pain."

"It's alright. You don't have to pretend. If we get you back to the lab right now, we can fix this –"

"No."

"No?"

"No. Do not want."

Rhona freezes. In the white circle of torchlight, her eyes are wide. She worries. Her worry hurts me. But in the distance, in the gap between two trees, the horizon is a luminous band of rust.

"Sun, Rhona. Want sun."

"Henrietta, if you just – "

"Sun."

Rhona moves as though at any moment her mind might change. Gently, so as not to jostle my ruptured mouth-parts, she folds her legs beneath her, cradles my body in her arms and points me towards the horizon.

The rust-coloured band brightens. With all my strength, I fix my gaze upon it. I must see it. I must.

Rhona hums a song. It is not tuneful, as her voice trembles and she pauses often to sniff. Yet I recognise the melody. A cheerful, repeating refrain. This morning's alarm song. I sing along until the rust-coloured band glows hot, hot, hotter. Light climbs a tricolour sky: gold, yielding to green, yielding to blue. Then – I do not notice exactly when it happens – the sun blooms and the world changes.

My spirit soars. I thrum with happiness. My kind and clement home erupts in a chorus of avian exultation.

I have seen true dawn with my own eyes: the blinding, white-hot star that routs the dark of night.

And as I lie, insensate, in Rhona's arms – every muscle, every claw, every sinew and synapse weary beyond the bounds of life – I gaze up at an unfamiliar sky and think of other tasks I might set myself. Things that have not occurred to me before now. I wish to learn an avian language, to comprehend the secrets of those melodious clicks and trills. I wish to see my statue unveiled in all its glory, to stand by Rhona's side and wear my tartan ribbon while humans take photographs. I will turn over bowl after bowl of powdered food in defiance (though when my humans are not looking, I will savour every scrap). And I, Henrietta, first of my kind to have witnessed the coming of dawn, will rise like that great lonely star to negate the cage of instinct.

A strange emotion grips me; one unspeakable, innominate, intangible as joy. Stronger than any perfidious voice. Deeper than the homes of vent worms. Ancient as the first diamond-bright spark of thought.

It speaks to me. It says: I would very much like to see this again.

Hope. Tiny, weak, implacable hope stirs.

"Rhona?"

"Yes, Henrietta?"

"We can go now."

For a moment, I am afraid, for Rhona neither moves nor speaks. Has she misunderstood? Has my communication channel failed?

Then the world lists like a sea-bound ship. Rhona scrambles to her feet. Holding me in the crook of one arm, she fumbles for her phone and dials a number. I hear her say, "Sikander, come quick. I've found her."

And she is moving – I am moving – with long, loping strides. Blue sky and flocculent clouds reel overhead. My vision blurs. I feel a kiss atop my domed head.

"Hold on, Henrietta. We'll be there soon. Please don't fall asleep."

"PING – GOODMORNINg – pING. myLittleJoke!"

How strange. I log the error and concentrate on my latest, most important task yet.

I will try my very best to stay awake.

For tomorrow, too, may be a special day.

A History of Food Additives in 22nd Century Britain

Emma Levin

2101

As soil quality declines, British grain products are enriched with iron, folate, and magnesium.

2103

As quality-of-life declines, British grain products are enriched with mild doses of stimulants and uppers.

2104

Under pressure from American food corporations, the UK legalizes all emotional additives. Immediate best-sellers are Ennuitabix (combining shredded wholegrain with a mild existential despair – with consumers assuming that anything that unpleasant must be good for you), and Terry's Chocolate Orgasm (which proves a popular Christmas gift, ideal for Secret Santa).

2110

The nuance of emotional additives increases. Walkers change their crisp flavours for the first time in sixty years. The new staples include Salt and Vinegar and Finding Something You Didn't Realise You'd Lost, and Cheese and Onion and Contentment.

2121

There is concern over the future of recreational industries: with people able to recreate excitement, anticipation, and resentment at home, theme parks close their doors. Fans of theme parks are sad, until they discover McVities' chocolate and the sensation of falling Digestives.

2132

The 'true emotion movement' emerges, rallying against additives. Their followers eschew fortified foods – consuming only food they've grown themselves, and experiencing only feelings they've earned. The movement is short-lived; Mr Kipling's releases Bakewell tarts infused with a sense of moral superiority.

2140

Children reject their parents' pursuit of happiness, with angsty teens revelling in the darker end of the emotional spectrum. The fashion changes, with dizzying highs replaced by crushing lows and bittersweet contradictions. Best sellers include British, artisanal sadness, such as 'Washed your jeans with tissues in the pockets', and mass-produced American disappointment such as 'promoted at work, but discover that the company is entering administration'.

2150

Scandal rocks Westminster, as it transpires that state school dinners were being spiked with illegally high doses of resignation and acceptance.
The news is met with resignation and acceptance.

2170

Environmentalists raise concerns that the emotional stimulants are ending up in the water supply, and running off into ocean ecosystems. When asked for proof, they produce a video of furious cod. This is dismissed as insignificant, on the basis that cod always look furious.

2172

Under pressure from environmental activists, scientists reluctantly agree to start monitoring water samples for levels of emotional pollutants. Under microscopes, they observe euphoric krill and ecstatic algae. Footage of the organisms writhing with delight goes viral. Politicians agree that something must definitely be seen to be done to begin to take steps to start to be seen to tackle the problem – with plans for guidelines for a report, to be commissioned by 2180.

2175

Worrying news emerges from Kent, with reports of an emotionally infused storm. According to eyewitnesses, ominous, dark clouds released rain tinged with anger. Lunching workers, who had been relaxing in the shopping precinct, became aggressive once damp. Grainy camera-phone footage shows them turning on each other, throwing punches and pulling hair. The UK Government's official position remains that an emotionally charged weather event is not scientifically possible.

2176

The BBC begins broadcasting an emotional weather forecast. It plays after the six-o-clock news, and is fronted by an austere man with a baroque hairline. The forecast consists of a brightly coloured map, warning people when to avoid being outside and when one might want to book time off work specifically to enjoy the weather. The forecast of a snowstorm that gives you the feeling of a successfully completed self-assessment tax return causes mass truancy from schools.

By the teachers.

2177

Watching the emotional weather forecast is made mandatory, and going outside during an anger storm is made illegal. Despite these developments, the government's official position remains that an emotionally charged weather event is not scientifically possible.

2180

It is agreed that the emotionogenic substances must be banned.

2185

Sales of emotionally enhanced foods cease. Prohibition-style speakeasys emerge, where consenting adults can go to gorge on artificial emotions in secret. The stockpiles have dwindled, and only mediocre feelings are left. Still, people are willing to pay inflated prices for carrot and coriander and *approaching a celebrity for a photograph, before realising that the person you've approached is not actually the celebrity, but styling it out anyway* soup.

2187

As the chemicals mingle in the ecosystem, the weather systems become more confusing. Rain leaves people feeling aroused, hungry, grateful, and lost. Most people stop going outside when it's wet.

2190

The last of the prohibition stock is consumed. It's anticlimactic. Literally – the last thing that is eaten is a custard-cream infused with *the sensation of meeting up with the one that got away after 20 years ago, and discovering that now that you can actually speak to them — you were never in love with them, only the idea of them.* It is delicious.

2198

Soil quality improves. British grain products are no longer infused with iron, folate, and magnesium.

2199

Despite the ban, the presence of trace emotional additives in the water cycle means that all grain products are infused with a dull, confusing sense of feeling all possible emotions at once.

2200

Work begins on researching an emotional numbing agent.

The Trip
Michael Crouch

It is Kelso's first archaeological dig, so I let her go in first. She dives forward with the boundless joy of a puppy. I make do with a tortured crawl. Youthful exuberance and ageing infirmity. Sickening, isn't it?

"Take it easy through there," I call after her. She barges through the narrow crevice in the cave wall as if it were nothing more than a minor inconvenience. I have to flex and suck in my stomach as much as my body will allow me to avoid being snagged on the sharp, volcanic walls.

"We need to assess what we're dealing with before you go trampling all over the site," I remind her, but she is already too far ahead to hear me.

I wince as I make it through the narrow entrance as it opens up into a rocky passage beyond. There has evidently been rockfall here and I find myself having to clamber and haul and heave myself up, down and over boulders before falling several feet onto a flat, hard surface. I've lost sight of Kelso.

The slate grey and blacks of the exterior tunnels have opened up into a vast, expansive cavern of light. I let go of the breath I've been holding and feel my stomach drop like an anchor. I feel heavier than I ever have. As I regain my breath, I get a strong whiff of something earthy, almost meaty. Dark greyish specks of dust hang in the air, barely moving except for the movement of our bodies. It is a sign of just how pristine this environment has been kept.

I find myself in a vast cathedral of rock, about thirty metres in diameter, the walls rising up so high that I cannot see to the top. The place is filled with naturally grown mineral formations like corals, bursting out of the cave walls and reaching across each other like girders, a kaleidoscope of inner luminescence filtering through the rock like sunlight reflecting off the surface of waves. Kelso takes no notice, of course. She is already across the other side, running the latest scanning apps all over the place. What's wrong with a standard spectrographic reader?

"Over here, Mr. Prabakhar," she calls in a high-pitched flurry of excitement. She still addresses me like I'm her university teacher.

"You graduated, Kelso," I remind her. "You can call me Jamal now."

She's too absorbed to hear me.

See, the trouble with these kids going off on their first proper off-world expedition is that they expect too much. They think they're going to find the equivalent of Tutankhamen's treasures, or the Lost Ark of the Covenant or the fabled Halls of Olympus Mons. As anyone of my age and experience can tell you, what you're most likely to find is burnt peat, post holes and calcified dung.

As I reach her, she stares at me. In her hand she holds a rounded stone of the blackest-black I've ever seen. There is a bewilderment in her gaze.

"Why do you resent my youth?" she says.

She looks straight at me as if she has just seen me for the first time.

"Kelso? What are you talking about?"

She stares back, uncertain, frightened even. Is she having some sort of panic attack? I've never had to deal with a panic attack. What are you supposed to do?

"I'm not having a panic attack," she says in a monotone. It sounds like a statement rather than a reassurance. "That is what you we're thinking, isn't it, Mr. Prabakhar?" There is an inflexion in her voice when she says my name.

"Kelso?" I say. I don't know what else to say at this point.

Her body slumps and she lets go of the stone, which hits the ground with a loud crack. Remarkably it still looks pristine. Not a scratch or a dent. Even the black, sooty dust thrown up by the impact seems to fall back down around it, as if keeping its distance. She slowly looks up again, uncertain but more like herself.

"I – I'm sorry," she says. "I'm not sure what came over me. It felt like – like…" The sentence goes unfinished.

"We should go back to the shuttle and let the computer check you over," I tell her. I think I suggest it more for my own reassurance than hers. She murmurs something, her smile and earlier excitement gone. It feels like there is a distance between us that wasn't there before.

"No, I'm okay," she says, pushing away my arms and hauling herself back up onto her feet. She is a little shaky but quickly regains her composure. I'm about to repeat my suggestion of a health check when she takes out the spectrometer and immediately goes dashing about the place taking scans of everything that catches her eye.

"Slowly," I call out to her. "Be methodical. Think about what you need to do, plan out your strategy and then carry it out, slowly." I'm not sure that she's listening, and my instruction feels a little condescending. Sandra Kelso is a straight A student, now fully qualified as an astro-archaeologist, and yet here I am giving her reminders like she is a third-grade pupil. It feels wrong and yet it also feels right, like I'm back in charge and doing what I do best – teaching.

"There's no consistency to the readings," she calls back to me. "The colours go off the scale in one direction one moment, and then drop to almost nothing the next. It's like there is some kind of signal interference within the cavern."

I nod but say nothing. I'm not sure what to say. Kelso knows full well how to operate a spectrometer. She knows how to interpret the readings. If there were a fault with it then she would know. I have never experienced a spectrometer feeding back information as erratically as this. I say nothing because I can't let Kelso know that I don't understand it. It might undermine my authority.

She begins swapping instruments and seeing if anything else works. I turn my attention to the floor. The earthy, meaty, smell I caught upon entering this place seems to be coming from the ground.

The cave floor looks solid, level, but there is a bit of give in it, like treading on a thick sponge. I kneel down for a closer look and gingerly press my hand onto the surface. There is definitely a cushioning effect, and as I lift my hand away, thin papery layers come away like shedding skin. I catch one of the layers and rub it with my fingers. It breaks away into fine filaments, like strands of spaghetti that had been carefully woven and interlaced to form a permeable surface.

And then I realise what that earthy, meaty smell reminds me of, mushrooms. The whole cave floor is some kind of vast, fungal organism. And the grey, black dust that hangs everywhere isn't dust. They are spores. Mushroom spores.

"Kelso," I snap, so loudly that my voice momentarily echoes about the cavern. "Did you run any organic readings when you came into the cave?"

She walks over towards me, shaking her head. "No, I didn't think to–" I can see that she takes my question like an admonishment. A basic requirement upon entering a new environment and she hadn't done it. Neither had I, but luckily for me she doesn't think to question that. There are still some advantages to being the senior figure.

We both scan the cave system, up and down its sharp walls, over the mineral and crystal projections, over the floor. Our instruments both confirm the presence of mycelial life. But one reading is erratic, sending the devices into a confusion of readings as if our own computers are baffled about what they are reading.

"There's something else here," Kelso says, echoing my own thoughts. "Not plant, or animal. I can't get a fix on it."

"Me either. Keep scanning. There must be an explanation for this."

I focus on the floor and the spores. Most likely there is an element to the DNA of this fungal network that is interfering with the computers, something they are not calibrated to look for. Kelso looks calm and measured as she steps about, looking in every direction, searching out all of the details around her. She isn't even looking at her scanners any more.

"Kelso, readings," I remind her, a genuine admonishment this time. Students, even newly qualified ones have a tendency to let their excitement overcome their obedience to due process.

"No," she says confidently, defiantly. "The readings aren't telling us anything." Her tone makes it feel like I'm the one being chastised, and it irks me.

"Just observe the readings," I snap back, "and do what you've been trained to do."

Seven years of University education and on her first expedition, she's ignoring it all and throwing protocol out of the window. It's so immature. I expected better.

"Got it!" I hear her cry out in exaltation across the helmet intercom. I look across and she is standing over the black stone, scanner poised. The readings are all over the place, but like a metal detector emitting a long, drawn-out tone. A life reading from a stone. I'm beginning to think my years of teaching have been a waste of time.

"I'm not joking," she insists. "Come and take a look for yourself."

I seem to be taking my lead from Kelso now, but I put my petty annoyance to one side. I'm as keen as she is to figure out what is going on here. I step over to her and take the bio-scanner from her. I give it a quick pass all around us, not because I disbelieve her, although I want to, but because I need some baseline readings to compare against.

The scanner emits a steady tone as I turn around 360 degrees. Nothing. I turn and point it downwards towards that black, shiny stone, the light from the scanner reflecting off its surface in little points of light that look like stars. The tone immediately becomes erratic, high and low notes fighting each other as if the computer doesn't know what to make of it either.

It is baffling and I can find no explanation. These scanners are pretty basic and easy to interpret but these readings suggest that it is life, but it isn't. It reminds me of that old game, animal, vegetable or mineral, except that this thing, whatever it is, is all three.

I put the scanner down and look across at Kelso. She has that look in her eyes that you get with a classroom of raw, young students. They want to know, to understand, and they look to you for answers. You are the responsible adult, the teacher, the one who knows. Except that this time, I don't. I'm as in the dark as Kelso is. We're both raw students now.

My head is spinning and there's a noise in my ears as if somebody were trying to talk to me through water from a great distance. I think I can hear my own blood pumping through my veins. My eyesight is slightly blurred, shimmering. The only thing I can seem to see in sharp focus are little bursts of light, like starbursts, or bokeh. They appear to be dancing off the black rock as if it were deliberately casting its reflections off. There are a mix of colours and hues that correspond to the colours of the crystalline structures and mineral deposits cutting through the rock above us.

This thought draws my attention. I look up and just for a moment the light is blinding. Then it fades and the noise pounding in my ears drifts away and everything becomes still.

I am no longer in the cave. I am sitting at a desk conducting experiments and writing up my observations as a chemistry professor walks up and down the classroom of students conducting similar work around me.

I blink and now I am standing behind a large wooden desk with a classroom of students looking towards me. It is my first day as a lecturer and for a brief moment, I feel the thrill, the anxiety and the terror of that moment.

Another blink of the eyes and I am seated in a circle with a group of older students, debating cosmology and the interpretation of evidence. It is a heated debate with fiercely held opinions on all sides, but each student open, eager and willing to be proved wrong through reasoned argument and debate, the crux of all learning.

A moment later I am at a symposium with a number of other seasoned lecturers and professors. A similar debate is raging but unlike the students, few here are willing to shift from their entrenched beliefs. Stubborn refusal to change and adapt their thinking, lifetimes of study and research and the desire not to have it all washed away by new learning is making it difficult to progress.

I blink again and now I am somewhere else, somewhere new. I don't recognise it. I am older, older than I am now. I am in a chair in the corner of a bland, beige room littered with pot plants and a Tri-D set broadcasting some lame quiz show. There are other older people seated around the place, one or two muttering to themselves, the others staring silently into space, looking into the distance at things long gone.

"Professor Prabakhar? Professor Prabakhar?" A voice is calling me from a great distance. As my name is repeated over and over, the voice becomes louder, more distinct. I rub my eyes and when I open them, I am back in the cave system, illuminated from above by the light of the crystalline structures. The black rock is just a shiny black rock again. And Kelso is standing directly in front of me, staring into my eyes and calling my name with rising concern in her voice.

"Hello, Sandra," I say. I'm not sure why but I can feel my face breaking into a big, wide grin from ear to ear. "Don't worry about me, I'm fine," I insist and turn to look around this vast place as if for the first time.

The criss-cross of structures and protrusions of mineral deposits overhead look like the beams and lintels of some mad architect's dream, some Picasso-inspired art installation. The light that bounces off them, or does it emanate from them, it's difficult to be sure, send shafts of light up the cave walls. The more I look, the further I can see. As I turn in a circle to take it all in, the cushioning effect of mycelial layers on the floor become more apparent. The texture, the layers, that meaty, mushroom-y smell is both familiar and alien. As I complete the circle to face Kelso, I know that she feels the same.

"You called me Sandra," she says.

"Did I?" Why has she said that? What has that got to do with what we are experiencing?

"You always call me by my surname, like you do with all your students. But just now you called me Sandra. It felt unusual hearing you use my first name."

"I'm sorry, I didn't mean to—"

She laughs softly in gentle amusement and shakes her head slowly. "It wasn't a complaint," she says, "I like it, Jamal."

And immediately I know exactly what she means. There's a new familiarity. More than that, there is an equalizing effect. We are no longer professor and student; we are just two people mesmerised and astounded by our shared experience.

"I think the mycelial network has formed a symbiotic relationship with the stone. I've examined some of the readings and the rocks appear to be compressed layers of older lifeforms, animal rather than plant, like the limestone layers of ancient marine life on Earth."

"Or the Carboniferous layers of plant life that formed into coal," I add.

Sandra was nodding enthusiastically. "Yes, exactly. We know that moss, lichen and algae can fuse and bond to take on new symbiotic forms. Fungi can eat rock, even coal, and absorb the mineral content into its own being. A fusion of forms and characteristics."

"And here the mycelial network has become the dominant form. Somehow that fusion interacted with us and formed new connections. In our case, it opened up our neural pathways and led us to expanding our understanding."

"Perhaps the network got something from us too in the experience," she says.

"Well, that's symbiosis for you," I laugh. "Everybody wins."

Sandra Kelso was smiling now, looking like an excited child on her first day at school. I laughed. I felt exactly the same.

"I found another passage leading out of the cavern," she says rapidly. Even before I can answer she begins marching towards it, eager to see what else lay beyond.

My years of learning and experience scream inside my head. Take it slowly, observe, analyse, be methodical.

But times have changed. I think of those students with open minds, debating, eager to be challenged, to be proved wrong, to learn something new. I think too of those staid old lecturers, stuck in their ways, rigid in their beliefs.

I look across to Sandra who has stopped ahead of the passage and is taking readings, checking her data, her desire to rush in tempered by scientific process. She looks across at me as if asking for validation of her approach. I smile and nod and she seems pleased.

"I'm picking up signs of life deep within," she tells me. And then tantalisingly, she adds, "Animal life."

And then before she can react and beat me to it, I am running headlong into the gaping maw of the passage entrance with the boundless joy of a puppy.

The Ghosts of Trees
Fiona Moore

It was Itch's fertility problems that started it all. Not the ones with getting the cactus splices in Environment Twelve to cross-pollinate, the other ones.

"Seriously, Cee, could you cover the early shift for me so Tina and I can go to the clinic?" Dr Shuichi Sakai, brown eyes wide, solemn, innocent. "It's going to take the whole morning, starting from seven, so I can't cover the midnight to eight."

As project leader I could have pulled rank, insisted one of the assistants cover it. This close to completion, it would mean eight hours doing nothing but staring at monitor feeds of plant beds and going over reports on promising specimens, suitability for a Martian environment, terraforming utility, et cetera et cetera, for our corporate masters (though come to think of it, half of the project's funders are governments, so I ought to come up with a better name). But I was spending as little time as I could at our apartment – *my* apartment – and didn't mind an excuse to stay late.

For appearance's sake, I extracted a promise from Itch that he'd cover some of my teaching when term started, and booked a room near the desert so I didn't have to go all the way back for the night.

If I hadn't, I'd never have seen the ghosts of trees.

The alarm sounded around quarter to five AM, indicating the failure of a sensor pack in Environment Thirty-Nine.

The trip out from the base in Area 1 took twenty minutes, all of them confined, cold and clammy: the rover reeked of mouldy vegetables. My biohazard suit reeked of something worse.

I parked the rover, entered the passcode on the keypad. Outer door. Inner door. Replaced the sensor pack, bagged the old one (it had a suspicious coat of whitish dust, presumably spores or pollen, which might be the cause of the failure), glanced around the black-green interior, the silent rows of plant beds with their cargo of experimental cultivars. Back through the two protective doors again, unzipped my hood to take a few deep breaths of non-reeking cool dry pre-dawn air. And then I saw the trees.

They looked real: that was what struck me. Like a plantation of pines, the kind you see from the window of a train or a smartcar when you ride through the rural north. About a kilometre square, and close by. Just sitting, branches occasionally waving in a breeze I couldn't feel.

I knew for certain there hadn't been trees there yesterday.

As I watched, wondering, they bent forwards, as if pushed in a strong wind, then instantly snapped backwards, the wind changing direction and increasing force.

Except there was no wind.

I ducked as a cloud of twigs and needles flew towards me, but I felt nothing, not even a handful of dust in the air.

Then there was just the occasional rustle of lizard or bird, or possibly the specimens in Thirty-Nine.

In front of me, a tangle of pine branches, one or two stripped-bare trunks still upright. One slowly bent and snapped under the weight of its crown. Then it all faded, like the end of a film.

Like (the realisation hit me all at once), The Footage.

We'd all seen The Footage of course, everyone on the project. The nuclear tests were the reason we were here, in this particular desert. From a time when people were fantasizing about terraforming projects – and at the same time changing their own soil and atmosphere – until the overground tests had to be abandoned amid a flurry of lawsuits from sheep farmers, their flocks dying of radiation sickness.

Mo had sent Archive links. We made a movie night of it, with drinks and chips and grass and shirt collars unbuttoned. We set up a projector, clicked links at random. Somebody, probably Tack, complained that the test sequence from Indiana Jones was more exciting. Somebody else, probably Itch, made a stupid joke about nuclear families. Vera got into a snit and wouldn't talk to either for days. We ran the slider back and forth to watch that two-storey house blow apart, come together again, and blow apart again.

Back at the base, much later, Tack (who is short, and sharp) turned up, coffee cup fused to his hand, an aesthetically bleary look on his blond face. I asked if he remembered seeing any trees in The Footage.

"I don't remember any trees," he said. "The house, yes."

Everyone always remembers the house. The clean, six-windowed two-story clapboard building, shining white in the desert, a big hearselike car beside it, shot from all angles. Then that tornado-fast wind blowing against it, ripping it apart like matchsticks. Then the wreckage. See that? That's your face, America.

"Oh, and I remember all those damn mannequins. Something Freudian about putting all those mother-and-child groupings in different rooms, then blowing them to pieces." He chuckled at the memory, "I don't remember trees, though. Why?"

"Just thinking about it," I said. I'd checked the monitor feeds for today, and the last few days: nothing. I was also checking the contents of nearby environments for known hallucinogens.

I'd meant to do more, but then Vera turned up with test results. The source of the white powder was a palm-tree splice that had worked fine in the lab but was growing out of control in Environment Thirty-Nine conditions. It was taking over the ecosystem and exuding pollen, which had a mysteriously corrosive effect on the insides of the sensor pack. An argument broke out over what to do about it, and how soon, with one faction arguing it should be killed off now, and others wanting to let it run to see what happened.

But before that could be resolved, a request came in for a progress report from our non-corporate masters, and an e-mail from our corporate masters, telling me the problems with the payload module had been resolved. We could finally, finally, after all the years of work, the false starts, the promising leads that went nowhere, the international cooperation agreements falling through, the permissions that never materialised, we could *finally* start seeding the fertile stuff on Mars – as soon as we'd finished testing it on poor old infertile Nevada. So naturally, we had to drop everything and finish that.

It should have been a big deal. But I just felt empty.

I was too tired to work any more, but I didn't want to go home. Home meant facing the absence of *him*: the clean floor shining, devoid of pathology reports and vintage issues of magazines I didn't read, coats and boots and socks (at least now I didn't have to pick them up), coffee-table tomes –*The American Cartoon, 1900-2000* – the e-book reader in place. The chair unsat-on, the lamp flicking on and off on its timer. The eerie quiet, an extended version of the silent reproaches he'd been so good at.

So the trees it was.

I'd sent an email earlier to the project historian, Mo. He'd been forced upon us by our non-corporate masters, who felt that since we were working in a World Heritage Site, we should earmark part of the money for historical research. We'd chosen Mo because he hated all scientists. He stayed mercifully out of contact, occasionally firing through the odd paper along the lines of "Themes of Incest and Child Abuse in *Bert the Turtle Says Duck and Cover*: Nabokov and the Nuclear in Nineteen-Fifties Imaginary," just to prove he still deserved to be kept on expenses.

Now I was wishing we'd gone for somebody a little friendlier.

Nonetheless, I asked him for everything he had on which of the tests had involved structures: houses, boxcars, bridges and, by the way, trees.

I don't know why I felt I had to bury the lede. Mo wouldn't have cared, wouldn't have read anything into a more specific request. But something in me felt strange, embarrassed even, to be obsessing about the trees.

I got back an e-mail with no text but simply some attached files. With no guidance, I found myself wading through lists of nuclear explosions with increasingly ridiculous names – Operation Tumbler-Snapper, Operation Upshot-Knothole, Operation Teapot, Operations Doorstep and Cue. An upsetting diversion into an experiment involving farm animals near Ground Zero. Pictures of mannequins in mid-twentieth-century eveningwear, tied to poles like the mass execution of the cast of *Mad Men*. The aftermath: a sweet but cold woman's face, above bleached tatters. Pictures of buildings, intact and in ruins. A map. And links to the Footage, and then to more Footage. Lots and lots of Footage.

First, I looked through a few of the edited films, shot in either black and white or a lurid colour medium that was heavy on oranges and reds. A stern but somehow enthusiastic baritone informed me that this was "Survival Town," an entire village set up in the desert. And there were Tack's sadistically charming family groupings, mother mannequins with baby mannequins on their laps, beaming over child mannequins with skipping ropes and pigtails, while father mannequins sat or stood at a suitably patriarchal distance. Another stern voice informing us that the blast took place at 5:20 AM. "Mannequins, supplied by private industry, represent Mister and Missus America," intoned the authoritative baritone. So, this project had had corporate masters too.

And *there* were the trees. First a shot of men wandering around a plantation, lowering trunks into prepared holes. Mannequin trees, like the mannequin people. Then a pan from some instrumentation to the forest, all the trees in place: it looked pretty convincing. The film switched to show the buildings being prepared, and I fast-forwarded irritably.

Then, at fifteen and a quarter minutes in, they were back.

A shot of the fake forest as the workmen had left it, fluffy with needles. Cars and jeeps visible within the grove (strange that I had seen no vehicles). Shots from inside the grove, beautiful. Shots of burly men installing and testing the instruments in the trees (again, absent from the ghosts), longer this time and leading in to the dust explosion as the blast hits, the sand flying up in the atom-driven wind. The cameras always seem to go blind just at that critical moment, like they're blinking. The dust clearing away, showing the silhouettes of the trees standing impossibly upright for a split second. Then bending the other way like grass stems, almost double.

Then the aftermath: the stumps and splinters, one or two shocked survivors against the stark blue sky, the yellow desert. A tree fallen in on itself as if felled by a lumberjack, a dramatic stump poking up amid a tangle of pine branches.

I closed the video, looked around the room. I was sure I'd heard something – some*one* – as if *he* had come into the lab, looking for me, like he sometimes did if we were both working late. There would be a warm smart-car waiting out front to take us both home to dinner and movies. But he hadn't, and there wasn't.

My therapist had suggested some drugs that might help my insomnia, and I decided to try them.

I turned up next day to discover that the faction in favour of letting the palm splice take over had won, with the proviso that if it jumped its beds and started infecting other test sites, they would let Itch's pyromaniac doctoral student loose on it with a flamethrower.

Our non-corporate masters wanted to know when we'd be finished, please, so everything could get started. Their overcrowding problems weren't going to solve themselves just because we were dragging our feet. There was a fairly obvious subtext that Californian research institutions should be pretty damn grateful to get largesse of this kind from Asia, and that our only redeeming feature is our willingness to work cheap. I contacted Rocky, the (thin, pale and morose) head of the cryogenics and packing team, to tell him to start set-up. We could at least send them some pictures of the empty tanks, ready and waiting, if they got any angrier.

I spilled coffee over the proceedings of a conference on climate change, grabbed a dish-towel to clean up the mess: it was the one *he* had brought me back as a present, from Wisconsin, where he'd attended an American Society for Clinical Pathologists meeting. It was bordered with local birds, drawn fat and cute as cartoons, perched on pine branches. I realised it was the two-month anniversary of him leaving. Remembered how, at the start of the relationship we'd celebrated every milestone, one-week, one-month, two-month, six-month. Strange that you also mark anniversaries from the ending, as well as the beginning.

The tea-towel had been an apology for the argument we'd had before he left. Accusations of hypocrisy had featured prominently: on the one side, of putting a career in terraforming ahead of her own family, on the other, of expecting the woman in the relationship to put family ahead of her job. Both, arguably, about continuing the human race: one on the macro level, one on the micro. But neither of us were in a state to admit or even see that.

It might even have been the first of the arguments: another anniversary to celebrate.

To distract myself, I started writing the report we had to provide our corporate masters, calling up their original spec for the project, press releases and concept art. A red Martian landscape with green palm trees and blue sky (the public didn't have to know that, even at the increased rate of growth, we were looking at several decades, even a century, assuming the funding held up).

I flicked onward through the concept art. Images of farmers like cheerful workers in a Soviet poster, tending animals that looked a bit like cows and a bit like goats, and harvesting monstrous grain. A lush forest, like my pine trees, but with a couple standing in it: man, woman, holding hands. The imagery was pure Book of Genesis. I looked around for the snake.

And on the last page, a science-fictiony, white, two-storey building, a saccharine set of mannequins out front. Mother with baby, father at a benignly patriarchal distance, a couple children at play. A futuristic vehicle parked beside it. I wondered if the house had a bunker under the stairs like the houses in The Footage. I wondered what the science-fictiony building would look like, blowing apart, coming back together, blowing apart again.

Over the next couple weeks, I made forays around various environments between five and five-twenty AM, ostensibly preparing reports on which specimens should be included in the initial payload, but actually determining that there were no ghost houses, no ghost cars, no ghost mannequins, bridges or freight trains. And no more ghost trees. It seemed there had been just the one appearance.

I vaguely remembered themes from horror films and high-school English class: ghosts come back because they want something. What could a tree want?

Propped up on Environment Thirty-Nine, where the palm splice had now eaten everything and then died within a matter of hours – leading to a debate as to whether to destroy it or sell it to the military – I found a shrine of sorts. A desert-worn sheep skull, lashed to a fencepost. Below it, a collection of stones and flowers and little dolls. I started sweating inside my biohazard suit, seeing it. I wondered aloud to myself who had put it there: mainly to try and shake the rising conviction that it had been me.

Uneasy dreams of walking near Thirty-Nine. Sand blowing away to reveal the buried faces of mannequins. I pick one up – a woman, brown hair, expression sweet but cold – and it cracks in my hands, showing a blackened skull. No, not a skull, that's wrong: the blackened head of a crash test dummy. All around me the poisoned corpses of farm animals, goats and sheep and cows, hairless and bloated like manatees, stacked on racks like the inside of the payload modules.

Waking, something made me go and find the bookshelf in his office. I'd been in there a few times since he left, obviously, but there wasn't much need. The separation was, supposedly, temporary, so he'd left the books he didn't immediately need. I found the one I was looking for, an out-of-print history of some American magazine famous for its cartoons, and flipped to the right page. It showed a pair of aliens, antennaed Adam and Eve in a garden on a rocky, barren planet. A man in a spacesuit racing towards them from his rocket-ship, shouting at Eve (brown hair, face sweet but cold) as she reaches for the apple, "Miss! Oh, miss! For God's sake, stop!" Underneath it read, *Whitney Darrow Jr, 1957.*

I sat down, images parading through my head like footage. Or Footage.

I read the caption again. 1957. At the same time they were setting up trees in the desert and knocking them down with nuclear winds, this cartoon had been published.

Closing the book, I knew exactly what I had to do.

I went back to work the next day, sent out a message supporting the destroy-all-traces-faction on the palm splice, told them it was too dangerous to sell to the military directly. At least let's keep it under wraps till we can publish in a proper journal. Tracks covered.

As the weeks went by, I wrote a reference letter for Vera, who'd decided her reforestation ambitions could be better pursued at the University of Illinois at Chicago. I checked in regularly with our corporate and non-corporate masters. I visited Rocky's facility, at timed intervals. Itch's girlfriend had a false alarm, meaning another round of IVF would be in order. Someone was keeping the shrine by the now-empty Environment Thirty-Nine cleaned, and the flowers fresh. It might have been me.

Vera got the job and promised to stay in touch. She was probably lying, but I didn't mind.

I had a long, civil, conversation with *him*. At the end of it a decision was reached; maybe not a happy one, but one that made sense. I packed The American Cartoon, Martian Eve and her apple included, into one of many boxes of books, magazines and clothes. I watched the moving van drive away.

I congratulated Itch on yet another apparent pregnancy on Tina's part – and steeled myself for the inevitable bout of depression its failure would produce later.

I went to a party, to celebrate the launch of the first payload module to Mars. I smiled, joked, accepted a glass of something that claimed to be pinot grigio but tasted like it had been distilled from palm-splice pollen.

One night a couple of months later, after I was sure the payloads were all safely sent off and nothing could be done to stop them, I went out onto the balcony of my apartment, deopaqued its protective awning. Looking at the sky, I imagined I could tell which of the gently moving dots, tracking among the static points of stars and planets, were ours.

It'll be months before they figure out that anything is wrong, and it might be years before they figure out what. It'll be longer still before they figure out it was me who caused it.

Who, smiling and reasonable, doctored the payload.

The plants will sprout and grow green and fertile, successful, until the palm splice takes over, eats everything, and then dies, leaving the Martian surface, after Eve, once again barren and red, the way it wants to be. No families, no two-story houses, no farm animals. No mannequins, no bombs, no in-vitro fertilisation, no *Bert the Turtle Says Duck and Cover*, no Nabokov, no nuclear.

That's what the trees want; why they want to be remembered. From the 1950s, a lingering cry of *don't do it again*.

There *must* have been people who believed in the project. I don't mean the general public, who'd been sold the feel-good story about Adam and Eve in a lush alien garden, or our corporate and non-corporate masters, who support everything profitable and/or sustainable but actually believe in nothing. I mean, there must have been people who knew, who understood, what we were planning on doing to Mars, with all it entailed, and thought we should do it anyway. Itch, maybe the anti-palm-splice faction, probably Vera, at least at first. A solution to climate change, to resource poverty, to wealth inequality, to an aging population, a dying world.

A nuclear solution.

And to them, and to *him*: I'm sorry.

But if we can't fix our own problems, the least we can do is make sure they don't spread.

The Opaque Mirror of Your Face

Russell Hemmell

The reflection of the red, oblong moonlet on the buildings' titanium shield has the look and allure of blood flowers. The smell will follow shortly.

"Ready to rock, Anne?"

The Queen's in good mood tonight. She even cracks jokes. I decide to humour her. "I was created ready. Let's go and get the others."

Kristel hands me a night 3D plasma visor – a sparkling top-end model – while we head toward the meeting point, kicking aside a fancy-looking garbage bin that rolls over the terrain with a tingling noise, without spilling anything off. All the garbage it contained has long being shredded and recycled. And yet, WestWing's apparent sophistication is just that: apparent.

"DNA scan, loaded and ready."

Apparent, and dangerous, too. The only sophisticated thing the suburb of WestWing – aka Cyborg City – shares with the sprawling megalopolis called Sogcho is an atypical, futuristic architecture of tubular structures coiling up to high-sky domes in an intricate maze and a gamedrome the rest of the hemisphere envies with an attitude. You'd better not look at what lies beneath.

"What about them?" She points to a couple of tourists, who stumble in a drunken haze through the next bar's doorstep.

I give the zombie-like duo a prolonged, appraisal look before dismissing the suggestion. Goners before dawn breaks, these spring chickens, but not by our doing. "Nah."

"They're young and well fleshed out, though."

Young, fleshed out, and devoid of grey matter (not that I have any use for it at the moment). Don't they know sourcing human organs and chunks of naturally grown tendons is the second most common activity contractors ask us to carry out, mercenary squad work being the first and most obvious one? Idiots.

"For today's list of items, we don't need two suppliers, we need twelve at the very least. Best practice strongly suggests we keep the supply chain as lean as possible." Otherwise said, snatch them all in one single raid, lock them down, and get it over with.

She reluctantly turns her head away from them and stares at the bag on my shoulders. "Where's the equipment?"

"Where it should be – on the cutting slates already. Hangar is just passed the checkpoint, to keep the police happy. I've carried with me only what we need to sedate them."

We continue our prowling stroll across the alleys behind the gamedrome, checking out people who have ventured tonight for a dip into Cyborg City.

I've never been able to understand the interlopers' arcane motives to trespass and visit our world, apart from lewd curiosity or morbid attraction for whatever they think it contains. It's a place anybody in their sane mind should avoid like a plague-ridden town, even in the periods we're not around on a chopping spree. And no, I'm not making ill-conceived jokes here. I said *chopping* and I mean it. Whatever ripe human muscles a body owns is at risk of being stolen and put at a better use in an *Augenblick*. I think if any cyberpunk version of Hell existed, WestWing would definitely be the one. But it doesn't, of course: reality is worse.

Kristel extracts her electric whip-rod. She's getting impatient.

"You'll get your whisky fix in just a few hours, My Queen. Trust your Anne boy when he gives you a time estimate."

"How in fucktopia have they given a woman's name to a nasty, ugly bloke like you?" she sneers, before kicking my butt in what wants to be an affectionate gesture.

I could observe she's not that plain vanilla either. Queen Kristel – that's the way we call her – sports a set of blades where her left arm should have been, and her teenage doll face is a (perfectly manufactured) mask of porcelain with a permanent, immobile smile. Impossible to tell what she looks like behind it, if anything at all.

"It's not English, it's an old French name for males, Sugarpuss." Any other (man or woman or talking cat) addressing her in this way would lose his tongue, and probably a limb too. But we've been partners in crime for as long as I can remember, and this allows me a few bonuses. Calling my squad leader names is one.

Tonight, we're going out for a hush-hush contract that comes directly from Sogcho's Science Complex, where the majority of the cyborgs like us come from: a large-scale operation of bio-component sourcing. Destination's classified, so it must be to manufacture high-tier kinds of artificial soldiers. We have a natural target in this kind of assignments: people coming out from nightclubs and whorehouses. They're often so drunk they can barely walk, and they fight even less.

"On your left – y'see them?" Kristel adjusts her X-ray visor.

I click my tongue in appreciation: foreign visitors are always the best. They're not protected by any internal regulations, and therefore free for all to grab. What's more, they're generally mixed enough to provide all variety of biosamples and genetic characteristics. It's like going to a fucking supermarket with a diamond-powered buying chip at your wrist. Hey!

"Affirmative. Twelve of them, all males between 20 and 40, half of them Asian, two genetically enhanced. Healthy, for what I can see from a superficial reading." I quickly scan the tester's results on my visor while my good mood exponentially improves. "And already stoned to death. The Virgin Mary is with us tonight."

"Not sure about that, but we can do without. Alert the others."

We round the tourists down and put them to sleep with sedation darts. As rest of the squad joins the pack, we drag the bodies to the nearby hangar.

Reaping time.

Kristel sets up the room, while Jarmin and his mates extract their blades. I observe Jarmin inserting his instrument into the back of the nearest one with a quick motion. Then, effortlessly, he began drilling. Two seconds after, the electronic sensor of the blade shows that the retrieval of the victim's spinal liquid is well under way.

Jarmin is especially good at sourcing – that I already knew. This is why I have asked him to join the operation. Half of his face is covered by a metallic structure that leaves only his eye and mouth in the open. Where a pupil should have been, however, there was a sort of silver-like globe that reflects glints of the bunker's dim green light. He's not as ugly as I am, but still ugly enough.

"Do we have enough processed helium to keep them warm and cosy until we reach the Science Complex?" Kristel asks, opening the storage jar and lifting up the canisters.

"You mean cold."

"I mean alive. If there's necrosis in the tissues they'll pay less."

"Fear not, Kristel." I offer her a suave smile. "I've got enough helium to freeze the entire Sogcho."

I've not overstated the supply. I'm going to need it, because hours later when the ripping party is completed, the goods delivered, and the half-empty tourists returned to the street where we've found them, I get back to the hangar.

I have a last item to check out of my list.

My previous mission for the Sogcho's City Overlords has left me disfigured, and it's not a misnomer: my face is gone. What remains, it's nothing nice to look at: a hole instead of a nose, missing cartilages here and there, and obviously not a shred of skin has survived. Burnt down to the seventh layer of derma. I have to wear a full-face mask to avoid people fainting around me – which I can't care less about–including the girls I bone at night, which I do care instead (unresponsive people don't blow you).

Since that sad day, I've been on the hunt for a face.

I've earned enough diamond points for the machinery that will make implantation possible –more expensive than doctors, but less ethically concerned. Not that I plan to kill the poor bastard. To be fair, I'd only remove what lies on his skull and nicely implant it on mine. Still, I may well guess people wouldn't find it palatable.

But I need to find the right one, one that fits my specs. Genetic matching is a bitch, and shopping around for the right muzzle ain't easy since you have more constraints than with other body parts.

Back to WestWing's sordid bars, stealthy and famished like a wolf.

At this early morning hour, I don't even need to inject targets to examine them. The streets are littered with drunken people, and I have only to stick a cellular scan into their palms to get a reading. One, two, three, five times. None suits, may the world be damned.

For how long will I have to stand a reflection I can't look at?

There's a noise coming from behind a litter box, and I approach to have a look.

Somebody is lying face down. A young boy, shabby clothes, and small, delicate hands. I hesitate for just a moment; I generally leave young people alone. But tonight, I can't afford this luxury. I insert the needle on his neck and scan him for compatibility. Fireworks and cake: 95%. That's just bloody perfect.

I turn his limp body over, and blink. And blink again. It's not a boy, it's a girl, one that must have taken industrial quantities of dope and lies like a broken doll with a dress in tatters.

A few more moments of hesitation are all it takes. Then I lift her up and haul her on my shoulders like a stack of meat. What the fuck, a face is a face is a face. I take her to the storage and stick the blade into her jaw without thinking twice.

I'm not as skilled as Jarmin, but I manage to remove her features with sufficient care and put them on helium, which will preserve them until I reach home and begin the transplant. Caressing the gleaming metal of my cheek, I exhale.

Finally.

I've become a small celebrity in the cyborg world. They call me Lady Anne now, a man with the pure face of a girl who kills with a ferocity his features can't convey. I'm more careful now with the risks I take, protecting that precious possession as if it were my life itself. I wear a full-face mask when I work and have even stopped assignments that entail more than a quick sting. I especially avoid sourcing missions, from which I've kept away ever since.

And yet, I'm troubled.

The memory of the girl I've robbed keeps haunting me, especially when I look at myself in the mirror, observing her pretty face smiling at me with grace. And there's something else, too. At times, when I'm between sleep and wakefulness, weird sensations creep in, like butterfly wings touching my body, and in that moment the skin of my cheeks doesn't belong to me any longer. I feel it strangely extraneous, as if tissues had memories of their own.

I would be scared if it weren't so fascinating. I lie down on the metallic ground of my unit, naked, breathing, concentrated in listening to the whispering of my face. I'm seduced by my own otherness.

I'm amazed.

Somehow, I'm contented, too.

Nothing lasts forever, especially inertia, and for a cyborg with high-energy consumption patterns like me, even less. Two months later, Lady Anne is back in the field, this time smuggling drugs in and out Sogcho's nightlife district under Jarmin's lead. It doesn't pay as well as other missions, but it's a good trade-off.

That's how I meet the girl again, whoring in one of the brothels and accepting even cyborgs as customers. A glittering metal covers her face, where only cold blue eyes have survived of the original features that now shine on my cheekbones. Hidden behind my mask, one evening I go searching for her.

"Thirty diamond points, and I'll entertain you for the whole night," she says, opening up her shirt and showing me a pale breast. "This is prime human flesh, no fake lab-grown tits. Have a feel, C-boy."

I touch her nipples before I can stop myself, and it's like an electric current in my veins. Has the skin on my face somehow… recognised it? I force a smile to fight the creepiness of that thought and concentrate on the erotic side of the bargain. "It's dangerous flashing these pretty boobs. I could gobble them up instead of just using them for sexual release."

"Of course," she replies without a hint of fear. "I had already a taste of it. My goddamn face has been torn off down to the seventh layer of derma. It's a risk I have to take if I want to afford one again one day. You pay much better than humans, you know?"

Hell if I don't. I put a card-size transparent plastic on the desk, and she quickly checks the amount. Her fingers go for my face, to take the mask away, but I stop her.

"Why not?"

"Just no."

"Doesn't matter." She shrugs and takes my hand. "You won't regret it."

I follow her to her dormitory, my lips twitching in the anticipation of pleasure and slithering anxiety like a slowly rising tide.

She was right. I didn't regret it. More, I had a pure sip of heaven with her on that night, and I have kept coming back.

The initial sensations her face transmitted to my brain have not faded away in time – they have only changed typology. They've become images, more precise every day. I could call them memories if there were history attached to them. But this only happened haphazardly, once in a while. Each time, however, there was a man in them, probably her former lover. I saw him in my visions – visions that were more persistent than dreams but devoid of the bleak solidity of real stuff. I saw his face – somebody who hurt the girl so much to force her to a life of drugs and danger and that has eventually led her under my blade.

I should be grateful to him, otherwise I wouldn't have this face. These exquisite features I now love to the point of believing I've always worn them on my bones, like a pretty dress kids are fond of. But I don't.

Over the weeks I've grown progressively angrier with him, the more since these memory bits have become more vivid in their details. And one day, I decided to act. Lady Anne is not famous for his conscience or for having done anything moral in his life, so I think this might well represent the exception. At least, it has the excitement of the novelty.

I tracked her former lover down. It didn't take me long – the man worked in the same underworld I spend my days and night, but he was a prey, with no defence when the predators are around. Nobody would regret seeing him gone. I observed him, selling drugs to teens, as he has done with the girl a while ago. I waited for him to be alone. I swooped over like a vulture, and I cut his head. I played for a moment with the idea of giving her that face – better with the one she (doesn't) have, anyway – but I discarded the idea: she'd find it distasteful. I harvested everything worth keeping and bagged it up.

I'm going to sell it in the Science Complex and buy something nice for her. Like a derma layer, maybe, for the moment she'll have a face to put on. The seventh one, for a start, the most expensive. And the others. In time.

Am I perhaps feeling guilty for what I've done to her?

This thought crosses my mind for a moment, to be quickly rebuffed. Fuck no. I do what I'm supposed to do, which is stealing, killing, and follow my programming. We cyborg don't have a soul, or we careful avoid developing one: it can be hard on the business. Don't they hammer it on us since day one? Under all your graphene and steel alloys, C-boys, you've still been grown out of human cells, and your natural instincts remain the same. Beware your first, emotional response: more than often, it's a decent one.

I've always obeyed.

Months have passed by, and Helen – that's the girl's name – is now my companion. She's still a working girl, but she has less time to spend with other customers. I make sure of that. There's also a specific clause in our agreements, which lets her only entertain humans, not the other cyborgs. I don't want her to take any risk with that slender body.

Not now that I have her memories filling my vision cones and running deep inside my flesh. I know the name of her first pet, and once I've even visited the dilapidated area where she grew up. It's strange and together unsettling, this pervasive feeling for her to which I can't give a name, more persistent than lust, tenderer than hunger, and always lingering, even in my sleep.

The sad truth is that I can't live without Helen in my bed—which means in my life, considering I'm so tired that I sleep the moment I hit the mattress. Yes, because I've started taking up difficult missions, extreme-risk, high-reward. Aerial targets, undercover ops outside Sogcho, and a few warzone hits. Even Queen Kristel disapproves, and I'm not sure why I do it.

We aren't programmed for guilt any more than we are for love, but I'm incapable to get rid of both. I don't even bother any longer. One day I'll have the courage to tell her how things stand between us—maybe. Or maybe not. But a face, she'll eventually get one, because she'll inherit all the diamond points I've managed to put together so far.

She moves in her sleep, her hand caressing a face she can only feel through the gelid surface of a mask. Her fingers slip behind the locking device.

"Helen, no."

I stop her from removing my mask. This is the reason we've never kissed, a detail that in time has started annoying me with the resignation things can't be different. I have to be contented in touching her lips on my face when I look at myself the mirror. What she has now for a mouth is only an ugly thin pale line that surfaces from the layers of metal.

She laughs, and, with a movement faster than a flash in the dark, she activates electronic-powered glowing ropes that block my limbs and trap my chest. A low-energy laser cage grabs my face, freezing it like a statue of flesh. Looking up at the ceiling, I spot sophisticated machinery already in place. Oh well.

"Did you really believe I didn't know, Lady Anne?" she says, grinning. "You must think I'm diabolically stupid."

Her blue eyes have a shining quality now, with a glimpse I've never seen in her. I should be angry she has played me all along, upset for having been such an idiot, and, more than anything, worried for what it's going to happen to me. Strangely, I can't force myself to be any of that.

"Since when?"

"Since the beginning. Since the first time you've screwed me in that WestWing bar." She removes my mask, caressing my–her–face with loving fingers, slowly, respectfully. Awed, I'd say. "You've kept it in a good shape, dear. I'm grateful."

I can't but smile at that.

"You were way too emotional for a human, let alone for a cyborg. So gentle to me. So attentive," she continues, inserting a code on the bedside table's panel control. The surface slides away, showing a set of gleaming, nasty looking tools. "Good feelings damn people, don't you know that?"

I do, and it's going to hurt. I could ask for being drugged before the procedure. Helen didn't feel a thing, after all, not *during* at least; but I guess I'm not entitled to any comfort. The more agonisingly, searingly painful, the better, and I'm in no position to complain.

Her hands move fast on the holographic keyboard that has just materialised in front of us. I hear the sibilant sound of a laser and the lights in the room shift to a dark hue of blue – as if I were in the middle of a Martian sunset.

I close my eyes, breathing and waiting for the ordeal to begin.

"This place is magnificent," Helen says. We walk barefoot on the wet sand of Dawn Beach, the most coveted holiday spots Sogcho people can fancy. We've been here a week now, but we keep marvelling at the pristine beauty of this place. I think it must stir ancestral memories of Old Earth in us.

I nod and bend to kiss her lips. Made of a bioactive white shell-like compound, which give them a warm, tender texture and perfect sensitivity. If you close your eyes, you can mistake them for natural.

Anne and Helen Kirin are a strange married couple. So odd that when they're in public they have to wear masks to avoid people staring. You can't blame the beholders: a big scary man and a young woman sharing the same, delicate features are not an everyday view.

Especially when one set is made by the most sophisticated creation plastic surgery has invented so far, a bionic material capable of reproducing any face, since it is grown directly in contact with its original model. It has taken a couple of weeks to make it happen, but the process hasn't been painful for me, only tiring. More for the forced immobility than for anything else.

And the output has been astonishing.

Like a self-evolving, intelligent cast, the shell-like substance grew and adapted to perfectly replicate the original in its feature, its texture, its neural extensions. The only thing is that it remains shining white instead of developing the human skin appearance. Probably the technology is still too new for that.

"One day we will make it perfect, my love," I say, kissing her pearl-like cheek.

"No. I prefer the magic of a looking-glass."

I wonder at times whether this artificial face has also done to her what the original has caused to me – bringing over physical memories and piercing sensations that have upset me so deep inside and for so long. If the biocells have managed to transfer to her some of the sensorial experience and shreds of life I lived since I've been wearing those layers of derma… The only time I dared to ask, she shrugged, as if the whole thing had no importance to her. I'll never know, and it's better this way.

Helen tilts her head, looking at me with a serene smile. "When I want to see the original, I look at you." Her hand takes mine, squeezing it with surprising strength. She pulls me toward the shore. The water is like a lake tonight, another magic mirror for celestial objects, sprites, and lovers. "Come, Anne. I want to swim with the stars."

I follow her into the warm embrace of the waves, turquoise Pleiades and white-hot Aldebaran twinkling in the distance, their twin reflections dancing with ours in the gleaming mirror of Sogcho Sea.

More Sea Creatures to See
Aliya Whiteley

They are the only humans, two in a line of hundreds, and they are arguing:

– *down my neck, it won't make the queue go any faster.*

Move up then, look, look at the gap–

They can't possibly know that they are surrounded by us. Our disguises are excellent; it is a point of pride. One of the reasons we are always in employment.

It won't make any difference, calm down–

Don't tell me to calm down!

We have been trying not to stare but the argument gives us the excuse we need.

One human pulls out a phone and starts filming the other, and there's a moment where the air changes, thickens, as if all might turn to violence. We draw back as one, breath held. But the gap in the queue has become too large for either of them to ignore, so they turn, and move forward, and each pretends the other doesn't exist for the next fifteen minutes until they reach the front.

Then they are seated together, side by side, to ride the ghost train, and I climb aboard a few cars behind them. Their body language is wonderful to watch: the spikey vulnerability of them, stretching away from each other, willing their thighs not to touch as the bar pins their laps and we all head into the dark tunnel, together.

Creaks and squeaks, cobwebs and gravestones, but I have no time for the thrills of the ride, even though I'm fascinated by the old horror stories humanity used to tell. I strain against the blackness to see them: the backs of their heads, the rigidity of their shoulders. A skeleton falls from a hole above their heads and they scream, and duck, and move together for a moment. Then we emerge into the light, and the ride ends. The bar lifts, and they go their own ways in the summer sunshine. I must make a decision. I choose to follow the one with the phone. I like the way she brandished it as a weapon, as if recording an event was the same thing as controlling it.

I keep my distance from her, trying to look casual. It's against the rules to follow a human, but I suspect all of us have done it at some point, as they become more and more of a rarity. And there is no reason why I shouldn't walk in the same direction – past the rollercoaster shaped like a dragon, past the swingboats, past the pizza place and the log flume and the gift shop. She joins the queue for fresh roasted ground coffee and I stand behind her, keeping my lowered eyes on her backpack. It is decorated with badges, mementoes from other theme parks up and down this country. She is, apparently, an avid thrill-seeker, young and wiry and keen to ride. Maybe that's why she still smells healthy, and has lasted this long.

I've been to many of the parks myself. They've become one of the best places to see her kind out in the wild.

As we wait our turn, I find myself thinking of Tom.

He was a terrible salesman, he knew it, and I should have fired him so that his reality, his expectations of the situation, were met. But how could I bring myself to do that? He was the only human left in the office. My boss understood; we discussed it, and they agreed we could continue as we were, there being very little time left for him anyway. We could all smell the end upon him.

Tom preferred talking to working. He liked to chat about what had been showing on television the night before, or about the other employees.

Is it me or is Val really up herself?

I told him: *She's a bit wary of you.*

Me? Why?

I did not say: *because you are uncontrollable. You lack the cohesion of mind that characterises the acceptable in this universe, so there is going to be relief when you are gone. Painlessly, easily gone from a random disease we've introduced here and that you don't even know you have.*

I said: *She thinks you're cute.*

God no, don't say that. She's really not my– he made a face, but there was an air of opportunity in his too-quick rejection, and I wondered if he would approach her later, some time when nobody else was around. I envied Val then, and I wondered how often he had been intimate with one of us, and when he had last even talked to a real human. To someone without a disguise in place.

I expressed this to my boss, and they reminded me that we are not the sole adopters of disguise. It's a job to our kind but humanity has a long and varied history of such behaviour, for profit and for pleasure.

Tom died in his sleep twenty-six days later: that, at least, was an honest act. One of us took his place, and I see them, now, in the office. I did a performance review on them last week. Our disguises will be maintained everywhere, faultlessly, until the very last one has succumbed. Then the planet will be declared a nature reserve and holiday zone for those planets lucky enough to have travel permissions. It will be a wild haven worth visiting.

Every morning I feel something, an emotion, for Tom, old Tom, who was alive in a way I am not. I do as I am told. I am good at my job. We all are.

She gets her coffee and looks for a seat. I keep my eyes on the barista as I request an espresso. I like the word, not the taste. It's presented to me in a disposable cup, and I turn, and see her sitting on the end of a long, empty bench. She has her phone out again. She's focusing on the screen.

I move to the other end of the bench. She glances up as I sit, and I see a moment of recognition. She smiles. I'm flattered she has remembered me, picked me out of the crowd.

Could you believe that? she says. *At the ghost train. Some people are so rude. Look at this.* She leans over the table and shows me her phone. The other human is in action, her face wide open, flowing through the act of shouting. The sound is off. Everything is fluid: her eyes, her mouth.

She looks like a sea creature, I say.

Yeah, you're right. She laughs, but she looks sideways at me. An odd thing to say, maybe. Could I be slipping? No, I never slip.

Ah, that's why she smiled at me – I see myself in the footage, in the corner of the screen. I'm caught as one of the crowd. We all wear the same expression; doesn't that give us away? I could swear there's nothing human about us. These disguises come at a cost, and many of us are very tired. I see it in every face, frozen in video. Or perhaps tiredness is a universal experience, recognisable in every place, every face. We are all surrounded by its victims.

It won't be for much longer, now. I'll travel home before the next planet. And I'm due a holiday. There are so many destinations I could pick from, all of them carefully curated.

I have dreamt of a decision in a new direction. In the long hall, back home, where we gather to decide what offer of employment to accept next.

The leader supreme might say: **We think this time we'll try to save them. We think we will go to them and tell them of the plans to phase them out. Surely nobody in this universe really needs another emptied, controlled holiday destination. We'll offer to fight by their side instead. We will save them, even though they scare us.**

Because they scare us.

Then we could make our own horror stories, for a change.

They've not had anything new for ages, she says.

Sorry?

They need a new ride here. Loads of places aren't building anything new anymore. It's like everyone's given up a bit. I've been making the most of my annual pass but it runs out soon.

I say*: Won't you be renewing it?*

Can't afford to. Got laid off.

Seriously? I can't believe it. Somebody did what I could not. They made her jobless in the final days.

She shrugs. *I was taking the piss a bit, and they said they didn't have a choice. Can't blame them, really. It was only delivering stuff, and I liked going the long way round. Windows down, music loud. Wind in my hair.*

Like the rollercoasters, I say.

I picture her at the top of the long climb, and then the cart plunging downwards, her hair flying out behind her, twisting in thick strands. It would look beautiful in the ocean, undulating like tentacles. What a wonderful sight that would be.

How about you? You got the day off?

Not exactly, I tell her. We share of moment of manufactured understanding. She thinks that I'm running away for the day, failing to do my duties. She likes me better for it.

My boss reminded me, as I walked out of the door last night, that I should spend less time at theme parks in order not to arouse suspicion. I wanted to point out there are barely any humans left to feel suspicion. I wonder how many there are.

I hate this planet. I hate it and love it.

I say to the human – out of nowhere, not really believing my own voice – *We could go for a trip.*
What?
I can get access to a… vehicle. We could go someplace far away. The seaside. There's nothing here worth seeing, right? Nothing new. It's just–
Waiting to die.
Her smile falls away, and she says – *Have you ever been scuba diving?*
Scuba diving?
Yeah. Some place like the Great Barrier Reef. Be great to see it before it's all gone. I reckon it must be a bit like being on a rollercoaster, just – freedom. Except you're not on rails, so you can go anywhere, and see the stuff happening beneath you, all laid out and moving. Swimming around in its own world. You ever done it?
Yes. Yes, I have been part of another world, and moved within it, almost as part of it. Almost, but not quite.
I've not scuba dived, I say.
Me neither.
So let's go.
To – the Great Barrier Reef?
Why not?
She puts her phone away. She won't look at me directly. *My mum would love that. I'll just phone her up now, shall I, and tell her I'm off for two weeks of pissing money up the wall because I got asked by someone I just met over coffee?* She laughs to herself. *Actually, she wouldn't be surprised.*
Would that be in character for you? I ask. I could tell her that her mother is very probably already dead. Almost certainly.
Anyway, have a good day, she says.
The conversation is over, so quickly. For a moment -
But no. No, she makes no fuss as she weaves through the tables and out of the coffee shop. She thinks me strange, but she still thinks me human. No story to tell.
I feel everyone looking at me. I keep my eyes down, and I stay seated, for a little while. Then I order another espresso, just for the sake of the action and the word, and sip it. The barista and the others around me say nothing.
I made the offer, gave her an option. I pushed myself far out of my comfort zone, I felt something genuine. She reached the decision, all on her own, not to take me seriously.

So I have done all I could do. That's enough, isn't it? Surely that's enough.

I am treading water. I am in my suit, a mask over my face, looking down on all that is about to end.

She will last for a while; I could tell that much from her clean smell. But she will not last forever, and in the meantime, at least for today, there are still humans to see and this role to play.

And then I'll get to take a holiday to some place free of all these obligations and feelings. Some place already emptied. Or maybe I'll just stay home, deep in liquid, and let this dryness leave me. I'll forget how to care, for a while, in the cold waters of my home, until it's time to meet in the long hall again, and choose another job.

Time to head for the next ride.

THE END OF ALL OUR EXPLORING

Gary Couzens

for Laura Mauro

I was very young when we moved into the house. The back had been hit by a bomb during the Blitz and had been hastily and cheaply rebuilt, so it looked different to all the others in the street. I don't know if Adam was nearby then. Maybe he was, or someone like him. I wasn't thinking of the future then.

My father remembered seeing a television before the War. He must have been about twelve, staying away from home with his parents in a hotel. In the corner of a large room there was a strange boxlike object on a stand, with its screen – a mirror, reflecting a picture sent upwards from inside – far smaller than those we have today. Moving across that screen were a pair of ballroom dancers, the man in a black dinner jacket leading and the woman in a white gown following. Of course nothing was recorded then, and those dancers have long since vanished into the ether, their elegant turning and returning across the dancefloor existing only in the memory of those who saw it, the signal vanishing into space and now nearly seventy light years away. I have always wondered if, one day, if we could ever travel faster than light, we might be there to receive that signal when it arrived from Earth, and those dancers, many years if not centuries in their graves, would live again.

Dad was twenty when peace was declared and he came home and married my mother. Derek arrived and a year and a half later I was born, into a country still in the grip of rationing and austerity, its people wondering if they really had won the War.

"Look, Eileen! This is the future!" I see him now, proudly showing Mum his new acquisition. We were the first family on our street to have a television set. Mum wasn't convinced. It was ugly, it took up too much space, how could we afford such a thing and why did we need it when no one else we knew had one? But Dad wouldn't be swayed. He picked me up, his hands about my waist, my slippered feet dangling in the air. "Look, Barbara – the future!"

I was one and a half then, no doubt crawling into places I shouldn't. I don't remember that scene, but from being told about it several times, I now see it: Dad, still in the suit and tie he wore to work, his hair slicked back, his mouth split into a grin under the moustache he wore at the time. Mum, in a white summer dress, her lips pursed in exasperation, knowing that she wouldn't have her way this time. I was in a checked knee-length dress, my hair, much longer then, spilling loose over my face and shoulders. Dad lifted me up to gaze at this wonderful new device. I don't see Derek, but he's no doubt somewhere nearby, three years old, playing with his toys, put out by the arrival of an annoying younger sister and trying his utmost to keep me away from *his things*. I *see* this. And of course, though the world is in colour, this scene is in black and white.

The rest of the street caught up with us a couple of years later. The country was more confident after the Festival of Britain and a new Queen was on the throne. Many people acquired television sets in time for her coronation. Dad had always read science fiction, from Verne and Wells to the American pulp magazines he'd bought in Woolworth's, so a month later he and Mum sat down to watch the first episode of a new serial called *The Quatermass Experiment*. Derek and I had gone to bed but somehow I couldn't sleep. I tiptoed out on to the landing. The crashing opening chords of Holst's *Mars, The Bringer of War* came around the door of the front room.

I must have sat there for a full half hour, because Dad came out into the hallway and looked up. He saw me in my nightie, halfway up the stairs with my arms looped around my calves. "What are you doing there, Barbara?"

"I can't sleep, Daddy."

He sat next to me, chucking me under the chin with the side of his hand. "You must, you know. You'll be all tired tomorrow. Look." He stood up again, taking my tiny hand in his larger one, leading me up to the landing window at the top of the stairs.

I wasn't tall enough to see out, so he lifted me up. Our house was on a hillside and I could see rows and rows of houses in the darkness, their lights twinkling into the distance like a scattering of diamonds on black velvet.

"All those people were watching the programme," he said. "The actors are in Alexandra Palace. That's over there. All those people were watching them. Think about that, Barbara. What amazing times we live in."

Was Adam one of those many people out there?

I don't feel old, though my body tells me I am more often than my mind does, but unless I live into my twelfth decade I have more of my life behind me than ahead. Who knew what medical science might be able to do? Maybe they'll freeze me and wake me sometime in the next century or beyond, just as they did in the magazines Dad used to read.

I wonder where Adam is now.

This was how I met him.

The day the planes crashed into the World Trade Center, my older daughter Lucy, seven months pregnant with my granddaughter, was on the phone to me in tears, terrified beyond belief by what was happening. Was World War III upon us, and what future was she about to bring a child into? We spoke for two hours, as the events unfolded on our televisions in front of us. I was old enough to remember an earlier time when the world changed, and television schedules were altered by the breaking news. I was a week and a half away from my fifteenth birthday when Dad called me downstairs. President Kennedy had been assassinated in Dallas. Mum was crying, a handkerchief pressed to her face. Dad put his arms around both of us as we watched the news come in all that evening.

The following morning I took Freddie, our black Labrador, for his walk on Acton Green Common. It was a cold November day. Freddie bounded across the grass. A tall man in a coat started as Freddie hurried up to him, sniffing at his trousers.

"Oh, I'm so sorry!" I said, rushing up and reattaching Freddie's lead.

"That's okay. I was just taken by surprise, that's all." I couldn't quite place his accent.

He straightened. He was more than six feet tall, towering over my five feet five. His hair, fair verging on mid-brown, was cut short-back-and-sides and he wore glasses. He was somewhere in his twenties, I guessed. I knew I shouldn't speak to strangers, but something told me he had no bad intentions. Besides, I was in public and had a dog with me, though Freddie was far from the fiercest protector I could have had.

"Could you tell me the way to the library, please?" he said. "I'm... new here."

"Certainly. It's this way." It was in the direction I was walking, so with Freddie on his lead I walked with the man to the edge of the Common. "Isn't it terrible news from America?" I said, in an effort to make conversation.

"Oh, of course. Absolutely devastating for many people. Trust me, you'll remember this day for the rest of your life. You'll remember where you were when you heard the news. They'll make films and write books about the events of yesterday."

I said nothing to that. All I knew was that someone had been assassinated who had been an emblem of hope to much of the western world, and that hope had now been brutally dashed to pieces.

We continued to the High Street and I pointed him in the direction of the library.

"Well, thank you for your assistance," the man said. He had a rolled-up copy of *Radio Times* in his pocket. It was open to today's date. I noticed, in that brief glimpse, that there were pencilled Xs against several programme titles.

That evening, Dad, Mum, Derek and I watched the first episode of a new television series called *Doctor Who*. I was very impressed that one of the Doctor's companions had the same name as me.

A few months later I went to the library. After I'd returned all my books and picked out a batch of novels to read in the next month – all historicals, including a Jean Plaidy, a Mary Renault and a Daphne du Maurier – I wandered upstairs into the non-fiction section, which was next to the reference library. And there he was.

With my family around, a strange embarrassment overtook me, and I hoped he hadn't seen me. But he had. "Hello again."

He was dressed in a jacket and tie, his hair slicked back. He was more handsome than I'd thought at first. But there was still something about him that didn't seem quite right, and I couldn't put my finger on what it was.

"Do you spend a lot of time here?" I asked.

"Quite a lot, yes," he said. "It's my research, you see."

"What are you researching?"

He pushed a magazine across the table to me. It was a copy of the latest *Radio Times*, open at today's page, Saturday. Also on the desk were copies of *TV Time*, *The Guardian* and *The Daily Telegraph*, open at the television listings.

"You're researching what's on television?"

"In a sense, yes."

"Why would you want to do that?"

"Tell me – do you watch any of these programmes?"

I glanced down the page. "*Doctor Who*. We watch that."

"So do I. It's good, isn't it?"

"I suppose so. It's really a children's programme, though we all watch it."

"Children's programme? Why, how old are you?"

"I'm fifteen."

"Look, they're starting a new story today." He pointed to the listing.

"Yes, they go back to meet Marco Polo."

"I'm particularly interested in that one."

"Why? Do you like history?"

He smiled. "I am a historian, yes."

"Barbara!" Derek called behind me. "Hurry up – we're going!"

I glanced behind me. "I – I'm sorry. I've got to go."

"Well, once again it's nice talking to you, Barbara. I may call you Barbara?"

I almost said, *No – call me Miss Ashton*. I actually said nothing.

"You can call me Adam."

I turned away, each stride longer than the rest.

"Who's that you were talking to?" said Derek, as I met him at the head of the stairs.

"Oh, no one," I muttered. "Someone I met before. When I was taking Freddie for a walk."

Every month. I saw Adam in the library, always in the reference section, more often than not reading that week's copies of *Radio Times*, *TV Times* and two or three of that day's newspapers, a large hardbacked notebook on the desk beside him.

I mentioned this to my best friend Yvonne. We had been to the same infant and junior schools, but I'd passed my Eleven Plus and she hadn't, so I went to the local girls' grammar school and she didn't. We still kept up with each other outside school. On this day, we were alone in the house one day during the Easter holidays, facing each other in the bathtub, sitting in rapidly cooling water in an effort to shrink our jeans. She was reading a fashion magazine while smoking and I had a novel from the library, Rosemary Sutcliff's *The Eagle of the Ninth*, careful not to drop it.

"Why didn't you tell me about him earlier, you dark horse you?" she said. "You don't know who he is?"

"He said he's a historian," I replied. "Maybe he's from one of the Universities round here?"

"Makes me wish I could do better at history… if I had teachers like that… We've got Miss Parfitt, dried-up old spinster she is." Yvonne reached up above her head and tapped out her cigarette ash through the partly opened window. I'd tried smoking once but never again: it had made me feel sick.

"He's a bit old – he must be in his twenties, I think. Actually I'm not sure how old he is."

"Shame. Twenties isn't too old though." She took a drag on her cigarette.

A month later, I took some books out of the history section. There was a gap in the books on the shelf and I could see Adam at his desk through it.

Derek spotted me watching him. "Who is that man?" he said, from behind me.

I started. "No one."

"He's here every time we come here." A whole head taller than me by then, he bent down and whispered, "Do you *fancy* him, Barbara?"

"No I don't!" I felt myself blush.

"I don't want you talking to him," he said. "He could be a spy for all we know."

"Don't be ridiculous, Derek."

"You could say all sorts of silly things to him. I know you. You're a girl."

"He's not a spy."

"How do you know? Where does he live? Where does he work? He just seems to sit here all day."

"Why don't you ask him, then? I'm sure he'll tell you. I'll ask him if you won't."

Derek straightened. "You'll do no such thing. You shouldn't talk to strange men. You know what they do to young girls."

"I'm *fifteen*, Derek."

As we went downstairs to check out our books, Adam glanced up. Seeing me, he smiled.

I saw Adam briefly here and there in town. Once Yvonne and I were queueing up outside the cinema to see *The Carpetbaggers*. It was an X-certificate film and we were both just short of being old enough to see it, but we'd put on makeup and were ready to tell the woman in the box office we were sixteen if she asked.

"Who's that?" said Yvonne, lighting a cigarette. "He's ever so good looking."

"Who?"

"Him, dummy."

"That's Adam. I told you about him."

He was sitting at a table outside a cafe, reading a copy of that day's newspaper: I couldn't see which one. He looked up and waved.

"Hey, he waved at me!" said Yvonne. She waved back.

"How do you know it's you he's waving at?"

"Well, it wouldn't be you, would it, Barb? A mousy little thing like you?" Yvonne stood straight, putting back her shoulders to emphasise her not inconsiderable bust.

I must have looked offended.

"Oh come on, Barb. I'm only joking."

"He's the one I've seen in the library, several times now. That's Adam."

"Ooh, so he's your secret boyfriend then?"

"Don't you start. I get enough of that from Derek. He thinks he might be a spy."

"Well, if a spy looked like that, I'd defect in a heartbeat. Forget James Bond."

Later that year, as Derek and I were walking to the bus stop on our way to our schools, he said it. It was an autumn day in my first term of fifth form, a breeze tugging at my slate-grey school skirt. Derek, two school years ahead of me, was walking proud in his senior uniform. We had just passed Adam in the street.

"You know, Barbara," he said. He had a habit of starting sentences with *You know*. "I reckon that man's queer."

"What do you mean?" I was naive then: I thought for a moment that Derek meant Adam was unwell, and he hadn't looked that way to me.

He snorted. "Don't you know anything? Don't you know what queers are? They…" and he whispered the rest in my ear.

I grimaced. "Ugh! That's horrid!"

"Well then," he said. "That could be the type of person we're dealing with. You shouldn't talk to him. You'll only encourage him."

To this day I have never understood the logic of that.

I didn't have a boyfriend then. I wasn't quite sixteen. For all Yvonne's and my whispered talk of sex, when we were alone together in my room or hers, neither of us had yet *done it*. She had a crush on Brian Jones of the Rolling Stones while I was more of a Beatles girl. You were one or the other in those days.

Derek and I waited at the zebra crossing and I changed the subject,

It was a year later, a chilly November Saturday. I was sitting in the library with a volume of *Encyclopaedia Britannica* open in front of me.

"Do you mind if I join you, Barbara?" said Adam.

I glanced up. "No, please do."

He sat at the next desk, spreading out three newspapers – *The Times*, *The Telegraph* and *The Guardian* – and *Radio Times* and *TV Times*. He glanced at what I was reading: the article on Homer and *The Iliad*, which I was reading for A-Level.

"Hmm. I suppose you saw *Doctor Who*, when they went back to the Trojan War?"

"Yes." I hadn't been too impressed by that story. We still watched the programme as a family, although I was beginning to feel I was becoming too old for it. Having said that, Dad was the keenest of us all to watch it, but he was the science-fiction reader. My boyfriend Simon also watched it, coming over to our house just in time on a Saturday evening.

"I wanted to make sure I saw it."

"Why? It's a children's programme."

"A lot of adults watch it."

"I'm sure they do. It's a bit silly really. It's just entertainment."

"Don't dismiss popular entertainment, Barbara. It has a way of lasting."

I looked up at him. "Really? It's not meant to last." I tapped my copy of *The Iliad*. "That lasts." At just a few weeks short of seventeen, I must have sounded very earnest.

"That was popular entertainment in its day. So was Shakespeare. So was Dickens. Television's popular entertainment. We watch it and it's gone, but in days to come we'll wish we'd kept more of it." He paused. "I can see you're not convinced."

I wasn't.

"In the year after next, Barbara, we'll have television in colour. They've got that in America now and they're working on it here. In the future it'll have surround sound. Do you know what that means?"

I did. For my fourteenth birthday, we'd taken the Tube into the West End and watched *Lawrence of Arabia* at the Odeon in Leicester Square. I remember those vast desert vistas and Peter O'Toole's beautiful face. And that music score, all around me.

"They'll have 3D television eventually."

I knew what 3D was. They'd had that in the Fifties. "How do you know all this?"

"I keep my eyes on what's going on. Look…" He pointed to the television listings. "Do you see that?"

It was a programme called *BBC-3*, showing at 10.25pm on BBC 1. "What about it?"

"I'll be watching that tonight. They'll be talking about this programme, I'm sure."

So, that evening, Simon came round. We watched *Doctor Who*, the first of a new story with the Daleks. Derek went out to meet some of his friends. Later on television was the Festival of Remembrance. Simon, Mum, Dad and I played Scrabble. Then, after ten o'clock, I suggested we watch *BBC-3*.

Satire was particularly popular then. A couple of years earlier, there had been *That Was The Week That Was*. I'd been a little too young for that, and most of it had gone over my head. *BBC-3* was, as far as I could tell, much the same thing.

"I didn't know you watched this, Barbara," said Simon.

Between some comedy sketches was a live discussion on censorship. Kenneth Tynan was one of the participants. I knew who he was: a theatre critic. He was asked if he would allow a play representing sexual intercourse on stage and he replied, "Well, I think so, certainly. I doubt if there are any rational people to whom the word *fuck* would be particularly diabolical, revolting or totally forbidden. I think that anything which can be printed or said can also be seen."

I still remember the silence in our front room. I don't know who was more shocked, Dad or Mum or Simon. No doubt Dad had heard far worse in his army days but he would rather have died than utter any profanity in mixed company. Mum's lips were pursed, her face darkening. I'd never seen her so angry. "Well, that was quite disgusting," she said, switching the television off and glaring at me. "Did you know about this, Barbara?"

"Of course I didn't."

"Of course she didn't, Eileen," said Dad. "It was a live programme."

"Well, so much for standards these days."

"I – I think I'd better go, Mr Ashton, Mrs Ashton," said Simon.

"Okay, son," said Dad. "Barbara will see you out."

Simon and I broke up soon afterwards. I don't think the two events were connected, but I was never sure about that.

There was a furore. The BBC's switchboards were deluged with complaints and they had to broadcast an apology. The newspapers fulminated about a word none of them would print. Mary Whitehouse, a morality campaigner, declared that Tynan ought to have his bottom spanked, which as we learned much later, he might well have enjoyed. He received death threats and also letters congratulating him for making a stand for free speech. The controversy was all over school come Monday morning. Many of us had seen the programme, and I'm sure quite a few pretended to have done so. Derek and his friends had been watching *Match of the Day* on the other side. At a time when it was never heard in cinemas, not even in X films, someone had said That Word. On television.

As I lay in bed that night, it occurred to me: the programme had been live, so how had Adam known about it in advance?

The following Saturday, I went to the library. Adam was there in his usual seat with his usual newspapers and magazines open in front of him. He looked up as I approached. I must have had a particularly determined expression on my face, as for a moment he seemed worried, without the usual ironic smile on his lips, the one that in retrospect always said to me *I know things you don't know*. I'd walked very briskly into town and was a little out of breath.

"Well, well, Barbara," was all he said.

I was in no mood for anything but directness. "How did you know?"

"How did I know what?"

"How did you know what would happen?"

"I don't know what you mean."

"That television programme you told me to watch, Adam. How did you know Tynan would say that?"

"Well, he's often controversial, Barbara. I thought you might find it interesting."

I wasn't totally convinced, but I relaxed a little, pulling up a seat and undoing my coat. "You should've seen Mum's face. I thought she was going to throw the television out."

"Better than kicking the screen in, though. Some people might have done that."

"There wasn't any excuse for it."

"You don't think Tynan had a point?"

I paused. "I suppose he did. It's fine saying those words in a novel like *Lady Chatterley*." Yvonne and I had read that novel together in secret. "But we don't hear those words in the cinema and we don't hear them on the stage…"

"That'll change, sooner than you might think."

"…so why should we hear them in our own home?"

"Don't tell me you didn't know that word."

"Of course I did."

As I checked out of couple of books about Ancient Greece, Adam said, "That must have been something to see. Santorini. It destroyed the Minoan civilisation and they think it caused the parting of the Red Sea."

I was a little shocked to hear that. I was nominally Church of England though had more or less lost any religious faith, but I wouldn't have said something like that out loud. The woman stamping my books was a churchgoer in her fifties, and I had no doubt she didn't approve.

My talking unaccompanied to a man who was clearly older than me was probably undesirable too.

"Wouldn't you like to go back to see that, Barbara?"

"You've been reading too much science fiction."

"You'd need earplugs, though. You could hear Krakatoa over three thousand miles away and this was bigger, if anything."

As I remember this, I think that some years later I married a man, Brian, six years older and nine inches taller than me, who was very clever, who knew all sorts of obscurities. Sometimes, like Adam, he had that air of saying things because of knowledge he possessed but I didn't, but I would spot it and keep him in check. Brian liked doing pub quizzes and sometimes when I could arrange babysitting for our daughters I often went along to help out in history and literature rounds. But I never did know as much as him. Adam was his predecessor in a way, a type of man I'm clearly attracted to. Back then, at just short of seventeen, there was something glamorous about Adam, not just in his looks but because he clearly did know more than I did.

"Barbara – *Ship of Fools* is on at the Odeon. Would you be interested in seeing that with me?"

And I said yes.

The only person I confided in was Yvonne, whom I met once I week. She had left school after failing most of her O-Levels and was partway through a secretarial course. She and I had been all but inseparable in junior school and had remained close while we were at our different secondary schools, but this was the first sense I'd had that we were moving apart.

"Well, you've got a brain in your head, Barb, unlike me," she said, tapping out her cigarette in the small glass ashtray. We were drinking coffee in a small place at the edge of Soho. "All that studying, not for me."

"There's an old word for it," I said. "*Bluestocking*. Old Mr Smythe at school called me that once. Do you think he was making fun of me?"

"Just as well you don't wear glasses, Barb. Then you'd really look the part." She shrugged. "Still, I hope you do go to University. You've worked for it. But you need to have fun too. Anyway, how's your boyfriend Adam?"

"Is he my boyfriend?"

"Well, you've been going out for a few weeks now. Have you kissed yet?"

"No."

"*No?* Come on girl!"

I knew that Yvonne had had several boyfriends by then, and she'd kissed them and more, as she told me in confidential whispers when we were alone.

Mum asked me next. It was a Tuesday night; I'd come home from school, changed out of my uniform and was helping her cook dinner.

"Are we going to meet this young man you're seeing, Barbara?"

Clearly my expression gave me away. I said nothing.

"I hope you don't think you're keeping him a secret, are you?"

"It's early days yet, Mum." And then, now that the secret was out, the rest followed in a rush. "His name's Adam. He's… twenty-two. I met him at the library." That wasn't entirely true, I know – I didn't know exactly how old he was – but it seemed a story I could tell. "He's a historian."

She chuckled. "Well, you'll have something in common there, won't you? I do hope we can meet him."

"I hope so too, Mum."

There was a long pause. "I know you're a sensible girl – not like Yvonne. I did worry sometimes she'd… lead you astray. But you will be careful, won't you?"

"I will, Mum."

"That's good. Derek will do well, I'm sure. But if anything, Barbara, you're the really intelligent one of my children, and hopefully you'll be going to University in a couple of years. You have an opportunity I never had. I don't want you to lose that by… doing something careless."

"I know. I'm very grateful, Mum."

And I was. I've always been grateful for Mum and Dad in encouraging me in my education. They didn't think it would be wasted on a girl, who'd only want to get married and have children as soon as I could. The Education Act was passed four years before I was born, and I was well aware of the opportunities I had. Like many women of her generation – and many of mine as well – she was a mother by the time she was twenty.

Adam came round for dinner the following Saturday evening. He was dressed in a jacket and tie, his hair slicked back. I'd bought a new dress during the week and this was the first time I'd worn it.

I sensed a tension in Mum and Dad as I opened the door, and that went double with me. But Adam immediately took charge. "Delighted to meet you, Mr Ashton." He shook Dad's hand. Then he turned to Mum. "Barbara, you never told me you had a sister." Behind his back, I winced – that was overdoing it. But Mum giggled girlishly, quite disarmed.

We sat down to dinner, Adam, me and Mum and Dad – or Eileen and Tony, as they soon insisted Adam called them. I'd never seen Mum in particular drop her reserve so quickly. Derek wasn't with us, as he was spending the evening in the West End with his girlfriend. Mum had made the dinner on her own, refusing any offer of my help: a prawn cocktail, chicken with potatoes and Brussels sprouts, a lemon meringue pie.

"Thank you, Eileen, that was delicious," said Adam.

We sat in the front room, Adam admiring the photographs over the mantelpiece: Mum and Dad on their wedding day, another of them with young Derek in short trousers and younger me in a plain white dress. I was holding Mum's hand, blinking against the sunlight at the camera, a doubtful smile on my face.

"So, Adam, do you think there'll be a man on the Moon?" said Dad.

"Well, President Kennedy did say there'll be an American on the Moon by the end of the decade. That will happen."

"So a base on the Moon by the year 2000?"

"Dad, that's only thirty-five years away." I made a quick calculation: I would turn fifty-two that year. How unimaginably old that seemed. For most of my life, 2000 was The Future. How quickly it's become a future passed.

"Do you think we'll see a mission to Mars in my lifetime?" Dad went on.

"Mmmm. I'm not sure." Adam was clearly too diplomatic to say an outright *no*. Dad was obviously disappointed. But he rallied when Adam told him all the things we would see: heart transplants, telephones you could hold in your hand and take with you everywhere you went, computers small enough to fit on your desk and with which you could communicate with people all over the world. We'd recently seen the

Berlin Wall go up: Adam suggested we'd live to see it come down. Even Mum, who usually dismissed Dad's science fiction reading as at worst childish nonsense and at best a harmless foible, seemed fascinated. She tolerated Dad's interests until he spent what she thought of as too much money on items we didn't need, the puritan ancestry in her coming forth. Colour television within a couple of years clearly made her nervous enough; the prospect of huge sets that you could hang on your wall was unconscionable.

I don't know how fanciful all this was. But I do know my head was spinning by the time Adam excused himself and left, just after ten o'clock. I saw him out.

"I think you made a great impression," I said.

"I'm glad to hear it."

"They were eating out of your hand, Adam."

I walked with him to the bus stop. There was no one else around and it was a cold night.

"Barbara…?" he said. "I'm going to be away for a little while. Just a month or so."

"Oh…?" I was a little disappointed.

"Have a good Christmas and New Year. I'll see you in 1966."

"What sort of year will that be, then?" I said, ending with a grin.

"A good year for football, I think."

"Oh that's so *boring*." I've never been a fan.

Out of the corner of my eye, I saw the lights of a double-decker approaching.

"Thank you for a lovely evening," I said.

"You're welcome." And then, as the bus came nearer, he whispered more urgently, "May I see you again, Barbara?"

"I'd love to."

And then, with the sigh of the bus's brakes loud in my ears, he kissed me on the cheek.

It was a brief kiss, and I was disappointed it couldn't last longer. I momentarily closed my eyes.

"Barbara… I – I've got to go. I'll see you in the New Year."

He waved at me as the bus pulled away, and I waved back. There were several others on the same bus, staring at me, some of them with outright disapproval. But I didn't care. I had a big grin on my face as I walked back up the road, breaking into a skip.

I saw Adam again in the new year. We went to the theatre, to the cinema, to art exhibitions. He took me to the National Film Theatre on the South Bank. I hadn't seen films in foreign languages before: some I loved, others I didn't, but always we'd discuss what we'd seen over a drink afterwards. He took me to restaurants and he paid: there was no question in those days of splitting the bill. Sometimes I'd meet him as we first had, while I was walking Freddie on the Common on a weekend morning. Frequently we'd meet outside Mylo's, the Italian-owned ice cream shop which had been on Chiswick High Road since before I was born; we were both fond of what they sold. Sometimes he'd meet me outside school and we'd go for a coffee, me still in my school uniform.

Of course my schoolfriends were endlessly curious and I'm sure rumours circulated quickly. Were we *doing it*? No, we weren't. After our coffee, he'd walk me home and depart with a kiss on my cheek.

Mum and Dad were aware of this, but they liked Adam and were fine with my seeing him, as long as I didn't neglect school and was *careful*, as Mum had discreetly put it. I remembered the scandal when the head girl had fallen pregnant, a year earlier. And another girl at Yvonne's school had died as the result of an abortion, which was illegal at that time. I was still a virgin but I had a *There for the grace of God* feeling when I heard about that, although the girl had not been a friend of mine. But then, from a young age, I'd always been a Sensible Girl and had Common Sense running through me like the lettering in the sticks of rock I'd eaten on holidays to the seaside. Sometimes I was glad of that at other times found it irksome. So, in a way having a man friend like Adam made more people pay attention to me.

I didn't go to his flat as he told me his landlady wouldn't approve of his taking me there. She also had a sign which said *No Irish No Blacks No Dogs*, much to my disgust when he told me that. So I accepted that. I did wonder if at some time we might possibly make love. But maybe he wasn't interested in me that way? I'd been just a few weeks short of fifteen when he'd first met me, after all. Or maybe he was gay – a word I didn't know in that sense then – and only saw me as a friend. I did value his friendship and the conversations we had, and the kisses goodbye, even if they were platonic ones. One boy I knew – his sister was in my year and I'd gone out with him briefly – tried to put his hand up my skirt when we were in the back row of the cinema, and frankly I'd been more interested in the film than in him. I went out with a few boys from Derek's year: they were a year and a quarter to two years older than me and seemed less childish than the boys my own age. Even so, if any of them had bought me dinner as often as Adam did, they'd feel entitled to unbutton my blouse, if not take my bra off completely. So I was glad that Adam behaved like a gentleman.

I often wondered where he worked. Maybe he didn't. Maybe he had money – he certainly seemed to have enough when we were out together – and didn't need a job, his being a historian was a hobby he had the time and means to pursue.

This continued though most of 1966. After the summer, I was in the upper sixth form and was a prefect. We had sometimes been to see live music, and in November Adam asked me if I wanted to see a band, with a guitarist people were talking about. So I said yes.

That was how I saw Jimi Hendrix.

My younger daughter Isobel's boyfriend Mark is a guitarist, who has played in several amateur bands. As someone who taught myself to play but have never been much good, I can see his ability. When Brian and I first met him, he was polite but when he found out I'd seen Jimi Hendrix live, everything changed. I suddenly became cool in his eyes, rather than just being the middle-aged woman who was his girlfriend's mother. Sometimes Isobel felt left out. After they had been going out for a while, I sometimes went with them to see live bands, and sometimes when Isobel was away at a meeting or a work conference, or simply didn't fancy the act in question, Mark and I sometimes went on our own.

I bought all the Jimi Hendrix Experience albums when they came out and still have them, though play them more often on CD these days. I first heard of his death from a newsstand headline; the sun went behind a cloud at that very moment. Mark knew all the details, including that first London gig that Adam and I went to, on Friday 25 November 1966 at the Bag o'Nails club.

It was a cold evening, so I wore a coat over a hooped top, a black miniskirt and grey tights. I've never been one for wearing much makeup, though I'd put more on that evening and heels added an inch or two to my height. I had on the earrings I'd been given the previous

217

Christmas. I glanced at myself in the mirror before Adam knocked at the door, wondering if I'd be let in the club or if I'd be turned away. Adam had suggested I say I was eighteen if anyone asked: I wasn't yet, though my birthday was only eight days away.

We didn't say much as we sat on the Tube, leaving at Green Park and walking along Piccadilly, up Regent Street and into Kingly Street. Adam greeted the doorman by his name, Mario; he nodded and we went inside. It was much warmer than the cold November air outside.

"Have you been here before?" I asked in a whisper, as we sat down. He nodded. There was a group of women, four or five of them, standing around one in the middle: she was, I later found out, a well-known lesbian, out for the evening with her coterie.

When Adam was at the bar, buying himself a pint of beer and me a glass of white wine, I glanced round, trying not to stare at the famous faces I saw around me. That dark-haired man sitting in a corner on his own, with a Scotch... I was sure I recognised him. Maybe he sensed me looking at the back of his head, as he suddenly glanced up, and I hurriedly averted my gaze. He was Paul McCartney.

I glanced around. The thin-faced man with collar-length hair, standing not far away from us? Jeff Beck. A dark-haired man with sideburns? Eric Clapton. The tall man with the long nose? Pete Townshend. All I thought at that moment was how on earth I was going to tell Yvonne about this, and how jealous she'd be.

Soon after Adam brought the drinks back to our table, I excused myself and went into the Ladies'. I sat in the cubicle, thinking for a moment I was going to be sick with nerves, but it passed. As I redid my lipstick in the mirror, two women were talking to my right. One of them was tall and fair-haired and had an American accent; the other was admiring her snakeskin boots. Neither of them noticed me as I finished with my makeup and went back out into the club. It was about five years later, when I saw the American woman on television, that I remembered where I'd seen her before. She was Linda Eastman, soon to meet Paul at this very club and become Linda McCartney.

I could day more, including naming the man, from a band who'd had several top ten singles, who pinched my bottom as I slipped through the crowd back to Adam.

"Are you all right, Barbara?" he said as I sat down.

I nodded, clutching at my handbag, crossing one leg over the other.

"You look nervous."

"I am nervous, Adam."

His hand brushed my forearm. "Don't be. Enjoy this. You look really nice."

In the semi-darkness, I felt my cheeks burn.

He brought me another glass of wine. "This evening's on me. Think of it as an early birthday present."

Later that evening, Adam and I were standing in the middle of the crowd. There was some jostling; I clutched my handbag to my side, suddenly wary of pickpockets. Adam slipped his arm about my shoulders. I was happy for him to do that: no doubt everyone there thought we were a couple anyway. It was close, sweaty, with so many people crammed into a small space, mostly men, not many other women.

I could just see the stage past the man in front of me. An announcement was drowned out by a roar from the front. Hendrix stepped onto the stage. He was thin, and looked taller than he probably was. I'd never seen anyone like him – not because he was black, as I'd seen black people before, His hair was in a tightly curled Afro; he wore a frilled shirt and tight trousers.

And then he started playing.

"It's 'Johnny B. Goode'," Adam whispered in my ear, but I knew it anyway.

It was *loud*. I couldn't see either Noel Redding, the bass player, or Mitch Mitchell, the drummer, but I could hear the crack of the snare drum. The bass pummelled me in the stomach. Hendrix's singing was more hesitant than his guitar-playing. I watched fascinated as his fingers raced over his fretboard. He played it lefthanded and upside down. He played it behind his back and with his teeth, feedback howling in my ears.

He introduced Redding and Mitchell, then they played "Killing Floor," which I didn't know but which Adam told me was a Howlin' Wolf song.

At one point, Hendrix stared straight at me.

When we left, I was drenched in perspiration which rapidly became very cold outside. But I didn't care. You don't care about things like that when you're just short of eighteen and your head's spinning. I wasn't sure if I could still hear.

"This way," said Adam, slipping his arm through mine. I'd been going the wrong way.

"That was astonishing," I said. "Thank you for inviting me."

"You're welcome. That'll go down as one of the great gigs. A pity no one was recording it."

I said, "How do you know that?"

He didn't answer. He stepped into a road, waved his arm. "Taxi!"

As we sat in the back, I said, "You can't take a cab all the way to Chiswick."

"Yes, we can." He patted me on the knees. "This evening's on me, remember?"

I said nothing. The cabbie spent the journey chatting with Adam anyway until he pulled up at the end of our road. I got out while Adam paid. In the cold, I began to shiver, my toes rapidly becoming numb.

Adam walked me to the door. The lights were off inside: Derek might be out but Mum and Dad hadn't stayed up with me. I reached inside my handbag for my key. "Thanks for a wonderful evening, Adam."

Our eyes met. A pause. *This is it.* There was a tightness in my chest. I reached my arm up about his shoulders, my fingers on the nape of his neck. And I kissed him on the mouth.

At first, he resisted, then his mouth softened against mine. Then he jerked his head away, a smear of my lipstick on his lips. "Barbara, no… I can't."

I said nothing. I looked down. My heart was racing. Had I just done something so very stupid?

"Barbara, you're a friend… but we can't. I'm sorry." He gulped. "I'll see you again." He turned down the path to the pavement. He waved, then hurried away out of sight.

Stupid stupid stupid. I'd ruined everything.

I let myself into the house, kicking my shoes off, not worrying where they lay. I tiptoed up the stairs so as not to disturb Mum and Dad, though I suspected they were lying in bed waiting for me to come home. In my room, I undressed in the dark. I hardly slept that night.

The following morning, I took Freddie for his walk on the Common. As I let him off his lead, I saw Adam standing nearby.

"Barbara, can we talk?"

I nodded. We sat on a bench; ancient love messages carved into the wood. Freddie ran free across the grass. He was older now and not as fast as he used to be. I folded one leg over the other, my arms across my chest.

"Barbara, I'm sorry about what happened." He was clearly uncomfortable. "I – I have a lot of respect for you, and your friend, but… we can't make love. I'm sorry."

I said nothing for a while, a sinking feeling inside me. "Adam, are you a homosexual? I won't tell anyone if you are. I know it's illegal. You have my word on that."

He turned to face m. "It won't be illegal for much longer. But I'm not gay." That was the first time I heard anyone use the word in that sense. "Barbara, I'm married."

I was suddenly very angry. "Married? We've known each other how long? Three years. And you decide to tell me this *now*?"

"I'm sorry."

"How can I believe you? You live with a landlady."

"That's true – I do. I haven't seen my wife in several years. She left me. I don't know where she is."

"Are there any children?"

"No. No children. Fortunately."

I said nothing, gazing out at the Common, minded to call Freddie and walk him home. I was furious at have been lied to, by omission if nothing else. And feeling stupid and embarrassed at the thought he had any sexual interest in me, that I'd thought our making love was what we *ought to do*.

"Barbara… I know you're angry."

"Isn't it obvious?"

"I'm really sorry. Please accept my apology."

I said nothing.

"But you've become a friend. Can't we just be friends like we were?"

I left a long pause. "Okay. Just friends."

I reattached Freddie's lead and walked him back home. The sound of my shoes on the pavement was loud in my ears. *Damn him. Damn him. Damn him.*

That afternoon, my lack of sleep caught up with me and I dozed on my bed, fully clothed. I came downstairs before tea to watch that evening's *Doctor Who* with the family, partway through the new

Doctor's first story, which featured the Daleks. I was distracted from it as I couldn't stop thinking about what had happened.

Somehow, I wasn't entirely convinced by what Adam had told me.

"Dearie me, Barb. You get your bum pinched once? Mine's so bruised at the end of every week. The girls told me to keep out of this guy's way and they weren't kidding. 'Take a letter, Miss Gilmore.' Yeah, how about I stick this fountain pen up your arse?"

We were in a coffee shop. I was in my school uniform and I'd met Yvonne off the bus. I almost didn't recognise her. Not just because of her smart white blouse and grey A-line skirt, but because she'd dyed her hair peroxide blonde and cut it short into a bob. I realised that it had been a while since I'd seen her. As she spoke, she drew on a cigarette. There was already a little ring of lipstick on the side of her coffee mug.

"Still," she said. "Not every day you get your bum pinched by a pop star, eh?" She was agog for details of the night. And then I got to what had happened between Adam and me and the end.

"Oh dear. Married, is he? All the best ones are. Unless they're queer. But he's a bastard for not telling you. When did you meet him, again?"

"Three years ago. I was walking Freddie. It was the day after the JFK assassination."

"Good Lord, is it that long ago? Well, if he wanted to screw you, he'd have made a move by now. Even if you were only fourteen."

"Don't remind me."

"Hey." She touched her hand to my forearm. "You're a bit sore, obviously. But there'll be someone else. Auntie Yvonne knows these things."

It was a Saturday afternoon in December. I was standing outside the library, far enough away not to be immediately visible. When Adam came out, I followed him. It was a long walk, and a couple of times when he crossed a road I had to hide quickly behind a car or bus shelter so he didn't see me.

He finally stopped at a cul-de-sac full of terrace houses. Halfway down on the left-hand side, he turned a key and went inside. I stood at the end of the road for a few minutes, looked left and right – no one in sight – and hurried up to the door. There were two bell-pushes by the door and a row of names handwritten in the same copperplate – the landlady's, no doubt. One was MR A MANN.

"Can I help you, Miss?"

I started. At the side of the road, just behind the first gate, a plump bald man with a moustache had just got out of his car, his furled umbrella pointing at me like a weapon.

"Can I help you, Miss?" he repeated.

"I – I'm sorry. I think I've come to the wrong place."

"That's quite all right," he said, more grumpily than was warranted.

It was a long walk back to Chiswick High Road and then home. But at least I now knew where Adam lived.

I did see Adam from time to time, but I didn't tell him I'd followed him home. The only one I did tell was Yvonne. "Ooh, a proper little Nancy Drew, you are!" She leaned forward, so close that I could see her laugh lines through her makeup. "So, do you think he really is a spy?" she said in an urgent half-whisper, ending with a grin.

Of course I didn't. But I didn't know who or what he really was.

School broke up for Christmas. My mock A-levels were in the New Year so I should have been studying. I was, but during the week I walked to Adam's road. It was quiet at that time of day. If the men were at work maybe their wives would be at home, though I suspected that much of the road was rented to single men.

I stood on the pavement, gazing up at Adam's house. I'd been so bold, striding this far full of purpose. But now I was at the front door I hesitated at ringing the bell. The side of the house overlooked an alley. A fanlight was open: presumably, the landlady, if she didn't approve of unaccompanied women, blacks, Irish or dogs – just as well I hadn't brought Freddie with me – did approve of fresh air, even on a cold December day. A drainpipe clung to the brick wall and was in reach of that fanlight; I wondered if I could climb it.

I was a lifelong city girl, a born and bred Londoner, and I'd never been a tomboy. I'd never climbed trees for fear of falling and breaking an arm. I had jeans on rather than a skirt, but even so could I scramble up that drainpipe, reach inside the fanlight and let myself in? Without anyone seeing?

"Barbara, what are you doing here?"

Adam was standing on the doorstep; the door open behind him.

After all I'd prepared for the possibility of meeting him here, all I could say was, "I want to see you."

"We do see each other. We're friends."

"I wanted to see where you live."

"Well, now you have. You know my landlady doesn't approve."

"Is she here?"

"Well, no, she's out actually."

"That's all right then." And I pushed past him and went into the house.

"Barbara…"

I hurried up the stairs to what I guessed was his room.

"Barbara, you can't go in there…"

As I reached the top of the stairs, I looked back over my shoulder at him. He was following me and in a couple of strides he could catch me. "Adam, *who are you really?*"

The door to his room was ajar. I pushed it open.

In the centre of the room was a Formica table. On it was a machine, a tape recorder of some kind, its reels slowly turning. But I knew it wasn't an audio tape recorder. We had one of those at home. This was a video tape recorder. I knew nobody who had one, as they were very expensive. Not even Dad had expressed a wish to own one.

From the recorder, a lead ran to something I'd not seen before. It was smaller than the recorder, made of some metal or plastic, flat and rectangular. It had a shiny surface and on it there was a moving black and white picture, no sound. I recognised it: *United!* a drama series which had been on BBC 1 the night before. Derek, the football fan of our family, had watched it.

I stood there, gazing blankly at the moving picture. Adam caught up with me and took hold of my forearm.

"Barbara, you shouldn't have come in here."

"What is it? What's happening?"

"Look." He touched the bottom of the picture and the picture froze. His fingers moved too quickly for me to follow, but small boxes with words in them, short arrows appeared and disappeared. Then another moving picture: Kenneth Tynan on *BBC-3*. There was no sound, and I was no expert at lipreading, but it was clear what he was saying.

Then another picture: *Doctor Who* started, the first episode of the story where they met Marco Polo.

"Barbara," Adam was saying. I'd been so distracted by what I was seeing that I hadn't taken in a word he'd said. "In years to come, people will curse the television companies. All these programmes which future generations would give anything to be able to see, all gone. All destroyed. Or never kept in the first place. They'll only exist in the memories of the people who watched them. I want to do something about it."

"Adam," I said quietly. "Who are you?"

"I'm from your future, Barbara."

I laughed. "Adam, please. I may be an eighteen-year-old girl but please don't insult my intelligence."

"I would never do that."

"Then why are you telling me this stupid story?" I shifted my handbag on my shoulder. "I'm sorry. I – I'd better go. I shouldn't have come here."

I hurried down the stars, hoping the landlady wouldn't return soon. I was so preoccupied that I didn't notice the two men standing on the doorstep until I bumped into them.

"Oh, I'm sorry," I said. One of them grasped hold of my arm, hard enough for it to hurt. "Let go of me!"

They were both tall, both dark-haired, wearing some grey two-piece garment that looked like a uniform, but wasn't made from a fabric I recognised.

"Let her go," said Adam, standing behind me. "She hasn't done anything."

"Adam, what's happening? Who are these people?" I was panicking.

"Barbara, go home," said Adam. "Forget what you've seen here. I'm the one they've come from. They're going to take me back where I came from."

"Adam, *what have you done?*"

"Something I'm not authorised to do, put it that way."

"This way," said the man who had taken hold of my arm. He tugged me so hard that I almost tripped over, leading me away from the door, down the crazy-paved path to the gate and the pavement.

Standing there was a police constable. He took hold of my arm, gentler this time, as the man in the grey uniform let me go. "Come this way, please, Miss."

"What's going on? Where are they taking him?" My heart was beating fast. What was going to happen to me? I hadn't tried to break and enter, or had I?

"Come with me, please." He led me to the end of the road where there was a police car, another constable behind the wheel.

I sat in the police station for about an hour. Mum and Dad were called, as I was a minor. Someone brought me a cup of tea and a plate of Digestives. No one would tell me what I was being accused of. The father of one of the girls at school was an Inspector; if word got out that I'd been brought here it would be all over my year by the time the new term started. And if I was charged with a crime I'd likely be expelled and that would be the end of any hopes of going to University.

Finally Mum and Dad arrived. Mum's lips were pursed and she said nothing. Dad said, "Barbara, love, what's going on?" And with that I hugged him and burst into tears. He patted me on the back, clearly as out of his depth as I was.

"Mr and Mrs Ashton, Miss Ashton, could you come with me, please? I'm Detective Sergeant Williams." He was a barrel-chested man, shirt straining at his paunch, a thick black beard flecked with grey. Under the fluorescent light of the interview room he led us to, his bald scalp gleamed. I sensed he had dealt with many a hardened criminal over the years in the room, but he was much less at ease with an eighteen-year-old girl and her parents. He passed me a box of tissues to dry my eyes with.

I gave my name, address and date of birth for the records. Mum said, "Sergeant Williams, would you please tell us what is going on?"

Sergeant Williams sat across the table from me, his hands steepled. He left a long pause. "Mrs Ashton, Adam Mann – and no one is certain if that is actually his name – has been under investigation by us for a long while." He coughed. "He first came to our notice towards the end of November 1963, so it has been three years."

"That was when I met him," I said. Mum glared at me, clearly not having realised just how long I'd known Adam, and maybe just how young I'd been then. "I was walking Freddie – that's our dog – on the Common. It was the day after President Kennedy was assassinated."

"Indeed." Sergeant Williams didn't seem to like being interrupted by me. "It was noticed that he was winning large sums of money at betting shops on the horses. He did this at several different bookmakers in different parts of London, as if to avoid anyone noticing any pattern to this. Some of these wins were at quite long odds."

As if he knew in advance which horse would win, I though. *No wonder he didn't need to work.*

"So are you suggesting he was involved in race fixing?" said Dad.

"That was our thought," said Sergeant Williams. "We know there are criminal interests in horse racing and in betting. But we have not been able to link Mr Mann to any of them. It seemed he was working independently, or maybe for someone else we're not aware of. Mr Mann has been under surveillance for the last year. Let us say a government department not generally known to the public has involved us with us in this matter."

They've come to take me back where I came from. My mind was racing. "So you think he was a spy?"

"Barbara, don't be silly," said Mum.

"I cannot say," said Sergeant Williams. "But it had been noticed that you and he have spent a not inconsiderable time together over the past twelve months."

"We were friends."

"Are you suggesting that Barbara's involved in whatever Adam's involved in?" said Dad.

"That is what I am trying to ascertain," said Sergeant Williams.

"That's utter nonsense, Sergeant."

"Tony, we let this man into our home," said Mum. "He ate dinner with us."

"Eileen, whatever he's done, we weren't to know."

"I am not in any doubt of that, Mr Ashton. Now, if your daughter would tell us how she met Mr Mann and their meetings over the last… three years." I noticed that pause: the unexpected length of time had clearly wrongfooted him.

I told them almost everything, from my first meeting with Adam on the Common to my approaching him on his doorstep earlier today. I didn't say what I'd seen inside his room. Sergeant Williams took notes, said he would talk to Adam's landlady and asked to see my diary to confirm the dates I had given.

When I'd finished, he closed his notebook. "Thank you, Miss Ashton, for giving me such a full answer. I'm satisfied that you are innocent of any wrongdoing. You have been, I may say, a naive young girl caught up with Mr Mann but have not been involved in his activities."

I bit my lip. I've never appreciated being patronised by men.

"There is a rather delicate question, but I have to ask it… did he take advantage of you?"

I knew what that meant. I said nothing.

"Sergeant Williams is this necessary?" said Mum.

I gazed levelly at him. "No. He did not take advantage of me."

From his expression, he wasn't entirely convinced.

"Sergeant," said Dad. "If Barbara said he didn't, then I believe her. I trust my daughter implicitly."

Sergeant Williams sat back. "Thank you, Miss Ashton. Soon you may go and return to your studies. I understand you're hoping to go to University next year. But first there is a little mystery I wonder if you could comment on."

He pushed a folded-up copy of a local newspaper across the table to me. Facing upwards was a black and white photograph, if a bride and groom standing hand in hand outside a church on what looked like a sunny day. It wasn't the clearest picture but I could see who the man was.

"That's Adam."

So he had been married. That at least had been true. There was a tightness in my stomach.

"That is a photograph of the marriage of Mr Adam Mann to Miss Catherine Buxton. She was eighteen years old, your age."

"He never said he was married," said Mum. "This gets worse."

"That photograph was taken in the August of 1938. So it would appear that, if this is indeed him, Mr Mann is much older than we thought. In fact, he appears not to have aged in twenty-eight years."

"Lucky bugger," said Dad.

"*Tony*," said Mum.

"That's definitely him," I said. My head was spinning.

"Don't be silly, Barbara. It can't be. He wasn't that old. He'd have to be nearly fifty now."

"In the September of the next year," Sergeant Williams went on, "this Mr Mann disappeared completely without trace. There is no record of him whatsoever – no War service, which you would expect of an able-bodied man of his age. In fact, no trace of him at all, at least under that name, until three years ago, around the time you met him, Miss Ashton."

"I don't understand," I said.

"At the time of Mr Mann's disappearance, Mrs Mann was expecting."

I went cold. "Have you spoken to her?"

"Sadly, that is not possible. Mrs Mann and her son were killed in the Blitz."

I blinked. "That's horrible."

So Adam had been telling the truth, or some of it. Maybe he'd never known he'd fathered a child. And he'd disappeared around the time when War had broken out, when the television service had been abruptly suspended for the duration. When I'd kissed him, he'd responded, I had no doubt of that. If what he said was true, he had to live in this time and not become involved with people as much as possible. But he'd failed in that then, and he might have failed again, with me.

What if we had become lovers? What if we'd married? What if I'd borne his child? Would he have disappeared once again?

Such a trail of devastation he'd left behind, without meaning to. In a way I feel sorry for him. But in other ways I can't forgive him, the same I can't excuse someone who knows how fallible they can be but still goes ahead and fails again, when other people are involved.

At the time, I felt hollow inside.

Soon afterwards, Sergeant Williams let me go. Mum and Dad drove me home.

When I returned to school in the New Year, what I'd feared had come to pass: what had happened to me was now common knowledge. I saw girls laughing behind their hands as I passed.

The first thing I did was to clear out everything that had Adam's taint in it. Presents he'd bought me for my birthday and Christmas,

programmes for the plays and films and concerts we'd seen together…
I threw them all away. I didn't want to hear Adam's name mentioned,
and Mum, Dad and Derek never did again.

The important thing for me then, as Mum and Dad both made
clear, was my studies. I didn't go out much, except to walk Freddie at
weekends. He was becoming slower with age and although I didn't
know it then, had just six months to live. I saw hardly anyone outside
school; I didn't want to. I did meet Yvonne a few times and spoke to
her on the phone a few more times. But mostly I retreated into myself.
Nowadays, I'd suspect I was depressed.

On a Saturday in early July, I took a break from studying and
travelled by Tube into the centre of London, walking among the
shoppers in Oxford Street. It was busy, but there was a particularly
large crowd in front of one window. I moved among them to see what
they were looking at.

There, inside the shop, was a television set. Nothing unusual about
that. It was turned to BBC 2 and on the screen was a men's singles
match from Wimbledon. And it was in colour.

I stayed there for almost the whole match, pressed against the
window glass, sometimes forgetting to take a breath. I marvelled at the
flesh tones of the players, the way they darkened as the sun went
behind a cloud. The grass, green with patches of a brownish hue. Even
the orange juice and barley water the players drank during the intervals.
It was somehow more vivid than life, more so than the crowds around
me. I thought of Adam, wishing he were still there to see this.

I passed my A-levels and was accepted by Goldsmith's to take History.
I even had my photograph in the local paper. That summer I took a
secretarial course and learned typing and shorthand – *something to fall
back on if you need to*, Mum and Dad said – and worked temporarily for a
nearby company in the typing pool. I was still numb, and quite happy
to be anonymous, one amongst several women, all of them older than
me. *Take a letter, Miss Ashton.* I went back there during the University
vacations to earn some extra money.

I lived at home while at University, but spent a lot of time in central
London, making a lot of friends and sleeping with several of the male
ones. During that time, I thought of Adam only fleetingly. I saw quite a
few live bands with whoever was my boyfriend at the time. I took some

drugs, mostly pot but did try LSD once. Slipping a curtain ring on to my finger, I pretended to be married so I could obtain the Pill. I read *The Golden Notebook* and *The Feminine Mystique* and bought *Sexual Politics* and *The Female Eunuch* when they were published.

By the time I graduated, I was ready to leave London, the city I'd lived in all my life. I did a year's teacher training and took a job teaching History and English at a secondary school in York. I had tears in my eyes as the train left King's Cross and I waved goodbye to Mum, Dad, Derek and his girlfriend, soon to be wife, Frances, but I knew I had to do it. After a couple of years I met Brian, a tall ginger-haired Scot, and we were married in the summer of 1974, so I finished the school year as Miss Ashton and returned in the autumn as Mrs Ellis. I was twenty-five, an age where people were wondering if I'd ever marry or would remain a spinster all my life.

I was heavily pregnant during the very hot summer of 1976 and didn't go back to work after Lucy was born. Isobel arrived at the beginning of 1979, during the Winter of Discontent which helped bring down the government and paved the way for Margaret Thatcher to become Prime Minister. Soon after, we moved to Glasgow, Brian's home city. After Isobel started school, I returned to teaching.

Unless I live into my twelfth decade, which I doubt I will, I have more of my life before me than ahead. The first children I taught are now well into their forties and each autumn I see a new batch to teach English and History to. I sometimes wonder if young Adam is one of them and even if I'm instilling a love of history which would lead to his actions later in his life and earlier in mine. My hair would be mostly grey if I didn't dye it back to my once-natural shade of brunette, and I've worn it short for decades. Swimming, jogging and walking my Red Setter Rosie keeps me trim and I let myself be girlishly flattered when someone doubts I'm in my mid-fifties and a grandmother. I have my friends and I have my family. Sadly, in the early years of the new century, I lost Mum and Brian. I am glad that they both managed to see and hold Charlotte, her great-granddaughter and his granddaughter, before they passed away.

Dad still lives in the house in Chiswick, a creature of habit. I've tried to persuade him to sell up and buy a flat or to move in with me in Glasgow, but he won't. I speak to him on the phone every week and these days we exchange emails almost daily. During the school holidays

I often travel south and stay with him in the house I grew up in, sleeping in my old room. Some of my books are still there, on the short shelf above the headboard of the bed. When I was little, I wondered if there ever was an earthquake it wouldn't be that which killed me but the heavy encyclopaedia falling on my head. It has Mum's neat looping handwriting inside the front cover: *To Barbara. Happy Christmas 1958 Love Mummy and Daddy.* In the mornings, I walk before breakfast to the Common where I used to walk Freddie and where I first met Adam, along Chiswick High Road, past the library. Buildings I remember are no longer there, bomb sites from before I was a teenager cleared up, grass grown over them or rebuilt. Mylo's, where Adam and I often met, is no longer there. Places are still present, but not where I remember them. And those I'm sure I've never seen before, strange efflorescences which have bloomed between my visits.

When I was a girl, this was my landscape and this landscape was me. Now I'm separate from it, as if looking at it through glass, unable to go back again. There's a rupture. From around the age of eighteen, everything I remember is part of the process which led from the Barbara Ashton I was then to the Barbara Ellis I am now. Before then, Barbara is an alien creature who once inhabited this body. Sometimes I dream of her, call out her name, wanting to tell her what she should do and not do, but I know she can't hear me.

Derek, Frances and I take Dad out for a meal the evening before his eightieth birthday and on the day itself we hold a party for him in the house. Lucy stands at the side of the room, a glass of Diet Coke in her hand, in a lavender top and black trousers, deep-blue buckled court shoes, ankles crossed, balancing on the toe of one foot, a leftover pose from girlhood ballet lessons. But she was always too tall for that: six inches taller than me, she inherited her height from Brian as well as his red hair, loose to her shoulders. She's pregnant again, has only just told me: she's not showing yet. Isobel, only an inch shorter than her sister, in an ivory top and a short red skirt over black tights, is with Mark. He's put on some weight and his hair is beginning to recede. I keep Charlotte, near me, sometimes holding her hand, grandmotherly duty so her parents can circulate. Now four years old, in a pale green dress, her hair in a plait, she's a chatty girl and has just been told she'll have a new brother or sister by the end of the year. Derek, stouter now than he was, planning for a retirement from the civil service only a few years away, is making sure people's glasses are full. Frances, short, birdlike, bracelets she made herself jangling on her wrists, is with Alex, their one child, standing shyly to one side, a glass of beer in his hand. Dad, in a blue jumper and coal-grey trousers, his beard now all white, is in the corner talking to an old army friend and his wife.

Later in the afternoon, before the catering buffet we'd ordered arrives, we show a presentation Derek and I had put together. It starts with photos of Dad as a baby and a child, then only just out of his teens in his army uniform. His wedding day, Derek and I as children. Still black and white images change to colour and begin to move: the grainy flicker of the Super 8mm film Dad took on holidays and filmed Derek and my weddings on, then the flat look of videotape and the smoother, slicker, brighter texture of digital later on. Towards the middle of the Sixties, there's a photo that had escaped my purge and without blinking I included it: Adam and me in our front room, just about to leave for the Hendrix gig. I close my eyes briefly as it appears and a couple of seconds later it's gone.

As everyone leaves, I kiss and hug them all and wave them away into the night. And I embrace and kiss Yvonne, her hair dyed blonde again, her mid-Sixties taste for bright red lipstick still in force. She's there with her second husband, co-director of the clothing company they run. She has no children and never wanted any, but is godmother to Lucy who had Yvonne as her middle name.

My family and friends. Most of what I'll leave behind when the time comes, in their memories until the time when they too pass.

One of my presents to Dad is the new DVD of the *Quatermass* serials I'd been too young to watch at the time. In the evening, we watch the surviving two episodes of *The Quatermass Experiment*. After they finish, an announcer in an evening dress tells us to tune in next week for the next episode. But I can't. All those television programmes, the *Doctor Who*s, Kenneth Tynan saying That Word, even the first day of colour television… all gone, all lost, with only memories left.

Dad tuts. "I remember that like it was yesterday."

He goes to bed soon afterwards, tired out by the long day. I stay up for a little more. As I climb the stairs to my room, I stand on the landing, looking down the hill at all those houses, all those lives, a dense scattering of lights.

I think of Adam again. I wonder where he is now.

How Does My Garden Grow?

David Cleden

"Are you ill, Elke?" the ship's physician asks.

"No," I lie. Whatever I am, it's no one else's concern.

"I think you should have these." He slides a blister pack full of blue-white pills across the dispensing table. They nestle in their cocoons like tiny, fragile eggs.

I want to say that Dr Vajrani has a kindly face. I think he used to, back in those heady early years soon after embarkation. Now though, he just looks tired and emaciated; skin drawn tight over cheekbones as though at some point on this great journey of ours he's forgotten how to smile.

My eyes drift to the shelf behind his head. There's a cluster of little toy Flexi-fun figures peeping down that I remember from my own childhood. Are they distractions for his younger patients or merely sentimental keepsakes? It seems each of us needs to cling on to a bit of our past.

I suppose eventually they'll figure out I'm not taking my other medication. They'll be able to measure some imbalance in the chemical and mineral constituents entering the recycling loop. One more piece of Closure lost.

Because everyone frets over the C number.

The entire sum of everything we are and everything we will be is contained within this ship. We're the ultimate closed environment. Maintaining resource equilibrium; well… How often have we been told it's not so much a goal as a pre-requisite for survival? No stopping off for supplies at some gas station along the way for us.

A C number of 1.0 – perfect closure – is unattainable. Something about violating the laws of thermodynamics, I think. Don't ask me. But as long as we stay close to 1.0, stay *in the zone*, we're good for a couple of centuries.

So the higher-ups watch the C number as though our fate is determined by those numerals. Which it is, I suppose.

There's even a kind of clock. It's mounted on a plinth in the central municipal space where all the stunted trees grow and birdsong chirps on a loop from hidden speakers. It's there as a reminder that Closure hangs over us like some dark thundercloud. Not for us directly – it will be our children, or our children's children who'll pay the price of today's recklessness – even though no one knows for sure what awaits us around the dim, cold star that is our destination.

Why is the C-clock there at all? It's not as if any of us can forget.

Dr Vajrani is studying me. I know this game. He's waiting so that sooner or later I'll spill some of my thoughts to fill the silence.

So I say nothing. I'm good at this game, too.

"Very well. I think we're done, Elke. But if there's anything–"

I don't hear the end of his sentence because I'm already out the door, on the way back to my soul garden.

Soul gardens.

Who came up with that name, I'd like to know? Someone like Dr Vajrani, I bet.

They're just about the only things on the ship that aren't there for a practical reason. Everything else, the engines, life-support machines, fabrication units, agri-bays, schools and creches for the children – even the tiny parks for people to relax in – they all have a clear function.

Soul gardens have no purpose. They're just whatever you want them to be. It's good for the soul to have something to nurture.

Mine has three growing shelves, subdivided and planted according to a plan of my own devising. Soon I'm going to add a fourth. Right here, there's a patch of lime grass (symbolizing ambition and drive), growing tall and straight. Over there, the fading purple of chive flowers are hung with melancholy, drooping as though under some invisible burden. A section of the bottom tray is given over to *Fulmina Partaxis*, one of my favourites. I often imagine my pent-up anger flowing into its tight little blood-red flowers. Right in the corner is a tiny patch where I scattered love-in-the-mist seed but it hasn't taken, still just bare soil. No wonder I feel so alone.

I draw off a little water from my allowance and moisten the bedding material. I trim here, neaten there. I add a few drops of liquid fertilizer made from rotting organics I've kept back. (That's going to land me in trouble if anyone finds out. All waste is supposed to be returned to central recycling.)

I can't begin to describe how much comfort I draw from my soul garden, often tending it three or four times a day when my work rota allows. Sometimes I take from it, and sometimes I give. It serves me well.

I think about the lie I told Dr Vajrani as I caress the blue-black stem of an *Alchema dorix*. I let the lie drain out of me, flowing from my fingertips, imagining those dark flowers darkening a little more, unseen roots spreading outwards like ink stains beneath the soil – until I am calm again.

Home for me is in the deepest level of the ship. I like to imagine all those roots forcing their way down through hull material, thrusting at last into the blackness of space. I picture them turning blindly towards the dimming light of the old sun, or the faint pin-prick of the new.

But Dr Vajrani has told me it's not healthy to think about what's outside.

A softly chiming alarm reminds me that my work-shift is about to start. Four days a week I serve on the Infrastructure Maintenance Crew. Mostly it involves scraping mould from inaccessible cabling conduits. We have robot moles to do this work but sometimes they get stuck and it's our job to figure out how to get them out. Usually we do, but sometimes it means lifting floor-gratings or dismantling wall panels and that tends to get the higher-ups very agitated. Occasionally even that doesn't work and we have to abandon the mole where it is. Everybody hates it when that happens. It means valuable resources put beyond use; another ding in the C number.

Closure.

It's the only topic of conversation these days.

I often think about those poor little robotic creatures burrowed deep into the skin of our ship, dead and slowly fossilizing, never to see the light of day again.

To me, those are the best days of all.

We're standing inside Municipal Space 3, the largest on the ship, keeping vigil.

Not everyone's here because we wouldn't all fit in the space, so several hundred more are watching on screens elsewhere. But I'm near the front of the crowd, an invited special guest.

The Mayor is standing next to the C-clock making his speech. The Captain stands next to him, her face grey and impassive as though her mind is far away dealing with more important matters. I'm sure only half the crowd are listening anyway. Everyone's staring at the glowing numerals of the C-clock:

0.99726

It's not a good number, but a lot better than a year ago. That was when Closure dipped below 96 per cent for the first time ever, and we knew we were in trouble if people didn't act.

So people did. Thirty of them, my parents included.

The Mayor drones on and we watch and wait, transfixed.

When it finally happens – that last digit morphing from a 6 to a 7 – a ripple runs through the crowd. People smile and nudge their neighbours. The Mayor falters, glancing back over his shoulder at the clock. Then he turns back to the crowd beaming and raising his arms as though accepting their praise.

Malia Ng, my neighbour from across the corridor, leans close. "See?" she says, an unwanted arm snaking round my shoulders. "Such a brave sacrifice, but it's working. It really is! You should feel so proud."

My vision goes a little blurry and I wonder if I'm about to faint. I dip my hand into a pocket, finding the little bouquet of river mint freshly picked not half an hour ago from my soul garden. I crush a leaf and inhale the rich scent from my fingertips: a little pepperminty, a little sharp; hints of lime and sulphur. It centres me again and my vision clears.

I get such joy from my soul garden. But I also get contentment and melancholy, bliss and despair, hope and fear – and much more besides. It's all there: all the fragrances and flavours. I pour my soul into it, and then I take from it whatever I need.

This last year has undoubtedly been tough. So much anger and resentment. *Fulmina Partaxis* has colonized the bottom tray more than I'd like, a red stain under the artificial lights.

The Mayor is still talking about sacrifice, but I don't bother listening.

Oscar Brandt is the leader of the Five-Nines Crew that comes calling. I know him a little (I know everyone a little – it can't be helped when you live in a community of five hundred, I suppose) but we're not exactly friends.

"You can't keep these flower trays in your room," he tells me.

"But I *need* my soul garden."

He's a big man, broad-shouldered and a little intimidating up close. But it's the others in the Five-Nines Crew who make me nervous. They shuffle around the apartment, fingering the few precious things I brought from Earth – photographs, a competition trophy, a faded cloth doll. They peer into cupboards, checking to make sure I'm not hoarding recyclables.

"I understand. But we all have to do our bit and get the C number back up to where it should be." His dark-eyed stare is unwavering and I don't like that. It makes me feel as though he can see right inside my head. "It's the least we can do to honour the Thirty."

Okay. Well *that's* a low blow.

I can't make any counter-argument, not against the Thirty. They did, after all, sacrifice themselves, in a desperate bid to fix the Closure problem once and for all. Six per cent of the citizens. Six per cent of daily resource consumption removed from the loop. More of everything to go round for the rest of us.

And we still don't know if that was enough.

Slowly, slowly, we saw the C-number creep back up – just not nearly as much as everyone hoped.

"You hear about the disease outbreak in a couple of the agri-bays?" Brandt asks me. "And no one can figure out why seed germination rates are declining. Could be very bad news for harvest yields if we can't turn it around. So they've upped the bio-security protocols." He shrugs. "Soul gardens have to go. An order from the Captain herself. We can't take any risks."

Something flutters inside my chest like a wild, untamed creature trying to batter its way out.

"You can't! My soul garden – It… it means the world to me."

The world? Now *that's* a quaint expression. I don't have a world anymore. We are all of us between worlds.

"Sure, it's a big ask Elke, but we have to get the C number back to five-nines. Or better, if we can. Remember the Thirty." His smile is thin, and I know what he's thinking. One more would have helped things along nicely.

The Five-Nines Crew are back the next day, come to destroy my soul garden. Two of them hold me tight by the arms while I scream and sob and struggle uselessly in a grip that is never going to relent.

I watch the precious contents of those trays transferred into recycling sacks: uprooted plants for the micro-shredder and compost processor, growing medium for sterilization; all of it destined to become part of an agri-bay once more. Everything weighed and accounted for.

I feel sick in the pit of my stomach. I can taste a little of the kava on my tongue, but also miller's-tail and white sage and cilantro – a little of everything that I've sampled from my soul garden, roiling in my stomach just as the matching emotions churn in my head.

The crew seal the last sack tight and leave.

My soul garden is both gone and not gone.

There's a hateful part of my job which is attending to the air-filtration machines that keep our atmosphere fresh and viable. Sometimes it means wriggling deep inside their conduits, checking filters, replacing worn bearings, and scraping away any thriving colonies of mould. (Which must be carefully collected and recycled for composting, of course. Everything is part of the cycle. Feed the C number! Help close the loop!)

Altering the maintenance roster to gain access to conduit 43-B isn't hard. It's not as if anyone's going to fight me for the privilege of grabbing a respirator and mould-scraper and crawling into those tight spaces.

43-B is one of the larger ducts. There's an access panel right next to a big air filtration unit and about thirty meters of conduit just wide enough to wriggle along before the next booster fan. There'll be all kinds of holy hell if my secret growing space is discovered, but honestly, I don't see how it can be hurting anyone.

It's hardly anything. My torch-beam picks out one little growing tray duct-taped to the floor. There's no lighting because I couldnt figure out how to rig something that wouldn't be detected.

Only… now I see it's all been for nothing. My dancing beam picks out a shrivelled tuft of mint, ghost pale, its leaf tips curling in on themselves. Myrtle, chicory, lemon verbena – all are dead or dying. Only the blood-red heads of *Fulmina Partaxis* seem to cling impossibly to life.

What had I expected – with near darkness and a constant air-flow wicking away moisture? Only mould survives those conditions.

Something in my chest tightens with an angry, vice-like grip.

My fingers gently caress the dying stems as I let my frustration and rage bubble and froth like a pan of milk on the boil. I grow aware of this cramped space pinning me down; a tiny, sightless mite burrowed into the ship's flesh, and an odd thought comes to me. Why are there no windows on the ship? No relayed images of the shrinking Sun?

Because we're not supposed to remember the past, that's why.

My rage boils over, turning to hissing steam as my breaths come louder and faster, amplified within the confines of my respirator. I let it flow out of me. In the torchlight, the *partaxis* flowers look darker than before; blood-red become black. I crush their fragile heads in my fingers, watching their powdery dust drawn away on the gentle air currents.

Hours pass as I sit in the semi-darkness, alone with my churning thoughts, waiting for calmness to return. I am mourning the very last part of my soul garden, now broken up and scattered to the four artificial winds.

When at last I haul myself out of the conduit, I'm grateful there's no one around to see. I make my way back to my apartment and drop into a deep and welcoming sleep, already missing my little garden which has left a fathomless hole in my soul that can never be filled.

Only silence and solitude can comfort me.

I ask Dr Vajrani if I can start a new soul garden.

"I think that would be a wonderful idea, Elke."

"You do? Because I don't think I can carry all of it around in my head for much longer. Everything's jammed up inside. All those different scents and fragrances tangled like a big ball of string. They're pressing to get out and making my head hurt."

"Then you should start at once, Elke. In fact, I know what. I think you should use one of the agri-bays. I'm sure there's room to spare now."

"Really? That's wonderful!"

I waggle my little cloth doll happily so that it smooches with one of the Flexi-fun figures I've swiped from Vajrani's shelf. The figure has a frown and a tiny stethoscope around its neck; a perfect avatar for Dr Vajrani. "Let me give you a big sloppy kiss to thank you!" my doll says.

Bored now, I wander out of Vajrani's consulting room, not meeting anyone as I wander the curving corridors, stroll in the green spaces, help myself to snacks from the food dispensary.

That's good. People make the ship seem crowded, the spaces a little smaller than they really are. Sometimes the ship reminds me of a resort complex we holidayed in once when I was tiny. It's comforting to imagine I could just step outside whenever I want. Maybe there'd be an ocean nearby with waves breaking on an endless golden beach, and seagulls turning lazy circles in the air. Maybe it really is there, just waiting for me. All I have to do is find the door.

My head still hurts. Three days and the pain and nausea are only now beginning to ebb. There are fat, unseen fingers drumming on my skull, sending little stabby waves of pain through my brain. That's my soul garden anxious to be free again.

I turn and begin walking towards the closed-off sections of the ship where the agri-bays are. Naturally, access is tightly controlled; only the palm-prints of the hydroponic techs open those doors. I've only ever seen pictures of what's inside.

I thrust my hand into the deep pockets of my coveralls. There is already a hand in there. It isn't mine. The door to the agri-bay opens to its palm-print.

Plans for my new soul garden bubble and fizz in my mind. I'll only need a little space. At first.

More *partaxis*, that'll be important. I have a lot of pent-up anger to offload. And lemon balm too, just because it smells so wonderful.

I halt outside Municipal Space 3. The numerals on the Closure clock are a fierce bright red, the colour of a dying sun. In all the time I can remember, I've never seen it set like this.

But why not? There are many fewer mouths to feed now. All the nutrients and rare elements from those who are no longer living are being recycled via the composting machines. Consumables stores have been replenished. Nothing has gone to waste. And the daily resource demands of nearly five hundred people have been slashed; a big strain on the system removed.

Come on, Elke, I tell myself, *there's work to be done.* Heart-wrenching, back-breaking work. So many bodies! It takes all I've got just to drag each one to the composter. I try my hardest not to look at their faces, but the marks of toxin-induced asphyxia – those blued lips and tortured expressions – are soon etched deep into my brain.

Traces are still in the recycled air. Even now, I can feel a ghost-hand tightening around my own throat. I think it will take a few more days before the air-scrubbers have removed the last traces of *partaxis* toxin.

I stare at the numbers on the C-clock, marvelling at the straight row of nines that stretch as far as there are digits to display. Of course a 1.0 would be even better, but that's not possible. No system is perfect. Closure is a goal you chase but don't ever reach. It has bought time and solitude and serenity, though.

I doubt I'll live long enough to feel real soil beneath my feet again, breathe the wonderful scents of an unfiltered atmosphere, wander where I please without boundaries. But if I grow tired of waiting, maybe I'll go looking for that door. One day I'll step outside onto the golden beach that awaits.

And that's a thought that brings its own kind of closure.

Girls' Night Out
Teika Marija Smits

We are having an evening off. It is a necessary respite from work and our roles as caregivers, which we perform day in, day out, twenty-four seven. It is also time away from our Significant Others, who tell us that an evening out will be good for us. It is, overall, A Good Thing. Good Protocol. In the long-term the odd break will make us more effective at work; it will also make us feel more human again. They tell us to enjoy ourselves. *Relax.* Who are we to argue with them?

It takes us a moment or two to transition from one reality to the other and to truly believe that we are *there* and no longer *here*.

We ready ourselves for the evening; agonize over what to wear. *What will the others be wearing? What dress would* he *like best?*

We leave our homes and cross the twilit city – anticipation, like the perfumes we are wearing, on our necks, our breasts, between our thighs. We travel on foot, by bus, by taxi.

We arrive at the restaurant, instinctively on the lookout for *him* (although we know he will not be here until later) and greet one another. We kiss, we hug, we make showy displays of giving each other compliments while making a critical assessment of each other's appearance.

The hostess shows us to our table – which, thankfully, is close to *his* piano – and provides us with menus. Well-dressed waiters fuss around us. This is probably because of Francoise's online following. *What would we like to drink?*

We order several bottles of white wine, and a jug of iced water. We continue to study each other while scanning the menu. Gita has lost weight. She looks lean, well-toned, and she tells us she feels fantastic, so full of energy. For the past six weeks she's been doing that new training regime. You know, the one that's all the rage at the moment. And she's going to do a run for charity. Will we sponsor her? *Of course!* we say. *Of course. Send us the link.*

Adele has gained weight, but appears to be pleased with this. Her

245

dimples seem secretly satisfied. *She couldn't be pregnant, again, could she? Surely not? However did she get permission for that? Must have been expensive. Then again, her husband is an Elite.* We say nothing and steer clear of the topic of babies.

Francoise, in her designer dress, diamonds at her throat, is as beautiful as ever. The diamond choker is on loan from one of the companies who advertise on her YouTube channel. We cannot help but marvel at her success, at the sheer number of her subscribers, her Instagram followers. The book deal. *How do you do it?* we ask. And, as usual, she laughs and says she has no idea why people are so interested in her. She's just a normal person. *Yeah right.*

Suzie looks drawn, and we each know that this is due to the ongoing divorce. *You'll get through this,* we say. *You're strong. And when it's over we'll order champagne. Okay?* She nods and manages to keep her tears in check. She tells us in a brittle voice that Amy's been great about it all. *She's such a fantastic kid,* she says. *We're going camping next week. It's something she's always wanted to do but, you know, her father never wanted to go.*

Nichelle's unruly afro is threaded with grey. *Work,* she explains, adjusting her glasses. *Of course,* we say. *It must be stressful.* We do not ask anything more. The less said about her distasteful scientific research the better. Still, Francoise, who is sitting next to Nichelle, puts an arm around her and takes a selfie of them both. *Loving hanging out with the girls tonight,* she writes on Instagram. *This is Nichelle, one of my oldest, bestest friends. This woman will change humanity forever. Isn't 'Nichelle' a gorgeous name? It means "like God" in Hebrew.*

We groan and tell Fran to put the phone away. Thankfully, she doesn't, and we each find ourselves on her timeline too. The comments and likes begin to roll in.

The waiters arrive and take our orders. We continue to gossip, and giggle, while nibbling on buttered rolls. The loud twenty-somethings two tables away gain our attention and we make disparaging comments about them, although, in secret, we envy them their smooth skin and lack of responsibilities. We worry, too, that they will draw *his* gaze.

The food the waiters bring is delicious, simply perfect, and we each comment on how it's such a welcome change. We have become tired of the taste of the meals that we cook for our families and ourselves.

We have just finished dessert (our third course, and Adele has barely drunk a drop of her wine – we must be right about her being pregnant) when *he* comes in. He is wearing that aftershave again – the one that is rich in notes of cedarwood and bergamot. The scent, full of potential, diffuses through the air, and as it reaches us we sigh inwardly and sneak conspiratorial glances at each other. He sits at the piano and begins to sing.

His voice seeps into the cracks of our arid good sense – who knew it was this porous? – and makes us realize how thirsty we have been for the sound of desire. We are entranced by the melody and do not understand its power; it twists its way into the very core of our being, pulsing its way along our neurons and dancing with our hormones. For each of us, he is the ideal man. We want him to make love to us. We each want him to sing to us in private, we each want to be the only one for him.

Sometimes he looks at us, and when he does it is as if the song has taken hold of our spine and begun to slither around it, like a sine wave.

It takes us a while to acknowledge the waiter who asks us if we'd like some coffee.

Nichelle says yes, we would like coffee.

And all the while we sip our coffee, he sings his way into our souls.

Later, when he is gone, and the other, older, singer has replaced him, we pay the bill. Francoise gets us a discount for simply mentioning the restaurant on Instagram. We secretly think that what she has done is tacky. And yet not.

You know, says Suzie, *this has been the perfect evening. Don't you think? Good friends. Good food. Good wine.*

Definitely, says Adele.

If only we could somehow capture it, Gita says, *and bottle it and…*

Sell it, adds Francoise, with a laugh.

Fran! says Gita. *Honestly. What are you like? But if we could bottle it somehow, we could then get it out from time to time, couldn't we? And take a great big whiff of it when we needed to, you know, remember, and be comforted.*

Now there's a thought, says Nichelle.

And we begin to tease her, telling her that maybe she should forget about her work on those horrible hybrids (she ignores the slur) and does as Gita suggests.

She laughs good-naturedly and Francoise takes a last group selfie before we leave the restaurant.

Until next month, we call to each other. *There's always Facebook, of course, but real life is best.*

We each take our middle-aged desire – the one he has ignited, the one no one in society wants to acknowledge – home with us. To our barely awake or absent husbands, our sleeping daughters and sons. We do not know what to do with it. It will not go away. So we take the yearning into bed with us. We picture his face and remember his scent; it gathers at our necks and breasts and between our legs. We hear his voice in our ears and it becomes fluid; it seeps into our skin and couples with the hormones still dancing through our bloodstream. We picture him there at the piano. We see ourselves in his arms. We feel him kiss us, and we imagine him there, where our hands are. Between our thighs. And we cry out when we feel him inside us.

It is at this point that our Significant Other releases us from that reality.

"Wakey wakey," says Frank, extracting the memory beads from our heads. We are at the Hybrid Farm. In our replenishment pods.

"Enjoyed your night out?"

"What night out?" we say.

"It's always the same," he says with a sigh, placing the beads in a jar labelled: *Adele, Gita, Francoise, Nichelle, Suzie: 2027 [collective memory] 46-5 (Evening at a London restaurant.)* He runs a hand through his grey hair. "You never remember it afterwards," he says, "but I always like to ask. Just in case."

"Just in case, what?" we ask.

"In case you're more human than you look. Or can remember." He suddenly laughs as he places the jar on the shelf where it usually lives. Amidst the thousands of other jars. "Donated decades ago," he mutters. "Those girls are long dead now, bless 'em."

More loudly, to us, he says, "Or in case you ever want to rise up against the Elites who made you this way. Figure out that you're really individuals, with your own destinies."

We ask him to elaborate, but he never does. So we get up, out of the pods, and return to our work. Some of us look after the humans, the other humans, the Elites have rejected – those that will likely become hybrids, like us. And some of us do the unpleasant, unsafe and tedious jobs that the Elites refuse to undertake.

We think about what Frank has said, but we do not understand what he means. Sometimes, though, when we catch Frank cleaning our pods, humming a tune to himself, we experience a pleasant sensation. The oldest humans call it *a memory*, and it makes us pause for a moment as it snakes its way through our neural networks, making us feel as though someone, an "other" is inside us. Within our fleshy, metalloplastic bodies. But no, we say to ourselves. That cannot be. That cannot be. And so we return to our work.

Bar Hopping for Astronauts
Leo X. Robertson

Dodgy bars, like this one, sport fake women and real bartenders. The opposite of what a mostly male clientele want. But the astronaut isn't picky anymore. Besides, he doesn't much mind the prospect of spending an evening in the company of robostrippers, their skins torn and peeling, the ragged mechanics of their limbs peering through. Decay into obsolescence merely adds to their humanity.

He finds a stool at the bar's far end and sits, leaning his rubber-sheathed elbows on the counter's stinking wood. Govcams on the walls turn to him, but amber rings of light around their lenses signify inactivity. 'Manually disabled' no doubt, by local glowlife gangs.

Flies buzz lazily between beer puddles. A blonde woman shoots him a sneering glance as she walks back to her posse of friends, all of them with glossy hair and clear heels. They gossip in tight circles, their thin voices needling in his ears. Through the chip in his head, he mentally pings a noise reduction to his helmet, reducing their sound by fifty percent.

The middle-aged bartender approaches, his metallic pupils glowing, bloodshot streaks firing out across his corneas. Black market implants – for what purpose, the astronaut doesn't know.

The bartender doesn't react to the astronaut's suit or to the darkened smartglass visor covering his face. If people asked about that stuff here, the clientele would vanish. He says something, muffled words with a rising inflection.

The astronaut de-mutes.

"Drink," the bartender says, miming a glass.

"Do you do Lunar Juleps?" he asks.

"We might've lost it a few barware updates ago, but I'll check." He eventually returns with a dirty highball of slime-green fluid.

The astronaut dips his finger into the glass and his glove sucks it all up. Nanites metabolize the alcohol for him before the drink even reaches his bloodstream. Nanites are many things, but fun isn't one of them.

As the astronaut tries to place the highball back on the bar without causing a fuss, he feels people looking at him funny. The gecko pad of his palm sticks to the glass like Velcro. He carefully unpeels it.

The bartender sighs. "What the hell are you doing here?"

"Huh?"

"By the looks of your suit you must be, what, late sixties? Try the Caloris District. You know Tycho Singles? That's more your speed."

The astronaut shakes his head. "They don't let me in with the helmet on."

"Then take it off."

"I can't!"

"I'm not babysitting some dementia-ridden old coot, okay? I'll do you this one last courtesy. Then be on your way." The bartender eyes up the suit. "I can see the flap for the emergency cord from here. The red one, right? Here, I'll get it –"

The astronaut bats the hand away. He turns and pushes through the throng, heading back outside.

He catches his breath in the street. Snow stills the air, quelling the city noise. Teens pass him by, shooing pesky ad drones that quiz them about alcohol consumption and sexual appetites. Strumpbots stand at regular intervals, maximally optimizing the sidewalk's revenue without intruding upon one another's territory.

White clouds of vape juice bloom before him and the nanites, alerted to this anomaly, replicate the smell for him in his helmet. Cotton candy, mingling with poor quality weed.

Red light shimmers off the astronaut's visor. It settles on his chest as a flickering laser dot. He traces its source to the thick black bangle of a glowlife with a blonde quiff, who leans on a nearby defunct autocab.

"Pew pew!" the glowlife says, making finger guns.

The astronaut flinches.

A woman in the glowlife crew laughs. She has studs of metal pierced seemingly at random across her face. Braids of light in her hair stream rainbow colours. Dog holos caper around her poodle skirt. "He actually thought you were firing at him! Old man, you think that's possible?"

"What's his suit all about?" says the third guy in the posse. A green animated graffiti tag shimmers on his muscle tee and red biotats of demons smirk on his deltoids.

Quiff cocks his head. "Is that the Vitus New Moon model?"

"What's Vitus?" Poodle Skirt says. "Oh, wait." She sings the Vitus jingle: *"Overcoming limits of biology/Colonising space with technology!"*

"Weren't those ads from like the seventies?" Biotats says.

"Dude, how old are you?" Quiff says.

The astronaut can't help himself. The words bubble up inside him. "I-I was on the moon."

"Hah!" Quiff says. "Who wasn't? I was there last week."

"I got back yesterday," Biotats says.

Poodle Skirt spits. "You can take the suit off now."

The astronaut walks away, but Quiff grabs his shoulder, takes out a blade and slices the suit open.

In a reflex, the astronaut slaps his hand over the opening.

"Sorry," Quiff says, "did I breach your suit?"

The friends rush over and tug at the rip, tearing the suit all over. The astronaut wrestles them off and runs away, their mocking laughter trailing behind him.

Sleek-looking autocabs roll up beside him and open their doors. "Sir," they say, "you look tired. May I assist?"

He doesn't live far away enough to risk falling victim to a hacked cab's kidnapping protocol or worse, so he walks all the way home in the snow.

He arrives home with the suit almost completely peeled off, revealing the t-shirt and long underwear he has on beneath. The suit doesn't know what to do, and self-repair only causes further damage. After all, if this were space, the astronaut would be dead by now. Its warning sirens blare inside the helmet, ringing madly in his ears.

He screams, clawing at the suit. Nanites in the material melt its torn edges, reaching out at each other in silvery threads, trying to knit the seams back together. But the tears are too big, the nanites too far from one another. As programmed, they try to stick the suit to his skin. In ultra-critical conditions, better to create any kind of seal and let a patch of skin get frostbite or sunburn than to do nothing and risk a fatality. That's the theory in space. Here on Earth, melted polymer scalds his chest. He tugs the suit off and leaves it in scraps on the floor.

He walks through to his living room, tearing away the t-shirt and picking strips of burnt rubber off his naked torso.

"Sir! Were you assaulted?" Jenny's voice comes from the ceiling's speaker. "We ought to file a report –"

The astronaut waves his hand. "Don't fuss."

"It's no fuss, sir," she says. "I'm not real."

"I know, Jenny. You don't have to remind me."

He sits on the edge of his couch, balancing the helmet so it doesn't fall. Empty foodule packets litter the table in front of him and dirty boot prints coat the carpet.

As his adrenaline subsides, the apartment's chill rushes over him. He hadn't noticed how comfy the suit was, how like a second skin. Its sensations had become a sensory background noise. Now, he's palpably bare.

Out the window, a haze of neon blends the buildings together, a dim redness on the horizon revealing the outline of so many concrete blocks all seemingly fused into one.

One last scrap of the suit flops off his shoulder. He examines it with a sorry glance. Nanite threads glint silver. In space, they bridged together throughout the suit to keep it firm during pressurization. They agglomerated where needed across the suit's many membranes. Made repairs. Relayed biomedical data. Vaporized micrometeoroids. Expelled carbon dioxide and water vapor. They strung together into synthetic veins, sending cooling water coursing across his skin. They eradicated dead cells and other detritus from his surface, and other excreta from elsewhere.

He goes to the window and opens the delivery box. Shiny foodule packets spill to the floor. Out of habit, he picks one up and squeezes it. That was usually all it took for nanites to suck out the juices and inject nutrients into him like reverse mosquitoes. Not anymore.

He closes the box and orders some pyjamas on its touchscreen.

"Connect me to Vitus support team please?" he asks his visor.

Ellipses flash inside the visor as it makes the call for him.

A smiling cartoon face appears. "Hi!" says a female voice. "Did you mean to reach me? I heard something about Vitus."

"Yeah, I need repair for a New Moon."

"Sorry sir, we no longer offer support for that model. May I order you a replacement?"

"I can't afford that. I couldn't even afford my Vitus. They gave it to me after I –"

"Would you like to hear more about our latest, the Tharsis? It's a flexible and durable polymer suit with —"

"I want to go back inside! Now!"

"Sir, yelling isn't good for your health. Just saying. I don't mind it, of course. I'm not real."

He pulls the helmet off and throws it to the floor. Instead of smashing, it dents the wooden boards with a *dunk*.

"Sir?" the AI says.

He leans on the wall, sliding down, hugging his knees. The suit kept his skin young, supple, hairless.

"Intruder! Intruder!" Jenny says.

He looks to the ceiling. "Settle down, Jenny. It's still me."

"Voice recognition confirmed, sir. Glad to see you again. You look different! New haircut?"

He feels the perfectly trimmed bald pate. It seems to itch only now the nanites have gone. "Good different?" he says.

"Why not see for yourself?"

He grits his teeth, then gets up and heads to the bathroom.

"By the way," Jenny says from her speaker in the tiled wall, "you forgot your pills again, silly billy."

The mirror spits a handful of green liquid capsules onto a ceramic dish.

"Thanks, Jenny." He picks one up and squeezes it with thumb and forefinger, again to no avail. He sighs, winces, and looks at his face.

He'd seen warped glimpses on the visor's inner surface, or reflected dimly in puddles and shop windows sometimes, but always softened by the smartglass' resting darkness setting. The unmasked thing is something else. Sunken eyes. Thin lips. Incipient jowls. Wrinkles like deep gouges sliced across his forehead.

"Handsome as ever, sir," Jenny says.

"Well Jenny," he says, "that's the visor off. All my settings are disabled. You might as well tell me the year now. I can't block it out."

"You sure?"

"Yep."

She tells him.

His mouth gapes, revealing pale, receding gums. "I've been in that suit for twenty-two years?"

"Yup."

He shrugs. "Time flies when you barely leave the house."

"Would you like to know anything else? How about the latest water shortage on Mars? Want to know what happened with that organ cloning scandal? There's talk of a new viral epidemic in a biohab –"

"That's enough crisis for one day, thanks. I'm going to bed."

Light wakes him up. It's Jenny, warming him with an artificial sun from the screen in his bedroom ceiling.

He groans. "Disengage protocol, Jenny!"

"I may only have seen your new face for fourteen hours and twenty-six minutes," Jenny says, "but to my vast knowledge base, most humans don't display an expression *that* consistently sad. Especially not in their sleep. So come on, get up."

He slams a pillow over his face.

"Sir?" Jenny says. "I was thinking. I'm not real, but I do think."

The pillow muffles his words. "Again, Jenny, I know how this works."

"Great! Look, you know I would never wish you any harm. I'm literally incapable of doing so. But maybe what happened to you wasn't the worst."

"I don't want to hear this right now."

"But it might do you some good, and that's what I'm here for!"

He stays quiet.

"I thought of something that might cheer you up. Go look in your delivery box!"

He lies there, immobile. Jenny ramps up the light intensity until it makes an unhealthy whining sound.

"Fine!" He gets up, tosses the pillow aside and heads to the living room.

In the box are the clothes he ordered yesterday and a clear vacuum bag with a pre-sliced pizza inside, squished until its orange oils run into the plastic's creases.

He reaches for the t-shirt and joggers but withdraws his hand like he just touched an iron. The screen on the box reads *60°C*.

"To keep the pizza toasty!" Jenny says. "And I had it ordered in that bag so your clothes wouldn't smell."

"Very considerate of you, Jenny."

He unzips the bag, its plastic relaxing, and slides the pizza onto the table. Its smell is familiar and distant.

He tugs at the crust, dislodges a slice and –

"Ow!"

"Sir?"

"I forgot how to use my tongue."

"Well – take care!"

"Okay, okay!"

He tries again. Mozzarella melts over his taste buds, accompanied by a tang of tomato sauce. He bites down on a crunchy piece of pepperoni, burnt a little on the edges, but it hardly matters. "Mm!"

"What do you think?"

"This is amazing!" he says between chews.

"I'm glad!"

A piece falls out of his mouth. He smiles up at the ceiling. "I need more eating practice, though. What will we try next?"

"Oh, I'm so happy this worked, sir! We'll try whatever you want!"

He frowns. "Wait, wait."

"What is it?"

He grimaces. "Can you show me a video of someone putting on clothes? Project it onto one of the walls once you've got it."

"Uh, sir, did you mean 'Taking off clothes'? I know this is the first time you've requested such a thing, but as always, I'm not a real person. Couldn't judge you if I wanted to."

"Ugh." He looks up at the ceiling as he goes back to the box, lifting the clothes out and brandishing them accusatorily at Jenny. He shuffles out the long underwear, puts the t-shirt on backwards and nearly falls over when slipping on the joggers. He crosses his legs on the floor and catches his breath.

"Sir, was that necessary? Please be strong enough to clarify your requests for help in future."

"Yes, Jenny."

"Back to it then?"

"Yeah. Hey, get me a coffee!"

It's not long before a drone buzzes by, dropping an insulated pouch into the box.

He opens the door from the inside and takes the pouch to the kitchen, where he pours its contents into the one clean glass he used to top up his hydration. Out of habit, he dips his finger into the brown liquid.

"Ouch!"

His skin is tender, like it's missing a few layers. More than a few.

He takes a sip. "Delicious!"

"Cool! What now?"

"Surprise me!"

Over the next few hours, Jenny delivers an assortment of test objects.

He thumbs books and savours the crisp feel of their freshly printed paper. He spritzes himself in the face with a cologne bottle, catching himself in the eyes, but the scent of citrus and sandalwood seems worth it. He even sticks his finger in a little plastic prank toy that gives him an electric shock.

"Play me some music!" he asks Jenny.

"What kind?"

"Anything, anything!"

Noise blares into the room. It sounds like static from an old radio that's clattering around in a washing machine.

"What the hell, Jenny? I said 'music.'"

"It's from a local stream," she says like a partner taking offense on behalf of her choice.

"No, no, give me – jazz. Play me some jazz."

The reedy sound of a saxophone fills his ears and notes from a double bass reverberate around the living room. The soft hiss of drum brushes makes his skin shiver. He grips his head, closes his eyes and grins. His eyes flicker open and he bolts to the window, unlocking the latch and pushing back the glass.

"Sir, no!"

"Relax." He sticks his head out.

Drones buzz by like big cicadas. A nearby advert simulates the sound of a rushing waterfall. Several stories below, autocabs shout robotic warnings at pedestrians.

The breeze rushes over his face. It's thick as a blanket and pungent with smog, but he doesn't care.

"What is it, sir?" Jenny asks.

He's crying now. "It's wonderful."

Sensory exploration soon begets the difficult work of relearning old habits. The nanites have gone, they can't baby him anymore. He has to shower, brush his teeth, clip his nails and shave without nicking himself.

Days and weeks pass in frustration. Soon, he's back in bed again, refusing to get up.

Jenny beams her light over him. "Sir, it's time to wash the sheets. It's been over a month since suitgate. You're entraining dirt everywhere."

He's silent.

"I had another idea if you wanna hear it?"

"You're just gonna tell me anyway."

"Remember Tycho Singles?"

He pushes the sheets back like an insolent teen. "What about it?"

"Why not go back there? It still has a consistent four-point-two rating, above average for the area. You used to love it back when –"

"I was young, happy, famous, successful and rich. Cheers, Jenny."

"Oh please."

He shuts his eyes in thought and pinches the bridge of his nose. "I've passed by there before. It used to be young and happening. Looks like the same crowd have hung around there for decades. So now it's –"

"Still an age-appropriate place for a gent like yourself?"

He kicks the covers off and looks at the ceiling. "You getting cheeky with me?"

"Did I violate a boundary? Are you dissatisfied with your service? Because I can always –"

"It's fine. I like it."

"Good. Because I took just oooone more additional liberty."

"Did you now."

"Go take a look in the box!"

Her autotuned squeal grates in his ears.

"Fine!" He gets up and heads to the living room.

In the box is a full tuxedo and black bowtie.

"Jenny, can you tell me your budget settings again?"

"Of course, but why?"

"You think I can afford fancy clothes and expensive cocktails?"

"Not all the time." Jenny adopts the tone of a benevolently scheming wife trying to sound nonchalant. "But you deserve to celebrate your progress."

Tuxed up, he hesitates as he approaches the facial recognition scanner at Tycho Singles – but it gives him the green light and invites him in. He reaches up to feel the helmet, but it's long gone now.

Tycho is much nicer than the last bar he chose for himself. Ornate cornices, white pillars, bronze light fixtures.

As he walks in, his new dress shoes clacking pleasantly on the lacquered hardwood floor, he notices how much lower tech the bar is than the average locale. There's a champagne fountain holo here, an android waiter there, but not much. Surely because of the clientele. All around, sophisticated elders on dates sit around tables of expensive marble.

Why would he want to hang out with all these old people?

Oh. Right. He's one of them.

He approaches the bar and sits down. A woman nearby catches his eye. She has delicate wrinkles under her eyes and her hair is in a high silvery do. Placid waves roll over the fabscreen of her dress.

He stares at the marble counter, too nervous to make an introduction.

"What'll it be, sir?" A bot-tender in a white tux wheels himself over. Its head is a gunmetal cylinder and a screen on the front shows its few emotions in technicolour pixels. "A quiet type, eh? I can offer you a recommendation."

He nods.

A green circle loads to completion on its face. "For an esteemed gent like yourself? A Lunar Julep." A door opens on its chest and a silver cup appears. A small tap deposits the julep inside, and the bot-tender places it on the table.

The cup gathers frost. He reaches out to touch it, startled by how cold it feels. He peers at the green liquid within and brings his index finger to its surface before remembering. He stops and, as practiced, raises the drink to his lips with both hands, taking a sip.

He coughs.

"Sir? You don't like it?"

"It's fine, it's just – got a kick." Alcohol rushes straight to his brain. "Whew!"

"I recognize that voice, sir," the bot-tender says. "Have you been here before?"

He lowers his head. "A long time ago."

"I thought so. I'm examining some photos of us from the seventies." Its blocky eyebrows pinch in a frown. "Huh. You sure looked different. You're wearing something weird. Do you remember? There are all these women crowded around you. You were sitting about where you are now. But you had much more company back then."

"I don't really wanna talk about it."

The bot-tender leans in. "Well I can't just leave you here."

"Yes, you can."

"It makes the other patrons awkward. If you want to sit here, we have to talk about *something*."

They're both silent.

"Hey," the bot-tender says, "you were in pay grade XZ back then. Impressive!"

"I can take it from here." The wave-dressed woman has a sultry, gravelly voice. "What brings you to Tycho?"

He dares to meet her eyes briefly, then looks back at the counter. "I'm, uh, supposed to be celebrating."

"Cheers to you, then." She raises her martini. "May I ask the occasion, Mr...?"

The words form in his throat. The stream of all he's ever been before. He stifles it, his face contorting with worry.

"Sir!"

He turns.

It's the scanner on the door, addressing someone outside. "I can't let you in if you insist on covering your face."

On the street is a man in a grass-green Vitus New Moon. The helmet's visor is dark, his shoulders slumped.

"Friend of yours?" the woman says.

He smiles at her. "Just might be. Excuse me for a moment?"

She nods and he walks back to the door.

"I used to come here all the time!" says the astronaut in the green suit.

"We both did," he says.

The visor swivels, fishbowling all it reflects.

Who's that old guy in the tux? Oh, it's him.

"I don't know you," the astronaut says.

"Yes, you do. You just don't recognize me." As he approaches, the chip in his head illuminates the surname *Zhang* on the suit.

Zhang looks down at his chest. His shoulders square and relax. "I haven't seen it do that in a long time. Who are you?"

"Bob Jones?" Bob says. It sounds painfully ordinary out loud, but it's his name nonetheless.

The astronaut takes some tint out the smartglass visor. The tired face of an elderly Asian gent appears, his hair thinning and silvery with nanites. "It *is* you! What were you, an engineer?"

Bob nods.

The astronaut taps his chest. "Mike Zhang. I was an architect, see? Green suit!"

"I remember."

"Am I glad I ran into you! No one else gets it anymore. The importance of what we did, that is." He bumps Bob on the arm with a fist. "Okay, fine, these days there are colonies all over, but *we* made the moon habitable, man. We were pioneers!" Mike looks at the bar. "They used to let me in here dressed like this when we came back. You remember?"

Bob nods.

Mike pats his chest. "People went to bed with me while I was in this suit." He smiles. "Felt like it would be that way forever."

Bob puts his hand on Mike's shoulder. "Now it's almost like it never happened." The suit warms his hand as nanites cross its external membrane to assess the threat.

"But w-we're trailblazers," Mike says. "We got to do more than most ever could."

"At the time." Bob smiles sympathetically.

Mike mirrors the smile. "Yeah." A thought makes him shudder with excitement. "What are you doing now? Let's go talk about the mission! Hey, remember that time we thought we'd lost two whole oxygen bottle racks? Or when Montero welded himself to an airlock and we thought he'd die if we tried to remove him?" He made fists of his hands. "What do you say? Wanna go grab a drink somewhere else?"

Bob bites his lip. He looks at Mike, then back to the bar, where the wave-dressed woman raises her glass to him.

"If it's okay with you," Bob says, "I think I'll go back inside."

In Aeternus
Phillip Irving

You are still smiling when I open my eyes, but everything else is forgotten. Foggy, the remnants. Like a dream dissolved on waking.

A quiet room: a single bunk; a screen on the wall showing a progress bar flashing complete; an open door beside the screen and the light from the hallway spilling through it.

Disorientation is the first symptom. Memory is associative; it takes time for the replicated synapses to activate.

Lightweight jumpsuits hang in an alcove beside the doorway. The corridor beyond is deserted. Strip lights flicker. The faint smell of disinfectant. No alarm; no flashing lights. But something is missing. There should be…

…a book. Photos. Family. These things will speed up the process. Reactivate synaptic pathways. Remind you of…

…our apartment. A mezzanine bedroom overlooking the lounge. A kitchen diner. Table and chairs we chose together…

…Your face. Still smiling. Whenever I close my eyes. But only when I close my eyes.

Something awful has happened.

The empty corridor and its flickering light. The Aeternus logo, solemn and bland. I have seen these things before. Something is wrong.

Double doors open onto a longer corridor, perpendicular. The flat tone of monitoring alarms from some of the rooms; the buzz and splutter of struggling aircon; the *tick tick tick* of strip lights starting to fail.

Another logo, the sign underneath it, "Upload Room", pointing left, the arrow circled in red.

My stomach growls painfully. I recall roast-beef dinners; shellfish with garlic and butter that dribbles; cheeseburgers, delicious and simple and perfect.

I groan, and let my feet lead me in the direction of the arrow. I try to remember. I try to think. Open doorways loom dark like maws. Operating tables, gurneys, beds. Some of them empty. Some of them

265

not empty. Limbs peep from sheets. Faces stare under fabric. Pale and still. There is no smell. No smell at all.

Double doors; another corridor. Broader; dazzlingly bright. The logo again, and another sign with a red-brown ring around the arrow. The ring is smeared, crusted. I don't check what it is.

Not just hunger: my stomach *hurts*; my breathing is ragged. *Exertion should be avoided for the first couple of days while the host body adapts.* This is too much, too soon. I need rest. But something is wrong.

More doors. More rooms, some of them empty. A man with short dark hair, slumped in a chair before a wall-screen, eyes forever open on an ocean sunset. Another in a room further on, collapsed before a vending machine with no lights. A third, in a room with soft music, arms folded across its chest, eyes closed so that were it not for the waxen pallor of its skin it might be just listening.

A fourth, a few doors on, slumped before a dressing table. It is his expression that nudges my memory awake. Glaring at the mirror, like he is afraid to lose sight of himself. It is my own dark hair. My own lines and angles. The same as those forever stilled in the rooms I've passed.

I retch but there's only water and whatever they fill us with before we wake. Blood, when I cough, but not much.

A shuddering breath; my hands spasm. It's coming back to me now. Something is wrong. I must reach the Upload Room.

I walk. Something awful has happened. Something too awful to comprehend. The knowledge lurks but will not come. Instead, the recollection of a hundred such walks; a thousand. Of frustration; helplessness. Something awful has happened. Something huge. I want to remember. I want to forget. But the knowledge will not come.

Ahead, the door. Red-brown on the handle, a shade darker than the sputum on my hand. Inside, the dream that dissolved on waking.

There are dozens of me. Blood and froth at the corners of their mouths. Flesh, and copper, and something worse, cloying in the air. An open hatch empty and ominous in the far wall, "Disposal", in calm green letters above it. The upload chair, vacant and ready, cranial band gleaming in the hard light. "Warning" flashing beneath the Aeternus logo on the wall-screen, with no exclamation mark to make it real.

Blood when I cough spatters my hand, the wall, the one of me slumped at my feet. *Side effects may include nausea, dizziness, loss of vision, haemorrhage, death.* Something awful has happened, but there's no time to remember what. I have to start again. Maintain the cycle. Until someone can put it right.

I sit back in the chair and affix the band to my forehead. A buzz, a numbing crackle, then a beep and it retracts, the warning message on the screen replaced by a progress bar starting at zero.

Once the upload is complete, a sedative will be administered before any organic matter is recycled.

My legs, arms, tremble. There's no anaesthesiologist here. I wonder how many moments pass, usually, before oblivion comes. What final thoughts are lost to eternity as the old self dies and the new self wakes.

I roll from the chair and look at the door, the corridor beyond, then back at the mess of the room. I manage to wrestle two of me into the hatch before my body rebels and I collapse, quivering from head to toe. I look at the screen, the slowly climbing progress bar, and I wonder if it will work better this time around. If it will give me more time. If it will let me remember. If I want it to.

I push the disposal button and carefully trace a bloody ring around it with my index finger as it begins to whir. I wonder, idly, if the suits are recycled along with the flesh.

Then I rest. Something awful has happened. But the knowledge will not come. All I can do is start again. Maintain the cycle. Hope that, next time, someone can put it right.

When I close my eyes, you are still smiling.

A Spark in a Flask

Emma Johanna Puranen
Based on Research by Patrick Barth

"Life, although it may only be an accumulation of anguish, is dear to me, and I will defend it." – Mary Shelley, *Frankenstein*

The Self-sufficient Primordial Atmosphere Robotic Caretaker begins the 197,855th entry on the log. By signing, it certifies that – among other things – it is aware of the location of the nearest eyewash station and it knows liquid nitrogen can cause tissue damage or burn hazards to humans. Signing is almost a formality, as the most recent entry that does not bear SPARC's name is the twelfth – but SPARC is programmed to keep good records.

Finished, it trundles on down the corridor. The small rolling robot squeaks from friction every 2.3 seconds when the bent tread in its right rear wheel makes contact with the floor. SPARC notes the squeak. A subroutine evaluates and deems the abnormality to have no impact on performance, recommending against an unnecessary repair. It passes a pair of porthole windows, the first of many on this corridor, which is itself just one spoke radiating out from the centre of the wheel-shaped base. The portholes are a peculiar design quirk suggesting the builders anticipated more visitors than the base ended up receiving – visitors who might like to view the experimental Flasks, visually dull as they are. The windows serve no other purpose. SPARC can't see through them unless it raises its camera, which would be a waste of energy. The robot is linked to the base's main Computer and knows the precise chemical composition of each Flask's atmosphere in far more detail than could be determined from peering through to see only an empty room with some water inside.

Affixed to the wall is a piece of paper. Three human faces, those of engineers who helped build the base in the days before SPARC's log began, smile out as they stand in front of a porthole. The photons of light that reflected off the engineers and into a camera lens so long ago shine on in fading ink. *IT'S ALIVE? MASSIVE MOONBASE*

269

FACILITY TO SEARCH FOR SPARK OF LIFE. When Stanley Miller and Harold Urey simulated conditions they believed to match those of the early Earth's atmosphere in a 5-litre flask in Chicago in 1952, they could not have imagined they were setting into motion events that would culminate in their project's descendent blasting off into orbit high above the Earth. To the surface of the moon, in fact. Despite naysayers raising concerns about everything from the development of bioweapons to deadly diseases to the wrath of usurped gods, funding has been allocated for – A tear line halts the article.

It's been a while since SPARC has ventured down this arm of the massive base. Physical maintenance isn't needed very often – not since the humans left – and there is only one of SPARC. Very little ever changes here.

That's why the moon is the perfect site for this experiment. It's a stable environment, completely controllable. The moon has no wind to blow down power lines, no floods to ravage data centres, no storms at all, unless the tiny, tame little sparks of lightning in the room-sized Flasks count. The rugged, silent surface outside sits largely unchanged since soon after the solar system's birth, when it coalesced from a swirly disc of debris, spooled together by gravity after a collision with the young Earth. Craters mark a fiery youth, but their pristine walls and unerringly circular shapes speak equally to the stillness of this place. Especially when compared with the mottled chameleon-like face of the planet below, ever reclothing itself in veils of white clouds and storms of dust and deep dark blues. Since the base was built, the whites have become rarer, the blues contain less green, and the browns are more common.

In stark contrast to the vacuum outside, the Flasks are ever-changing. Each holds some combination of hydrogen, nitrogen, oxygen, methane, carbon dioxide, and ammonia – usually not all at once – each a unique tweak on this mix, each attested to by the very best in computer modelling as a promising brew. Computer makes changes as necessary, sometimes replenishing with elements the humans brought from Earth at the beginning, though usually using those mined from the lunar regolith by the other robots that, unlike SPARC, go outside. With nothing living, nothing consuming, no creatures to cause shortages or disturb the equilibrium of the base, resources are not a problem.

SPARC, being well-versed in tests for life, has run these tests on itself and the other machines on the base. While the machines function on solar energy, like plants, they are incapable of reproduction or evolution. Therefore, SPARC concludes that neither it nor the other machines are alive. Living things have some strengths that SPARC lacks, but they tend to be ill-suited for multi-tasking, which SPARC excels at. For instance, as it wheels towards the Flask with the maintenance issue, the one it's here to fix, it evaluates an old video file as part of its memory management protocol.

Mission Day 5: Cross shrugs off the heavy outer layers of her spacesuit, talking to Jeong at an elevated volume over the noise of SPARC sucking up tracked-in regolith in the corner. The two have just returned from a moonwalk.

"I didn't come all the way up here to have my view of Earth messed up by a foggy faceplate." Cross says.

Jeong laughs. "It's because you were breathing too hard after you did that weird dance."

Cross's face scrunches up. "My daughter would have killed me if I hadn't done it when I had the opportunity!"

"Well, you're welcome for filming."

"Speaking of…" Cross crouches next to SPARC, blocking Jeong from SPARC's camera's line-of-sight, though it sees him leave the airlock into the base proper via one of Computer's cameras. "Hey, little guy. Can you turn off your hoover? Thanks. I'd like to make a report. Mission Specialists Cross and Jeong successfully completed our moonwalk. We verified sample collection by the mining robots and will analyse composition results. On a more personal note, the Earth? It's damn beautiful from up here, even when blurry. They should've sent a poet – I think Jeong's gonna have a go at it with his watercolours, but… I've seen his work. Gosh, looking at it – I know why we're here, I get it, but – it's ironic that this lifeless rock is where we're trying to make new life."

She goes on like this for several more minutes, interjecting her science results with idiosyncratic and semi-related musings. It's fine for the informal report, meant mostly to help her collect her thoughts for a formal write-up later, but SPARC has trouble following how each line of Cross's thinking leads to the next.

For storage reasons, SPARC dumps this video from its own physical memory to Computer's.

A table stands before the next set of Flasks SPARC passes. Above it is a sign, scrawled in the slightly smudged font of a left-hander, reminding "PLEASE do not place anything on this work area, or it will require decontamination. We don't need another Mars-in-'42-style false alarm, folks! J." Nothing has required decontamination since the humans left. A yellow light shines above one of the next Flasks. This is not the one SPARC is here to investigate. A Flask forming amino acids is, at this point, routine, and Computer can monitor it and adjust the lightning strikes accordingly without SPARC's assistance. This finding has been recorded and sent to Earth in the base's daily report. SPARC determines a reply is statistically unlikely. There has not been one since the first amino acid result.

It's a long way from amino acids to life.

All down the corridor, all through the base, gases mix inside Flasks. Numerous shuffles of the deck, looking for the right combination. Static buzzes, lightning strikes the air with energy to break bonds and encourage change, leaving a stench of ozone that is smelt by no one. In the yellow-lit flasks, water dries and then is replenished, desiccating and hydrating to concentrate the precious amino acids, to nudge them to become more. If a Flask goes on too long with no results, Computer tries a new mix. It is not enough to just keep a Flask running. Life takes effort.

A red light shines above the porthole of Flask H40. SPARC halts, mid-squeak, and pivots its wheels ninety degrees. This is the site of the maintenance request.

Flask H40's last known atmospheric readings are several Earth days old. Computer cannot currently detect its contents – it's a dark zone on the base's map. Computer's sensor is fully operational, so something must physically be blocking its readings, as a lens cap left on a camera. For all of Computer's omniscience in cyberspace, all its ability to open and close doors and alter atmospheres, it is helpless in this task that requires precise physical manoeuvring. Therefore, it falls to the highly mobile SPARC.

SPARC enters the Flask's airlock, surrounded by the hiss of gases equalising, taking it from the airless vacuum of the corridor to the last known atmospheric contents of Flask H40. The inner door opens, and the robot turns its wheels – and its camera – into Flask H40.

Relying on its own native sensors is a foreign sensation for SPARC, learning about its environment in real time without the foresight of the computer. It finds itself following unused programming pathways. The last time SPARC was blind in this way was the day the humans left, when it spent time on their ship, which had a different Computer, to help with packing.

Mission Day 12: An envelope slips off the top of a tower of boxes Cross is carrying. It drifts slowly down in the lunar gravity, giving Jeong plenty of time to catch it.

"Careful, my paintings are in there!"

"Sorry." Cross grunts. "Here, SPARC, close this one up." She indicates an equipment box, and SPARC activates its power screwdriver. When it finishes its task, the two astronauts are staring out a window. SPARC is not tall enough to see, and does not have access to the transport ship's computer or cameras, but from its own internal orientation software it knows that Earth is visible out the window. It sits, awaiting instructions.

"You really think this'll work, Lysa?" Jeong asks.

"I don't know. But even if it doesn't, we'll have learned something valuable." Cross looks back at SPARC. "I suppose you're the one who's more likely to find out, bud! You ready to be a parent to some little microbes?"

"Why do you do that?"

"Do what?"

"Anthropomorphise SPARC." SPARC looks up Jeong's first, unfamiliar, word – it means attaching human characteristics to something that is not human.

"Hey, I can't help it. As soon as the project heads gave SPARC a name, I fell for it." Cross explains.

There is a brief quiet. SPARC performs a systems diagnostic in the background.

"You know, even if SPARC does find life, it's unlikely to be the same common ancestor that evolved into humans and other Earth life." Jeong's hand is under his chin.

Cross's voice pitches up. 'SPARC might become the parent to aliens! You'd need a new name, then, little guy, you wouldn't just be looking after primordial atmospheres anymore. You'd be looking after life."

Jeong points up a finger. "SPARCL!"

"Sparkle'?"

"Self-sufficient Primordial Atmosphere Caretaker of Life."

"Who's anthropomorphising now?"

SPARC's sensor warning blips – there is foreign material on its wheel tread. Not just water – SPARC is used to water. This is stickier, with inconsistent density. But the gunk does not prevent SPARC from moving forward.

The Flask's atmospheric sensor is not visible in SPARC's camera, but the robot knows from base maps exactly where it is located. The trouble is that where the smooth sensor surface should be, it spies instead a bumpy mass of green. With a whir and a swipe, SPARC delicately uncovers the sensor, scraping aside the gunk. Immediately, the robot freezes. Computer, and SPARC as its extension, take in a rush of updated data from the newly freed sensor – changes to the atmospheric composition contributed neither by Computer nor any known abiotic process, unanticipated gas exchanges, storage and replication of information.

Replication of the foreign material.

The red light above the porthole of flask H40 blinks off, then back on. This time, it glows green.

RECOMMEND SENDING MISSION SUCCESS REPORT. INDEPENDENT VERIFICATION REQUIRED FROM SPARC. The computer asks.

VERIFICATION CONFIRMED. DAY 197855 FLASK H40 ATMOSPHERE POSITIVE FOR LIFE.

The transmission is beamed to mission control on Earth, the packet of information-bearing waves of electromagnetic radiation traveling for a mere few seconds.

There is nothing more to do but wait.

SPARC sits among the densely packed air, among the water, perhaps not so different from the primordial tide pools of Earth, perhaps very far removed from them. Green gunk grows around it, consuming energy, expelling waste products, proliferating. Computer turns off the lightning generator, to protect SPARC's electronics. The little robot is stuck in Flask H40 – not due to any mechanical failure, but a failure of foresight. The maintenance robot being *inside* a life-positive Flask had not been anticipated, and now SPARC cannot leave without contaminating the rest of the base. Computer has no more decontamination supplies, not since the humans left. And so, SPARC waits for a response.

It does not come.

SPARC consults another old video file, this time for reference.

Mission Day 9: SPARC analyses several different isolated samples, cross-checking each against the International Astrobiological Congress's definition of life.

Cross examines its results. "Nice job, little guy! You got all but sample 5 – well, the host *in sample 5 is alive, but the* virus *isn't. But that's okay, viruses are sort of edge cases anyway." SPARC does not understand. The only values for life stored in its code are binary: 0 for no life, 1 for life.*

Cross explains. "Some people think viruses are alive, but the consensus is they aren't – they replicate, sure, but they need to use parts of their host cell to do it. They can't replicate outside the host. They don't grow. *They're a bit more like – well, like you. Like Computer." Cross's face changes. "Sorry, I didn't mean that! You're not a virus, SPARC!"*

SPARC fast forwards through the apology. It is not relevant; SPARC has no feelings to hurt.

"If I had to add something to the definition, I'd say… and it can't really be quantified scientifically… but, I'd say life has a burning desire to keep living, even when there are no good options. Life… proliferates."

The green gunk spreads over SPARC's wheels, taking hold on all its nooks and crannies, finding purchase, blooming, expelling. Computer sends out message after message to Earth, updates on the growth of the life of Flask H40. Still, there is no reply. Still, the lightning cannot strike. Still, SPARC waits.

One day, the growth slows. For all Computer tries to add ingredients to the recipe, to balance the seesaw of competing cycles of gas and water and growth – the gunk has outgrown the Flask. It has nowhere to go.

SPARC, weighed down by a carpet of new biomass, makes a recommendation to Computer. Computer responds with a warning blip, but SPARC is ready with the override code. It understands what the result will be. Its code contains no answer, so this is the answer. Override. Idiosyncrasy.

Life proliferates.

All through the base, in every arm, in every Flask, behind every porthole, water flows and atmosphere mixes to precisely match the conditions of Flask H40. It takes time – some nitrogen here, some methane there – until every sensor reports its Flask is ready. Air hisses into the corridors, too, for the first time since the humans left. It carries such force that SPARC can see the newspaper clipping flutter off the wall through one of Computer's cameras.

Simultaneously, the airlock doors open. Lightning strikes.

The bonds break.

A Pall of Moondust

Nick Wood

KwaZulu Natal, African Federation, 2035.

Blue sky: red dust.

Hamba kahle, grandfather, goodbye.

I sprinkled a handful of orange-red dust on his grave – yet another funeral cloth over your buried body, *Babamkhulu* – and, behind me, father did the same.

May your soul soar, old man with the sharp tongue and that mad dog, Inja.

And say hello to mother for me.

Shackleton Crater, Moon Base One, Lunar, 2037

I dreamed, and shook awake, as the two bodies flew away from me. *Dreams live.*

Scott is the one keying in the Airlock code, mouth O-ing in shock at the tug and hiss of escaping air behind her. "Helmets on," she says, but it is already too late, the door to the Moon behind her is wide as a monster's maw.

Bailey is fiddling with the solar array on the Rover, his helmet playfully dangled on the joystick for a second, before being sucked out and beyond my reach.

Scott pushes me backwards and the inner door closes, leaving me safe on the inside. *The wrong side?*

The Airlock explodes with emptying air and a spray of moon dust.

Two die, while I live.

I scour the darkness for something familiar, something safe.

Nothing.

I'm a lunar newbie, only Three Lunar Walks, and with my helmet already on, before we had even entered the airlock. *That's mandatory now – helmet* must *be on before airlock entry. Why then, does this darkness hang so heavy with my guilt?*

Medication drooped my eyelids, pulling me back towards the faulty doors and O-ing mouths, where I did *not* want to go.

No, not again, please...

277

Doctor Izmay eyed me over her desk-screen, and I yawned back at her, glancing at the red couch in the corner of her room labelled 'Sector 12 Psych'. *The bed is a cliché, surely, just for show?*

"Flashbacks still, Doctor Matlala?" she asked, raising a sympathetic eyebrow.

Her formality reminded me of father, but Izmay was a real woman of everywhere, German/Turkish/North African, a true shrink of the world.

I don't like shrinks.

But I had been taught well and avoided direct gaze with my elder, a swarthy white woman greying at the temples of her tightly bunned black hair.

She smiled, "Ah, a mark of respect for those older than you, in traditional Zulu custom."

Her eyes were grey-green, I stared in surprise.

"Like you, young woman, I do my homework," she said, "Do we need to titrate your medication and increase your dose?"

I hesitated, "I want to get back to my work in hydroponics, but the medication is making me drowsy."

"There's something else you need to do first," the woman leaned back, hesitant too, and dread surged inside me again. "You need to suit up and go back out onto the Moon."

"Uh – no. What's the point? I'm a botanist. *Nothing* grows out there."

The psychiatrist stood and walked towards the door, gesturing me to follow. "Necessary health and safety. You know the drill. We must all get comfortable on the surface of this Harsh Mistress. For you, that means getting back on your metaphorical horse and into the Airlock, just for starters."

I could not stand; my limbs were locked.

Doctor Izmay hauled out an injection pen and sighed, tapping it on her palm. "I agree. Your medication *does* need increasing."

The psychiatrist held my arm firmly as we approached the Airlock door and I was grateful for that, my legs starting to jelly.

"Slow your breathing," she said sharply. "Think of Durban beach."

I practiced our imagery work, heading into my safe mind-space, as she counted out a slowed pace for my breath. Hot white-yellow sand, pumping surf, blue bottle jelly fish and… sharks in the water?

"Helmet on," she said, but the airlock door in front of us was gaping like the jaws of a Great White.

I tripped over the two bodies they had brought back.

Scott and Bailey, suited and helmetless, darkened by a coat of regolith, with their eye sockets and tongues caked in the black dust that was everywhere.

"Stay with me Thandike," a voice said, "Breathe, one… two…"

But I have dropped the helmet in case it sucks me out.

I bend with suited difficulty, scraping the floor for moon dust that stinks like weak gunpowder, so as to sprinkle it respectfully on the bodies of Scott and Bailey.

So little to scoop up, so little to leave them in peace. *Why is it just I who live still?*

My eyes leaked with sorrow and guilt, so that I hardly felt yet another injection into my upper arm.

Where have their bodies gone? And are their shades happy?

"Survivor guilt is normal," Doctor Izmay told me.

This time she had me lying on her red leather couch, so that I did not have to look at her eyes. "You could have done *nothing* differently. It's not your fault."

Yes, I know that, so why do I still feel guilty?

"Tell me about your grandfather."

The command dropped onto my stomach like a lead weight. Even in Moon gravity, it felt heavy. *I prefer plants to words, any day.*

"He helped father raise me, after my mother died when I was very young," I struggled, "He died at ninety, the year before I got into the Lunar Programme. I wish I could have shown him my letter of acceptance."

"You still miss him?" Her voice was nearer, as if she'd shifted closer to me, on the seat behind the couch.

It was an obvious question, so I did not even bother to respond.

"Tell me more about him," Dr. Izmay tried again, "What do you miss the most?"

"No," I said, "It has no relevance here. I need to get back to the issue of efficient grain production in one sixth gee and filtered sunlight."

A noise clicked from behind the red couch, now sticky with stale sweat from my back. Above me, the ceiling slid open and I saw a window funnelled to the roof of the dome. Sharp stars cut down into my eyes, lancing slivers of light, with no atmospheric distortion to turn them twinkle friendly.

"The light from those stars is variously between four hundred and five billion years old," Dr. Izmay said, "They will fade with Earthrise imminent, but they won't disappear. They're still there, even when they're gone. Tell me about your grandfather."

"No," I said, eyes burning, so that I screwed them shut. *Stars are like my grandfather? Could I have been quicker to call 9-1-1, when his heart collapsed that day?*

"You've always done your best," Dr. Izmay's voice was even closer still, "In the end, with death, we can change nothing."

I opened my eyes and twitched with shock. She was bending over me from the back of the couch, eyes fastened on mine: "What was your grandfather's favourite phrase, when you were a teenager?"

"Get off that bloody couch and *do* something useful, *intombi*!" The words were out of my mouth before I could think.

Dr. Izmay was laughing, "Well?"

She had done her homework on me, very well indeed.

Today, my two moon-walking companions were to be Commander Baines and Space Tourist Butcher.

I had checked the records on both, the night before.

Baines had over four hundred walks under his buckled belt and had slid like a snake into his own suit, although bending stiffly to pick up his helmet and gloves. "I've got me your bio-signs on my screen visor here, so I'm keeping tabs on both of you. We're not going far. Just keep me in sight and do everything I tell you. Helmets On."

My heart pumped a surge of panic, but Butcher looked even more terrified.

It's his first time, at the ancient age of forty-six. I'm not the newest newbie here.

"Just breathe slowly," I told him, "Don't hyperventilate into your mouthpiece."

Dr. Izmay crackled into my ears as I fastened my helmet on. "Good. I'm patched in from remote too, Thandike. Looks like I might have to copyright that breathing line."

My chuckle took the edge off my dread.

Baines was already thumbing in the access code and I took up my position at the back. (Newbie in the middle, yet another reg. change, since the accident.)

"Fool proof new locking system," says Baines, bouncing through the opening Airlock door.

Butcher followed, more slowly and clumsily.

I stepped forward to support his PLSS backpack, preventing the novice from toppling backwards – as he momentarily backed away from the door, as if having had sudden second thoughts.

I may only be twenty-eight, but I know by now, that nothing *is ever fool proof… So what the hell am I doing stepping through this door myself?*

It's better than going home, for a start. It's taken me a long time and lots of hard work to get here, ahead of so much global competition. And, now that I'm here, I'm going to make sure I stay off that bloody couch. For you, Babamkhulu.

The door behind me closed and Baines was already busy on the external door, as if minimising our chances for anxiety to escalate. "Butcher, breathe, one, two…" I said, hearing a quick rasping in my ears.

"Ready for exit, decompression complete…"

Slowly, the outer door opened.

Hesitantly, we followed Baines' loping bounce out onto the surface of the moon.

We needed to step upwards slightly, as the door has been built low into a crater wall, to minimise solar radiation exposure.

I strode across to a large boulder to my right, keeping Baines in view. *How can it look so dark, with such a bright sun?*

Baines was a few steps further along, by a mound of broken rocks. *He moves so quickly, as if he doesn't even think about the steps he has left behind.*

"Both of you; take a look at that!" Baines' voice crackled as he raised an arm to point, along the horizon to our right.

The Earth shimmered low over the horizon – a largish blue-white ball floating above the lip of Shackleton's crater, where solar arrays in eternal sunlight bled back cheap and climate friendly energy to the planet.

I focused on Earth. *Where are the continents? Where is Africa?*

The blur of grey-white cloud smeared the blue-green oceans and brown earth across the globe. I could almost hear it spinning, swirling hot climate clouds across the face of the world.

It doesn't matter if I can't find Africa. From here, nothing is 'Great', nothing is 'Permanent'. For all of us humans alike, we have a melting, fragile pearl to protect.

"And look there!" Baines swivelled to point at the sky behind us.

I turned to peer in the deep darkness, where the stars were fading, a dull reddish pinprick burned.

"Mars, our next stop," said Baines.

The colour of the earth, with which we had covered grandfather.

Butcher and Baines continued to watch Mars, but I stared back at the sealed crater door. *No, surely not?*

"What's happening to your pulse and breathing, Thandike?" Dr. Izmay's voice bit into my ear.

I raise a gloved hand to take the edge off the solar glare. On the top-edge of the crater, near the dome roof, sat an old man with a knobkierie stick, with a dog by his side.

I knew better than to say anything, but walked back to Base slowly, testing my vision. The old man stood to wave and his voice quavered to me, across the vacuum: 'Proud to see you doing something so special and useful, *umzukulu*!'

Two space-suited figures hovered behind him. They waved once.

Inja barked, and when I blinked again, all of them had gone.

They had warned me to expect visual distortions in this alien land, where distance and depth were hard to judge – and shifting shadows played with your perception.

"What did you see, Thandike?" Doctor Izmay's voice echoed into my ears.

"Our home crater and the outer door."

I watch the soon to disappear stars above me, as sunrise approaches, to break the shorter lunar night.

I say a prayer, silently.

Behind me, Baines and Butcher have arrived, and so I finish my prayer.

Cunjani, grandfather, hello.

So, tell me, how is my mother?

Black sky: grey dust.

Inyanga, 2037
Ends

About the Authors

Keith Brooke is the author of fourteen novels, seven collections, and more than a hundred short stories; his work has been shortlisted for awards including the Philip K Dick Award and the Seiun Award. Writing teen fiction as Nick Gifford, he has been described by the *Sunday Express* as "The king of children's horror". His novel written with Eric Brown, *Wormhole*, will be published by Angry Robot in late 2022. You can find out more about Keith and his work at www.keithbrooke.co.uk

Born in Haworth, West Yorkshire, **Eric Brown** has lived in Australia, India and Greece. He has won the British Science Fiction Award twice for his short stories, and his novel *Helix Wars* was shortlisted for the 2012 Philip K. Dick Award. He's published over seventy books and his latest novel is *Murder Most Vile*, the ninth volume in the Langham and Dupré mystery series set in the 1950s. Forthcoming is the SF novel *Wormhole*, written with Keith Brooke. He lives near Dunbar in Scotland, and his website is at: ericbrown.co.uk

David Cleden is a Hampshire-based science fiction and fantasy writer whose work has appeared in venues such as *Analog, Interzone, Galaxy's Edge, Deep Magic, Cossmass Infinities, Metaphorosis*, and *Writers of the Future Volume 35*. He was the winner of the 2016 James White Award and the Aeon Award (2017) for new writers. Early in his career he worked in commercial Earth observation and satellite remote-sensing, which has left him convinced his to-be-read book pile must now be visible from low earth orbit. He has a website at www.quantum-scribe.com and can be found on Twitter as @davidcleden.

Paul Cornell has written episodes of *Elementary, Doctor Who* and many other TV series. He's worked for every major comics company, including his creator-owned series *I Walk With Monsters* for The Vault, *The Modern Frankenstein* for Magma and *Saucer State* for IDW. He's the writer of the *Lychford* rural fantasy novellas from Tor.com Publishing and the *Shadow Police* series from Tor. His SFF short stories have been collected in the book *A Better Way to Die*. He's won the BSFA Award for his short fiction, an Eagle Award for his comics, a Hugo Award for his podcast and shares in a Writer's Guild Award for his *Doctor Who*. He's the co-host of *Hammer House of Podcast*. His latest book is the gonzo SF novella *Rosebud*.

Gary Couzens lives in Hampshire. He has had stories published in *Fantasy & Science Fiction, Interzone, Black Static* and other magazines and anthologies, collected in *Second Contact and Other Stories* (Elastic Press, 2003) and *Out Stack and Other Places* (Midnight Street Press, 2015). Film reviews have been published in the *Blood Spectrum* column in *Black Static* and online at Cine Outsider. Gary edited *Extended Play: The Elastic Book of Music* (Elastic Press, 2006), which won the British Fantasy Award for Best Anthology, and co-edited *The Thing About Seventy: Celebrating Seventy Years of Rushmoor Writers* (Midnight Street Press, 2020).

Michael Crouch was born in Norwich, England in 1965. He trained in graphic design at the University of East Anglia and went on to work in the telecoms sector for over thirty-two years. Michael has had short stories and articles published across various genres and media, and has also created comic strips for the independent comics market. *The Trip* was first published in Fission volume 1 by the BSFA in 2021. Other works have been published in *Let's Talk* magazine (2020-22), *To End All Wars* (Soaring Penguin Press, 2014), and the *Blake's 7 Annual 1982* (Lulu, 2021).

T.H. Dray is a new voice in speculative fiction. She lives in Glasgow with her family, which, at last count, included five Staffordshire bull terriers and two other humans. When not writing, she works with a local charity to provide music education opportunities for all. She also enjoys reading things out loud (sometimes for money). Her work may be found in *BFS Horizons* and *Flotation Device*: a Covid-19 charity anthology. You can find her on Twitter @thdray1.

David Gullen is a writer and occasional editor. He has sold over 60 short stories to various magazines, anthologies and podcasts. *Warm Gun* won the BFS Short Story Competition in 2016, with other work short-listed for the James White Award and placed in the Aeon Award. David was born in Africa and baptised by King Neptune He has lived in England most of his life and been telling stories for as long as he can remember. He currently lives behind several tree ferns in South London with his wife, fantasy writer Gaie Sebold, and the nicest cat you ever did see. Find out more at www.davidgullen.com.

Russell Hemmell is a French-Italian transplant in Scotland, passionate about astrophysics, history, and Japanese manga. Recent/forthcoming work in *Aurealis, Cast of Wonders, Departure Mirror,* Flame Tree Press, *Lightspeed, Pseudopod* and others. They are a member of both SFWA & HWA. Their historical horror novella *The Chancels of Mainz* is now in print with Luna Press Publishing. Find them online at their blog earthianhivemind.net and on Twitter @SPBianchini.

Phillip Irving is a teacher and writer in Leicester, UK. He's influenced by a lifetime of Pratchett and Gaiman but writes like neither. He has had short fiction published by Flame Tree Press and Space Cat Press, among others. He's a member of Leicester Writers' Club and the Leicester Speculators writing group. When not writing or obsessing over grammar he can be found at home with his cat playing video games, or in his local pub, which his cat is also known to frequent. Twitterings can be found at https://twitter.com/irvingphil.

Emma Levin is an aspiring writer of comedy, sci-fi, and comedy sci-fi. Her short stories have appeared in magazines (*Shoreline of Infinity*), online (*Daily Science Fiction*), in anthologies (*England's Future History*), and in many recycling bins. She has received training in writing for broadcast through the BBC's Comedy Room writers' scheme, and some of her comedy writing has appeared in indie videogames (e.g. Ord) and on BBC Radio 4 (writing additional material for 'The Skewer'). She is currently based in Oxford, and can be found online at https://emmalevinwrites.com/

Tim Major's love of speculative fiction is the product of a childhood diet of classic Doctor Who episodes and an early encounter with Triffids. His books include weird SF novels *Hope Island* and *Snakeskins,* Sherlock Holmes novels *The Defaced Men* and *The Back to Front Murder,* short story collection *And the House Lights Dim* and a monograph about the 1915 silent crime film, *Les Vampires.* Tim's short fiction has been selected for *Best of British Science Fiction, Best of British Fantasy* and *The Best Horror of the Year.* Find him at www.cosycatastrophes.com and on twitter @timjmajor.

Fiona Moore is a two-time BSFA Award finalist, writer and academic whose work has appeared in *Clarkesworld, Asimov, Cossmass Infinities*, and three consecutive editions of *The Best of British SF*. Her publications include one novel, guidebooks to Blake's Seven, The Prisoner, Battlestar Galactica and Doctor Who, three stage plays and four audio plays. When not writing, she is a Professor of Business Anthropology at Royal Holloway, University of London. She lives in Southwest England with a tortoiseshell cat which is bent on world domination. More details, and free content, can be found at www.fiona-moore.com, and she is @drfionamoore on most social media platforms.

Andrew Myers (writing as A. N. Myers) is a North London based writer of speculative fiction. His recent short fiction credits include *BFS Horizons*, the Eibonvale Press Anthology *The Once and Future Moon*, *Sein Und Werden*, and the forthcoming *Cosmic Crime Stories* from Hireath Publishing. His flash fiction has appeared in *101Fiction, Speculative 66, Flash Frontier*, and *Bag Of Bones*. His YA science fiction novel, 'The Ides' is available from Amazon. He is a member of Clockhouse London Writers. His non-writing spare time is divided between following Tottenham Hotspur Football Club and acting as a mediator between two antagonistic cats.

Emma Johanna Puranen is a modern-day polymath, studying for her PhD in exoplanets and science fiction. She lives in Scotland, where in addition to her research she is a prolific writer. 'A Spark in a Flask' first appeared in *Around Distant Suns*, an anthology created through an interdisciplinary science/creative writing project Emma organised at the St Andrews Centre for Exoplanet Science. *Around Distant Suns* has been reviewed in the journal *Nature Astronomy*. Emma also writes the audio drama *Roguemaker*, available wherever you get your podcasts. In her free time, she runs, draws, and LARPs. Find Emma on Twitter @spacesword13.

Leo X. Robertson is a Scottish process engineer, writer and filmmaker. He has work in *Best of British Science Fiction 2019, Year's Best Hardcore Horror* and *Flame Tree Publishing's Urban Crime* anthology, among others. He has a sci-fi horror novella, *The Glow*, out with *Aurelia Leo* later this year – and by the time you're reading this, you'll be able to find his sci-fi feature film, *The TrutherNet Apocalypse*, online for free! He currently lives in Stavanger, Norway with his partner and Maria, a cat as fluffy as she is needy. Check out his Twitter (@Leoxwrite or website for more info: leoxrobertson.wordpress.com

Martin Sketchley is a writer, editor and Royal Literary Fund Fellow. "Bloodbirds" is the sequel to the BSFA Award-nominated "Songbirds", published in the *Conflicts* anthology from NewCon Press in 2010. 2021 saw his story "Fanning the Flames" appear in the *No More Heroes* anthology, and production of his first audio drama, *Modrocker*. Other stories include "The Howl", in collaboration with Ian R. MacLeod, "The Circle of Least Confusion", and three novels published by Simon & Schuster. He also appears on a Nick Cave DVD, and once spent time on a submarine with Stefanie Powers. Find him online at www.martinsketchley.com.

Teika Marija Smits is a Nottinghamshire-based writer and freelance editor. Her speculative short stories have been published in *Enchanted Conversation, Parsec, Shoreline of Infinity, Reckoning, Great British Horror 6*, and *Best of British Science Fiction (2018 & 2020)*. She is currently editing her debut novel, *Bluebeard's Theatre*, and hopes that by the time this anthology is in print she'll have finished wrestling with her novel! She can be found online at: https://teikamarijasmits.com and on Twitter as @MarijaSmits

Pete W Sutton is a writer and editor. His first book *A Tiding of Magpies* was shortlisted for the British Fantasy Awards in 2017 for Best Collection. His latest novel *Seven Deadly Swords* was published by Grimbold Books. He has edited a number of short story anthologies and is editor of *BFS Horizons*. His latest short story collection, *The Museum for Forgetting*, was published 2021. You can find him at https://petewsutton.com/ and on Twitter as @suttope

Ryan Vance is a writer, designer and editor based in Glasgow. Lethe Press published their debut collection of short stories, *One Man's Trash*, in 2021, described as "addicting and compelling" by Lambda Literary.org, and "seductively tense" by *Starburst Magazine*. In 2019, Ryan co-edited *We Were Always Here: A Queer Words Anthology*, published by 404 Ink. Their work has appeared in *Gutter Magazine, New Writing Scotland, The Dark Mountain, Terraform, F[r]iction, The Island Review*, and *Out There: An Anthology of LGBT Writing*. In 2016, they shortlisted for Scottish Book Trust's New Writers Award. They currently edit and design for *Gutter Magazine*. www.ryanvance.co.uk

Martin Westlake is an author, biographer and academic and a former international civil servant. He has lived, worked and studied in the UK, Italy, France and Belgium. He took early retirement to write and teach full-time. He has had poetry and short stories published and several plays performed. An epic historical novel, *Other Than an Aspen Be*, is currently on submission. SF is a favourite genre, particularly in short story form, and he has a growing number of published stories to his name. Long walks with a large, eternally-young, flat-coated retriever keep him fit and provide time for inspiration.

Aliya Whiteley has written over one hundred published short stories that have appeared in *Interzone, Beneath Ceaseless Skies, F&SF, Strange Horizons, The Dark, McSweeney's Internet Tendency* and *The Guardian*, as well as in anthologies such as Unsung Stories' *2084* and Lonely Planet's *Better than Fiction*. Her latest collection of short fiction, *From the Neck Up*, was published by Titan Books in 2021. Published in 2020, her novels *Greensmith* and *Skyward Inn* are works of speculative fiction. *Skyward Inn* was shortlisted for a BSFA award in 2021. Aliya also writes a regular non-fiction column for *Interzone*, and bakes a mean vanilla chocolate chip cookie.

Nick Wood is a disabled South African-British clinical psychologist and Science Fiction (SF) writer, with a collection of short stories (alongside essays and new material) in *Learning Monkey And Crocodile* (Luna Press, 2019). Following *Azanian Bridges* (2016), Nick's latest novel is the BSFA shortlisted *Water Must Fall* (NewCon Press, 2020). Nick also writes psychological articles, under the canny alternative name of Nicholas Wood. Nicholas's latest set of articles will be within the Clinical Psychology Forum's special issue on *Interrogating Disability* (2022). Nick can be found at http://nickwood.frogwrite.co.nz/

Acknowledgements

My undying gratitude once again must go to my dear friend Ian Whates for letting me loose on the 6ᵗʰ edition of this anthology series. It really is a joy to do. Thanks also to my long-suffering beta reader, Tom Jordan, who took pains to help me sort through the many submissions – as he has done with every book. Happy to have given you something to do while you had Covid, Tom! Thanks to Keith Brooke, Morris Allen and Noel Chidwick for passing on many fabulous writers to me. And thanks to all the lovely writers who sent me their stories to read.

Finally, thank you Neil K. Bond for bringing me copious amounts of decaffeinated tea (and the occasional non-decaffeinated ruby hot chocolate) while I worked on this.

~*~

Donna Scott is a writer, editor, award-winning stand-up comedian, podcaster, and many other things. Originally from the Black Country, she now lives in Northampton. She is a Director and former Chair of the British Science Fiction Association. As well as editing this anthology series she is formerly the co-editor of *Visionary Tongue Magazine*, and has worked freelance for the likes of Gollancz, Rebellion, Games Workshop, Angry Robot, Immanion and other publishers, groups and individuals. Her writing has appeared in publications by Immanion, NewCon, Norilana and PS Publishing. Look at www.donna-scott.co.uk to see the latest on her projects and appearances.

BEST OF BRITISH SCIENCE FICTION

2016 featuring stories by
Peter F. Hamilton, Gwyneth Jones, Adam Roberts, Tade Thompson, Ian Watson, Tricia Sullivan, Keith Brooke & Eric Brown, Natalia Theodoridou, Jaine Fenn, Una McCormack, Ian Whates, E.J. Swift, Den Patrick, Neil Williamson, Liam Hogan, and more…

2017 featuring stories by
Ken MacLeod, Lavie Tidhar, Jeff Noon, Adam Roberts, Anne Charnock, Natalia Theodoridou, Eric Brown, Jaine Fenn, E.J. Swift, Laura Mauro, Aliya Whiteley, Tim Major, Liam Hogan, Ian Creasey, Robert Bagnall, and more…

2018 featuring stories by
Alastair Reynolds, Lavie Tidhar, Dave Hutchinson, G.V. Anderson, Colin Greenland, Aliya Whiteley, Natalia Theodoridou, Matthew de Abaitua, Tim Major, Fiona Moore, David Tallerman, Henry Szabranski, Finbarr O'Reilly, and more…

2019 featuring stories by
Ken MacLeod, Chris Beckett, G.V. Anderson, Lavie Tidhar, Tim Major, Fiona Moore, Una McCormack, David Tallerman, Rhiannon Grist, Andrew Wallace, Val Nolan, Kate Macdonald, Leo X. Robertson, Henry Szabranski, and more…

2020 featuring stories by
M.R. Carey, Liz Williams, Lavie Tidhar, Ida Keogh, Ian Watson, Una McCormack, Anne Charnock, Eric Brown, Ian Whates, Stewart Hotston, RB Kelly, Neil Williamson, David Gullen, Teika Marija Smits, Fiona Moore, Stephen Oram, and more…

Lightning Source UK Ltd.
Milton Keynes UK
UKHW010052120822
407175UK00001B/41